A WINTER WEDDING

Amanda Forester

sourcebooks
casablanca

Published by Sourcebooks Casablanca, an imprint of Sourcebooks,
Inc.
P.O. Box 4410, Naperville, Illinois 60567–4410
(630) 961–3900
Fax: (630) 961–2168
www.sourcebooks.com

Printed and bound in the United States of America.
RRD 10 9 8 7 6 5 4 3 2

To my family, who has been amazingly supportive. And to Ed, who makes me believe in love.

Prologue

London, December 1810

DEATH CAME ROWING UP THE THAMES. IT WAS TIME TO strike—now, when their English king was at his weakest. No doubt conquering Britain would prove challenging, but it would only make the reward sweeter.

The man sitting in the stern of the small boat pulled his thick Carrick coat tighter against the cold and wet. Wind buffeted the little craft, blowing waves over the edge as rain pelted his face like tiny needles. The smuggler before him strained against the wooden oars. He had hired the man for a few shillings. The smuggler was working hard rowing against the wind and could no doubt use help, but he had no intention of providing it.

"Hurry up," said the man in the thick coat. The sooner he was finished with this business, the sooner he could return to his warm seat by the fire—or better yet, the warm doxy he'd left in his bed. He was as much a loyal supporter of the emperor as any, but rowing up the Thames in a storm was not exactly what he had in mind.

"Me mum wouldn't approve o' this 'ere work," muttered the smuggler.

"Put your back into it, man."

"Few jobs 'round these parts for a working man. Fewer still if you be an honest one." The man at the oars seemed to need to explain his involvement in the scheme.

"Fortunately, you have no predilection toward honesty," said the man in the thick wool coat with no fewer than five capes.

"What's that now?"

"We're here. Look lively. Tie her up." Though they were hidden beneath Westminster Bridge, the man in the Carrick coat disembarked from the tiny skiff with the elegance befitting his person. A group of smugglers were huddled beneath the bridge, waiting for their arrival, along with a young man, clearly of a different class. Johnny strolled toward him, looking too cocky by half in his footman's livery.

"What are you doing, coming down here dressed for serving table?" the man growled at Johnny.

"It's under my coat," Johnny defended.

"I can still see it, you fool. Put up that collar!"

Johnny bit back a rebuke and did as he was told.

"Take these to the warehouse," the caped man commanded the man in the boat and the other shifty-eyed smugglers who had come to help for the prospect of a few coins.

"You got something for me?" Johnny asked as the smugglers began to unload crates of French wine.

The caped man handed over a packet that contained a small note and a wad of blunt. Johnny took it with a greedy grin.

"You know what to do."

"Yes, sir," said Johnny with more eagerness than the man in the Carrick coat liked to see. He preferred people in a more downtrodden state. Cheerfulness was unnatural.

"What kind of wine you got here?" asked Johnny with too much curiosity. "Maybe I'll take some back with me."

"This ain't that kind of wine. See you don't drop it!" the caped man called to the smugglers, who did not give the impression of overall sobriety. "And, you"—he drew nearer to Johnny—"watch Marchford. That duke's got more interest in our goings-on than what's good for him."

"Can you tell me what this is all about?" Johnny whispered.

The caped man motioned the lad closer and then pulled a pistol from his coat pocket and stuck it almost up the boy's nose.

"W-what's this?" Johnny stammered.

"It's for blighters like you, who don't know when to keep their traps shut." The caped man returned the pistol to his pocket and dismissed Johnny with a wave. The lad took off running, the smile drained from his face.

The crates were loaded in the wagon on the road above them and a tarp pulled securely over the crates. One of the burly smugglers glanced around, but there was no one else out in such weather. He put his hand to his cap in salute and drove off into the stormy night.

"Glad to have that delivery made," muttered the talkative smuggler.

The caped man climbed back into the rowboat once more.

"Think he knows what's really in those wine bottles?" asked the smuggler.

"Not a chance."

"What are they going to do with it?"

"What do you think?" asked the caped man, his hand finding his pistol once more. This smuggler was too sharp-eyed and loose-lipped.

"You think Napoleon will sit on the English throne?"

"I know it." He gave the smuggler a smile and cocked the pistol. It was time to take care of some loose ends.

One

JAMES LOCKTON, THE DUKE OF MARCHFORD, WAS A marked man. He heard voices coming and pressed himself against the wall, edging slowly away, careful not to make a sound. One wrong move would seal his fate.

He had tried to escape his doom, hiding at his country estate like a craven coward. It was only the pressing needs of king and country, and the early opening of Parliament to deal with a severe crisis of governance, that drew him back to London. He had hoped December would find Town desolate of company, but with the return of the members of Parliament came their families, and with their families came...

"The Duke of Marchford is sooooo handsome," cooed a young feminine voice.

"Better yet, he's dreadfully rich," said another lady. "What I wouldn't give to be duchess of this hall."

"Do you think we should be wandering about, Mama?"

"No, of course not, but do you think we should come all this way without an introduction to the duke? Do you really think I care a whit about that spiteful old dowager? No!" exclaimed the baroness. They were growing nearer.

Marchford knew the baroness and her daughters were coming to visit his grandmother, but he hardly expected them to make a search of the house. He darted up a servants' stairwell and into a long hallway of bedrooms. He walked quickly toward the main stairs but stopped short at the sound of their whining voices. The woman had the audacity to come up to the private rooms! If they cornered him in the hallway, there would be no way to politely avoid introductions, and then he would be forced to dance with one or both of the sour-faced girls. He could think of no worse fate.

"We'll flush out the duke," crooned the baroness, her voice growing louder, "say we got turned around in the house and secure an introduction. I swear I'll not set foot from this place until you both have been asked to dance at tonight's ball."

Nothing to do but run.

He spun and dashed down the hall on light feet. Taking a risk, he opened one of the doors and slipped inside, closing the door carefully to avoid the conspicuous click of the latch. Now if only the bedroom were empty, he could possibly survive the night.

A small, feminine shriek behind him laid waste to that grand hope.

"Your Grace!" demanded Penelope Rose. "What on earth are you doing in my bedroom?"

"Shhhh, I beg you, Miss Rose," whispered Marchford, relieved it was only his grandmother's companion and not one of those marriage-minded females. "I am glad it is only you. You gave me a fright."

"I gave *you* a fright!" Penelope wrapped a serviceable robe around an already modest dressing gown.

Penelope Rose was the companion to his grandmother, the Dowager Duchess of Marchford, and was the only one in a series of companions who had lasted more than a week. She stood with her hands on her slender hips, and her long brown hair, which was usually pulled back in something of a severe knot, tumbled down around her.

Marchford gave Penelope a cursory glance, then looked back once more. He had never seen her with her hair undone, and the transformation was remarkable. Her hair was a lovely shade of chestnut brown and fell in loose waves all the way to her waist. It was luscious and thick and he had the sudden impulse to touch it. She had worked as his grandmother's companion for almost a year, but he doubted he had ever truly seen her before this moment.

"I am dressing for dinner. You must leave at once!" Penelope glared at him. He may have been experiencing an epiphany regarding her true form, but the only thing he saw in her large brown eyes was irritation.

"Forgive me, Miss Rose. I would not intrude on your privacy if it were not a matter of desperate urgency."

"What is it?" Pen's tone changed instantly. "Is it the spymaster?"

Penelope was one of the very few people he trusted to assist him with his work for the Foreign Office. He was slow to trust, but she had proved her worth, helping him flush out French spies who had infiltrated English society. It was one of the many things he valued about her. Yet in this case, his distress was of a more personal nature. "Worse. The baroness and her daughters."

Pen raised an eyebrow. "You are intruding on my privacy to avoid forming a new acquaintance?" Ironically, her attempt to chastise only enhanced her growing appeal.

"Have you met her daughters?" he defended, all thoughts of any other lady, save the one before him, banished from his mind.

"I have."

"Would you like to spend an hour dancing with either of them?"

Penelope's lively face struggled to maintain her general reserve until she gave up and rolled her eyes at him. "I suppose I must concede the point."

"Besides, should you not be with my grandmother during their visit?" He stepped toward her, sensing he was gaining the advantage.

"Sudden headache," she said quickly, on the defense. She sat on the trunk by the foot of her bed.

"Couldn't stand them either, eh? And now, because you failed to keep them entertained, they are running amok in my house." Marchford claimed a chair by her dressing table and stretched out his long legs; he was sitting in her private boudoir and enjoying every minute of it.

"Do not make yourself comfortable. You cannot stay here. It is highly improper!" She put her hands on her hips.

She was right, of course, he had no business being in her room, but he was finally seeing Miss Penelope Rose in a more natural state, and he had no interest in making a hasty departure. "I certainly can't leave, not with them about."

"You best get accustomed to female attention. After all, you are unmarried, young, and a duke." Penelope listed his attributes as though they were an indictment against him.

"If I cannot even be safe in my own home, entering the London season a targeted bachelor…" He made a strangled sound. "Why, my life will not be worth living. I must find a wife. And soon," he added gloomily.

"Ah, the horror of it all." Pen clasped her hands to her breast in mock sympathy. She was teasing him, but he enjoyed it. How many others would dare to mock the Duke of Marchford? Only the adorably frumpy woman before him.

Marchford ignored her sarcasm. "I need at least a fian-cée, someone who will not plague me. Someone who does not whine or cry or do other feminishy things."

"Feminishy?" Penelope raised an eyebrow.

"Someone sensible. Someone who can stand up to my grandmother without causing a scene. Someone like…" Marchford met Pen's eyes. Her ancient dressing gown looked every bit the wardrobe of an old maid, but her hair…that beautiful hair. Why did she tie it up in a lump on the back of her head? What other charms might her old clothes be hiding? Marchford guessed her ill-fitting clothes hid a shapely body, and those expressive brown eyes revealed intel-ligence and humor.

"Someone like you," said Marchford. It was meant only as a joke, and yet as the idea turned around in his mind, it became more desirable. Becoming engaged to

Penelope would solve his problem of being hunted as a bachelor, and they could continue working together to catch spies, and…he suddenly had a great desire to unwrap the rest of the questionable package before him to see what delights lay underneath the hideous dressing gown. "What do you think? It would get me out of a jam."

Penelope's eyes widened and her mouth dropped open. He had surprised her if nothing else. In a blink, her reserve returned to her face. "I beg you would not speak such nonsense."

"I am in earnest. You are a sensible girl. You get along with my grandmother. You can hold intelligent conversation. You are…sensible."

"You said sensible."

"It is one of your better features."

Penelope's eyebrows lowered. "I thank you for that unmitigated praise."

"Miss Rose, will you or will you not consent to be my wife?" Suddenly the question that had begun as an impulse became gravely serious. Penelope was the perfect wife for him.

Penelope flushed and sputtered. "The difference in our stations…"

"If it means nothing to me, it can be nothing to you." He leaned forward, admiring her large brown eyes, which widened, only enhancing her appearance.

"I—I beg you would not tease me! I know you are just funning with me. Besides, if I were ever to marry, it would be for love, not to save a man from the marriage mart."

"That is grievously unkind of you," said Marchford

lightly, careful not to let her see any true disappointment. He leaned back in his chair. It was unfortunate about her attachment to love, for love was the one thing he could never offer.

Though he had spoken the words admittedly in jest, he was surprised how much her rejection stung. He had never proposed before and had always expected that when he did, even if it was admittedly backhanded, the girl—any girl—would fall over herself to say yes.

But Penelope was not just any girl. She was apparently the only girl in society who did not wish to marry him. And now, thanks to her dratted voluminous hair, she was the only girl he could imagine sharing his bed.

"Well, must dash," said Marchford, leaping from the chair. The voices of the baroness and her daughters had long since faded away. It was past time to make his exit. To let her see the sudden turn of his mind from playful banter into serious attraction would be fatal.

"I am sure you will find a suitable bride soon," said Penelope with an apologetic tone. "You have much to offer."

Was she trying to let him down softly? Did she feel sorry for him? His pride howled in pain. "Thank you," he said stiffly, listening at the door to ensure the hallway was empty.

"Any girl would be pleased to accept your offer."

"Not any girl apparently," muttered the duke.

"I do apologize, but I refuse to marry any man just so he can avoid awkward conversation."

Marchford turned on her with a desperate need to change the direction of the unfortunate conversation.

"If you will not oblige me, then it is your responsibility to find me someone who will, someone who meets the criteria I delineated."

Penelope flushed again and avoided his eye. "I can contact Madame X, the matchmaker, if you would like to engage her services to help find a bride." She was a dreadful liar.

"Hang it, Miss Rose. I know Madame X is nothing more than a fictional character you and my grandmother created. Now I want you, not my grandmother, but you alone to find me a bride. What is your going rate?"

"Exorbitant!"

"A little vague, but I am certain my solicitor can draw up the papers to your liking. Good day, Madame X!"

He stomped down the hall, taking a deep breath of cool air. She would get dressed, tie up her hair, and everything would go back to normal. Yes, normal was good. Miss Rose was his grandmother's companion, nothing more.

Yet something warned him it was too late. He would never be able to see Penelope Rose the same way again.

Two

PENELOPE ROSE STARED AT THE DOOR WHERE THE Duke of Marchford had left. Had he just…? It wasn't possible that… Had he just asked her to marry him? The Duke of Marchford, the biggest matrimonial prize in all of Britain, and consequently the whole world, had just entered her private bedchamber and proposed marriage.

Marriage!

Penelope put a hand to her chest to try to stop her heart from beating at such a rapid clip. She must be sensible. Was that not the highest praise he could offer her, after all? He was only in jest; it was not a true proposal. How utterly awkward and foolish she would have appeared had she accepted like a ninny, only to have him have to explain it was all in fun.

Thank heaven she hadn't done that.

But what if she had? And what if he had agreed? She could be married. Her, Penelope Rose, the confirmed old maid—the one ignored by every other suitor who passed her by to get to her more attractive sisters—could get married at last. And to a duke no less!

She gloried in the fantasy: Being announced at tonight's ball as the fiancée of the Duke of Marchford. Putting the newspaper clipping announcing her engagement next to the clippings she kept for each one of her four sisters. Standing up beside him in St. George's, saying their marriage vows. Reveling in the look of envy from every girl who ever ignored her as a nothing companion. Perhaps that last thought was beneath her, but she was indulging in fantasy and could not help herself.

She thought that might be the best part, but her imagination continued onward. She and Marchford—*James* she would call him now—arriving home. He would carry her to his bedroom—*their* bedroom. He would slowly unfasten her gown…

"Hello, miss!" The maid entered the room, carrying her new blue gown. "Got it all pressed and ready. Are you all right, miss?"

Penelope jumped up and fanned herself with her hands. The room was unbearably hot and she feared her maid might guess she had been lusting after the master of the house, the duke himself! "I am fine."

"You look all red in the face."

"It's nothing. I…I was standing too close to the fire."

"But you weren't nowhere near the fire, miss."

"I'm fine!" Penelope cursed Marchford. It was all his fault for putting treacherous thoughts in her head. First he mocked her by proposing marriage in fun, and now she was supposed to find him a wife. Fie on him!

"Now you look right mad, miss," said the overly observant maid.

"Thank you for your observations as to my countenance," said Penelope crossly.

"Oh no, I done said too much. I am always opening my mouth and out pops the first thing I think. No good, it is. They say I'm not ready to wait on any of the real ladies until I learn to keep my mouth—oh!" The maid put her hand over her mouth, realizing what she just said.

Penelope sighed. Since she was only a companion, she was a training subject for a young maid who was not ready for "real ladies."

"I'm so sorry, miss. I didn't mean it like that. I can go get another maid if you wish." She turned to leave, but Pen called her back, struggling to remember the young maid's name.

"Abigail is it?"

"Yes, fancy that. Me named Abigail wanting to be an abigail." She giggled. "I'm afraid I'm not too good at it."

"I appreciate your candor. We will get on quite well, you and I." There was no point in getting the young maid in trouble. "But I won't be wearing the blue gown. One of my old ones will do."

Penelope could not bear to have Marchford think she was putting on a new gown for his enticement. He had pretty girls falling at his feet, and she would rather wear sackcloth than be numbered as one of them.

"But this is the one Her Grace bought for you. And it's mighty pretty," objected Abigail.

"Yes, it is. But I will wear one of my old gowns tonight." Penelope was firm. The Dowager Duchess of Marchford was desirous of seeing her more elegantly

attired and had bought her a new wardrobe, with
Penelope's share of the proceeds from their Madame X
matchmaking business. Using their combined talents,
they had created a lucrative business creating matches
for society's elite under the pseudonym of Madame
X. It had allowed them to remain in London despite
Marchford cutting off funds to try to force his grandmother to retire to the Dower House in the country.

Abigail's face fell, but Penelope refused to relent and
was dressed in a lavender gown of her mother's that
had faded into something of a gray. Penelope resisted
all attempts to dress her hair and instead twisted it back
herself into the usual knot. It was not attractive, which
was entirely the point. One could never accuse her of
putting on airs or trying to seduce the duke.

The Duke of Marchford was waiting for the ladies
in the drawing room to leave for the ball and rose
when Penelope entered. Despite her best intentions,
she caught her breath when he approached.

If ever there was an image of the perfection of man,
the Duke of Marchford personified it. He was tall,
broad in the shoulders, and trim in the waist, which
was perfectly accentuated by the superb cut of his
double-breasted bright-blue frock coat and formfitting
slate-gray trousers. His features were dark and chiseled,
with a long nose and a square jaw, but not so brooding
as to be out of fashion. Add dark brown hair and mysterious gray-green eyes, and he was every young lady's
dream beau. Despite considerable effort, Penelope had
given up the hope of finding fault with his appearance.

In contrast, Penelope Rose knew very well she was
undeniably plain. The only brunette sister in a family

of blond beauties, Penelope watched as first her older sisters then her younger sisters all found husbands. Pretty could make up for a lack of dowry, but poor, plain sisters? They became companions.

As the companion to the Dowager Duchess of Marchford, Penelope held very little status to the members of the *haut ton* and was accordingly ignored. She was not a servant but was hardly a member of their set in society. She hovered somewhere between shabby gentry and honored servant, and, as such, held no place in either world.

"Miss Rose." Marchford acknowledged her with a nod of his head. "You are looking…" He paused as if trying to find the right words. "You appear quite yourself tonight. Very good of you."

Good of her? "Yes, quite. You are looking very well." She stopped before she admitted how utterly handsome he was.

Marchford regarded her with an interest that made heat slither up the back of her neck. They had lived under the same roof for almost a year, but she could not remember him gazing at her with such intensity. She wondered if something about her was out of place, and she smoothed a nervous hand over her hair to ensure everything was pulled back tight.

Marchford cleared his throat as if trying to change the subject, even though he had not said a word. "Please, sit. I am sure my grandmother will be down shortly."

Penelope perched on the edge of a chair, ready to take flight if the need arose. Marchford also sat, stood up again, walked aimlessly around the room, then sat down again in the same chair.

"I do not wish to be married," he blurted.

Penelope stared at him.

"I mean…that is to say…" Marchford stammered, as if surprised himself that he had spoken out loud. "I have no inclination toward the married state. It all seems a bother to me, but I shall have no peace until I do."

"Ah, the burden of being young, titled, and rich," said Penelope without mercy.

Marchford scowled at her. "You would not care to be chased about for nothing more than your money and your name."

"I will consider myself fortunate, then, never to have been chased at all." Penelope did not bother to keep the sarcasm from her voice.

She expected a stinging retort, but it never came. Instead, Marchford gave her such a look as she had never seen before. It was quite disconcerting.

"Perhaps someday you will be chased and you can tell me your opinion on the matter." Marchford's tone was soft and low.

Penelope's jaw dropped, and she struggled to find something to say. "I…I wonder what is keeping Her Grace."

"My grandmother moves in her own time and does what she will."

A twinge of fear had Penelope calling the butler to bring her coat. If anything she was overly warm, but she knew the gown she wore would bring offense to Her Grace, and she had tangled enough with the aristocratic Marchfords for one day.

"Oh, Penelope. What have you done to your hair?"

Antonia Lockton, Dowager Duchess of Marchford, swept into the room, elegantly attired in an azure-blue silk gown, which perfectly matched the sparkling blue of her eyes. Her white hair was ornately coiffed and bejeweled in an older style, which befitted her advanced years.

"Is it out of place?" asked Pen, once again smoothing her hair back to the harsh bun.

"Could you not have dressed it up a bit?" asked the dowager. "You would not know it to look at it now, James, but Penelope has the loveliest hair. It is so long and thick and—"

"Enough!" roared Marchford, surprising both ladies. He cleared his throat. "I'm sure Miss Rose's hair is fine indeed, but that is utterly irrelevant, and besides, we are late." He stalked out of the room, calling for the carriage to be brought around.

The dowager's eyebrows elevated considerably up her forehead then slowly fell back down into a knowing look that made Penelope squirm. "I see," she said, looking between Penelope and the retreating form of the Duke of Marchford. "I see."

After a relatively short carriage ride, they arrived at the home of Mr. William Grant, one of Marchford's closest friends. Marchford handed both of them out of the carriage, Penelope unusually conscious of how his gloved fingers closed around her hand as he helped her out.

He escorted them into the house for the Grant ball, his grandmother on one arm and Penelope on the other. Heads turned when they arrived, many interested in the arrival of the duke. It was not unusual, but the attention irritated Penelope, possibly because she was still chewing on his "utterly irrelevant" comment regarding her hair.

They relinquished their wraps to the butler, bringing a gasp from the dowager. "Penelope Rose," chastised Antonia. "What are you wearing?"

"A gown. *My* gown," Penelope clarified. She raised her chin in defiance, despite the fact that she had intentionally hidden the gown under her coat so the dowager would not discover the insubordination before it was too late to make her change her raiment.

"Should have had the maids burn them," the dowager muttered. "James, talk some sense into her."

"She looks fine," said Marchford absently. A weaker, more lackluster defense one could hardly imagine.

"What nonsense!" Antonia rapped her cane with a crack on the marble floor. "The gown is perfectly hideous and you know it."

"Yes, of course, it is horrid," said Marchford in an aloof manner. "But if Miss Rose finds it sufficient, who are we to quibble? You should not go about changing things that are better left as they are. The gown is perfectly good enough for Miss Rose."

Penelope stifled a gasp. If this was his attempt at support, she hoped to never experience his censure. Of all the dreadful things one could say, she could not imagine anything more crushing.

"How can you be so beastly—oh look, here is Lord Langley." Antonia's tone changed instantly with the arrival of her former beau. Antonia and Lord Langley had shared a romance in their youth and had only recently begun to speak to one another again. From the look of Langley's wide smile and quick step, their friendship was indeed rekindled.

"Ready to take them all at whist, my sweet?" asked Langley, offering his arm to Antonia.

"I'm off to the card room," said Antonia, and she left them without a second look.

"I hope you have given some thought to finding me a bride as soon as may be," Marchford whispered to Penelope as he led her into the ballroom.

"Oh yes," said Penelope, keeping her tone even. "I have some lovely ladies in mind for you."

He sighed audibly. "Well, let's get this over with."

"I will ensure that they are 'perfectly good enough' for you." She gave him a vicious smile, but he was looking ahead and did not see. Before the night was out, he would pay dearly for that comment. Oh yes, that son of a duke would pay.

Three

MARCHFORD LED THEM INTO THE FESTIVELY DECO-
rated ballroom awash with the colored silks of the
ladies' gowns and the well-tailored coats of the men.
Hundreds of candles twinkled in the drawing room,
boldly embellished with sprigs of holly and bright red
bows. It was perhaps a little provincial for London
society, which viewed Christmas as a quaint tradition
of the common populace. But Penelope, herself raised
in the country, loved it. Having spent three refined
Christmastides in London after her parents died, she
had missed the annual festivities.

Though it was proper for a lady to be escorted into
the ballroom, Penelope noted that Marchford failed
to release her hand once they were inside and instead
covered her gloved hand with his protectively. She
knew it was an oversight—he was not attending to
her in the least—but the continued contact warmed
her straight down to her slippered toes. Her unwanted,
inappropriate, and utterly inconvenient response to
him was clearly his fault.

The Duke of Marchford pressed forward into the

room, taking her along with him. All heads turned when he passed, but his aloof manner kept all but his intimates and the outrageously bold from approaching. It was December in London, so society would have typically been limited, but Parliament had been required to open session early. The crowded ballroom revealed the season was also getting an early start.

"Where are we going?" Pen whispered.

"Card room. Or better yet billiards. Only safe place."

"Coward," she hissed.

"They are looking at me like a prized goose, shot and plucked, and hanging by its neck in the shop window."

She smiled at the analogy. Served him right for being so handsome, and amusing, and blasted good company. The ladies in the ballroom had noted his movement from one side of the room to the other, and began to drift toward him in ever shrinking orbits until they fell willingly into the gravitational pull of the unmarried duke.

"It is your own fault for remaining a bachelor," chastised Penelope in a low voice. *And for being undeniably attractive*, she mentally added.

"No, that is entirely your fault," he returned in a seductive undertone.

His reference to his mock proposal sent tingles down her spine, and she wrenched her hand away from his arm to prevent herself from falling into his arms and declaring that she would marry him within the hour. Curse him!

Taking advantage of an unprotected duke, a lady wearing a gown so sheer Penelope did a double take before averting her eyes slid up to Marchford and giggled something in his ear. He acknowledged her with a tight smile but turned to Pen with haunted eyes. *Help!* he mouthed to her. Women circled like buzzards around carrion.

It was dangerous to stand between a marriage-minded miss and her ultimate prize. Pen was met with glares from determined maidens who saw her as interfering in their plans to corral the duke into conversation, marriage, and bed, in any order. One lady elbowed her. Another trod on her foot, trying to vie for Marchford's attention.

Penelope considered abandoning him to his fate, but she could not stomach the thought of leaving these women in command of the ultimate prize. Besides, what if his horror were to turn to interest? She was filled with an emotion unfamiliar to her, but it was definitely not jealousy. No, not that at all.

"Your Grace, please recall you promised to lead in Lady Devine's niece." Penelope's pronouncement was met with glares from the ladies and a look of relief from Marchford.

"Yes, of course. You all will excuse me." Marchford gave a slight nod of the head and detangled himself from their clutches.

"Here is my first matrimonial suggestion," said Pen in an undertone as they picked their way through the guests back to the entryway. "Frances is the niece of Lord Admiral and Lady Devine, a nicer family you could not hope to find. Frances will make her debut this season and is expected to do very well. You could save everyone a good deal of fuss and bother by making an offer before she needed to complete the season."

"Quite a business for you, this Madame X," observed Marchford coolly.

"Indeed," replied Pen without apology.

"Though I do thank you for extricating me from that situation." His eyes warmed and he inclined his head to her.

"Glad to be of assistance," said Pen lightly. Her conscience pricked her momentarily, for she knew he would not thank her for the young lady she was about to connect him to; yet one look at his infuriatingly handsome face was enough to set her back on her devious course.

They reached the entryway and were relatively alone as they waited for the Devine family. "Forgive my curiosity," continued Penelope. She had tried to resist asking but could not contain herself any longer. "You hardly are in need of a matchmaker. Why not find your own bride?"

"No!" Marchford was so emphatic it startled Penelope. "I do not want a romance, only a bride." Gone was the amusement from his eyes. He was serious in his aversion to love. But why?

Penelope reached out to touch his hand but caught herself in time. Lord Admiral Devine and his family arrived at that moment, distracting him from her awkward gesture. Marchford was naturally acquainted with Admiral Devine and his wife, and the introduction to Frances was quickly made. Frances was quite pretty and quite young, maybe fifteen at best, and her gown was the pinkest pink Pen had ever seen.

Penelope was shamelessly delighted. Marchford less so.

"May I have the honor of leading you into the ballroom?" asked Marchford politely.

Frances giggled and clapped her hands. She stepped away momentarily to give her wrap to one of the footmen.

"I fear I am robbing the nursery of its brightest ornament," Marchford hissed in Pen's ear.

Pen stifled a laugh.

"Since I will be occupied for the near future in unavoidable conversation, do keep your eye on Jonathan, that footman."

"Why?" asked Penelope.

"Something shady about his footwear. Do not forget the only reason I returned to London at all is to discover the spymaster."

Marchford's request was a serious one. He had been engaged in flushing out French spies from society for the past several years, both abroad and at home. The fact that he trusted Penelope with such work made a happy thrill run down her spine.

"Which one is he?" she asked, keeping herself from giggling and clapping her hands in excitement in the manner of a certain youthful debutante.

"He is taking the child's wrap now."

Frances returned and Marchford led her into the ballroom with the look of a long-suffering saint. Penelope refused to feel guilty.

Penelope loitered for a few minutes, watching the footman take coats as guests arrived. He was not doing anything of any particular suspicion. Soon, however, he handed over his duties to another footman and disappeared through a side door, which Pen guessed led to the servants' passages.

Penelope followed her quarry down a servants' stairwell at a discreet distance. No member of society could do the same. That was the nice thing about being a companion; one could go almost anywhere and nobody would notice. Or if it wasn't nice, at least it was helpful.

The footman, an attractive man of at least six feet tall, walked down the corridor with a swagger of confidence he would not have dared show in the drawing rooms upstairs. He entered the kitchen and Pen followed, the heat warming her face even before she entered the room.

He selected a tray that held three decanters of hard spirits and began to refill them. It was winter, and the cold put the guests in mind to drink.

Penelope found the harried cook to give the impression she had some business below stairs. "My mistress, the Duchess of Marchford, requests tea to aid her digestion," Penelope said to the cook. "I have brought her special blend." Pen reached into her reticule and handed a pouch of tea to the cook.

"Yes, miss," said the cook without a second look at Penelope.

Penelope busied herself with the teacups while watching the footman out of the corner of her eye. He filled two of the decanters but not the third. The only odd thing she noted was one bottle was labeled "Whiskey" and two were "Brandy." Perhaps he was offering two types of brandy?

He headed back upstairs with his tray. She decided to test his disposition and turned quickly to step out in front of him, causing him to nearly lose his balance.

"Watch it, you careless, little…" He stopped short

when he realized she was not a member of the kitchen staff, but the look of venom he bestowed upon her revealed that beneath the cheerful disposition beat a calculating heart. He knew just how much he could get away with. As a guest, he could not verbally berate her, but as a lowly companion, he could certainly attempt to make her feel her place with a demeaning look.

"So sorry," said Penelope.

"I'm sure you are," he said with all impudence. He turned and swaggered his way back up the stairs. He straightened his shoulders when he reached the ball-room door and entered the ballroom the very picture of poise. She watched him until her own tray became heavy, and she went in search of the dowager.

The regal Duchess of Marchford was playing whist and, by the devious glint in her eye, winning most atrociously. Her partner, Lord Langley, was smiling in a genial sort of way. Penelope placed the tea beside the dowager, who glared at it as if Penelope had offered her hemlock.

"And what is that?" asked the dowager.

Penelope knew she would not be pleased, but she needed to keep up the act. Working with the duke for the better part of nine months had taught her as much. "Your tea, Your Grace. I know how you like tea in the evenings."

"At home." The dowager's voice was like ice.

"Yes, of course," said Penelope. "I will ask a foot-man to take away the tray."

"And Sir Gareth is speaking to the wrong chit. Fix it," demanded the dowager with a wave of her hand. Marchford was not the only client of Madame X that evening, though Penelope was more inclined to offer actual help when it came to her other clients.

Penelope followed the dowager's line of sight and noted Sir Gareth speaking with a young lady, which unbeknownst to him was not the one she intended him to marry. Sir Gareth moved away from the object of his attention, presumably to acquire refreshments, and Penelope intercepted.

"Good evening, Sir Gareth," said Penelope. "I see you have made the acquaintance of Miss Reeves."

"Yes, charming girl." He gave an interested smile.

"Quite. I do not think I have ever seen a girl quite so beautiful. And so much admired. I do not envy her future husband." Since Miss Reeves had the moral compass of a serpent, Penelope felt the interference was justified.

"Why is that?" Sir Gareth was startled at the comment.

"Why, with a bride as young and beautiful as she, one would always have the need to guard the roost."

"I see. Yes, you have a point." From Gareth's tone, it was clear her shaft had hit home. He had recently been appointed to an important post overseas and was facing extended trips abroad.

"Ah, I see Lady Jane across the way. I have been looking for her, poor dear," said Penelope, thinking quickly to set her plan in motion.

"Has something happened to Janie?" Sir Gareth coughed and corrected himself. "Lady Jane."

Penelope smiled. Sir Gareth and Lady Jane had been friends since childhood. "It is not common knowledge, since she certainly does not wish for a scandal, but Lady Jane is no longer engaged."

"Truly?" Gareth sounded hopeful, a good sign.

"Yes, but I must ask for your confidence. I understand the groom was found wanting." Since the man had lost his fortune at cards and slept with half of London, Penelope considered him very wanting indeed. Lady Jane had called off the engagement but feared societal retribution.

"Indeed, the man was utterly unworthy of her," he said with a shake of his head.

"Quite. Still the whole affair has been lowering. She has been remembering happier times. She speaks of you a great deal when she talks of her childhood."

"Does she speak of me?" Gareth turned to her and gave Pen his full attention.

Penelope smiled. "Quite positively."

"How kind," said Gareth, gazing in the direction of Lady Jane. The music started again and brought Gareth back to his senses. "Oh, I am engaged to dance with Miss Reeves." And with that he walked away.

Penelope sighed. The matters of the heart were most difficult to manage.

Which reminded her, she needed to find the duke. He was nowhere in sight, a sure sign he had run away, and Pen had an idea where.

She walked down an empty corridor to Grant's study. She heard voices behind the closed door, knocked, received silence, so she opened the door herself. "If you are attempting to hide from your company, you should lower your voice," she chastised.

"Miss Rose!" Marchford stood at her entrance. "You abandoned me with an infant!"

Grant laughed and beckoned her inside, shutting

the door behind her. "Marchford was regaling me with horror stories of the life of a bachelor." Grant was a remarkably handsome man, perfectly attired in a coat of dark burgundy superfine, with the blond curly hair and blue eyes of a Nordic god. When the *ton* looked to fashion, they looked to him.

"Was it so terribly bad?" Penelope asked innocently, trying to hide a smile.

Marchford stepped closer, his eyes a mixture of amusement and outrage. "I see you are enjoying my discomfort. I thought you were supposed to be of help, but you left me when I was most needful."

"I was following the footman as requested." Penelope had to turn away from those light gray eyes before she could be drawn once more under his spell. A change of subject was needed, and she knew she could speak openly to only a few—the spy hunters of London. Mr. Grant, though resistant at times, was one of them.

"Ah, all cloak and dagger, mystery and intrigue," Grant accused Marchford. "You cannot go anywhere without running afoul of a traitor or two. I begin to rethink our acquaintance."

"Difficult times, my friend," said Marchford. He sat on an upholstered settee and motioned for Penelope to sit next to him.

"The war, you mean?" asked Penelope. She hesitated, unsure if she should sit so close, but she did anyway, unable to resist.

"Oh no, every good Englishman loves a good war. It's this mad king that's got us in a twist," said Grant with his unfailing good humor. He claimed a leather chair next to them.

"King George?" asked Penelope, trying to focus on the conversation rather than how close her thigh was from touching Marchford's. Everyone knew their aging monarch, King George III, had taken ill once more and now his sanity had quite left him.

"Yes," said Marchford. "This special early session of Parliament has been called to discuss this matter and debate the merits of naming the Prince of Wales as regent."

"Love the prince," said Grant. "Great parties, nothing but the best. Though I fear his household management skills may be slightly lacking."

"Indeed," said Penelope and held her tongue. The Prince of Wales was notorious for living a profligate life. His numerous affairs were legendary and Parliament had already been obliged to bail out his debts to the shocking amount of 161,000 pounds.

"And some believe the entire discussion is grounds for treason," continued Marchford, lowering his voice and leaning even closer to Penelope. "So the entire situation must be handled with care."

Penelope swallowed hard, willing herself not to react to his closeness nor the warm smell of his coat. She focused on the conversation and had no doubt Marchford was deeply involved in the "handling" of the situation. "But what does all this have to do with enemy agents in London?"

"Napoleon no doubt views our current crisis as weakness and an opportunity to act. I fear there may be some sort of plot brewing."

"What sort of plot?" asked Penelope.

"If I knew that, I would not have risked coming

to London to find out." Marchford's tone was grave, but there was a mischievous smile in his eyes when he regarded Penelope.

"Try not to cause a scene at my party. It is my poor wife's first ball as hostess," Grant said with a smile. "Which reminds me, I must return to my duties as host. I shall leave the world of espionage in your capable hands. Evening!" Grant slid from the room with a fluid grace, an easy smile on his lips.

Marchford turned to her and their knees accidently touched. "Oh!" said Penelope, and they both jumped back to the edges of the settee.

Penelope coughed and struggled to find a benign topic of conversation. "The footman is an arrogant fellow. Not sure where his lay is, but I think he warrants further observation."

"His lay?" Marchford's eyes were dancing.

Penelope cleared her throat at being caught using thieves' cant. "I am only trying to assist your investigations."

"Yes, I do appreciate it. I only wonder at what point I corrupted you." Marchford leaned forward again, a sly smile playing about his lips.

Of course he was only teasing, but it would take a woman stronger than she not to melt when his voice rumbled with seductive thunder. She took a quick breath. "Not corrupted in the least. I merely wished to do my duty for my country."

"If you have a plan, Miss Rose, I am willing to do anything you wish."

Penelope stilled a sigh. How many young ladies of the *ton* would give anything to hear those words from the duke? *Anything she wished…*

"Miss Rose?"

Penelope was startled out of a happy revelry to find the object of her distraction staring at her intently. "Yes. Right." She cleared her throat. "We should continue to watch the footman, but we also must return to the business of finding you a bride."

Marchford's shoulders slumped. "A bride. What bother."

Four

PENELOPE WALKED OUT OF THE STUDY WITH Marchford, her emotions swirling around like the couples dancing the quadrille. She was not certain whether she was still irritated at the duke or not. Should she help him find true love?

His fingertips brushed across her back as he led her down the corridor toward the ballroom. Heat radiated from the place of his touch. Perhaps it was important to see him married as soon as may be for her own sanity.

"I think you will like this next one," said Penelope, adopting her most businesslike tone and trying to squelch any physical reaction she might have to him. "You are acquainted with Lady Jane, the sister of Lord Wynbrook?"

"She is engaged," said Marchford without a shred of interest.

"She was, but she found the groom lacking and broke off the engagement. Lord Wynbrook has contracted with Madame X to find her another groom before the scandal hits."

Marchford stopped at the end of the corridor, raising an aristocratic eyebrow. "So if I was to make an offer to Lady Jane, you would collect quite a windfall."

"Yes, quite." Penelope knew better than to meet his gaze. If she had to find a match for Marchford, at least it could benefit her as well.

"Well then, I shall propose to her as soon as may be"—he lowered his voice—"to please you."

Heat ran up the back of her neck in a most disturbing manner. "Yes, well, that would be quite obliging."

"Your humble servant." Marchford offered her his arm, and she once again entered the ballroom on the arm of a duke.

They were quick to find Lady Jane sitting by the wall on the edge of the ballroom.

"I should like the carriage," Lady Jane was telling her sister when they approached. "Let us find our brother and leave at once."

"Lady Jane!" said Penelope. "You look lovely this evening."

Lady Jane looked nothing of the sort. It had been a severe disappointment, discovering her fiancé was less than worthy. The disreputable man had not taken well to the dissolution of their engagement for, as the sister of the Earl of Wynbrook, Lady Jane was well-dowered. He had made an ugly scene, threatening scandal. Lady Jane's brother had hired Madame X to find a replacement groom—and fast.

"You are acquainted with the Duke of Marchford?"

Lady Jane rose and gazed at them through dreary, half-closed eyes. "Yes, of course. Good evening, Your Grace."

"Good evening, Lady Jane."

They stood in awkward silence for a moment, staring at each other with equal looks of polite disinterest.

"Good evening, Lady Jane." Sir Gareth chose that moment to arrive with a wide, eager smile. "Forgive the interruption, but would you care to dance?"

"Oh!" Lady Jane's eyes flew open and she gave Sir Gareth her most becoming smile. "Yes, indeed, I would truly love to dance."

"Now he takes the bait," muttered Penelope.

Penelope and Marchford watched them dance away.

"Do you think I should wait for them to complete the set before I propose?" Marchford whispered in her ear. His breath warm on her skin.

Penelope's treacherous body responded immediately. Their eyes met and she had to force herself to look away. "Forgive me my error. But I have others in mind, do not despair."

"Too late for that. Perhaps your matchmaking skills are not up to the task." His tone was aloof, but his eyes were dancing. Was he sharing a joke or laughing at her?

Now she could name this emotion he incited within her: Irritation. Frustration. Exasperation tinged with malicious rage. "I have the perfect lady for you." She smiled sweetly at the duke. "The Princess Alexandra of Austria. Of course, I could never count her among my acquaintance, being only a lowly companion. She would only deign to speak to an illustrious person such as yourself."

Marchford gave her a suspicious glance, as well he should. They approached the princess from the side.

She was wearing an enormous golden turban adorned with jewels and a giant purple plume.

"Did you ever see such gaudy decorations?" the princess was commenting to the elegant person of the Comtesse de Marseille.

"Simply dreadful," intoned the comtesse, society maven and vicious gossip.

"I cannot understand why the Grants are held in such high society. After all, he married only some countrified thing with some scandal attached to her mother. Clearly, she was beneath him. No telling the oddities of English society," said the princess with haughty disdain.

Marchford shook his head, and they walked past the princess and the comtesse without a second look.

"Are you trying to make me a match or convince me to join a monastery?" growled Marchford.

"Thinking of taking a vow of celibacy?"

"Are you taking an interest in my carnal habits, Miss Rose?"

"No!" She turned away from him and plucked a fan out of her reticule to cool her flushed skin. Dratted man, he had done it to her again.

"I have just the lady for you." Penelope attempted to keep the sarcasm at bay.

Marchford gave her a false smile. "Joy and rapture."

"Lord Wynbrook has a friend, the Earl of Darington, who is staying with them."

"Let me guess, Lord Darington has a sister."

"Yes! I have yet to meet her—"

"No."

"Now, how bad can she be?" It was a rhetorical

question. If Darington's sister was half as bad as her reputation, this would be perfect. "Besides, I am running out of suitable potential brides. You are a duke, you know. Your bride must be the daughter of an earl at the very least. You cannot marry a commoner."

"Can I not?" Despite their light banter, his question seemed surprisingly honest.

They reached Lord Wynbrook, who greeted them with a warm smile. "Marchford, Miss Rose, you are well met. Allow me to present Robert Ashton, the Earl of Darington, and his sister, Lady Katherine."

The young Earl of Wynbrook was a handsome man with chestnut hair and flashing, bright eyes. Lord Darington, on the other hand, was a tall man with dark hair and brown, sunken eyes, dressed all in black. Katherine wore a shabby white muslin gown and had brown hair pulled back into a severe bun with sharp features and intelligent eyes. Both she and her brother were quite thin, making Penelope wonder if they were naturally that way or if they had recently survived some sort of deprivation. With him in black and her in white, they appeared solemnly monochrome in a sea of festive color.

The appropriate bows were made, with neither Darington nor his sister saying a word.

"Darington has just returned from years at sea, commanding the *Lady Kate*. Came back plumper in the pocket than he left," said Wynbrook with a smile.

"You served in the Royal Navy?" asked Penelope, attempting to start the conversation.

"Yes" was his monosyllabic reply. Unlike his more amiable friend, there was no smile in Darington's eyes.

Theirs must have been a sad life, but still, they were titled, in London, and with a bit of blunt about them, so they were definitely marriable potentials—once you got past the icy stares.

"Admirable," commented Marchford, joining the conversation with his own brief reply.

"And will you begin a London season this year?" Pen asked Lady Katherine.

"No. I do not wish to enter society. And I certainly I do not wish to be married. You will excuse me." Lady Katherine turned on her heel and left.

Penelope was forced to hide her smile behind her fan. Marchford's face was a perfect mix of horror and insult. She gloried in her revenge for a moment before the words of her grandma Moira came to mind. *Revenge is as sweet as a sheep turd. Those who delight in it end up with a face full of sh—* This is where Penelope's mother would cut off her Scottish grandmother's colorful adage. Perhaps it was time to stop this game.

"It was nice to meet you, Lord Darington. Forgive us, but I believe we must see to my grandmother," said Marchford, extricating them from the awkward situation. His placid countenance had returned, though with the aristocratic veil of injured pride.

"I believe we should give up finding you a bride for the evening." Penelope sighed in defeat.

"Thank heaven!" cried Marchford with considerable animation, quick to recover from his matrimonial setbacks.

"You are horrid."

"Indeed, I am. I'm glad you have finally noticed.

Now we can get back to more serious matters. Where is that footman?"

"The card room, I believe. Oh bother. I forgot to ask someone to collect the tea tray from your grandmother. She will no doubt be cross at me. And I have not found anything suspicious about the footman, other than he is arrogant and serving two decanters of brandy."

"Perhaps we should investigate?" He gave her a sly smile.

Penelope could not help but smile in return. "I have a plan."

Marchford offered his arm. "Lead on!"

~

Marchford reluctantly released Penelope's arm when they reached the card room, careful not to make eye contact with anyone in a dress. Unlike Penelope, with whom he enjoyed a certain feeling of safety, many other young ladies would pounce upon the slightest encouragement. Thus, a ducal aura of detachment must be maintained.

He stayed behind while she moved forward toward the tea tray. He had been relieved to see her dressed much the same as always, in her worn-out gown and simple bun. Yet he could not help but continue to imagine her with her hair down—and maybe her dress down too.

He stifled a growl. He must get control of himself. Miss Rose was his grandmother's companion and his hired assistant in his important work for the Foreign Office. Their relationship was purely business and contractual. Nothing more.

Penelope picked up the tea tray and walked up to the footman, who was pouring golden liquid from one of his carafes for an elderly gentleman. "Jonathan," she accosted him. "Her Grace, the duchess, is not inclined for tea tonight. Could you take this tray down for me?"

"Not likely," the footman hissed in a manner he would never take with any other guests of the party. "Why don't you make yourself useful and do it yourself?" The footman sidestepped Penelope, but she stepped in front of him, stopping him with her tray.

"It is getting heavy. Can you take it? I don't want it to spill."

"Can't. Got my own hands full. You blind?"

"What seems to be the difficulty?" Marchford had seen enough. Penelope was right; the footman was at least rude if nothing else. "Here, I will take your tray, and you can take the lady's tea service."

Marchford reached for the decanters, but the footman was not going to relinquish his prize readily. "No, Your Grace. You don't need to do that. I will call for some assistance for the lady." He glanced around, but Penelope had already told two other footman they were needed in the kitchens. It would take them a few minutes before they returned.

"Thank you so much." Penelope all but tossed her tray at the footman, and Marchford held out a hand for the tray of liquor, but Jonathan held on.

"No, it's no trouble. Please, Your Grace, I can carry both."

To Marchford's surprise, the footman managed to take her tray in one hand and balance it on one shoulder, while the other tray he likewise carried on the other shoulder. One had to admire the footman's determination and ingenuity, but his clear desire to retain possession of the decanters only raised Marchford's suspicion.

Penelope glanced at him with large eyes, a clear appeal to do something. He could not resist her silent plea—he could hardly resist her at all. Hoping Grant would forgive him, he grabbed the edge of the tea tray and shoved it up, spilling the contents with a crash of broken china.

Penelope's mouth dropped open. People stopped their games and turned to stare. Marchford grabbed the tray of decanters from the footman's grasp, and they left the footman thin-lipped in the middle of shattered china and a puddle of tea. With the focus of the assembly momentarily diverted by the cracked crockery, Marchford was able to discreetly slip Penelope back to the private study, alone now save the tray and three bottles of spirit.

He placed the tray on a small round table. The decanters were a fine set of cut leaded crystal with ornately engraved gold inlays. Even the bottoms were of gold, engraved with intricate patterns. Nothing seemed out of place, except two were labeled "Brandy."

"Why two of the same liquor?" Pen asked, her focus on the bottles.

Marchford was more interested in watching her intelligent face as she worked over the puzzle of the decanters. Forcing himself to focus on the task at hand, he found a glass. "I am agreeable to a test." He poured himself a splash of one and sampled it carefully in his mouth before swallowing. "Good. Very fine. Expect nothing less from Grant."

"And the other?" asked Pen.

Marchford poured the liquid, but Penelope stopped him.

"Look. When you pour, there is something I can see in the bottle," exclaimed Pen, her eyes alight with the delight of discovery.

Marchford was enchanted. She was not dressed to entice; in a plain muslin gown and a requisite old-maid lace cap, her appearance was utterly lamentable. Yet her wide-eyed excitement made him momentarily forget the task at hand.

"You are not even looking at it," protested Penelope.

"Decanters…right," sputtered Marchford. He turned the bottle slowly and squinted through the faceted glass. There appeared to be an inner tube also made of glass. He looked over the decanter at her with a growing smile. She returned it with a grin of eager anticipation.

Forcing himself to get back to business, Marchford made a further inspection of the bottle. On the bottom, he found a small, round stopper within the engraved gold. Carefully removing it, he discovered a glass chamber inside the decanter and within a small twist of a note.

"Penelope, you are lovely tonight. Absolutely brilliant." Marchford meant every word. Carefully, he opened the note and spread it flat. Penelope leaned in, her brown head close to his. He caught a whiff of her perfume—or more likely the lavender soap she used. It was more intriguing to him than any exotic fragrance. He had to remind himself to read the note.

Another delivery tonight. Four bells.

"It appears people were using this decanter to pass messages," said Marchford. "Ingenious really."

"It is a clever contraption. But why not just pass a note hand to hand or even just talk briefly at the ball?" She leaned closer to inspect the note.

"It would be beyond my capability to pretend to know what passes for rational thought in the minds of my enemy," muttered Marchford, also leaning toward the note—and her. "But there is always a chance of being overheard or seen. This way, information can be passed between them or to the footman, without them ever being seen together."

"What do you think the footman knows?"

The footman! "Don't know, but I'm going to find out." Marchford was already heading to the door. His long stride outstripped Penelope as he approached the ballroom. A quick glance told them the footman was not present. He quickly inspected the card room and the dining areas. Jonathan was not to be found. Once again he needed assistance from Miss Rose. "Fastest way to the kitchens," Marchford demanded of her.

"Follow me," said Penelope, guiding him to a small side door that led to a servants' passage down to the kitchens.

He paused only a moment. He had hardly ever entered his own kitchens, let alone those of a friend. He burst out into the heat and bustle of the kitchens, which came to a complete halt at the presence of a duke in their midst. Jaws dropped; a dish hit the floor; a scullery maid squeaked in surprise.

"Jonathan the footman," Marchford commanded.

"He went outside," faltered the cook, pointing to the side kitchen door.

Marchford ran out the door, up the steps, and out to the alley behind the house, hoping Penelope would have the sense to not follow. She did not.

"Stay here," he commanded her, pulling a small pistol from his coat. Nothing could happen to her. Nothing.

He heard the scuffing of boots on gravel ahead and proceeded into the darkness of the alley.

Five

PENELOPE WAITED IN THE FREEZING COLD FOR
Marchford to return. As demanded, she went no farther than the kitchen steps and stared into the darkness
where Marchford had disappeared. Despite the apparent danger that led Marchford to pull out his pistol,
the prominent thought in her head was: Just where did
he hide said pistol? His coat was formfitting enough
one would think there would be a bulge somewhere,
and yet he appeared the very figure of a gentleman in a
perfectly cut coat. He must have had his coat cut with
the express purpose of concealing weaponry. Did he
always carry it? Shocking.

Pen waited for a moment, squinting into the dark
and listening past the soft musical strains of the orches-
tra that floated beyond the walls of the ballroom. It
seemed impossible that any true danger would lurk
here, by the walls of the Grant home. Yet Marchford
was always wary of foreign agents, and he had been
right to suspect the footman.

A sudden shout pierced the night followed by
a gagging cry. She was running into the dark alley
before she could think. Marchford! Was he hurt?

She ran forward into the blackness. The winter air was cold and damp. She breathed hard and her lungs complained. Where was he? She stilled and listened in the dark. Footsteps, grating on the rocks and gravel, echoed off the alley's walls around her. Was someone running away or toward her? She spun around just as a black-caped form knocked into her hard and sent her sprawling to the ground.

She shrieked and rolled over onto her back. A figure loomed over her. It bent closer, reaching out. Penelope shouted for help and grabbed a handful of dirt and gravel, throwing it into the man's dark face.

"Ow!" The man stood up. "I say, Penelope. Rather unsporting to blind me."

"Marchford?" Penelope breathed a ragged sigh of relief. "I thought you were trying to kill me. Why did you run into me?"

"I didn't. Must have been the man I was chasing. Are you hurt?" He reached down and, without warning or preamble, neatly picked her up in his arms.

"Oh!" squeaked Penelope, surprised to find herself in the arms of the duke. She wrapped her arms around his neck in a natural reaction. "I…I'm fine."

"You sound breathless. Are you sure you are all right?"

Her sudden difficulties in breathing had more to do with his holding her than her being knocked to the ground, but she could hardly express that sentiment. "Just give me a moment to collect myself."

"You are safe. No need to fear." His words were soft and tender.

Penelope could not help herself. She rested her

head briefly on his shoulder. His coat smelled of fine cloth and gentleman musk. She breathed deep, relaxing into the intoxicating scent, before remembering her place. "I am fine now. I can stand."

"Are you certain? If anything happened to you..." The sentiment hung in the frosty air unfinished. He had not yet set her down.

"I am well," she assured, though in no hurry to be released.

Finally he allowed her to regain her feet, but then surprised her by making a cursory inspection of her body, running his hands down her sides. "Does anything hurt? Are you injured in any way?"

Despite the bitter cold, she warmed at his touch. She wished to invite him to continue to search for injuries but censored the comment. "No, just jostled a bit. Was it Jonathan who hit me?"

"No, no, I am certain it was not he."

"Then who ran into me?"

"The man who got away." Marchford was solemn in his disappointment.

"The footman got away?"

"No. He's here."

"Where?" Penelope struggled to see in the almost impenetrable darkness. "Shall we question him? He is the link to whoever was passing messages in the ballroom."

"Yes, I know. Unfortunately, others in the ballroom also knew that and disposed of a certain problem."

"How so?" Penelope attempted to walk past Marchford in the dark alley. The duke blocked her path but not before she caught a glimpse of something that stopped her cold. The footman was lying on the ground in an awkward position, a pool of something dark around his throat.

Penelope grew suddenly chilled, which given the freezing wind slicing through her muslin gown, was surprising only because she didn't think she could get colder than she already was.

She turned away, not wanting to see more. "Is he dead?"

"Quite dead."

Penelope took a ragged, cold breath. The man was dead. Dead. Her mind reeled and the ground began to tip. He was alive just a few minutes ago. How could such a hale and hearty lad suddenly cease to exist?

Marchford put an arm around her waist and pulled her close to his body, propping her up, which was odd since she hadn't realized she was starting to fall. Before she had seen the body, she had not known herself to be the fainting type.

Marchford walked her away from the body. "Take a few slow breaths." Penelope did as he suggested, slowing her breathing, feeling the cold, damp air fill her lungs like a restorative.

"This is not your first corpse," she whispered.

"No. The first time I found a dead body, I cast up my accounts all over my boots."

"Waste of good food," muttered Penelope, trying to keep the contents of her stomach where she'd put it.

"I was more thinking of my boots."

Penelope could not help but smile. With another breath, she straightened her backbone and attempted to pull away from the duke with a shiver. "I can walk on my own now, thank you."

"Yes, of course," he said. He removed his jacket and put it around her shoulders. It was warm with his own heat and smelled intoxicatingly of him. She breathed deep again, and his arm returned to around her waist, as if it belonged there. She could not help herself from leaning into him, accepting his warmth and strength.

Marchford led Penelope down the stone steps, back into the kitchen. "Are you ready?"

"Yes," said Pen, pulling away and handing him back his jacket. Appearances must be preserved. He nodded in understanding and put his jacket back on, hiding his pistol somewhere in the mysterious coat. Within the kitchen, the air was shockingly hot and pungent with the smells of food in various states of preparation and waste. All were silent again as the duke returned. The butler, having clearly been notified of the strange goings-on, greeted Marchford with a bow.

"Your Grace, how may we assist you?"

"Inform Mr. Grant there is a situation with the footman and rouse a constable. I will meet Grant in his private sitting room." Marchford leaned toward the butler and whispered something further in his ear.

The generally reserved butler stared in shock, his eyes wide. "At once, Your Grace," he finally managed and bowed again to take his leave.

Marchford led Penelope up through the servants' stairs to avoid company. Penelope noted he put his arm around her once more. She was not about to protest. Marchford led her deftly to the private sitting room.

"I am quite well," insisted Penelope, but she did not resist when a glass of brandy was placed in her hand.

"Of course you are," said Marchford mildly, and he poured himself a glass.

Not generally one for hard spirits, as befitted a young lady raised by a country parson, Penelope decided that, considering the shocking events of the evening, it may be permissible to have a few sips. The brandy seared a hot trail down the back of her throat. She was not sure if it was considered restorative, but the unpleasant sensation did shock her back into the present, so she supposed the object of the libation had been met.

Within minutes, Grant strolled into the sitting room, followed by his young bride, the renowned beauty Eugenia Grant, who entered with a hand protectively over her growing midsection.

"Marchford, what have you done now?" asked Grant. "I knew when they said you had a situation there must be something dreadfully wrong."

"Now, perhaps, it may not be as bad as all that," said Genie with a kind smile that lit her deep blue eyes.

"The footman has been murdered," said Marchford.

The Grants shared a look between them.

"Then again, my dear, you may well be right," said Genie sincerely.

Grant smiled at his new wife, then shook his head at Marchford. "I told Genie you were a bad risk to invite. Always intrigue with you. Why, a body's not safe within fifty feet of you."

"I cannot believe such a thing would happen," exclaimed Genie.

"Now don't upset yourself," soothed Grant, leading his wife to a high-backed chair by a warm fire. He had her comfortably settled with her feet propped up on a little footstool in seconds. "Wanted the ball to be memorable, didn't you? When word gets out you hosted a real murder, no one will ever forget!"

"I do not think Mrs. Grant wishes to be remembered as being the hostess to a murder," said Penelope, reading the horrified look on Genie's face.

Grant shrugged. "No one will miss the next party. Too interesting."

"You are rather taking this in stride," commented Marchford, taking a seat on the settee next to Penelope.

"No reason to get upset," said Grant in his affable manner. "Knew something was smoky when I saw those shoes. Man up to no good, I'm sure."

"Shoes?" asked Genie.

"Too nice by half," said Grant. "Custom pair by David and Clark. Now how would an honest footman be able to pay for those? He wouldn't. So he must be a dishonest one."

"So that is why you had me follow the footman," said Penelope, feeling the need to hazard another sip of brandy. Only Grant, with his impeccable knowledge of all things fashion, could have noted such a detail.

The butler entered and presented the Watch. The constable's eyes bulged at the glittering array of honored personages present. Pen felt sorry for the man to have to interview the duke. The Duke of Marchford could be an imposing man when he had the mind, and he quickly took control of the interview, answering the questions of his own posing, which he felt most relevant. The constable then turned to Penelope, but Marchford interceded.

"I have already told you what you need to know about her involvement. You needn't involve the lady who is clearly overwrought with the proceedings of the night." Marchford shifted closer to her on the seat and leaned forward so that he was partially blocking her view of the constable—or the constable's view of her.

"No, no, I can answer a few questions," said Penelope, needled by the suggestion her precious nerves were at risk.

"This person who hit you, Miss Rose. Did you get a look at him?" asked the constable.

"No, I fear I did not. He was wearing a dark cloak and cowl. I saw nothing of his face. It all happened so fast."

"Lucky to be alive, miss," commented the constable.

Penelope stilled. He was right; she could have been killed. No wonder Marchford had been so concerned with her welfare.

"Enough questions," demanded Marchford, putting his arm around her and resting it on the back of the settee in a protective gesture. Though his arm was not touching her—that would be insupportable—Penelope was keenly aware of his arm's presence near her shoulders. "You know where to find me if you should require any further information," continued Marchford.

The constable bowed and left them in silence.

"Do you know who killed the footman?" asked Grant when the four of them were alone in the sitting room.

"No, but I know he was assisting in some clandestine communications." Marchford related to the

Grants their findings about the brandy decanter. "Can you tell me where the decanters came from?"

Grant shook his head slowly. "No, can't quite place it. Got a lot of presents for the wedding. Genie, you know?"

Genie also shook her head. "No, and I wrote notes for all the gifts. I do not recall this one. I do not believe we have had it long. Isn't it strange? I saw it before, but I thought it something you had acquired, my dear."

"And I thought it a wedding gift," said Grant.

"It may have been added to your household without your knowledge," suggested Penelope.

"Oh dear." Genie put a hand to her cheek. "Truly, I must run a more competent household."

"No, no, I would forbid you change a thing." Grant rushed to her side. "Are you tired? Do you wish to rest, my love?"

"I confess, with all the festivities and the dreadful news about the footman, I do feel a mite worn." Genie stifled a yawn.

"To bed!" cried Grant, helping his growing wife out of the chair. "I shall put the solving of this mystery in your capable hands, Marchford. Good night, my friends!" Grant ushered the sleepy Genie out of the room.

"We must also get you home," said Marchford, offering Penelope his arm.

Penelope typically resisted all attempts at coddling, but she owned the prospects of a warm bath and a soft bed were inviting. She took the arm of the duke with a soft sigh. He would take her home. He would keep her safe. She should be comforted, but deep within she knew…

She wanted more.

～

The man in the thick Carrick coat raced down the cobblestone streets, whipping his horse to keep up the pace. What did he care if the beast broke a leg on the uneven ground? The nag wasn't his anyway, and his need was pressing. He must get to the men before four bells or all would be lost.

He turned down narrow, muddy streets and into the rookery of St. Giles. It was shocking how little distance there actually was between the spacious town houses of the landed gentry and the crowded slums of London. They were practically neighbors, but no resident of St. Giles would dare to trespass on the pristine streets of Mayfair, nor would any Town gentleman dare to step into the narrow, crooked streets of St. Giles.

The man in the Carrick coat soon gave up on the horse and continued on by foot, navigating the narrow paths, slogging through rancid filth. Most men in such a coat as his would avoid coming into the rookery for fear of robbery. This man, however, was known to the local thieves, and they wisely let him be.

This was the perfect hiding place for anything you wanted to have disappear. He entered the small warehouse where the crates smuggled in from France were stacked under a large amount of debris. The man sighed in relief; the crates were still there.

An elderly man with a sloped back entered the

room and gave a quick bow. "'Ere to move the barrels, gov'ner?"

"No, we have changed plans. No deliveries tonight."

"Right then," said the old man, and he shuffled away.

The man in the Carrick coat sank onto the crates in relief. He was in time. The mission had not been compromised. He pulled out a pipe from his large coat pocket but suddenly jumped off the crate in horror.

Light a pipe? What could he be thinking of? He eyed the crate with suspicion.

He was a smuggler, but his cargo was rather more dangerous than wine.

Six

THE COMFORTABLE TOWN CARRIAGE LUMBERED SLOWLY along the streets of London. Considering the momentous events of the evening, Penelope gave herself leave to lean back against the velvet squabs and rest her feet upon the foot warmer. She reveled in the warmth, gradually bringing her frozen toes back to life. Marchford, sitting across from her, remained somber and his posture rigid.

"What an eventful evening," commented Penelope, not knowing where to start. The entire day had been a series of emotional flips centered on the forbidding man sitting across from her. She wondered what put such grim tightness about his mouth.

"Yes. I appreciate your help. Though had I known such danger was nigh, I would never have requested your assistance." Marchford frowned more severely.

Now she understood what was irritating the man; he was reprimanding himself for unwittingly putting her in danger. It was actually quite kind that he was so disturbed. "You had no way of knowing a murderer was about."

"No, I did not." He spoke the words as a curse upon his ignorance.

"Surely you cannot blame yourself."

"I most certainly do."

"Nonsense. Besides, I was never in any real danger." She glanced at Marchford to judge his reaction to that statement. He remained impassive. "It was the poor footman who was the only target. He had not the kindest of hearts, but I do feel sorry for him."

"Do not waste your sympathy. He was a traitor to the Crown and got nothing more than he deserved. Though I wish he had revealed the identities of the conspirators before he died."

"He must have known something of importance," agreed Penelope. "What do you make of the note?"

Marchford shook his head slowly. "I am unsure. Since our enemy clearly suspects we are in possession of the note, whatever was going to happen at four bells has almost certainly been changed."

"So where do we go from here?" Tracking down spies was only part of the question. The word *we* reverberated within her chest. Was there any form of *we*?

"I would like to review everyone you can remember with whom the footman spoke, everyone to whom he gave a drink. Tomorrow we can have the servants interviewed, see if they know anything. Perhaps Grant can be of service in our inquiries." Marchford was all business.

"I believe Jonathan had only worked there a short time. I should ask Genie to speak to her housekeeper and get the references he provided. Perhaps they can be of assistance," Penelope responded in kind. Ironic that discussing traitors against the Crown was the safest topic of conversation.

"A capital idea," said Marchford, leaning back on the squabs, his body more relaxed. It was good to see him let go of self-recrimination.

"I am glad you approve." Pen smiled and let her eyes half close under the gentle rocking of the carriage. It had been quite an exciting evening, and she was more than ready to find her bed. Memories flooded back of what happened earlier when they were in her bedroom. What would have happened if…

Pen forced her eyes open and sat up straight. The Duke of Marchford had become an amiable acquaintance and had trusted her to assist with his investigations for the Foreign Office. He also had hired her to help him *find* a bride, not *be* his bride. He was a duke, after all, and she was, in the end, nothing more than his grandmother's companion. She must not let her imagination carry her into unrealistic flights of fancy.

She cleared her throat. After his kindness to her, she repented her mischievous suggestions for a mate. "I regret we were not able to find you a suitable bride tonight, but do not lose heart. We shall continue the search."

"For some reason, your words only bring a sense of doom to my poor heart."

"I am certain your heart will recover," Penelope clipped in return. She had the wretched realization that she owed him an apology. "I do apologize if some of my suggestions were not suitable, but the season is starting early since Parliament is in session. I am sure there will be some new—"

"No debutantes." The duke was firm.

"I beg your pardon?"

"No doe-eyed teenagers with fribble in their heads and spots on their faces."

"They don't all have spots," protested Penelope. "Besides, the most beautiful young ladies are generally engaged before the end of their first season. You need to consider those just entering society."

The duke shook his head. "I would rather have a wife with something in her head worth saying than a chit with a beautiful face and not one intelligent thought. And what on earth made you think Devine's infant niece would make me a suitable match?"

Penelope looked away and straightened her skirts. Silence fell within the carriage. Though she could not meet his eye, Penelope could feel the heat of his intense glare in the dim light of the carriage lantern.

"You knew she would make a poor match." The duke spoke in a low voice. "You did that on purpose." He leaned forward.

"It…it was a suitable match. You are on quite friendly terms with the Lord Admiral," Pen defended weakly, still unable to look at him directly. She hated that she was not a better liar.

Marchford moved across the carriage and sat next to her, causing her heart rate to jump. "You purposely attempted to connect me with the most unsuitable matches possible!"

"No…yes!" Penelope turned to him, tired of trying to maintain the facade.

"Why?" Marchford's voice raised and he leaned closer to her. "Why would you do such a thing?"

"Because you said my mother's gown was horrible." Penelope's voice also rose.

"I intended no insult to your mother. I'm sure she looked very well in this gown, *fifty years ago* when it was first made." He gestured down her body.

"Well! This gown is hardly fifty years old," she defended, her mind doing a quick calculation and coming up with a shockingly high number. "And even if it is a bit mature, it is still very serviceable." She leaned closer to the infuriating duke.

"Serviceable? The style is utterly outmoded, no matter how much you have attempted to have it redone. Why, the flounces are practically falling off." He slid closer and touched a flounce at her knee. The traitorous fabric fell off in his hand.

"You tore my gown!" She shouted in outrage, leaning still closer.

"I barely touched it!" The air crackled around them.

"You said this horrible gown was *good enough for Miss Rose!*" Penelope's voice caught, betraying the hurt she had felt at his thoughtless comment.

Marchford stilled. Only then did Penelope realize they were so close. Her heart pounded but whether with anger or something else she did not know.

"Did I truly say that?" Marchford's voice was soft, his eyes wide and black in the dim light. "I meant only to support you. I apologize for my hurtful words." He put his gloved hand over hers.

They leaned toward each other, their faces mere inches apart. Time seemed to still, to stretch on slowly. He moved closer, ever so slowly, as if in a dream. Penelope closed her eyes.

A sudden bump in the road jostled them apart, breaking the trance.

Marchford removed his hand and cleared his throat. "Yes. Quite. Very sorry if I offended." The cool exterior returned.

"And I apologize for my petty revenge."

Marchford pressed his lips together, but the mirth could not be contained. "I can't believe you paired me with that poor child—or that vicious princess." He leaned back and chuckled.

Penelope joined him. She was relieved he was taking it in a humorous light. She laughed partly because of her disastrous attempts at matchmaking and partly because she was nervous at what had almost happened between them. Or perhaps it was only in her own mind?

"I shall make a more honest attempt at trying to find you a bride," promised Penelope, unsure how she felt about this.

"It is important to find someone quickly," replied Marchford with an equal lack of enthusiasm. "I do not care to be stalked at the next ball as I was tonight."

"I shall put my mind to it after I see to your grandmother's nighttime routine," said Penelope.

They rattled along in the carriage for another full minute before they both realized something.

"The dowager!" gasped Penelope.

"We left her at the house," groaned Marchford, and rapped on the top of the carriage with his cane to give directions to the coachman to return to the assembly.

"I cannot believe we forgot her," said Penelope.

"I cannot believe you did not remind me," chastised

Marchford. "You know I am quite dependent on you to remind me to collect my grandmother."

Penelope smiled, remembering how she first met the duke and his grandmother. It had been less than a year ago when she found the Dowager Duchess of Marchford had been left behind in church, sleeping in the ladies' retiring room. Penelope had waited with the dowager until the duke arrived and berated him severely for leaving his grandmother behind. The dowager duchess was impressed by her pluck and offered Penelope the position as her companion on the spot.

"Yes, I suppose I am quite good at reminding you of your responsibilities to your grandmother. I thought perhaps my example would influence you to take more responsibility, but instead I fear I become more like you."

"Dreadful," said Marchford with a delicious smile.

Penelope was glad the darkness of the carriage hid the heat in her cheeks. "I can think of nothing worse."

It did not take long to return to the home of Mr. and Mrs. Grant. By unspoken agreement, they had no intention of telling the dowager they had mistakenly left her behind. They found her sitting at a game of whist, her blue eyes shining, a clear sign she was winning. Lord Langley, also a shrewd card player, sat across from her; together they made an astute team.

The dowager duchess played a card with a smile, her white hair gleaming in the candlelight only adding to her beauty. She had been lauded as the most ravishing lady of her day and through the refining of the years had emerged quite elegant, with the glint of fire still burning in her eyes. She took the trump, winning the last rubber of the game. The dejected couple forfeited their prize, forcing Marchford to look away so as to maintain the illusion that he did not know the amounts (shocking indeed!) that were laid down on the dowager's whist table.

"Are you ready to retire for the evening?" the duke asked his grandmother in a manner most solicitous.

"Did you remember me at last?" she asked with a malicious smile. "I wondered how far you both would go before you remembered to return for me."

Marchford and Penelope shared a glance. They were in for a scolding now.

"I would have been pleased to see her home in any case," said Lord Langley. He smiled in such a way at the dowager that Penelope almost felt inclined to blush. The pair of them were acting more like young lovers than the elderly grandparents they were. With a great-grandchild on the way for Lord Langley, Penelope felt sure he should not have given the dowager a wink. And as a woman who had buried three successive Dukes of Marchford, the dowager had no business returning it.

Marchford cleared his throat. "Shall we leave?" he intoned, frowning with a distinctively aristocratic air.

His grandmother, queen of the aristocratic set-downs, merely laughed in his face. "Do not take such a tone with me. You must learn to live a little."

"Children today." Lord Langley shook his head.

"La, but they would have been shocked by one day in King Louis's court," returned the dowager.

The fact that King Louis XVI had lost his life in part due to the excesses of his reign was not something

Penelope chose to address. Instead, she and the duke gave the dowager her precedence and followed her and Lord Langley out of the ballroom to the waiting carriage. Here, Lord Langley whispered something to the dowager that made her giggle.

Giggle.

Penelope was so shocked she could not find words. Marchford's eyebrows clamped down over his eyes. They glanced at each other, their suspicions shared.

Lord Langley on the other hand smiled broadly at them all. "Marchford, if I could have a word with you." The two men held back a moment while the ladies entered the carriage.

"Not now. Not now," said Marchford, briskly ending the audience and striding away from Lord Langley as if the man were a contagion. "Come see me later. Next month, perhaps."

Penelope wondered at this. Marchford's glower remained for the ride home. He was silent, but the dowager chatted freely, in a lively mood, until Penelope was inclined to ask if she was febrile, yet in truth she had never seen the dowager looking so well. Nor Marchford so ill.

"What is wrong?" she whispered to him when they finally returned to Marchford House and the duke handed her out of the carriage.

"My grandmother has taken utter leave of her senses."

Seven

PENELOPE'S DAY BEGAN WITH THE POST—FOUR LETTERS from her sisters. Her married sisters. Her beautiful, blond, vivacious, married sisters. Reading the letters brought a new adjective to mind. Not only were they blond, beautiful, vivacious, and married, but they were now all in expectation of a blessed event.

The Rose sisters had taken London by storm three years ago. After their parents died, their aunt brought them out in London. The Rose sisters soon made heads turn, all blond-haired, blue-eyed beauties...all except Penelope. She had supported her sisters, first her two elder, then her two younger, as they all found husbands, no one happier than her that they found true love. It was getting left behind that was less appealing.

Penelope was pleased, she reminded herself firmly. Very pleased. She would be an auntie again. Her elder sisters, Amelia and Sophie, were expecting their seconds; for her younger sisters, Mariah and Julia, it would be their firsts.

And for Penelope, there would be no babies at all.

Pen recalled once again Marchford's joke proposal

of yesterday. It was her only proposal and it was only in jest. Even if he had been serious, she would certainly never enter into a marriage of convenience. She may be on the shelf at age twenty-six, but she still had standards.

She pulled out her copy of Debrett's *Peerage of England* and flipped through the annotated pages. She and her sisters had used the volume as a sort of shopping guide for finding titled husbands. Penelope had made meticulous notes, adding sections for the respected landed gentry, and had used the volume with great success in finding brilliant marriages for all her sisters. She continued to use the volume to make matches in her new occupation as Madame X, society's most exclusive matchmaker.

The only person Penelope had not been able to find a match for was herself.

Dressed in sensible attire, her hair pulled back in a sensible knot, Penelope walked down to breakfast with every intention of having a sensible day. All aspirations toward sensibility were lost, however, when she entered the breakfast room.

He was there.

They were hardly alone, with the footman standing at attention on the side of the wall, but she was keenly aware of Marchford's presence in the room. Nothing between them had changed, and yet after their experience last night, she had difficulty looking at him in the same way again.

She had barely entered the room before the barrage began. "The Devine ball is fewer than three days away," Marchford accused over his eggs. It was barely nine in the morning, and he was still in a foul temper from the night before.

"Should I apologize?" Penelope selected some breakfast items for herself. She would not allow his ill temper to distract her from her meal. It would be insensible, and she was never that.

"Yes. Quite. I am obliged to go," said Marchford glumly. "I cannot insult Lord Admiral Devine by not attending his wife's Christmas gala."

"Dreadful. I can clearly see why you blame me." Penelope took a long sip of hot chocolate to avoid Marchford's cold stare.

"I do not blame you for the invitation," he began.

"Am I responsible for the Christmas holiday, then? All that merrymaking and jolly times—what rot. How astute of you to lay the blame at my doorstep."

"That will be all, Charles," said Marchford, dismissing the footman who had begun to snicker. "The Devine Christmas gala is something of a tradition. She is German aristocracy, you know, which somehow requires a tree to be carted inside and set ablaze."

Penelope put down her fork in surprise. "They set a whole tree on fire inside the house?"

"Not intentionally—except for the Christmas of 1804, though I rather think that was a mistake. The point is to attach candles all over the limbs of an evergreen."

Pen frowned. "What has burning a tree to do with Christmas?"

"How the blast do I know?" Marchford gave her an irritated scowl. He was certainly in an ill temper. "The point is I must attend, and now with the early start of the season, the gala will be a crush. Everyone is in a frolicking, blasted good mood."

"Appalling."

"The truly appalling thing is that I remain unwed, unengaged, and utterly unattached." He spoke each word as a crisp indictment against her.

"Utterly insupportable," agreed Penelope.

Marchford's frown deepened. "Truth is I need to find a wife in order to avoid the machinations of marriage-minded females and their utterly vicious mamas. All this holiday joviality and matchmaking nonsense—it's plain gone to her head. It can be the only explanation."

"Explanation for what?" Penelope was confused.

"Nothing, nothing at all. I can only hope it comes to nothing," he added in a mutter. "But more to the point, you cannot possibly throw me to the wolves without feeling the slightest bit of remorse."

"Of course not." Penelope revealed a packet of papers she had prepared for him. She should, perhaps, have shown him earlier but had been nettled by his accusatory tone. "Allow me to present six potential brides, all of the highest character and from some of the most established families."

"Oh. Well then." Marchford accepted the papers with a look Pen found unreadable. If he was not pleased by her efforts, she could do nothing more for him. She had stayed up late the night before, the excitement of the events at the ball making sleep impossible. Instead, she reviewed her annotated copy of Debrett's and created profiles of potential brides for Marchford. She had found the work calming after the unsettling events of the evening. She made practical checklists, rated numerous young ladies on essential qualities, and prepared a report of her top candidates.

She enjoyed bringing something as messy and confusing as falling in love into rational control. Turning the affairs of the heart into something tangible and quantifiable was comforting. Though when it came to making selections for Marchford, none seemed to quite fit. Beyond checklists and calculated evaluation, she had difficulty with the notion that any of these ladies would find themselves the wife of the scowling man before her.

"No. None of these are suitable." Marchford tossed the papers down on the table after only the briefest examination.

"What?" asked Penelope, her eggs wiggling on her fork halfway to her mouth. She had expected at least to be able to finish her breakfast while he selected a bride—and yet she could not deny a wave of relief.

"They are simply not suitable." He picked up her papers and began to thumb through them, tossing them down once more with each rejection. "Too young, too old, too empty-headed, too many freckles, too well dowered, and too, too…oh I don't know, but this one has too much of it at any rate."

"Too many freckles? Too well dowered?" Penelope had never heard of such a thing.

"I have no need for a well-dowered bride, should leave her to my friends who do. As for spots, I believe that speaks for itself."

"Well!" Penelope paused to collect her speech into something more refined than telling the duke to go to perdition. "I regret to tell you that you have rejected the most eligible ladies in London." And she was mighty pleased he had.

"Then perhaps you need to start looking at those *ineligible*, for none of these will do. In the meantime, I am still stuck attending the gala as a marked man. I have a most pressing need for a wife, and you have failed to provide a suitable candidate." His gray-green eyes pierced into hers. He wanted something from her, but what, she could not name.

"Your idea of suitable is rather elusive," defended Penelope, though in truth she only felt relief that he had not selected any of the potential brides. He was correct that none of them would do, though she would never admit to it.

"I am the Duke of Marchford," he said in a grave tone, accepting from the butler the newspaper that had just been ironed to prevent the ink from staining his precious hands.

"Yes, yes, quite." Penelope took another sip of cocoa. She returned to the comforting feeling of finding him odious to think so highly of himself. Of course half of London—particularly the female half—all seemed to agree with his self-aggrandizing assessment. The man was literally being stalked by eligible females, but Penelope had not the least amount of sympathy for him.

"For the price you are charging me for your dubious services, I expect nothing less than a suitable bride." Marchford unfolded his newspaper.

"I just presented you with six choices, and you refused them all. And one without even giving me a hint of why she was unacceptable."

"That last one snorts when she laughs."

"Does she really? Had I but known, I would have never have suggested her." Though her words dripped with sarcasm, it seemed to pass by Marchford unnoticed.

"The point is, I cannot attend the Devine gala unmarried still."

"If you wish to be married within three days, you may have to settle for the chit who snorts."

"I do not believe you are treating this situation with the gravity it deserves." He looked over his paper at her.

"I would never contradict you," Penelope said sweetly. She was quite enjoying herself.

Marchford folded his paper with a great rustle. "This is not simply a matter of my own personal interest. I cannot conduct the investigations necessary in the service to my king if I am constantly being hounded by females wishing to become the next Duchess of Marchford."

Penelope was forced to concede he had a point. "I shall redouble my efforts, though it might help if you could…"

"Lower my standards? Marry the next female who walks into the room?"

"It would make my job easier."

The Dowager Duchess of Marchford glided into the room with a radiant smile.

Penelope and Marchford exchanged a glance and a smile. "On second thought, perhaps not," murmured Penelope.

If the dowager heard her, she gave no hint of it and

instead sat down to her coffee and crumpet with clotted cream, with a gleam in her blue eyes that signaled she was up to mischief. "Good morning, children. Lovely day, is it not?"

Marchford's eyes narrowed and he disappeared behind his newspaper again. Penelope was suspicious. In all the time she had lived with the dowager, she had always taken breakfast in her room. The dowager's presence here in the breakfast room was greatly suspect. Adding to her alarm, Penelope had never seen the dowager in such a fine mood without it heralding some discomfort for either her or Marchford.

"Yes. Lovely day," came Marchford's detached voice from behind the paper. "Anything in particular that makes it admirable to you, Grandmother? Perhaps the cold or the damp or maybe even the ice?"

The dowager's good humor never faded. "Yes, and the snow. Do not forget it looks like snow."

"You despise snow," reminded Marchford.

"Me despise snow? Whatever gave you such a notion?" Antonia stirred her coffee and attempted to look innocent.

"Because you have told me so every winter that I have been alive." Marchford glanced over his paper.

The dowager waved an elegant hand at him like she was batting a fly. "Bah! What do you know of it? I used to race sleighs down country lanes before your father was even a twinkle in my eye. Ah, the times we had." She smiled and savored her crumpet as if she were eating ambrosia.

Penelope was truly concerned. Anything that had the dowager this pleased could only spell trouble.

Marchford refused to look beyond his paper, and she suspected his bad humor was directly related to the dowager's good one. Whatever had Antonia so pleased was clearly putting the duke in an ill temper.

"Anything new happen to put you in a good mood this morning?" asked Penelope.

Antonia smiled radiantly. "Yes, I suppose you could say so."

"Please do not hold me in suspense," said Penelope. "Will you not share your good news?"

"I was going to wait, but if you must know…" Antonia gave them both a wide, gracious smile and waited for Marchford to slowly lower his paper. "I am going to be married!"

"Married?" Penelope set her cocoa down with a clank, almost spilling it on her lap. Married? Of all the things she thought she might hear from the dowager's lips, marriage was not one of them.

Marchford was silent. His features hardened into stone, but it was evident he was not entirely caught unawares. No wonder he had been so irritable this morning.

"Forgive me," said Penelope, "but who is to be the groom?"

The dowager looked at Pen as if she were daft. "Why, Lord Langley of course."

"But you and he are always fighting," observed Penelope.

"So true. You see we are already acting like a married couple."

"Marriage, Grandmother? Why marriage?" Marchford's voice was strained.

"The thing to do," said Antonia lightly.

"At your age, I think it would be the thing *not* to do," accused Marchford.

Antonia's eyes flashed. "Are you insinuating you think me old?"

"No, not at all." He wisely disappeared behind his newspaper with an irritated shuffle.

"So you are going to marry the Earl of Langley?" Penelope was still struggling to make herself clear on the facts. "The same Lord Langley who broke your engagement so many years ago?"

Antonia looked down her regal nose. The remembrance was not appreciated. "Yes, indeed. He may be unworthy of me, but I will have him just the same." There was something definitely malicious twinkling in her eye. "Now I must dash. Langley will be coming by to take me riding in Hyde Park."

"Riding in this weather?" asked Penelope.

"Oh yes, for I have it on good authority that the Comtesse de Marseille does a morning constitutional in the park in her curricle." She glanced down at a rather large emerald surrounded with smaller diamonds on her finger. "A shame I cannot wear this outside my glove. Ah, well, can't be helped. No need to come with me Penelope." She paused as if seeing Pen for the first time. "What *are* you wearing?"

Eight

PENELOPE DECIDED TO PAY AN EARLY CALL ON HER friend Genie Grant. She wished to know how her friend had survived the shock of the night before. Genie had been married to the affable Mr. Grant for less than a year, and this had been her first great soiree, supposedly establishing herself as an accomplished hostess. Instead, her home was the scene of a murder.

Besides, Penelope needed an escape from Marchford House. The atmosphere between the dowager and Marchford had grown so chilly, going outside in the sleet was a welcome relief.

"Oh, thank you for coming!" Genie rushed to Penelope and held both her hands.

"I was not sure if you were seeing visitors."

"Oh, I'm not. But you are my friend." Genie gave her a smile that was truly lovely. She was a stunning girl with blond hair and blue eyes, a great beauty, but so unconscious of her looks that her disposition remained sweet. She was a rare creature, beautiful both within and without.

Penelope smiled in return. She was no great beauty

and knew it perfectly well, but Genie was so kind Pen could not begrudge Genie her looks.

"Come. Sit. I'll ring for tea and cakes. What a dreadful business with the footman. I cannot imagine why anyone would want to kill him. He seemed such a likable fellow." Genie motioned for Pen to sit next to her on the settee.

"I fear he may have been connected with some underhanded doings," said Penelope.

Genie shook her head and clasped her hands over her enlarging midsection. A happy event for the Grant household was clearly in the works. "So sad. I have heard there are spies among us, but why would anyone target this household? Surely they know Grant is not privy to any information they could want."

"I don't know either. Grant is a friend of Marchford's. It may be enough to put him under suspicion. I suppose the agents from the Foreign Office were here to ask questions."

"Yes, they spoke with the housekeeper and the butler. Can you imagine, they believe the references he provided were forged?" Genie spoke as if faking a reference were the worst thing she could imagine.

"Shocking," agreed Pen, though she could imagine things far worse. "I was hoping you might be able to shed some light on your footman so we may untangle this mystery."

"Indeed, we must find who killed him. I shudder to think there was a murderer wandering about just outside my kitchen door."

"There was possibly a murderer wandering about your drawing rooms."

"No!"

"Only someone at the party would have known we came into possession of the decanter that had the hidden message."

"Oh, yes." Genie grew pale. "I had not thought of that."

"Of course, it might not have been that at all, just someone passing by," added Penelope hastily, wishing she had kept her own counsel. One thing she had learned about expecting mothers was that they were not to be upset.

"You are very kind," said Genie in a voice that told Penelope she saw through her good intentions. "There is someone who may be able to help give us insight into the nature of the footman." Genie rang the bell and asked to have Jem called to the salon.

"You still have Jemmy?" Pen asked doubtfully.

"But of course!" replied Genie with a tense smile. Jem was a street urchin whom Genie, with her overly kind heart, had rescued and brought into service. The girl was quite unsuitable for service, but once Genie got it in her head to do a thing or save a person, she could be quite tenacious. Just ask Mr. Grant, whose intended desire to remain a bachelor for life was put to shambles within weeks of meeting her. Genie was like that—so very sweet but a force of nature few could stand against.

Jemima Price entered the salon with a skip in her step and a tear in the sleeve of her maid's costume. "Hallo!" The child ran up to Genie in a manner much too familiar for a maid.

"Miss Jemmy," said Genie with a look to remind

Jem of her manners before company. Penelope had the distinct impression the girl was not being treated as a servant but rather a distant relative or a loved pet. "You know that poor Jonathan was killed last night. Can you tell us anything about him that might help us understand why?"

"He was a lout for sure. Worst kind. Sweet words but dark on the inside. Do anything for a bit o' blunt." Jem's accent was so clearly from the rookery slums of London she was always a challenge to understand.

"What makes you say that?" asked Pen.

"He was a cunning shaver, t'be sure."

Pen looked at Genie for translation but she was no help. "What do you mean, Jemmy? And please use words I might have a chance of understanding."

"Oh, right. Sorry. I forget myself. I am trying to improve, honest."

"Yes, yes, you are doing well," soothed Genie. "Now tell us why you had a low opinion of him."

"He'd make himself scarce when there's work to be done and always be back afore he could get caught. Canny cove he was."

"Did you ever see any friends of the footman? Did you know any of his associates?" asked Pen.

Jem thought a moment but shook her head. "None never came for him that I know. He may come from seafaring folk—always whistling a shanty."

"Did he ever speak of any family?" asked Genie. "We should send his things somewhere."

"Nah. But check under the grate in his room. I saw him hide something there once."

"Thank you, Jemmy. You have been very helpful."

Jemima gave a broad smile and ran from the room, ran back in, gave a sweeping curtsy, and ran back out.

Genie sighed. "I know you are thinking I should not have her as a maid, and I know you are right, for she is not quite acceptable."

"No, but she is an observant little scamp, and that alone is worth her wages," reassured Penelope.

Genie smiled faintly. "I suppose now you want to see this grate."

"How did you guess?" Penelope returned the smile.

Soon the two ladies were in the footman's room. It was a small space at the bottom of the house, though like everything in Genie's household, the furniture and bedding was comfortable and generous. No servant of hers could claim deprivation from the creature comforts.

Under the bed was a small grate. It did not look clean and both ladies hesitated, with Pen finally deciding to sacrifice a handkerchief to pull the thing up. She did so with surprising ease and found a leather pouch. Penelope poured the contents into her hand and gasped.

"Oh my stars!" exclaimed Genie, staring at the gold coins in Penelope's hand.

"What are you paying your help?"

Genie could not suppress a laugh. "Not this! Look, twenty franc pieces with Napoleon on the front."

"And pieces of eight as well."

"He was involved in something." Genie straightened with a hand to her back and a slight grimace.

"Indeed. And I have kept you too long. May I take this to Marchford?"

"Please do. However Jonathan acquired it, I fear it was not by respectable means."

"Of that, dear Genie, we may be sure!"

❧

Marchford rustled papers about in an irritated manner. He must find the persons responsible for passing messages and killing the footman. He flung maps and notes and letters across his desk in some vain hope something would make sense. Surely nothing else in his life did.

He was in need of a wife, and yet there was none in whom he had the slightest interest. He must admit that Miss Rose had done a perfectly adequate job of supplying him with potential candidates—the second time at least—but absolutely none would do. Unfortunately, whenever he attempted to consider a perfect bride, the only image that came to mind was a picture of Penelope with her hair down. The vision came to him at the most inopportune times. He tried to keep her at an emotional distance, but it failed more often than it worked. It was enough to put any man in a foul temper.

To make matters worse, his grandmother had taken complete leave of her senses. Married? Impossible! It was unseemly for a woman her age. Unseemly, irresponsible, incomprehensible, and worse yet, utterly beyond his control. Total control of himself and his surroundings was the only thing that had ever kept him alive.

"Good morning."

Marchford jumped back and reached for his pistol,

pointing it in the direction of the voice. A small figure stepped forward out of the shadows. He knew this figure. Marchford took a moment to collect himself before answering. "Good morning, Mr. Sprot."

The old man stepped forward slowly and made his way to a wingback chair by the fire. Marchford pocketed the pistol and sat next to him in a matching chair. Mr. Sprot graced him with a paternal smile.

Mortimer Sprot had been an old, thin man when Marchford had first met him. The passing years had not been kind, making Mortimer thinner and more decrepit. The wrinkles of his face were deeply etched, his clothes loose over his wasted frame. He appeared frail and very much as if he would need assistance simply to rise from the chair. Yet here he was, sitting in Marchford's private study without being announced. His presence in the house was undoubtedly unknown to anyone besides the one to whom he wished to speak.

"I thought you had retired," said Marchford.

"Troubled times, Your Grace," said Sprot.

"I believe that is what you said to me when we first met," remembered Marchford. He had been assigned a post with the British consulate in Cádiz, the type of position they created for unwanted brothers of dukes. It was sufficiently prestigious but conveniently out of the way. Sprot had recruited him for the Foreign Office. It had given him purpose. Sprot had made Marchford a spy catcher. Marchford would have been content to live out his days working for the Foreign Office on the Continent had he not been called back to London when his brother, the previous Duke of Marchford, was on his deathbed.

"I am sure you are correct," said Sprot in his calm voice.

Marchford reclined back in his chair with a sigh. "I thought I had retired."

Sprot shook his head. "Apparently not possible in this game. Thought I could myself until my replacement turned up a traitor. Can't trust anyone but myself." He gazed at Marchford with intense black eyes. "And you."

"What is it you would have me do?"

"We have gained disturbing information that Napoleon is planning a large invasion to take London," said Sprot in his soft-spoken manner.

"Here? Impossible."

"Our enemy sees us as weak, vulnerable. Our current crisis in leadership is having a toll on our overall effectiveness."

"I am doing what I can with Parliament. Unfortunately our options…" Marchford did not have to express the well-known truth that King George's irresponsible son was not of the same caliber as his father.

"Yes. That is why our enemy is emboldened. There appears to be something brewing, some sort of attack or sabotage. Intercepted correspondence refers to 'the event,' something that will happen here I believe."

"What is their plan?" asked Marchford.

"That is what I hope I can rely on you to discover. We need to find those involved in this. The stakes are too high. We need to find the London spymaster."

"I understand."

He understood he would need Miss Rose's help, and that could prove difficult. He needed to focus on the task at hand—and not Penelope.

Nine

PENELOPE RETURNED TO MARCHFORD HOUSE WITH SOME trepidation. The disagreements between the Duke and Dowager Duchess of Marchford were legendary. Not that either party would express their anger in a verbal manner; there would not be any disagreeable scenes at Marchford House. No, their cold anger seeped through every word until the entire house was frozen solid.

Relations had improved of late between Marchford and his grandmother, but Penelope judged it would not take much to return to the frozen wasteland she initially endured when she first came to serve as the dowager's companion.

Penelope was thus pleased to learn that the dowager duchess was entertaining when she returned; it was always safer to be with the dowager in company. The Earl of Wynbrook had come to thank the dowager for connecting him with the elusive Madame X.

"I am pleased to tell you that Sir Gareth proposed to Janie last night," Wynbrook was telling Antonia when Penelope entered the sitting room. "The engagement will be published in the papers tomorrow!"

"My best wishes to the happy couple!" exclaimed Penelope. She was pleased Sir Gareth had responded to her gentle push in Lady Jane's direction.

"I shall tell Madame X that you are pleased with her efforts for dear Lady Jane," said the dowager. "I am glad she was able to act quickly to prevent social disaster." Antonia gave Pen a knowing smile.

"Indeed, quite so!" exclaimed Wynbrook, who was as animated as any brother would be to see his sister settled and respectably off his hands. "And I hear I am to wish you much happiness too, Your Grace!"

"You hear correctly," said the dowager with a broad smile, placing her hand where he could see the large ring.

"I have come with strict instructions to discover your plans for your wedding date," said Wynbrook. "Jane does not wish to conflict. They wish to have the engagement ball before the end of the year."

"Yes, she really must. Will she be married from home or church?"

"Home, I believe."

"I was married from home, but that was well before any here were born. I thought to grace St. George's this time, but I fear it is not seemly for a woman of my age to do such a thing."

"Nonsense!" roared Wynbrook, which of course was the only appropriate thing to say.

The duchess smiled as radiantly as any bride. Wynbrook conversed easily about wedding plans, though he left the debate about the best warehouses for the wedding clothes to the ladies.

Midway through the visit, the butler entered and

intoned that Penelope was needed elsewhere. Pen knew exactly why she was being called. Her presence was requested by the Duke of Marchford.

And the duke waited for no one.

Penelope walked to the study, her heart an annoying flutter. Why should a simple meeting fluster her so? She decided she must be annoyed with him. When she entered the study, the Duke of Marchford was at his desk, focused on his papers, and did not bother to look up, let alone stand, at her presence, further irritating her.

"You might have waited until our visit with our guest had concluded," she chastised.

"Guest?" Marchford looked up over some notes and a map. "Do you refer to Wynbrook? Nonsense. He came to visit my grandmother anyway."

Penelope bristled under the assumption, albeit correct, that her presence was not sufficient to draw such visitors. "If I am of no great import, then I shall retire to my room and work on my correspondence. I am quite delinquent with my sisters."

"Now don't fly into hysterics."

"I assure you my uterus is where it ought to be."

The comment was assured to break Marchford's concentration, and he looked up, perplexed. "Your what?"

"Uterus. You made reference to it with the ill-advised hysterics comment. You are aware that the word hysterical comes from the Latin root word meaning *uterus*, based on the odd notion that insanity in women is brought on by a wandering uterus."

Marchford stared at her and said nothing.

"A strange idea indeed, for everyone knows insanity in women is clearly caused by men."

Marchford raised one dark eyebrow, a smile playing on his lips. "And what of insanity in men?"

Penelope took a seat in a burgundy-colored leather chair before the desk and examined the papers littering the top. "I can only assume they are born that way."

Marchford chuckled. "Your conversation is nothing if not educational."

"Is that why you summoned me away from morning callers? To discuss madness?" Penelope smiled in return. She could not help but enjoy sparring with the duke.

Marchford leaned back in his chair, the smile still on his lips. "Yes, actually—the madness of King George. With Napoleon at our backs, it could not have come at a worse time."

"How can I help?" Penelope was all business.

"I would like you to speak to Mrs. Grant. I know the Ministry has already been there, but perhaps you can find something of importance they overlooked."

"I've already done that." Penelope pulled the leather pouch of coins from her reticule and plunked it on the duke's desk, explaining how she had come by it. He listened attentively to all she had to say.

"Very well done, Miss Rose," said Marchford with genuine warmth in his eyes.

Penelope smiled at his unmitigated praise. It was rarely bestowed and therefore worth the earning. Something in the intensity of his gaze heated her core.

Marchford cleared his throat and focused back on his papers. "Now if only you could be as successful in managing my grandmother."

Penelope's smile faded. "Your grandmother is certainly old enough to make up her own mind on the subject."

"No one would debate the fact that my grandmother is of age, Miss Rose. What I would like is some enlightenment as to why, after fifty years of living as the dowager duchess, she would suddenly decide to wed again."

"I wish I knew, but I was as much surprised as you, though she did seem intent on sharing her good news with the comtesse."

Marchford narrowed his eyes. "My grandmother is a proud person. To have been left at the altar by Langley early in life would have been a severe blow."

"Though she more than made up for it by marrying a duke afterward," Penelope reminded him.

"Perhaps she seeks to redeem the one stain on her otherwise flawless record by showing the world that even the one man who dared to spurn her can be made to come around."

Penelope leaned back in her chair. "A rather cynical view of marriage, even for you."

Marchford shrugged. "Marriage is nothing but a social contract, generally initiated to increase wealth or status or in this case repair a reputation. How would you explain it?"

Penelope leaned forward again, trying to find some humor in his eyes to say that this was all in jest, but she could not. "Do you not believe in the awakening of two hearts when they fall in love? Perhaps she has rekindled a love from when she was a young girl. You must concede the possibility of true romance."

"Romance?" He shook his head and folded his arms across his chest. "Utter rubbish."

Penelope's heart crashed to the floor with his dismissal. She knew not why, but she desperately needed him to believe in the possibility of true love. "But you must allow that true love is a possibility." Penelope pressed her point. "There are many cases of people doing remarkable things all for the power of love."

Marchford's cool reserve stiffened into something more like cold disdain. "Yes, people do the most remarkable, irrational, unsupportable things all for an ounce of lust, easily enflamed and just as quickly extinguished."

Penelope jumped up from the chair, her heart pounding. "I think it perfectly odious for you to disregard the most pure, most important of human experiences into something so trivial—and to assign such shallow motivations to your grandmother," she added, almost forgetting the topic of the discussion.

Marchford stood as well, forcing Penelope to look up at him. "Think what you like, but I have only known this 'most important of human experiences' to cause pain to all involved, and as for my grandmother, I can only say that I have known her much longer than you. I have no intention of allowing such a distraction now when I need to focus on the important work at hand."

"On what grounds would you stop this union?" asked Penelope, trying to redirect her thoughts toward Antonia and not her own disappointment at his words. "There can be no grounds for denying her your blessing to marry a peer of the realm. Besides, have you not considered how beneficial this marriage would be for you?"

"For me? How so?"

"She would naturally move to Langley Hall, leaving your household open for your potential bride. Have you not tried to force your grandmother to decamp for the Dower House in the country ever since your return from Cádiz? You wished to free your household from her influence so you could bring in a wife who could take over command of the household management without her interference."

"Which could never happen in her presence." Marchford was pensive.

"Quite so." Penelope was not so blind to her mistress's faults that she did not recognize that Antonia would never hand over the reins of control to what she considered her household. She hoped this new perspective would prevent war from breaking out once again between grandmother and grandson.

Marchford frowned from the effort the consideration of this new perspective brought him. "Perhaps," he said slowly.

"Besides, can you not consider for a moment that perhaps she has fallen in love?"

"Love is not an emotion she knows anything about," said Marchford more coldly than either expected.

Penelope could think of no reply. Gone was the amusement in his eyes; only pain rested there now. Her anger receded, leaving only sorrow for whatever had occurred in his life to turn him so violently against love.

"Forgive me." Marchford shuffled the papers on his desk in a businesslike manner. He grabbed hold of the leather pouch of coins and bounced it in his hand. "We need to find out more about these coins."

He changed the subject so fast Penelope was almost dizzy from the sudden turn. "If we cannot determine where he got them, perhaps we can learn something from where he exchanged them. He certainly could not have spent a gold franc in London without raising suspicion. You said something about a naval connection with the footman?"

Penelope nodded, keeping the discussion on safe topics. "Perhaps Wynbrook's friend, Lord Darington, whom we met yesterday, could help. He is a sea captain and would presumably know where to exchange money."

"Good thinking. We shall ask for his assistance." Marchford spoke in a clipped tone. "Second, we need to find who was using that decanter at the ball to pass messages. The decanter itself must have been a special order. I have already gone around to a few glassmakers in Town, but when I asked questions, they appeared nervous and stopped talking. All I gleaned was that the maker had died. Don't like it."

"What do you mean?"

"Something has them spooked, and they don't want to tell me. I did discover the name of a glassmaker who died recently, but I doubt going to his widow myself would garner the information I want." Marchford met her eyes in a manner that raised her pulse. "I need you."

Penelope took a sharp breath. She wished to remain aloof and rejected the thought that she too had fallen under the spell of the handsome duke. And yet she knew if he asked, there would be little she would not do for him.

"What would you have me do?"

Ten

"ARE YOU GOING LIKE THAT?" ASKED PENELOPE.

"You find fault in my appearance?" Marchford held himself at a rigid hauteur.

Penelope had woken early and met Marchford at the prescribed time. The plan was to appear to be common folk to induce the widow of the glassmaker to talk. Marchford felt Penelope would be more successful in securing this audience, hence his request for her presence. However, if Marchford was attempting to appear as one of the masses, or even shabby gentry, he was far from the mark.

"You look perfectly acceptable if you are going to White's, but for trying to get real people to talk to us, it is a bit much." In truth, Penelope enjoyed the image of the superbly attired Duke of Marchford a bit too much.

"You are suggesting I am not a real person?" Marchford inspected his bright-blue coat of superfine with disapproval. "This is of inferior quality. Besides, I will wear my greatcoat over it."

Penelope rolled her eyes. "No, you are not a real

person." She shook her head and muttered, "Inferior quality indeed."

"You suggest I further degrade my appearance?"

"It would be helpful."

"I live to please you."

Penelope's breath caught, and she let it out slowly, turning away. She wished there were more behind his idle words than just talk.

"We cannot all have garments such as the one you wear." He looked her up and down in a manner that raised her temperature. "I thought Grandmother gave away all your old gowns."

"I bought them back," said Penelope.

Marchford stopped and turned toward her, eyebrows raised. "You actually paid money for this... this...thing?" He gestured to her plain muslin frock.

"Are you criticizing my mother's gown again?" Penelope's voice raised an octave.

"Never!" The duke held up his hands in surrender. "Not at all. You look very...sensible."

Sensible. There it was again. Would she ever do something insensible?

Penelope donned her old wool coat, warm and *sensible*. Marchford led them out the door to the stables.

"Willie, my good man," Marchford greeted the stable master. "I do appreciate the cut of your coat and that cloak looks quite warm."

Willie, a sturdy man in his forties, lifted his bushy eyebrows in surprise and paused a moment before replying, "The missus made them for me. I'll pass along the compliment."

"Ah, thank you, do that. In fact, if it is not too

presumptuous, I should love to own that coat and cloak myself, though I know you could hardly wish to be parted from them since they were made by your dearest wife."

"Wouldn't go that far," said the stable master slowly, as if trying to make sense of the duke's strange statements.

"Then perhaps I might persuade you to make a trade. My coat was not stitched by hands quite as loving or with as much care, but—"

"Done!" The stable master was already stripping off his brown cloak and his mud-green jacket and handing it to the duke.

Marchford traded his blue superfine and brushed wool greatcoat for the stable master's attire and turned to Penelope, his eyes demanding approval.

"Some improvement." She knew better than to let him feast on too much praise. "Now do you have any vehicle of a simple nature?"

The stable master ran down the list of fashionable carriages, and it was clear no such modest vehicle existed in the stables of a duke, so they were for a moment in a quandary.

"You'll have to hire a hack for us," the duke told the stable master.

Willie bowed and departed just as the most modest of conveyances rolled slowly into their drive, being pulled by a swaybacked gray horse. The curricle was of such disrepair it more resembled a hay wagon. Penelope assumed it must be a tradesman making a delivery and was therefore shocked when Lord Darington jumped down.

"Lord Darington." She curtsied. "What a surprise to see you again so soon. Good morn to you."

"Goodness, my man. Were you robbed?" asked Marchford, surveying his questionable equipage with alarm.

"No, nothing like that." The stern expression on Darington's face gave him the appearance of being older than his age. His clothes would best be described as adequate, plain, sturdy, functional. She could appreciate the sentiment but knew that, among his peers, his attire would be considered woefully insufficient.

"M'sister has a morbid fascination with cost savings," continued Darington. "This was quite inexpensive." Considering the condition of the carriage, Penelope thought any amount to be a crime. His cloth also must have suffered from his sister's "morbid" sense of thrift. With a flash of unwanted insight, she wondered if this was how the dowager felt looking at her older gowns.

"I should say." Marchford shook his head in disbelief.

"I came to give you a report regarding the question you asked me yesterday." Darington got directly to the point.

"Yes, thank you. I appreciate your swift attendance to this matter."

Darington shifted his eyes to Penelope and back to Marchford in a silent request.

"Do speak freely. Miss Rose is my associate in these matters," said Marchford.

Penelope's heart soared. His *associate*. It sounded important.

"I took the description of the young footman to

several moneylenders along the docks. One knew him, had been changing money for the past four months. Doubloons and francs mostly."

"Where would a footman get such loot?" asked Marchford to no one in particular.

"Smuggling most likely. We have a blockade, but society wants French wines, and so many look the other way." Darington's voice was bitter with disapproval. "Quality gets what quality wants."

"Any talk on who killed the footman?" asked Marchford.

"Talk yes, but nothing definite. Most figured he was involved in something shady, and got killed for his troubles."

"Thank you, Lord Darington, you have been most helpful," said Marchford. "Please do forgive me, but I wonder if I might borrow your…err…carriage for a few hours at most. We should be very glad to have my groom drive you home."

Darington lowered his eyebrows in an intelligent glower. "In disguise are you? Very well."

"You do not wish to know why we are traveling together in such a manner?" asked Penelope. Darington lacked a natural level of curiosity.

"I can think of only two reasons why you would travel in disguise. First, you are proceeding in some sort of romantic adventure in which you do not wish your identities to be known until the elopement is finalized."

Penelope's mouth dropped open and she struggled to find an appropriate response.

"Second," continued Darington, "you are proceeding to search for the murderer of the footman and feel you should be more successful appearing as a common man than a duke. Either way I will not interfere. If the first, I ought not, and if the second, I should not."

"Well said, my friend." Marchford gave him a smile. Penelope wished he would clarify any confusion regarding an elopement, but Marchford went on along a different train of thought. "I shall confer with the stable master and let him know the change of plans."

Marchford strode off into the damp, early morning fog, leaving Darington and Penelope alone in the dark gray mist.

"There is no elopement." Penelope felt the need for a quick clarification. "No romantic adventure." *More's the pity.*

"If you say so," said Darington without emotion. "Speaking of romantic adventure, is the dowager duchess available for visitors this morning?"

Penelope could only smile. The dowager would not be ready to receive guests any time before noon. "I fear she does not receive anyone so early."

"I understand she helped Wynbrook by serving as an intermediary between him and a matchmaker."

"Yes, we do know a matchmaker, but she remains quite elusive and does not want her identity known."

"I see. Do you know how she may be contacted on a matter of business?"

"I can assist you and take your request to her. Are you looking for a wife, my lord?"

"No!" he exclaimed with more power than was necessary. "Looking for a husband for my twin sister."

"The sister who chose this conveyance as a Town coach?" asked Penelope, hoping for a negative response.

"Yes. Lady Katherine."

Penelope swallowed dashed hopes. "I believe she indicated at the ball her desire never to wed."

"Precisely why I have come," he said as if the conclusion was obvious. "Kate does not wish to wed. But it is time. She should marry."

"Indeed, all women should be married." Except, of course, her own spinster self.

"How much does it cost?" Darington was clearly a blunt man, quick to get to the heart of business. A sea captain too long she guessed. So Penelope told him, assuming he could not afford the going rate. He did not even blink. "I accept your terms."

"So do you have a particular man or type of man in mind for your sister?"

"Breathing."

Penelope smiled, but Darington's face was so impassive she hardly knew if he was attempting humor. "I shall guarantee that all of Madame X's grooms are in the land of the living. Have you any other attributes you would like to mention?"

"Whatever the standard kit is will do for my sister."

"Standard kit?"

Darington shifted on his feet. "Acceptable society, plump in the pocket, modest in vice." He crossed his arms before himself. "In truth, it would be good if her intended groom were of modest habits. She has no tolerance for men who suffer from moral failings."

"You want a young, rich, English gentleman who does not chase women or drink in excess?"

"Or smoke or take snuff," Darington added, utterly missing the sarcasm in her voice.

"And where would you think such bastions of society would congregate?"

"Honestly, I have no idea. If I did, I shouldn't need to call the matchmaker, would I?"

Penelope could hardly argue with his logic. "I shall relay the message to Madame X."

"Thank you for taking this case," said Darington. "I understand my sister can be…challenging. Has her own mind about her is all. Good gal."

"Yes, of course." From their brief introduction, Penelope would have to say she would make a most difficult case.

Marchford reappeared out of the thick, cold fog along with the stable master, happy and warm in his new greatcoat. "We are all arranged," said Marchford. "Willie here will take you back home in the town coach if that is acceptable."

"Quite. I fear you will not be as comfortable in this contraption," said Darington with utter candor.

"You have a wonderful sense of understatement, Lord Darington. I wish you a pleasant day."

Darington bowed and followed the stable master into the mist, leaving Penelope and Marchford and the broken-backed horse.

"Adventure calls," said Marchford with a gleam in his eye.

Eleven

It was a frigid morning. The roads were slick, and Marchford could see his breath in the frosty morning air. His horse and buggy were hardly fit for the icy cobblestones. He should have been freezing in his insufficient coat, and yet, sitting next to Penelope Rose, Marchford felt inexplicably warm.

"Now I know why you wanted to leave so early this morning," commented Penelope with a flash of humor in her eyes. "Mortifying if anyone saw you driving this curricle."

Marchford realized he should have been appalled at driving such a contraption down the London streets, but his only thoughts were of Penelope. At a bump in the road, Penelope was jostled closer to him, her arm touching his. She did not move away, leaving him to guess why. Was she cold and merely seeking warmth, or did she enjoy his company?

"So tell me where we are going," said Penelope in a most nonchalant tone. Perhaps she had not even noticed she was touching him. He rejected that notion as dreadfully lowering and decided she must be seeking heat. An understandable motive.

"We are going to find the widow of a certain Jimmy McDoogle. Whether he is the man who made the decanters I do not know. Everyone I spoke to, however, was dreadfully suspicious of society, hence the disguise." It was good to focus on facts and not the faint smell of lavender that clung to her.

"We certainly have succeeded in being unrecognizable," said Penelope with a smile hovering around her lips.

The curricle jostled and slipped on the cobblestones, and Marchford wrapped an arm around her to ensure she did not slide off the questionable vehicle. They continued going at a slow pace, but Marchford's arm remained around her waist, holding her close to him, protecting her from harm. Penelope said nothing and stared straight ahead into the gray London fog. He considered removing his arm, but it stayed there of its own accord.

They arrived at the home of the widow of Jimmy McDoogle in an area of Town that might generously have been considered working poor. The sign outside was old and hanging sideways by one hook. Unlike other glassworks, there was no shop outside; this was purely a work site of sand and glass and heat.

Marchford scanned the area for potential dangers, but none were readily apparent. Even the pickpockets had decided to stay indoors on such a frosty morning. He jumped down and helped Penelope to do the same, his hands around her small waist for the briefest of moments before he set her down. Why the simple act distracted him he could not say.

He opened the rickety wooden door and stepped inside. The workshop was shockingly hot compared to the cold outside. The ovens were working in the back, and the smell of coal and the sweltering heat was almost unbearable. A man in rolled up shirtsleeves and a red, sweaty face walked up to them.

"I have business with Master McDoogle, but I hear he passed," said Marchford.

"Aye," answered the muscular man. He wiped his hands on a gray apron and came forward. "I'm his brother. What's your business, gov'ner?"

"I would like to know about one of his last jobs. He made a special decanter I believe."

The man's face darkened. "Don't know nothing about that. I was in the country, see? I only came to Town after he was killed. I came to take care of the shop, that's all."

"I understand there is some question of how your brother died."

"Nah, there ain't no question. He was killed. Don't care what no magistrate says. My brother was killed, but he's dead now, so just leave it at that and get out of this here shop."

They were being kicked out and he needed to think of something fast before the interview was over. The heat, such a contrast to the cold outside, was making him almost dizzy. He glanced at Penelope only to have her roll up her eyes and fall in a dead faint directly into his arms.

"Penelope!" Marchford would wonder about that later. When she fell into his arms, he called her Penelope, not Miss Rose. He had no right to use her name with such familiarity, and yet when she fainted, she was his Penelope.

He scooped her up in an instant. She was surprisingly light. For some reason, he thought such a formidable lady would be heavy with the weight of her own practicality. She was not. She was just a young woman, one who felt nice in his arms. One who also was unconscious. His heart pounded with true concern. "Quick, fetch some smelling salts or a restorative. Go man!"

"Penelope!" he shouted. "Penelope?" he whispered.

She opened her eyes a sliver, gave him a sly wink and closed them again, allowing her head to loll against his shoulder. Relief swept over him, so powerful he had to cough to hide the smile that came over his face when the man ran back in.

"Got no smelling salts, but I found gin."

"Widow," hissed Penelope through her teeth.

"She needs a woman's touch," said Marchford, taking the hint. He held her closer.

"Aye, come follow me. Molly will set her right." He led them through to the back of the workshop, past giant gaping ovens of molten heat. He opened a door and went up a rickety wooden staircase to a small apartment above. The home was cramped and dingy. Marchford was reluctant to touch anything in the small room, but he lay Penelope on the couch, which had probably seen its best days before the first Duke of Marchford had cut his teeth.

"What's happened? Another accident?" A thin woman with gray hair pulled back in a loose bun rushed in from a back room separated by a blanket.

"Naw, just a woman fainted is all," said the brother. "This is my brother's wife, Molly."

"Probably the heat, or possibly the cold," said Marchford with purposeful vagueness. The key to getting good information was to distract your opponent as long as possible so as to sneak the questions in the back door. "I do hope there has not been a fit of apoplexy."

"Shoo!" said Molly, sending Marchford aside and her brother-in-law downstairs. She assessed the nature of Penelope's ailments by the time-tested manner of feeling the forehead and taking the pulse.

Penelope must have decided it was time to make a recovery and did so with such a fluttering of the eyes and soft mewling that Marchford was tempted to kneel beside her and hold her hand against what must be death throes. Molly, however, was made of sterner stuff and stood once more, muttering something about the sensibilities of some ladies. Penelope raised herself gracefully from the couch and put a hand to her forehead.

"I do apologize. I do not know what has gotten into me," said Pen weakly.

"Fainted. There now don't you worry none. I have something that will fix you fast." Molly turned to the corner of the apartment that served as the kitchen. Behind her back, Penelope shot Marchford a glance.

"No need. Here, I have everything she needs." He drew from his coat pocket a flask of whiskey belonging to the original owner of the garment.

Penelope frowned at him and Marchford merely shrugged. It must be better than whatever Molly was preparing. Yet their hostess was not easily dissuaded from her mission.

"Here smell this." The quick-moving Molly brought a wadded-up piece of linen on a stick.

Before Pen could back away, she took a whiff and her face contorted into a facial expression Marchford had not thought humanly possible. Tears sprung to Penelope's eyes and she started to cough. A morbid curiosity made Marchford want to sniff the offending rag to determine for himself just how bad the aroma must be. Penelope began to gag and Marchford decided against it.

"Thank you for your help," croaked Penelope when she could find words once more. "That is quite powerful."

Molly placed the rag back into a glass bottle with a stopper. "I used it whenever my kids told me they were feeling poorly. I had well children as a result."

Marchford did not doubt it.

"Good thinking," said Penelope, taking the lead. Marchford felt certain Molly would be more comfortable speaking to a woman, and retreated toward the door to give the women some space.

"How many children do you have?" asked Penelope politely.

"Five. Most are grown now, though one came late in life, still underfoot."

"I am sorry to hear of your recent loss."

Molly nodded. "They killed my Jimmy they did."

"What makes you so sure it wasn't an accident?"

"'Cause it weren't no accident. He worked by the oven his whole life, never once got more than a tiny burn. He was real careful, always. Not right what they did to him."

"We are trying to find the men who might be responsible. Can you tell us anything about who may have killed him or the last project he worked on, a decanter?"

Molly shook her head. "He was never one to talk about his work. 'Cept he said it was quality he was working for."

"Did he say anything else?"

Molly shook her head. "His last project was difficult. Not your standard fare. He worked late to get it done before the man returned. Made three sets, very fine work."

"Three sets? Are you sure?"

"Sure I am. Saw them myself before that bastard in the Carrick coat claimed them. Oh, he must have thought he was very fine with all them capes on the back."

"Did you see what he looked like?"

"Nah, I was going out as he was going in. Never looked up to see me. Wrapped in a muffler and stocking cap. He shorted us too. Took them pretty works and ran."

A young boy darted out from underneath a tablecloth and ran across the room and down the steps. Penelope and Marchford were surprised, but Molly took it in stride.

"My son," said Molly in a straightforward tone. "He is always underfoot, getting in the way. Now if you got what you came for, I should go back to trying to make gruel into something that resembles a Christmas pudding."

"Thank you. You have been helpful." Penelope stood and walked to the door.

Marchford reached out to shake Molly's hand and pressed a crown into her palm. "For your troubles."

She removed her hand with suspicion and stared at the coin, her bottom lip trembling. "Well now, I prayed for a Christmas pudding and the Good Lord done answered my prayers."

Marchford handed her another coin. "The Good Lord would like you to have a Christmas goose too."

Penelope gave him a smile that he could have basked in for days. The warmth radiating from her eyes surged heat through him, even thawing his numb toes.

Back in the wagon, he returned Penelope's smile. "Very well done, Miss Rose. You have a certain knack for deception." He meant to compliment, but Penelope's frown told him he had missed the mark. He was generally adept at conversation, but with Penelope he was just as adept at making gaffes.

"Thank you, Your Grace. How delightful you find me an accomplished liar."

"I meant it as a compliment."

"Try insulting me then. You might have better luck."

"At any rate, we now know more than we did before." Marchford retreated back to the business at hand. "Several sets were made, that is important. We will need to go look for them. I wish they could have identified the man in the Carrick coat."

Penelope turned to him with a face of a cat who had caught a mouse. "I bet I know who would know his identity."

"Who?"

"The boy. I bet you anything he would have seen quality coming and hid somewhere in the room to hear what happened."

"Good idea! Shall we interview the lad?" Marchford slapped the reins in a vain attempt to make the horse move faster.

"I doubt he will talk to us."

"So if we can't talk to him, how does this help us?"

"We cannot talk to him, but I know somebody who can!"

Twelve

When they returned to Marchford House, the duke went about seeing to the return of the dubious curricle and Penelope went into the house. Despite the cold, she had enjoyed the adventure, though whether it was because she wished to serve king and country or because she simply enjoyed being near a certain duke, she thought best not to examine too closely.

In her room, she found a maid once again removing her older gowns from the closet.

"Sorry, miss. Orders of the duchess. She weren't happy to find you bought back them gowns and asked me to burn them."

Pen was hardly surprised. The duchess was adamant in her abhorrence of the old gowns. Penelope handed the maid a coin from her reticule. "I will give you something to burn but leave the rest. I will ensure the duchess never sees them again."

It was not that Penelope was afraid of the dowager, but she had learned long ago that avoiding unnecessary conflict could only lead to her general peace and contentment. So it was with such felicitous musings that Penelope traipsed up the rickety stairs with an armload of unsuitable garments past the housemaid's quarters to the attic.

It was as attic-y an attic as could be and had she been a younger girl it would have been the sort of place she would have loved to explore. It was lit only from a few dormer windows and was filled with trunks and bags and bandboxes and mysterious crates. Old furnishings were covered with white sheets against the dust, which along with the cobwebs gave the place a deliciously spooky feel.

Penelope looked around for a suitable place to store her undesirable frocks. It was perhaps recalcitrant to hang on to her old wardrobe, resisting the new ones purchased by the dowager, though with Penelope's own share of one of Madame X's triumphs. Trouble was the new garments were so much more stylish, so fashionable, that it was a dramatic shift from her usual drab ensembles.

In her old gowns she could hide, recede into the background. In her new gowns…she was not even sure what she could do. What she did know was that the dowager was serious about sending her gowns to the poorhouse or the burn pile, and if she wanted to keep them, they must be hid.

Besides, the ones she kept had been her mother's gowns. They still smelled faintly of her perfume. When she wore them, she felt close to her mum, almost as if she had become her mother. Penelope leaned against a trunk, turning over a new thought.

Was this why she was holding on to the gowns? Trying to fill the gaping hole left by the death of her mother by trying to become like her? Even dress like her? She must admit she had taken a rather mothering role with her sisters. Somebody had to be the sensible one to set everything to rights. Just like Mum.

Oh Lord, I do not know who I am anymore. She had always been one to take care of people—her sisters, the dowager—but now with them all joining the ranks of matrimony, she was hardly needed. Who was she now?

Trust in the Lord with all thine heart; and lean not unto thine own understanding. Proverbs 3:5. It was one of her father's favorite verses and was quoted often in her home. Followed by her grandma Moira's addition, *It may no' work out the way ye plan, but it may just work out the way He planned.*

Penelope brushed past old chairs and furnishings covered in white sheets to an old forgotten trunk in the corner. By the layer of cobwebs, it was clear the trunk held nothing of current use and should be a successful storage place. Opening the trunk, Penelope found a lovely gown in an older style, complete with an old-fashioned long corset and side panniers folded underneath. Penelope wondered if it had been the dowager's gown from a bygone era. It was a fancy one, with more ribbons and frills than Penelope would have expected, and in a most shocking color of deep rose pink. How would the dowager have appeared in such a gown?

Penelope continued to explore the contents of the trunk and found another gown of emerald silk. Underneath was an exquisitely painted fan, a bottle of perfume, and an ivory-handled brush and comb.

Penelope wondered at these items and decided these things must not have been Antonia's but from some lady who had died. Why else would one pack away a half-used bottle of perfume?

In a corner of the trunk, Penelope found a little velvet box. Inside was a darling miniature of a young woman. Penelope mentally reviewed the long line of family portraits in the gallery, but she was certain she had never seen her before. The young woman was a raven-haired beauty with large, dark eyes and an olive complexion. Her mouth was alluring with a half smile and full rose lips, as if she wished to share a secret. Her dark eyes held a come-hither look that must have conquered the heart of any young man with the ability to draw breath. She was exquisite.

But who was she? And why was she hidden away in a trunk in the Marchford home?

At the bottom of the trunk was a large rectangular object wrapped in brown paper. Penelope doubted she could remove the package without ripping the paper, so she left it be, curious as she was.

Getting back to the business at hand, she repacked the trunk. She laid out her own gowns, folding them and carefully adding them to the trunk. Fortunately, there was room for her own things, but now her interest was focused on this new mystery.

Penelope flung a white sheet over the trunk and slipped the velvet box in her pocket. She never thought twice about taking the miniature. If pressed, she would be forced to confess she had a shocking propensity toward curiosity. The adage of what had happened to certain cats of similar disposition had been reviewed for her in her younger years on multiple occasions. However, her natural inclination toward solving mysteries and generally poking about in other people's business had not yet killed her.

But the day was still young.

⤜⤒⤝

Penelope had just finished changing clothes into something the dowager would consider "suitable" when she received an urgent summons to join the dowager in her sitting room. The carriage of the Comtesse de Marseille had been spotted outside.

The Comtesse de Marseille, notorious society gossip, could ruin almost anyone with the raise of an eyebrow. Penelope could not find a single person who did not secretly loathe and fear the comtesse, yet her word on fashion, art, music, theatre—anything of any substance—was considered authoritative. It was said that when the patronesses of Almack's disagreed whether or not to grant a particular person a voucher, they inquired of the comtesse.

"Thank goodness you look presentable," exclaimed Antonia when Penelope entered the room. "Sit there." The dowager pointed to a wingback chair. "No, no, sit over here on the settee."

Penelope had not seen the dowager in such a state since Marchford had cut off her extra pocket money. Though the announcement had only just been published, Penelope had no doubt that news of the dowager's engagement had spread to the outer banks of the Thames before noon and then scurried throughout the countryside by teatime. By the end of a week, the news would no doubt spread to the outer reaches of Scotland and even to Napoleon himself, who if the rumors were to be believed, enjoyed reading a bit of gossip as much as any society matron.

Despite her reassuring words, Penelope was not certain how the *ton* would react. The Dowager Duchess of Marchford herself held much sway in society, though she had been a widow for longer than many had been alive. Marriages in the mature years did happen, but not often. The question on everyone's mind was why. Why now?

The comtesse was coming for a story. She was looking for gossip. Whether the impending nuptials of the dowager's would be met with praise or censure depended largely on the opinion of the comtesse. And that depended on the story they were about to tell.

"Forgive me, Antonia," said Penelope in a soft voice. "But everyone will want to know why you are getting married. Why are you?"

"Do you not know?" Antonia's sharp, blue eyes softened and she spoke in a whisper. "Because I love him. I always have."

"The Comtesse de Marseille," the butler intoned.

"Antonia!" A tall, thin woman swished into the room with an air of elegance. Beneath a stylish hat with a wild plume of ostrich feathers, her silver hair was coiffed so elaborately it reminded Pen of an earlier time, when monstrous wigs were the fashion.

"Cosette," answered the dowager in an airy voice. The two societal mavens moved together with a swish of silk and kissed the air around each other. "How are you this morning?"

"Very well, thank you, my dear. Now tell me all. Are you so very poor it has come to this?" The face of the comtesse may have appeared sympathetic, but her eyes gleamed with malevolent delight.

Penelope had thought herself accustomed to the bluntness of the comtesse, but this greeting surprised even her.

"Goodness no, my dear. Wherever do you get such notions?" said the dowager with an outward calm Penelope found admirable. Antonia motioned to the tea table and they all sat around it.

"Enlighten me *s'il vous plaît*. Why would you, of all people, consent to be his wife?" The comtesse passed on the cream and sugar; she preferred her tea as black as her soul. "Have you been beguiled by this Madame X for whom you have been acting as agent?"

"I think it wonderfully romantic," said Penelope, trying a strategy to change the story from the dowager being so impoverished she had to wed to something less incriminating. "Her Grace was engaged to be married to Lord Langley many years ago, but their parents had a feud and intervened, breaking off the engagement."

Penelope was telling a censored version of the story. Truth was Antonia, for all her stature now, had begun life as the daughter of a simple country gentleman. Langley's parents had not thought Antonia suitable, but this particular truth was not helpful to their current situation.

The comtesse regarded Penelope as if just noticing she existed. "Romance? Bah! How much like a gothic novel, And you know, my dear, how much I despise novels."

"No, no, nothing like that," said the dowager, flashing her eyes at Penelope. "But Langley did make me an offer many years ago."

"Indeed, he did," said Penelope, changing tack. She had made a mistake by trying to appeal to the comtesse's romantic nature. Clearly the woman had been born without such feeling. "Lord Langley entered into a binding contract. He suffered as a result of breaking it and begged Her Grace to end his misery by consenting to be his wife."

A slow smile crept on the face of the comtesse. "Why, you are a sly one, Antonia. Even after all these years, you are holding the man accountable. Good for you!"

Penelope and the dowager exchanged a glance. They had successfully achieved the support of the comtesse.

"Now tell me." The comtesse smiled over her teacup at the dowager. "Who is this mysterious Madame X?" The comtesse stayed only a few minutes more, trying to wheedle out as many clues to the identity of Madame X as possible, yet Antonia remained stoic. Penelope was not sure what would happen if the truth regarding Madame X were discovered, but she was certain it would not end well for her.

They both sighed in relief when the comtesse left, taking with her the biting censure that surrounded her like an aura.

"Thank you, my dear. You have been a true treasure to me." The duchess paused and regarded her with a critical eye. "I fear I am going to have to let you go."

Penelope's heart dropped. "I beg your pardon?"

"I said you are fired!" The dowager rapped her cane on the floor with a loud crack for emphasis.

Penelope's heart pounded. "Is this because I abandoned you yesterday with your visitor? I am sorry if the duke called me away. Was the conversation very dull?"

"No, this is not because you ran off with James. Yes, I know you two are working on some dark dealings, which is in part why you are officially no longer my companion."

"I understand." Penelope stood and brushed out her skirts, focusing on the material and keeping her head down so the dowager would not see the tears that had sprung there. The dowager was a hard woman, but Penelope had thought they had become so much more than an old duchess and her companion.

"Now sit down. Do not get yourself in a pet. I stopped thinking of you as my companion months ago. I consider you my friend." Antonia's severe face cracked into something of a warm smile.

Penelope's head shot up and the tears that had threatened spilled down her cheeks. The warmth of a compliment, particularly one from a lady who rarely bestowed them, curled up happy inside her heart. "Thank you, Your Grace." She sank back down onto the settee next to her.

The dowager reached out and handed Penelope a lace handkerchief, clasping her hand. "Antonia."

Penelope blotted her eyes. "Antonia. After losing my family, I could not ask for more than being welcomed here."

"Oh. Well. Yes, yes of course." The dowager pulled another handkerchief from the mysterious place old ladies keep handkerchiefs and blotted her own eyes. "Yes, and that is why I need to speak with you. It is time for you to find your own family," said Antonia firmly. "You have found husbands for everyone but yourself, so I have a business proposition for you."

"You do?"

"I will contract with Madame X at her usual fee to find a marriage partner for your own self."

Penelope didn't know whether to laugh or cry. Finding a husband for herself was the one thing she couldn't do. "I did try once but was unsuccessful, as you see. If I had entertained any offers of marriage, I would not have ended up your companion, forgive me for saying."

"You were so busy helping your sisters, you did not take the time to help yourself," accused Antonia, making a valid point. "It is the beginning of a new season. Let this be a new beginning for you too."

"I have had several seasons already," said Penelope, trying not to be irritated at reiterating her personal failure.

"No. You never did." Antonia was adamant. "First you were busy taking care of your elder sisters. Then when your younger sisters made their debut, you in turn took care of them. When was it ever your turn? When did you ever have the new gowns or a maid to devote to your hair?"

"There were five of us girls, all landing on my aunt's home quite unexpectedly. She took us in and introduced us all in society." Penelope felt the need to defend her family, but the truth was the dowager was right. No one had taken the time to ensure she wore a new gown or did her hair to its best advantage. Not even herself.

"Now is your turn, your time." Antonia was firm. "You may stay with me until the wedding, but after that, I shall insist you find a groom of your own."

Thirteen

THE NEXT FROSTY MORNING MARCHFORD SAT BESIDE
Penelope in the lumbering town coach. They were going
to try again to get information out of the glassmaker,
but this time Marchford refused to travel in anything
less than the comfortable coach. Despite the importance of their task, he was considerably more interested
in the lady beside him than the plan she was concocting or the dubious creature who sat across from them.

"Now are you certain you understand what you are
to do?" Penelope asked their passenger with a slight
quiver of anxiety.

Jemima Price, guttersnipe street rat turned upstairs
maid, smiled sweetly. "Yes'm, I got it right. I is to ask
about the glass bottle thing that the spy had."

Marchford could not help a painful sigh from
escaping his lips. The urchin was likely to give more
information than she got.

Penelope's lips tightened and she ignored him.
"Well, yes, we are trying to get that information, but
you must not say anything about spies. Wherever did
you get such a notion?"

"The Duke o' Marchford's a spy catcher." Jemima's voice trembled with delicious intrigue. "I heard Mr. Grant say so."

"Upstairs maids may overhear things they should not repeat," said Marchford severely. "I wonder very much as to your ability to be discreet." He looked at Pen when he said it, but she turned her head so the edge of her outmoded bonnet blocked him from view.

"Aye, I knows. I can be very lip locked I can," assured Jem.

"Now remember you are pretending to be a chambermaid who broke a bottle," coached Penelope. "You are afraid and you are wanting to find another. You need to find as much as you can about who purchased them and where they went. Is that clear?"

"Yes, yes, and then I says how I can nick the bob to pay for the loot."

Another audible sigh escaped Marchford.

"No, no, please I implore you would not say anything like that," begged Penelope.

"All right." Jem's smile never dimmed.

"The glassmaker has a son about your age. I'm not sure the name, but I think you will be most successful if you talk to him. If you need to encourage discussion, give him this crown."

Jem's eyes widened as Penelope produced the heavy coin. "All righty," she said randomly, not attending to anything Penelope was saying.

"Now listen, Jem, listen!"

Jem's eyes snapped to attention, though they kept sliding down to the coin in her hand.

"Try to get a name or an address of the man who

commissioned the bottles. Anything identifying will do. Then come tell us what you learned. Do you understand?"

"Yes'm," said Jem, her eyes stubbornly fixed on the crown.

Marchford sighed to the point of groaning and Penelope finally threw him a severe glance. Petty though it was, he could not help but feel he had won by succeeding in drawing her attention.

"We shall have to drop you several blocks away. Do you think you can manage walking a bit on your own?" asked Penelope.

"Aw bless you, ma'am. I've been everywhere in this here Town on these here feet. And look, now I gots shoes!" She held up her feet to show them.

"Good gracious," muttered Marchford, turning away from the offending little feet.

The carriage rolled to a stop and Jemima jumped down with a smile. "I'll do right. I'm a kinchin mort!"

Penelope smiled and waved, watching her skip down the street. "Whatever did she mean by that, I wonder?"

"If my understanding of the thief cant serves, it means she was trained as a young girl for a life of pervasive criminality," Marchford said cheerfully.

"Oh." Penelope's mouth formed a perfect round circle, causing Marchford to catch his breath.

"I doubt we shall see her or that crown again." He needed to focus on something other than Penelope's rose-colored lips.

"Now have a little faith. Besides, neither one of us could be as persuasive as she. No matter how we might pretend poverty, we cannot carry it off as convincingly as our young Jem."

"True." The word was an indictment.

"And we certainly could never get a young boy to talk to us," added Penelope.

"Also correct. Of course, it may be she who does most of the talking."

It was Penelope's turn to sigh. "She does mean well."

"Does she?"

"You did not have any better ideas," accused Penelope.

"Which is the only reason I agreed to this travesty. If it all goes terribly wrong there is very little we can lose. The spy already knows I have the bottle and that I am looking for him."

"Perhaps our young Jem will surprise you." Penelope spoke as though she was trying to convince herself. She shivered in the cold of the coach. The weather had turned bitter and outside it was starting to sleet.

"I am rarely surprised, so it would be a novelty at least." Marchford rapped on the ceiling to get the coachman's attention and gave him leave to go to a nearby pub to get warm while they waited. He then reached for the blanket they kept in the carriage and spread it over Penelope.

"Thank you," said Penelope, tucking the blanket across her lap. "You are very kind."

Marchford attempted to guard himself against the warmth of her compliment, but it was too late. "No thanks needed," he said gruffly. "Only sensible thing to do."

"Then we should both share the blanket and put it over the foot warmer so we can try to not freeze." Penelope scooted dangerously close to him and shared half the blanket.

His treacherous mind considered other ways two people could avoid freezing. They were alone in a coach with a blanket. Marchford folded his hands together before him and grasped them tight to remind himself to remain aloof. It may be his imagination, but he swore he could feel her warmth on his side even through multiple layers of cloth and coats.

"Oh!" exclaimed Pen. "With all this excitement I just realized something."

"Which is?" He had ridiculous hopes that somehow it involved getting closer.

"It is Christmas Eve. Happy Christmas Eve to you."

"Oh. Christmas." What a disappointing answer.

"Have you no sense of the magic and wonder of Christmas?" Penelope's face lit up. "Tell me about how you celebrated Christmas as a child."

"Church," was his monosyllabic answer.

"Yes, but beyond that," Penelope pressed with a childlike gleam of anticipation in her eyes. "I look forward to Christmas every year. When I was a girl, we celebrated the twelve days of Christmas by giving each other little gifts every day, starting with Christmas and going till Twelfth Night. Since there were five of us girls, we would draw names out of the hat to pick who to give a gift. Some of the days we gave to each other and some of the days we gave to our neighbors, especially those less fortunate."

Penelope paused, looking at him expectantly. If she

hoped he would share happy reminiscences, she was much mistaken. Marchford had nothing to say, so she continued. "Mother would always bake plum pudding on Christmas and king's cake on Twelfth Night. She would hide the bean and the pea inside the cake and the people who found it were the king and queen for the evening's festivities. After dinner, father would read from the gospels of Christ's birth and we would sing songs and play games, like the twelve days of Christmas. You know, seven swans a swimming, six geese a laying."

"No, indeed, I was not aware any family actually did such things," Marchford said stiffly. He kept himself emotionally removed from the pain of childhood remembrances. It was best that way.

"We were only country folk after all, so our amusements must appear rather shabby to such a worldly man as yourself." Penelope glared at him, and he guessed she interpreted his reserve as arrogance. To correct her would be to reveal himself, so he said nothing.

"What were your family traditions?" Penelope asked, unable to leave it alone.

Marchford gave her a cheerless smile. "Every year my mother would make an attempt to decorate the house for Christmastide—green bows, holly, red ribbons, and the like. And every year my grandmother would order the servants to take out the decorations and burn them. Christmas decorations were considered a hallmark of low society. Of course, anything my mother wanted my grandmother considered low society." He spoke quickly. These were not remembrances on which he wished to dwell.

"That is dreadful." Penelope's expressive face turned from irritation to sympathy. "I had no idea the dowager was so displeased with your mother."

"If I told you my grandmother loathed her, it would be an understatement."

"But why?"

This was a topic he never discussed. Never. And yet in Penelope's eyes, he saw compassion without pity, and without intending to, he began to talk. "Grandmother chose my father's first wife, and my half brother Frederick was the result. It was not that my father was unhappy, but he was not in love with her, a situation he sought to remedy after his first wife died and he began looking for a second. His second wife, my mother, he loved. An inexcusable mistake for a duke."

"What makes you say that? Your grandmother did not approve?"

Marchford shifted on the velvet seat. "My mother was not what my grandmother considered suitable."

Penelope pressed her lips together for a moment in thought. "But surely they must have put aside their differences for Christmastide, if only for the sake of the children. What did you and Frederick do for Christmas?"

"Mostly listen to Mother and Grandmother argue. Father would disappear to the club. There would be a huge row over what food would be served. Figgy pudding would be ordered and then thrown in the rubbish heap. Frederick and I often went without supper because the menu could never be decided." He couldn't keep the bitterness from his voice.

"I am sorry," whispered Penelope, placing her gloved

hand on his. "This year we shall have to make up for what you lacked."

Something in his frozen heart began to melt, and he clenched his teeth against an unmanly show of feeling. To remain aloof was the only safe option. "I assure you there is no need." But he took her hand in his own and held it.

"Indeed, but there is." Penelope's voice was inviting, and he struggled against its seductive warmth.

Marchford rubbed his gloved thumb along her hand. She gave his hand a small squeeze and he returned it. Her rich brown eyes met his. "You are a kindhearted soul, Penelope Rose." He spoke in a low voice, as if not wanting to admit it even to himself.

She parted her lips to say something, but no words came. He leaned forward, her full lips beckoning him. She leaned toward him and every rational thought died. The only thing that made sense now was Penelope and drawing her close to him. He moved in for the kiss.

Suddenly, the door opened and in hopped the cursedly prompt figure of Jemima Price.

"Jem!" Penelope jumped away, releasing Marchford's hand and smoothing the blanket off her lap in a flustered manner. "Are you all right? Tell us what happened!"

"Talked to the son o' the glassmaker. He was a peery cove, looked cutty-eyed at me."

"Is that so?" Penelope turned a bewildered eye to Marchford.

"He was suspicious of you?" asked Marchford, serving as translator, though the only thing on his mind was how to get the urchin out of the carriage and return his attentions to Miss Rose.

"Yes, ma'am. Told him the flam about breaking the bottle, and I could tells he weren't buying it. Nothing to it, so I started to blubber and say I was an orphan and I needed to find another bottle or they would kicks me out of the house and I gots nowheres to go."

"So what happened?" asked Penelope her attention on the girl, ignoring Marchford.

"Well, Georgie, that's the glassmaker's son, he tells me he's half an orphan too cause of this man that ordered the bottles and he says his father was killed for it."

"Did he know who killed his father?" asked Marchford, attempting to focus back on his work.

"Well, yes and no. When the man came to pick up the bottles, his father wasn't quite done. The man was terrible angry. Said they made a deal. Threw a fit, so Georgie says. His father gave the man the sets he had, and then delivered the last set the next day when he was done. Georgie delivered them himself."

"Where?" Marchford and Penelope asked together, leaning forward.

"Didn't want to tell me."

Marchford and Penelope both leaned back in disappointment.

"So I said it was probably where I worked anyways and asked what address he took it, and he says I should know where I work for the heaven's own sake. And I says I knows where I butter my bread, but does he. And we went round until he said that if I don't know the address of Lord Felton then I deserve whatever I got for being nothing but a buffled-headed mop-squeezer. Then I told him—"

"Enough," commanded Marchford, but he gave the girl a smile. "Without resorting to telling us the full extent of the insults exchanged, was there anything else he told you about the person who commissioned the glassware?"

"No. We got too loud and his mum came down and run me out with a broom. Here's your crown, ma'am. Didn't need it."

Penelope took the crown from Jem's hands with a smile, throwing Marchford a triumphant look. "Thank you, Jemima. You have done very well indeed."

Jemima's smile brightened the coach.

"Might I even say surprisingly well?" Penelope glanced again at Marchford.

He nodded in assent. She deserved to win this round. "I concede defeat and admit surprise."

Penelope handed him the coin. "To remind you that there are people out there who may surprise you yet."

"But I have you for that," he said in a low voice. He turned to Jem and handed her the crown, her eyes growing as wide as the coin. "For services rendered. A grateful nation thanks you. And a merry Christmas," he added as an afterthought.

Jem snatched the coin and was utterly absorbed by her newfound wealth. "Thank you," she said in a reverent voice.

"Thank you," whispered Marchford in Penelope's ear, delighting in the blush that pinked her cheeks. How he could ever have thought her plain he could not say. She may not be a striking beauty, but she was handsome in a way he quite preferred.

"Do you mind if we stop somewhere?" asked Jemima. "It ain't far."

"Certainly," said Marchford, happy to drop her anywhere if that meant he was alone once more with Penelope. He jumped out to retrieve the coachman and soon they were rolling along. Following Jemima's directions, the coach drove them nearer to St. Giles. A modest bakeshop stood next to a humble butcher.

Jemima hopped down into the slush and looked from one to the next, but finally decided on the butcher and walked inside.

"What can she be buying?" asked Penelope. "Surely she knows she will have plenty of food at Grant's table."

"I confess some curiosity," admitted Marchford. So they both stepped down from the coach, Marchford lifting her briefly down and over a freezing puddle.

"Thank you," she murmured, turning the brim of her bonnet from him to conceal what may have been another blush.

Inside the shop, Jemima was arguing with the shopkeeper about how much the crown would buy. She had her eye on a large goose, but the shopkeeper was holding out for more.

"Jemima, what do you want with a goose?" asked Penelope.

"Oh, it isn't for me. I just know how many St. Giles folk will be hungry this Christmas, and I wanted to fill their stomachs with goose and pudding."

Penelope put her hand to her mouth to stop a gasp. Tears sprung to her eyes. She glanced at Marchford, who was admittedly surprised by Jemima's generosity but delighted with Penelope's reaction. He knew what Penelope wished, and he would deny her nothing.

"I see you are taking this surprise thing to heart," he commented dryly. In a manner of moments, Marchford had financially arranged with the butcher and the baker to send to the address provided by Jemima a veritable Christmas feast, though he did not doubt he was feeding persons of dubious repute.

The smile Penelope graced him with was well worth the price. When they walked out of the shop, the sleet turned to soft, gentle snow, fluttering gracefully down.

Jemima shrieked with joy and stuck out her tongue to catch the flakes, racing around them as if moving faster would help her get snowflakes.

Marchford reached out a gloved hand and took Penelope's hand in his. She smiled, snowflakes gracing on her long, black eyelashes like tiny crystals. She was beautiful. Simply beautiful.

He must beware.

Fourteen

AFTER THEY DROPPED OFF A HAPPY JEMIMA PRICE AT Grant's town house, they drove slowly back to Marchford House. The snow was beginning to fall in earnest, and Penelope could not help but stare at the beautiful white flakes out the carriage window. The coal-dusted London streets were brightened with a white blanket of snow, lifting Penelope's spirits.

She turned back to Marchford, sitting silently beside her. She wondered if he would initiate any more of what had passed between them earlier, but he was looking at nothing in particular, a frown marring his otherwise pleasant countenance. He was no doubt thinking about the problem of tracking down foreign spies, while the beautiful landscape passed by his window unnoticed.

A lump of emotion caught in her throat at the thought of his generosity to provide a happy Christmas for others though he, with all his riches, had never experienced one. How difficult it must have been to feel the brunt of the feud between his mother and grandmother. If there was one thing she was determined to do, it was to provide this man with some happy memory of the Christmas season.

Her eyes were drawn to his lips. They appeared soft yet firm, and she could not stop herself from wondering what it might be like to kiss those lips.

"What do you make of Lord Felton being named?" asked Penelope in a fluster, trying to change the focus of her own traitorous mind.

"Not sure. I am thinking on that. He could be a co-conspirator. And yet the decanters were found in Grant's house too, so Felton could be yet another innocent."

"How do we determine whether he is involved or not?" She tried to look at something other than how his lips moved when he spoke. She must not reveal her damning curiosity.

"I would like to get into his house, look around." He glanced at her briefly, then turned back slowly and caught her eyes, holding the gaze.

Penelope was very much aware that they were alone in a large, plush town carriage. Pull the curtains and they could have complete privacy. Despite the cold, her temperature rose. "Little chance of that," replied Penelope, fighting to keep on the topic of conversation. "He has not entertained for years, as far as I am aware."

"No, he swore he would never host another ball after the last debutante ball for his daughters. Had seven of them. None too pleased about it. Now his estate will be entailed off to a nephew whom he apparently loathes."

"Sounds charming. I don't suppose he is in possession of a Carrick coat?" asked Penelope.

"Half of London is in possession of a Carrick coat.

Even me." Marchford drew her attention to his coat, which she had not noticed until then. It was indeed a black Carrick coat with multiple capes. He held up an arm to invite investigation, then placed it down on the top of the plush carriage seat, his arm now resting on the squabs above her shoulders. He was not touching her, but she felt drawn to him just the same.

"Could you call on Lord Felton?" asked Penelope, trying to pretend she was utterly unaffected by sitting so close to him.

"Unlikely. He is a prickly man, never had much to do with him. Can't think of any reason why I should pay him a visit."

She slowly leaned back against the squabs, his arm now touching her shoulders. She thought he would pull away. He did not. His green eyes sizzled with intensity.

"I do not see a way forward. Do you?" he asked.

Penelope stammered in response. Was he talking about trying to get into Felton's house or something else entirely?

The carriage rolled to a stop and before Penelope could think of a response, the door opened and the coachman announced that they had arrived. Penelope sprung out the door, gulping the frigid air to clear her head.

The dowager duchess was in a bit of a state when they returned from their expedition.

"It will all be ruined, nothing else that can be done. We shall have to cancel their engagement ball," declared Antonia, accepting a glass of something strong from a sympathetic butler.

"What is ruined?" asked Penelope as she and

Marchford joined Antonia in the sitting room. She glanced at Marchford, but he accepted his paper from the butler without comment. If they had shared anything in the coach, it was now gone.

"The engagement ball for Sir Gareth and Lady Jane," said Antonia dismissively, irritated at having to explain herself in what, apparently to her mind, should be obvious.

"What has happened?" exclaimed Pen. "Surely they have not decided to call off the wedding."

"No, of course not."

"Then what is the problem?"

"The snow! Have you not seen it?"

"Forgive me, but how does the snow prevent there from being an engagement ball?" Penelope was lost. She glanced at Marchford, but he had disappeared behind his paper.

"Lord Wynbrook lives on top of a large hill. Lovely views, but in winter, if the roads freeze, which they are sure to do, the road becomes impassible by horse and carriage."

"Oh." Slow realization dawned on Penelope. "That is a problem."

"Indeed it is. And do not think we'll be seeing a pound of our fee until the engagement ball has formalized the deal."

"Surely we can move the location, rather than cancel it."

"But where? It should be a relative to host, and they have none in Town besides Lord Felton, and he has sworn never to host another ball as long as he draws breath."

"Of what relation is Lord Felton?" asked Marchford, taking sudden interest in a conversation that until then had no claim on his attention.

"He is a second cousin to Lord Wynbrook and his sisters," said the dowager.

Marchford and Penelope exchanged a glance.

"Too bad Lord Felton has sworn never to host again. I remember his ballroom as being quite fine," said Marchford, casually turning the page of his paper.

"Yes," said the dowager absently. "His drawing rooms are superb."

"Too bad it is not possible," said Penelope with a sigh.

The dowager narrowed her eyes. "I wonder," she said.

"Now don't you go bothering the man," chastised Marchford.

"I would not consider it a bother. I would consider it an opportunity to be of service to his niece," defended the dowager.

Marchford looked up over his paper. "Only you would even consider asking such a thing."

"It would be quite the social coup if you could obtain Lord Felton's consent. No one has seen the house in years," commented Penelope.

"Everyone would come," added Marchford from behind the paper.

"Penelope, ring the bell. I'm going out."

"Shall I go with you?" asked Penelope rising.

"No, no, stay here with James. I think I shall do better alone." Antonia bustled out of the room with a determined look.

Marchford lowered his paper, revealing a smile. "Well played."

"I shall not be surprised if the ball is rescheduled for Lord Felton's drawing rooms by the end of the day."

"The notice of the change in venue shall be delivered within the hour, you can depend on it," said Marchford with a wink.

Pen smiled and wished she would not flush every time he looked at her. It was most disconcerting and might give the duke the wrong impression. Or worse, he might get the *right* impression that, despite all efforts to the contrary, she found the man irritatingly attractive. And then he would be insufferable. "We can inform people at the gala tonight."

Marchford's eyebrows fell over his eyes. "I had forgotten the ball is tonight. I thought you were going to provide me with a wife."

"You rejected my proposed candidates," defended Penelope.

"A poor excuse for leaving me to the machinations of marriage-minded females."

"Someone has been distracting me with trivial matters, such as saving the kingdom from foreign threats."

"Ignore the bastard." The corners of his mouth twitched up.

"I shall remind you of that comment in the future," returned Penelope, trying to suppress a grin. She did enjoy sparring with the duke—more than she should. In truth, it was time to discuss not only his future but hers.

"If that is all, Miss Rose." Marchford rose to quit the room.

"Actually, I wished to ask a favor." Penelope shifted uncomfortably in her chair. She did not wish to raise this topic but felt she must.

"Odd timing for it."

"Perhaps you would like this one, since it involves my removal from your presence."

Marchford raised an eyebrow.

"Your grandmother's wedding will be soon. I shall stay for the wedding, naturally, since she has family coming to visit, but after that, I thought to decamp in Bath. I was wondering if I might be allowed to take the coach to Bath and have the groom return it."

Marchford stared at her as if she had turned into a changeling before his eyes. "Bath? Why on earth would you be going to Bath?"

"Well, I should think I need someplace to live. London rents are a bit steep, but I have some money on my own to live with some independence in a place with more reasonable accommodations. I have been in correspondence with a man in Bath who has a small apartment that I believe shall fit me nicely."

"But why would you abandon the duchess? Surely you would not leave my grandmother alone!" Marchford glared at her.

"Your grandmother is getting *married*." She emphasized the word as if that would help him understand. "She will have company enough without me underfoot."

"Fine then, stay here. No need to move to Bath."

"Surely you understand I cannot do that."

"No, I certainly do not." Marchford's voice took on a growl of displeasure.

"You are an unmarried man. I am an unmarried woman. We are not related to each other. Without my service to the duchess, there is no reason for me to stay and every reason for me to leave."

Marchford crossed his arms. "No. It won't work for me. I need you here. Your insights have proven invaluable. Do you forget that a spy is still among us? You need to stay at your post until this crisis is averted."

Penelope sighed. She wished there was a way for her to continue to stay with the duke, but what this ill-advised attraction needed was a dose of reality to bring it to ground. "I am sorry to disappoint, but I cannot stay. I am certain you understand what the rumors would be if we continued to live under one roof."

"Yes, well, I suppose if you put it that way," grumbled Marchford. He folded and refolded his paper with emphasis. "But if there was a relationship between us, then the need for propriety would be met."

"What are you saying? You cannot suddenly decide I am your long-lost cousin."

"Will think of something. Must!" Marchford protested. "I am to White's. I shall return to escort you ladies to the Devine ball." He stood and strode out of the room, the newspaper tucked under his arm.

Penelope leaned back in her chair. What was the man going to do? And why was she so hopeful he would somehow find a way for her to stay? Pen took a long breath and let it out. As much as she may wish to stay with the duke just the way things were, it was not to be. The dowager was leaving, along with Penelope's reason to be in the house, and Marchford needed to find a society lady to wed.

It was all for the best—though she knew no matter how many times she told herself those words, she would never fully believe it. Penelope looked idly around the room, committing the beautiful furnishings to memory. Wherever she lived next, it would not be so opulent. The room was quite elegant, but it was also Christmas Eve and not one single sprig of holly or festive ribbon could be found in the entire house. It seemed a shame not to acknowledge the Lord's greatest gift.

Penelope once again felt sorry for the young future duke, whose Christmases had been so cheerless. Of course, it was never too late to have a merry Christmas. If the angels could surprise the shepherds with the joyful good news, perhaps she also could herald the great event? Penelope stood and surveyed the room with devious intent.

Did she dare?

Fifteen

PENELOPE SHIFTED FROM FOOT TO FOOT, WAITING anxiously for the duke and duchess to complete dressing for the gala and meet her in the drawing room. To appease the duchess, she wore an emerald gown with a champagne overdress of the most gauzy material, giving her the impression of floating in a cloud. The neckline plunged and the new stays cinched up her bosoms such that she was literally spilling out the top. She even let the maid curl her hair in a more becoming style, all in an attempt to compensate for the festive desecration of the orderly drawing room.

Marchford was the first to arrive. He entered the drawing room and came to a full stop. His jaw dropped, his eyes only for her.

"Do you like it?" asked Penelope a little too anxiously.

He stared at her in silence a moment more before finally responding. "Yes, quite. Indeed. Capital." His voice was stilted.

Penelope was gratified. "Let me be the first to wish you a happy Christmas Eve," said Penelope quickly, shoving a cup of wassail into his hand. She was certain her decorating would be better appreciated with a warm drink. Marchford must have agreed because he took a generous draught.

"Try these as well." Penelope nearly forced a rum butter tart down his throat. The tarts alone were so filled with rum-soaked fruit that it was a heady mouthful.

"Delicious." Marchford's voice was soft and low.

"What the blazes!" The dowager stopped at the open doorway and wandered in slowly, turning around in a full circle to note the full extent of Penelope's handiwork. Holly branches graced the chandeliers, tied on with red-and-gold bows. Ribbons of red velvet and sparkly gold decorated the room. Evergreen boughs with red holly berries and thick gold bows hung over the windows and doors. An abundance of candles had been brought into the room, making it unusually bright and cheery. Her eyes narrowed at Marchford. "James! What have you done?"

"I fear I am responsible." Penelope offered wassail and tarts, but the dowager refused. "I wanted to show you how we used to decorate our house every Christmas Eve. It is a present for you," Penelope added nervously.

The dowager looked around at the glittering candles and the festive ribbons. Her face was stern.

"It is a going-away present since you will soon be married and I will need to leave," Penelope added, hoping that if she reminded the dowager she was leaving, this indiscretion might be forgiven.

"I never took to decorating for Christmas," said the dowager with disdain.

"I do hope you like it. I am sure if you had done

the decorating, it would be improved." Penelope added in a little flattery, hoping to soothe the dowager's ruffled sensibilities.

"Yes, well. You did very well for your first attempt," said the dowager. She accepted a rum butter tart and could not help but smile. Antonia had been in a good mood ever since returning with the news that she had convinced Lord Felton to host the engagement party. "I am pleased to see you finally dressed respectably."

With so much of her décolletage on view, Penelope hardly felt respectable. She shuddered to think of what her father would say, who preferred his daughters to wear high necklines. He was, after all, a clergyman and their father.

The butler arrived cautiously but was instantly reassured by the dowager, who invited him to note some improvements to the festive decor she wished him to make. He ushered them to the carriage with the duchess leading the way.

"I think she might have actually liked how I decorated the drawing room," whispered Penelope.

Marchford's eyes had been fixed on her since he entered the room. "You decorated the drawing room?"

❧

The Devine Christmas gala was an annual event for those hardy few in society who remained in London for the holiday. With the early opening of Parliament, more of society was present than ever before, making the Devine gala quite the event. The gala was designed to be a glittering festival of the season and it succeeded in every way.

Glass icicles hung down from the chandeliers with small candles inside, lighting the wondrous orbs. Fresh holly was festively displayed with red velvet ribbons tying the bundles. Marchford had not lied about the tree—a huge evergreen was prominently located, lit with multiple candles, and festooned with red bows. The effect was enchanting and slightly scary, but most dangerous of all was the numerous sprays of mistletoe hanging in different locations, waiting to catch unsuspecting guests in romantic encounters.

The dowager had declared her the height of fashion, but Penelope felt she was the height of something else entirely. She preferred her more conservative frocks, in which she was nearly invisible. However, she knew enough about society to understand the smallest sign of insecurity or doubt would be pounced upon, magnified and exploited, so she held her head high. She would not show weakness, even if she did look like a highly paid courtesan.

The dowager and Marchford were instantly engaged in conversations when they arrived, so Penelope walked across to the refreshments, noting that heads turned. Odd. Were they mocking? She was sure she did not wish to know. She still had a job to do as the infamous Madame X. Penelope smiled to herself. What would all these highbrow members of society's *haut ton* do if they discovered the exclusive matchmaker to society's elite was none other than a lowly companion?

In a flash, Penelope realized that she knew something precious few others were privy to: She was Madame X. And yes, Madame X would definitely wear this type of gown to a Christmas Eve ball. Her self-assurance rose within her, and by the time she had crossed the ballroom, she was no longer pretending the confidence she portrayed.

"Miss Rose." Lord Darington approached and bowed before her, his sister by his side. "I believe you are acquainted with my sister, Lady Katherine."

The young woman accordingly curtsied. "Call me Kate," she said without a smile.

"And you must call me Penelope. I understand you are new to London. How are you enjoying your visit?"

Kate raised one eyebrow. "Delightful." But her tone and manner gave Penelope the impression that it was anything but. "Would you excuse us, Robby?" Kate turned to her brother, who was standing mutely beside her. He bowed and disappeared into the crowd without a word. "I understand my brother has contacted you regarding my matrimonial prospects," said Kate bluntly, her tone accusing.

Pen was not unaccustomed to having the object of the matchmaking scheme be quite out of sorts when the truth was discovered, so her tone was not surprising, though her blunt manner in the middle of a crowded ballroom was a surprise. "Perhaps we should find a quiet corner? I believe the balcony boasts a fine view of Town," suggested Penelope.

"I am agreed."

Penelope led Kate to a side balcony. It was not snowing at the moment, but the snow on the ground lightened the entire view of the streets before them. Though the chill air was refreshing after the heat of the crowded ballroom, it was soon going to be uncomfortably cold. "Your brother did make an inquiry with Madame X to find you a suitable match," began Penelope.

"I do not mean any offense, but I have absolutely no inclination to marry. In truth, I am quite set against it," said Kate.

"Is there something in the institution that offends you?"

"The prospect of handing over my money, my future, my very freedom to a man of any sort makes me ill. No, I shall never marry; on this fact I am entirely resigned."

"I shall relay your feelings to Madame X." Penelope was used to people denying they wanted to be found a spouse, but never had anyone declared such an adamant intention to never wed.

"I thought you were Madame X."

Penelope was caught off guard. No one had ever considered her to be the mastermind behind the operation. "Whyever did you think such a thing?"

Kate shrugged. "Truly, it makes no difference to me. Either you are Madame X or you are in her employ; either way I would like to redirect your efforts."

"In what way?"

"I have no need or inclination to wed, but my brother must marry. He has a title and no other living family to take his place. If he dies, the title dies with him."

"I see. So you would like Madame X to find your brother a wife instead of you a husband."

"Yes. I am glad you are of a quick understanding."

Penelope paused at Kate's blunt statement, unsure

if it was praise or insult. She hoped Lord Darington would prove a more willing subject for matrimonial schemes. "Any particular guidelines in terms of the type of young lady your brother would be most suited for?"

Kate gazed up, thinking over the question. "She must be of a serious nature, not vibrant or chatty. She must be able to bear children, though I suppose it may be difficult to determine this beforehand. Perhaps a young widow with children, though Robert would not care to have children underfoot, particularly if they were not his. Perhaps a lady who had conceived children but they had died, but not died through illness; we do not need sickly brats."

"So the perfect wife for your brother would be a silent, serious woman who had not only lost her husband but her children as well?"

"Yes! Perfect!"

Penelope opened her mouth and closed it again. Her attempt at sarcasm had been entirely lost on this cheerless lady. Not usually at a loss for things to say, she was unaccustomed to her present speechless condition. What a description for a prospective wife! With the two taciturn siblings, an aggrieved wife might make their household the grimmest place in Town.

"I shall pass this on, but you must understand, there may not be many young widows whose children have also passed away."

"Yes, well, tell Madame X to do her best. If you cannot find these characteristics, just go for someone pretty. But no one who will speak insistently, I beg you, or I may be forced to cut out her tongue myself."

Penelope smiled at what she assumed must be a jest, but Kate's face was somber, leaving Penelope with the distinct impression Kate was being sincere. "Perhaps we should return to the party so we do not freeze," suggested Penelope, though the cold she now felt had little to do with the outside temperature.

They both returned to the celebrations, with Kate's expression outright hostile any time a man dared to set foot within three yards of her for any reason. Penelope made her apologies and left Kate to find some warmth from the chill that pervaded her very soul. Good thing Madame X was fired from finding Lady Katherine a husband. That was one lady who Pen would have to agree was not suited for marriage vows.

She stood by the wall as she usually did in these glittering ballrooms. Yet this time, her eyes searched the crowd looking for no one but Marchford. When she found him, he was in conversation with Mr. Grant.

But his eyes were on her.

Sixteen

"WHY DON'T YOU ASK HER TO DANCE?"

Marchford was startled back to present awareness. Grant had caught him staring at Miss Rose. Again.

"Ask whom to dance?" Marchford's only defense was to play innocent.

"Miss Rose. The bosom you've been gawking at all night. Got a pocket handkerchief if you feel the need to drool." Grant gave him a wicked grin.

"I am not staring."

"I said gawking and I'll stand by it. Not that I blame you. She does look quite different in those Town togs. Grandmama pick them?"

"Yes, I believe so." Marchford started to look around the room at anything but the infernal figure of Miss Rose, now shown to perfection. It was hardly his fault. He had seen Miss Rose almost every day for the past nine months, but he had never seen anything like this.

Where had she been hiding that cleavage?

"So go over and ask her to dance. Quick, before all her dances are claimed."

"No, no, if I dance with her, I would have to dance with all the debutantes here."

"Dreadful!"

"You mock, but I know for a fact you were set against marriage not long ago."

"And now I am happily caught in the web of matrimony!" Grant gave one of his mad grins. "So are you set against finding a wife and producing bouncing little heirs?"

"Not at all. I'm trying to get married, if only to stop being stalked by ladies determined to be the next duchess."

"So why not ask *mademoiselle décolletage* to marry you?"

"What?" Marchford turned to address his friend. "How much rum punch have you had?"

"Why not ask for her hand?" Grant persisted.

Marchford sputtered. "She is the companion to my grandmother. It is simply not done."

"Well, if being a duke doesn't give you the right to marry where you will, what does? Did not your father marry for love the second time around?"

Grant's arrow of mischief sunk home, but perhaps not in the manner he expected. Marchford was reminded of the fighting between his mother and his grandmother. No one should have to endure that, especially not a child. No, he had learned from his father's mistake. He was determined to enter into a marriage in which no love was required.

"Being a duke means I must be responsible. I cannot do as I like. I must serve the greater good."

"What rot!" exclaimed Grant with a laugh. "You are only trying to avoid heartache."

Marchford was spared having to make a reply by the arrival of their host, Lord Admiral Devine.

"Happy Christmas, my fine friends!" The admiral joined them with a merry twinkle in his eye. "What a crush! My wife will be so pleased." Nothing was more important to a hostess than the number of guests.

"Did you receive my warnings?" asked Marchford, taking command and changing the subject. He needed to focus back on his mission and forget the mysterious case of the growing bosom.

"Yes, indeed. Come, let us talk." Devine motioned to a side door and they all entered a small, private study, closing the door behind them. "I think we can all rest well tonight. I have commissioned a safe in which to place all documents of a sensitive nature."

"A safe? Intriguing!" said Grant in a manner that suggested he was not taking it as seriously as Marchford thought the moment required.

"Indeed! Not only is it impossible to open without the key, but it also has a secret compartment that can only be opened by…well, there is a trick to it that I shall not share to anyone. In that compartment are the codes for our spies abroad."

Marchford was impressed. "I am pleased you are taking caution."

"Quite so, quite so. After the last time I hosted a ball, I have learned to be cautious." At the last Devine ball, coded letters containing information about the foreign spy service had been stolen out of his desk. "See, here is a drawing of the safe. She is a beauty."

Marchford looked over the detailed drawing and was impressed. The diagram indicated the safe was three feet high by two feet in width, with an ornate steel-and-iron case around it. "Looks secure."

"I shall boast and say that it is."

"Good." Marchford shook the admiral's hand and walked back into the ballroom with Grant at his side. He knew Grant was grinning mischievously and attempted to avoid eye contact. It was no use.

"Now then," began Grant, not taking the hint. "Your information is secure. You can have no more worry tonight. Time for a little fun."

Marchford said nothing, but he had little hope it would deter Grant.

"I wonder where our ravishing Miss Rose has got to."

Marchford already knew. Without conscious intention, he scanned the ballroom until the lithe form of Miss Rose was found. She was speaking with Mrs. Grant, which was a shame, because Grant was sure to notice.

"Here we are, come along." Grant began to move toward his wife, dragging Marchford along with him.

"I cannot simply indulge myself. Somewhere even in our midst a traitor lurks. I must remain awares," Marchford protested.

"Indeed you must! Never let it be said that on this fine, snowy Christmas Eve, you were anything less than gravely miserable, a trial to friend and foe alike. I am only encouraging you to inflict poor Miss Rose with your sour disposition. Not quite charitable I admit, but there you are. Happy Christmas, ladies!"

Mrs. Grant was positively glowing in the candle-light. Miss Rose, in contrast, was not the kind of beautiful that turned men's heads, yet she was the only lady he wished to see. Her brown eyes sparked with intelligence, and there was something about her mouth that spoke of a secret that rested there. Her figure was flawless and more on display than ever before. His eyes had a terrible inclination to drift down to her ample bosom, and his hands itched for just one touch.

"Your Grace?" Penelope's eyes were now filled with irritation. Had she been talking to him?

Marchford glanced at Grant, who was merely laughing at him, without making any attempt to hide it. Marchford cleared his throat. "Yes, indeed."

"Yes, indeed?" asked Penelope. "Most people say 'happy Christmas' in return, but I shall have to amuse myself with 'yes, indeed.'"

"Your decorations were quite a surprise," he said, trying to change the subject by mentioning the new decor of his house, which in truth he had not noticed in the slightest. He forced his eyes once again from her bosom. "A nice surprise." Much like her assets now firmly on display.

"I am glad you liked them," said a mollified Penelope.

"I also want to thank you for all your assistance," he said in a low voice. "You have been quite useful."

It was quite a crush and Penelope stepped even closer to avoid being in someone's way. "You know how delighted I am to be of some use." Her eyes were laughing at him, and he deserved it.

"I hope…it is my wish that you…" Marchford struggled to find the right words. It was difficult when his focus was constantly being challenged by her plunging neckline and her rose-colored lips. How was a man to think?

BOOM!

A huge explosion rocked the entire house. Marchford grabbed Penelope around the waist with one hand and with the other drew his pistol, shielding her between the wall and his body. Even in this moment of crisis, his body delighted in her soft, feminine curves pressed against him. It was the spark of a beginning, but of what would have to wait. They were under attack.

"What was that?" demanded Penelope, slightly muffled from her face pressed against his coat collar.

"Don't know," said Marchford as he scanned the room in an instant, looking for danger. Women screamed; the music stopped; people began running in random directions. He could not see any damage nor the location of the explosion. Admiral Devine ran past, waving his arms, calling for people to remain calm. Marchford darted after him, not letting go of Penelope's hand for an instant.

"The safe! Where is it?" demanded Marchford, even as smoke began to pour into the ballroom from doors leading downstairs.

"Downstairs, in the cellar. Not again. Not again!" Admiral Devine hustled toward the door leading downstairs as the kitchen staff ran upstairs, away from the choking smoke.

The chaos was causing panic. The footmen ran to dump water on the burning tree. An elderly man was knocked down in the crush. People were going to get hurt. Marchford whistled loudly. It was not the most gentile form of communication, but it was necessary and effective.

People stopped and heads turned in his direction. "Please proceed in an orderly fashion to the exits," he commanded in a loud voice. "Gentlemen, please assist those who may need it. Once outside, the footmen shall deliver your cloaks and arrange for your carriages as soon as possible."

His calm words brought order back to chaos, and everyone began to do as he suggested. Despite his outward appearance, he was breathing hard. He had learned long ago to keep his emotions in check, particularly in times of crisis. And yet the black smoke gave him pause. He could face almost any trial, but being stuck in a burning building was something that made even him nervous.

Penelope squeezed his hand and gave him a confident nod. He had almost forgotten he held her hand. She believed in him, and it steadied his nerves.

"My grandmother?" he asked.

"I will see to her. Do not worry."

He knew she would take care of things. It was what she always did. He squeezed her hand in return and hoped it would express everything he could not say. In a blink, she let go of his hand and disappeared into the crowd.

"Where is the fire? Where is the fire?" Admiral Devine shouted at the kitchen staff as they evacuated up the stairs, coughing and sputtering, their faces blackened. No one could say, except that it had not originated in the kitchens.

"Is there another way down there?" asked Marchford.

"Follow me," boomed the admiral, and he followed him first outside the main door and then around to the back. They stopped short at what they saw.

A huge hole, low to the ground, had been blasted in the side of the redbrick town house. They ran to it and stared into the gaping hole, squinting into the acrid black smoke.

"My safe!" cried Devine. "It's gone!"

Seventeen

IT HAD BEEN A LONG NIGHT. PENELOPE HAD ESCORTED the dowager back home, though she would have preferred to stay with Marchford while he investigated the explosion. She had learned that a huge hole had been blown into the side of the house. Instead of trying to crack the safe, the thieves had chosen to remove the entire thing.

Penelope woke late to a cold, gray Christmas morning. It was a stark contrast to the cheery Christmas mornings of her childhood. Penelope put her feet on the frozen floor and took a deep breath of cold air. She walked to her closet undeterred. She would bring some joy into this house if it killed her. Her hand passed over the sensible frock she wished to wear and instead landed on a modish morning dress of white muslin with a bright red sash.

She met Marchford downstairs in the hall. He was dressed as well as ever, but his eyes were tired and she wondered if he had gotten any sleep.

"Did you find the safe?" she asked.

He shook a tired head. "The thieves used a wagon

to haul away the safe. We followed the trail through London. Searched all night, tried to follow tracks of the wagon in the snow, but we lost it. We think it went somewhere in the direction of St. Giles." His voice was grim.

"Do you think it was regular thieves or the work of foreign spies?"

"Undoubtedly the latter." Marchford rubbed his forehead in a tired motion. "No average thief would have access to as much gunpowder as what must have been used to blow that hole. We are lucky the whole house wasn't collapsed or consumed in flames."

She reached out to touch his arm. "This was not your fault. You are doing everything you can."

"Am I?" he asked, but his eyes softened toward her.

Antonia joined them and they were soon bundled up from head to toe for the requisite trip to St. George's for Christmas Mass. Marchford escorted them into their reserved box and they sat mutely in the cold church. If Penelope wished for Christmas carols, she was disappointed. This was St. George's after all, not some country parish. Yet even the staid reverend could not diminish the good news of the birth of the baby Jesus, who came to forgive the sins of the world and restore all to a relationship with their creator.

"God must truly have loved us to send his only son," whispered Penelope. "I can't imagine giving away my child to save the life of another."

Marchford frowned, as if the concept was a new one. "Nor I."

"That's why I love Christmas so much. It reminds

me that there is hope." She wished so much to share this hope with the dejected man beside her.

The dowager hushed them like errant children, and Penelope returned her attention to the service.

Upon their return, Pen made her way to the kitchens. She found willing allies in the cook and kitchen staff. Together they decided on a menu of roast goose with chestnut stuffing and celery sauce, marmalade glazed ham, pork and cranberry pie, and spiced prunes, with plum pudding and hot rum cream for dessert.

She might not be able to fix all the problems facing the Marchford house, but at least she could ensure their Christmas table, and that of the many domestics within their employ, would have a feast for supper. Returning upstairs, she surveyed the festive touches added to the dining room by the butler, who had been emboldened to include his own exquisite touches.

"I see you have now corrupted my entire staff." Marchford strolled into the empty dining room, surveying the crystal dangling orbs and silver bows with a critical eye.

"Should I apologize?" asked Penelope.

"Indeed, you should. I am in no mood for cheer."

"But that is when you are most in need of it."

Marchford merely shrugged. His usually bright eyes were dull and tired. "Since the thieves most likely are using the Rookery of St. Giles as a base of operations, I am amused by the prospect that, with my misguided philanthropy, I provided a hearty meal for the agents before they carried out this plot."

"No, no, I'm sure you did good." Penelope stood

beside him next to the long table, beautifully decorated with crisp, white linens and pure-white china
with gold accents. "I have something for you," she
added, wishing to change the subject and lift his spirits.

"You do? Why? Oh, right, that Christmas thing."
He answered his own question with a dejected mutter.

"I was going through some trunks in the attic,"
Penelope began.

"Why on earth would you be rummaging through
my trunks?" asked Marchford in a manner that could
only raise Penelope's defenses.

"I was hiding certain garments from your grandmother
to prevent them from being burned," she explained.

"That's my girl," muttered Marchford, though
she was not certain if he was referring to herself or
to his grandmother.

"As I was saying, I found this miniature and
I wondered if you knew who it was?" Penelope
handed him the miniature and was surprised at his
immediate reaction.

Marchford gasped and stared at the tiny picture. He
shook his head and muttered something Penelope's
tender ears should not have heard. She wished to ask
who it was but held her tongue, allowing Marchford
to stare at the picture in peace. He leaned against a
chair for support, closed his eyes, and held the miniature to his chest. "Where did you find it?"

"In a chest, far back in the attic, with a gown I
believe she is wearing in the picture."

He stood up tall, his eyes intense. "Where? Show me!"

Within minutes, they were in the attic, lit dimly
with pale blue light from the dormer windows.

Penelope showed him the trunk and he opened it slowly. He removed the gown with reverent hands, pausing to breathe in its scent.

"Was she a lost love of yours?" Penelope asked softly, swallowing down any inappropriate jealousy. She had no claim on this man.

Marchford gave a half smile. "Yes, in a manner of speaking." He removed the other items with gentle hands. A fan, a bottle of perfume, an ivory-handled brush and comb. Underneath it all was a large, rectangular object wrapped in brown paper. Marchford did what she had not dared and removed it from the trunk, slowly unwrapping the portrait.

"I thought this was burned," he whispered. It was a portrait of the same young woman. She was quite handsome, with an olive complexion, black hair, large dark eyes, and a wide, full mouth. The artist had captured a look of devious amusement. It was an enchanting picture.

In fairness, Penelope could easily see how Marchford would fall in love with such a beauty. In truth, who would not be tempted by her charms? Penelope pushed aside a flood of envy. Of course Marchford had experienced previous loves, and of course he would do so again. And when he did fall in love again, it would be with a divine creature like the one painted before her. It would not be…her.

Penelope cleared her throat and asked, "When did you know her?"

"When I was young." His voice was soft. He reached up to touch the cheek of the lovely lady.

"Yes. Quite. I am glad to have reunited you

with her," said Penelope with something less than
candor. She had never seen Marchford—safe, stolid
Marchford—so entranced. It was not a vision she
enjoyed. Handsome, young, rich, titled men fall in love
with beautiful ladies. Those were the facts she knew
all too well. She did not need to watch Marchford
make love to a portrait to have the point driven home.

"I shall leave you to have some privacy for your
remembrances," said Pen, feeling she had already
overstayed her welcome—or at least her tolerance.

"Thank you, Penelope," murmured Marchford.

Pen stilled. The man never called her by her
given name.

His eyes met hers. "This was my mother."

᭡

To see his mother again was the best Christmas gift
he had ever received, though in truth he had received
very few presents in his life. Over time, the memory of
her had faded and his vision of her image was obscured.
He remembered her soft voice and the smell of her
perfume—which still clung to her gown—and now her
image was renewed in his mind. Penelope had given
him back the image of someone he thought lost forever.

"Your mother!" Penelope's surprise was evident.
She sank down on the floor beside him. "There is no
record of her in the house." Penelope was referring to
the fact that his mother's portrait did not hang in the
gallery with the other family members.

"No indeed. My grandmother did everything in
her power to ensure that all memory of my mother
was erased. This portrait should be hanging now in the

gallery, but my grandmother would rather be buried alive than allow such a travesty to occur."

"I understand your mother and your grandmother were not the best of friends," prompted Penelope gently.

"My father's first marriage was an arranged alliance to Sophia of Lincolnshire. She was a lovely creature but did not survive childbirth with my elder brother, Frederick. My grandmother moved back into the house to care for Frederick, and my father took to the Continent for a grand tour. In Spain, he met a very beautiful lady. She was the daughter of the Earl of Wainwright and a very famous Spanish courtesan. My father fell madly, passionately in love with Belicia, Bella he called her, and they were married." Marchford paused for effect.

"Oh my," whispered Penelope. Marchford was the grandson of a Spanish courtesan?

"Can you possibly imagine the feelings of my grandmother when he returned with his new Spanish wife?"

"I am surprised the house was not rocked off its foundation."

Marchford gave a humorless laugh. "Very nearly. Grandmother was furious. It was all the talk. My grandmother refused to acknowledge my mother and to this day denies the legality of the marriage. In truth, she repeated this sentiment so often that I grew up with the strong impression that I was a bastard son and my father had brought home a mistress. One of the first things I did when I gained my majority was to travel to Spain to determine once and for all whether my birth was legitimate."

"And was it?"

"Oh yes, quite. The marriage was performed by an English minister for the British consulate to Spain. I found the register."

"It must have been difficult to grow up this way."

Marchford leaned back against the trunk. "My grandmother refused to leave Frederick to the care of a woman she despised, and consequently, we all ended up living together, one big, miserable family. My grandmother was supposedly raising Frederick and my mother supposedly raising me, though in truth they left most of the actual child care to a series of nannies and governesses, to whom they gave conflicting instructions." Marchford inspected the bottle of perfume as he told a tale he had never verbalized to anyone before now.

"I believe the primary reason they remained in the house was to fight. My mother planted flowers; my grandmother ripped them out. My mother redecorated the parlor; my grandmother refused to set foot in it. It all played out in society with different members of the *ton* taking sides. My father attempted at first to effect compromise and peace in his household but eventually gave up and spent most of his time at his club or hunting."

"What a dismal childhood." Penelope's voice was warm with understanding, but he could not look at her.

"It was not all bad. Frederick and I would secretly meet and play together when we should have been taking naps or focusing on our studies. Freddy was a marvelous companion, and though I'm sure he was often told that I was of inferior blood, he never once made me feel slighted.

"He was an excellent older brother, weak as he was. He had a fever early in life, and his body never fully recovered. Though his illness occurred before my father brought home my mother, my grandmother even laid the blame of that on my mother's doorstep. I think it offended my grandmother greatly to see Frederick remain so weak and me grow strong and healthy. The offense of this I could never overcome in her eyes."

"I cannot believe she was so hurtful to you!"

"When I was ten years old, my father died in a fire in his hunting box." Marchford closed his eyes, remembering the moment when the news had reached the household. His mother had collapsed on the floor, crying. His grandmother proceeded to scream at her for being overly dramatic. His mother had screamed right back.

"That must have been very difficult for you," said Penelope softly. She put her hand on his. It was warm and comforting, and he paused a moment simply accepting the comfort she provided. He had never told anyone this story. His oldest friends already knew and nobody else would dare to ask. A part of him wondered why he was telling Penelope now. She was nothing more to him than his grandmother's companion. And yet she was more—much more.

"After my father's death, it all became very ugly. I was sent away to school, and my mother was left to duel it out with my grandmother. It did not last long."

Marchford continued his tale, slowly turning his hand until Penelope's rested in his. It was natural, right. "One day they called me in to a small parlor at

Eton where my mother was waiting. She hugged me tight and told me she loved me and that she was going away for a little while but that her love remained."

Marchford paused to ensure his voice was steady before he continued. "It was the last time I ever saw her."

Penelope closed both hands around his. "I am so sorry. Whatever happened to her?"

"I am not sure. I attempted to find her, but to no avail. My grandmother also hindered any attempt. I wrote many letters that were never answered. Later, I discovered my grandmother had paid the school to ensure no letter was ever posted."

"How cruel!" Penelope squeezed his hand. Her eyes blazed. "I am so sorry. I had not thought the duchess to be so mean-spirited."

"I am glad you are finally seeing her from my perspective." He hazarded a glance at Penelope, who looked at him with nothing but compassion. "Though to be fair, I believe she thought she was doing right by me. She believed my mother to be a poor influence on me, and in truth, there may have been something to it."

"How so?"

"When I gained majority, I attempted to follow my mother's path. When she left England, she was not alone but in the company of a German prince. After that, she had an alliance with the King of Spain until his wife objected. I fear she had a variety of liaisons until the trail grew cold, and I could no longer discover any word of her."

"You believe she has died?" Penelope's voice was soft yet strong. This was something he had never verbalized, yet she gave him the strength to speak of this long-denied pain.

"It is most likely. I have never received any word from her. Not even when Frederick died and I ascended to the dukedom. I can only assume she has passed."

"I am sorry for your loss." In Penelope's eyes, he saw honest compassion and understanding. Her parents also being deceased, he knew she truly did understand what it was like to be without one's parents.

Marchford sat on the dusty floor of the attic on Christmas day with his grandmother's companion and the image of his mother. It was a strange day. "When I returned on holiday from Eton, I found all trace of her was removed. All questions regarding her whereabouts were rebuffed. It was as if she had never existed. I was never allowed to express…" He paused, unsure how to proceed. His grief at his mother's absence became an illicit thing. He could not voice the loss. Except, apparently, with Penelope.

"I understand." Penelope took a deep breath and looked down. "I have never shared this with anyone, but after my parents died, we were in a bit of desperate straits. My aunt took us in, but we all knew it was only for a short time. After that, we were to be on our own. One of us needed to marry and marry well, but we were still in mourning. It had not been long enough; we should not have entered society when we did, but we could ill afford to wait another year."

"You did what you had to do." Marchford gave her hand an understanding squeeze.

"Did we?" Penelope looked up with big dark

eyes. "I have never felt entirely comfortable with the decision to pretend our parents had died earlier than they had. Perhaps that is why I clung to my mother's outmoded frocks. If I could not show my mourning, I could at least keep her close."

A lock of brown hair fell out of place over her eyes, and Marchford gently pushed it back, his thumb tracing along the edge of her forehead. For the first time he felt he had someone who understood. He leaned forward, breathing in her clean scent. Her eyes widened and she leaned closer to him.

"Thank you." He slowly kissed one cheek. "This is for bringing back the memory of my mother." He kissed the other cheek, lingering at his work. "This is for sharing a piece of yourself."

He attempted to pull back, but Penelope's eyes flashed and his intention was arrested. "You have shared with me also, so I should return the favor." She leaned in and kissed him softly on the cheek, spreading warmth throughout his body.

His heart, generally something beyond his notice, began to beat. He could not tell if it was faster than normal since, until that moment, he had not been aware he had a heart at all. He leaned closer, his eyes focusing on her soft lips the color of the pale sunrise through the London haze. He paused, allowing her a moment to retreat. She did not. He could not.

Their lips met.

Slowly their hands found each other, intertwining their fingers. He pressed forward, his lips softly brushing hers. It was a chaste kiss as kisses went, but it was a kiss. A kiss with Penelope Rose.

Propriety forced him to pull back. She said nothing, but he could tell she was thinking furiously. He wondered what he could do to make the little crease between her eyebrows disappear. So he kissed her again, this time putting one hand on her cheek. He wondered desperately if she tasted as good as her scent promised. He moved forward and deepened the kiss, his arms wrapping around her and pulling her close.

He needed her, was drawn to her with a power he could no longer resist. He had wanted to kiss her for so long now he pulled her closer, one hand running down her back, his tongue sliding along her lower lip.

"Oh!" She pulled back and put her hand over her mouth.

He cursed himself for going too far.

"Well now. Well, well," she said, a deep pink flush gracing her cheeks. "I think we have thanked each other sufficiently, don't you think?"

Not even close.

"I believe I should be going." Penelope struggled to untangle her gown enough to stand, and Marchford stood to give her assistance. "I am glad you have found something that was lost to you." Her eyes grew soft once more but hardened an instant later and turned away.

"I cannot thank you enough," he said in a low voice, meaning it sincerely in every way possible.

"We have thanked each other enough with…with a Christmas kiss of friendship!" She turned on him, defiant, as if daring him to contradict her.

"I am new to these traditions, so I thank you for sharing them with me. Tell me more about the Christmas kiss."

"We did it wrong." Penelope crossed her arms.

"Did we? I am more than willing to try again until I get it right." He stepped closer.

"There was supposed to be mistletoe." She frowned, scolding him.

"Ah, yes, you are right. You must forgive me since I am new to this. Next time—"

"No, no." Her eyes widened and she stepped back. "No need for a next time."

"But I do so want to get this Christmas tradition correct. You did promise me a happy Christmas."

"Did I, Your Grace?" She edged away even more.

"James. If we are going to share the traditional Christmas kiss of friendship, then you definitely need to call me James."

A smile played along her lips. "As you wish. James." She said it slowly as if trying it out. "I suppose you should call me Penelope."

"Penelope," he said in a voice that was almost a whisper.

She swallowed. "I must go." And she fled the attic. Marchford took the portrait of his mother and followed at a more sedate pace. It was suddenly very important that he find mistletoe.

He smiled broadly, filled with Christmas cheer.

Eighteen

"JAMES IS IN A VERY STRANGE MOOD," COMMENTED Antonia, giving Penelope a critical eye.

"Is he?" replied Penelope, trying her best to ignore the banging and focus on her knitting. They were in the sitting room before Christmas dinner. Usually, it was a dignified affair. Tonight strange things were afoot.

"He smiled at me." The dowager frowned.

"He did?" Penelope chewed her lower lip.

"And wished me a merry Christmas."

"No!"

The dowager raised an eyebrow. "What have you done to him?"

"Me? Nothing! I've done nothing!"

Banging came from the dining room.

"What on earth is that boy doing?"

Penelope slouched in her chair. She knew exactly what Marchford was doing. The telltale banging could be heard coming from the drawing room. He was hanging mistletoe.

"I think I should check on the dinner." Penelope

dashed out of the room toward the kitchen. She had kissed him. *Kissed* him. A friendly kiss. Is there such a thing as a friendly kiss? And now the duke had gone and lost his mind. Along the servants' corridor, she overheard the staff discussing the strange behavior.

"Where did His Grace find so much mistletoe?" asked one of the upstairs maids to the footman.

"And why is he hanging it all over the place?" asked the footman.

"That's quality for you. They're all cracked," said a scullery maid.

"I'll crack you if you don't stop your yapping and get back to work," shouted Cook. "And you, not you again. Get out. Out!"

Cook came at Pen with a broom.

"I beg your pardon?" asked Penelope, taking a step back.

"Oh laws, not you, Miss Rose. That dratted dog thing."

Looking around, Penelope noted a matted mass of wet fur scurrying around people's feet. Cook tried to sweep the little dog up the stone stairs, out into the snow, but the beast would have none of it, ducking around the broom at the last minute and running between legs back into the hostile kitchen.

"Poor thing. He's probably cold and hungry," said Penelope.

"He can be poor and hungry outside my kitchen!" demanded Cook.

The animal took refuge behind Penelope, his large yellow eyes pleading for help. He had a funny face, as if he had run into a wall and his face was flattened.

He put up a dirty paw to beg. "But it is Christmas," suggested Penelope. "We are to provide a home for the weary traveler."

Cook gave her a withering look. The scullery maid muttered something again about quality being touched in the head and this time Cook did not correct her.

"That thing will have fleas, miss. Can't stay here," reasoned Cook.

"Perhaps I could give him a bath?" suggested Penelope. She hoped another member of the help would actually *help*. But not one would meet her eye, and all became very busy.

She ended up kneeling on the floor, covered with towels, washing a bedraggled dog in a large bucket. With the liberal use of a jar of soap and a comb, along with some meat treats to gain compliance, she began to reveal the image of her rescued friend.

It was a gray mop.

Further drying with a towel revealed an unexpected surprise.

"Blimey. I reckon that dog is a cat!" exclaimed a maid.

The cat meowed loudly to the stunned kitchen, proving his felineness.

"That done be the largest cat I ever saw," said one of the grooms, coming in from the cold.

"What are you gonna name it, miss?" asked a footman.

"Miles," said Penelope without a second thought. "Because there are miles of cat here."

The kitchen staff laughed and all gathered around the Christmas cat-dog. After a hearty feeding for the cat and some debate over whether Christmas syllabub or wassail punch should be served at dinner, and it being decided to prepare both, Penelope returned upstairs, a large bundle of damp cat in her arms.

Upon reaching the main floor, Penelope found a labyrinth of danger. Somewhere was the dowager, who must be avoided at all costs—a stray cat in her pristine household would be an abhorrence. And somewhere else lurked the duke. To make matters difficult, he had hung a maze of tiny bundles of mistletoe overhead. Not content with simply hanging it in doorways, he had constructed a web of string from which dangerous bundles of mistletoe hung at random intervals.

The real question was, did she want to get caught?

Well, did she? Clearly she had much too much cat in her arms for rational thought. Penelope took a breath and stole softly across the hall to the main stairs, one eye looking for the duke or dowager and the other eye nervously glancing above her. Miles, the enormous cat, chose that inopportune moment to make a rather large meow, which echoed loudly down the hall.

"What was that?" came the voice of the dowager from the sitting room.

"I shall go see," replied the duke.

Nothing for it but to run. And run she did, except when she got to the stairs, she encountered a difficult problem with her hands full of cat, her wet slippers slick on the marble floor, and a meowing animal who did not appreciate the ride. She stepped on her skirts and went down on the stairs with a bump and a hiss.

"What the blazes..." Marchford stood above her. "Is that a dog?"

"No, actually," said Penelope, trying to untangle her foot from the hem of her skirt. "It is a cat."

"A what?" The dowager walked up and poked the damp creature with her cane before Penelope could pick it up again. Miles growled, looking more disreputable than ever.

Marchford glanced between the dowager and Penelope, his eyes narrowing. Penelope sighed. So much for her Christmas cat. She was certain she would be told to remove the beast, but the dowager just then noticed the web of mistletoe above her head.

"My stars and garters, what have you done?" exclaimed the dowager.

"I have mistletoed the house," said Marchford defiantly. "I have decided that if I choose to decorate my home like a tradesman, I shall do it to distinction."

"You have decided what?" the dowager's voice was like ice.

"Too bad you have seen your Christmas present early," said Marchford, swiftly changing the subject.

"My present?" asked the dowager, slightly mollified, looking back at him and Penelope and the monstrosity in her arms in a distracted way.

"Yes, your present," said Penelope. She had no idea where Marchford was going with this, but she took his lead.

"The extremely rare Peruvian jungle house cat," said Marchford.

"The Peruvian jungle house what?" The dowager rapped her cane on the marble floor in irritation.

"The jungle house cat, from deepest Peru," said Penelope. For all she knew it could be from Peru.

"That is a dog," dismissed the dowager.

Miles, the Peruvian jungle house cat, meowed in complaint.

"Is that really a cat? I don't want that thing," exclaimed the dowager.

"I can keep it until later," suggested Penelope.

"You can send that Peruvian beast back to—"

"Oh look, mistletoe!" declared Marchford. Penelope almost jumped into his arms, but Marchford turned and kissed his grandmother on the cheek. Penelope took the clue and picked up her skirts and ran up the stairs.

"Merry Christmas to all!" she called as she fled. She made it to the door of her room, where she intended to deposit the scraggly cat, but just as she reached out with one hand to open her door, he chose that moment to jump and run.

"Come back here," cried Penelope. Miles skittered across the floor and dashed up the hall and back down, finally pushing open a door and racing in. It was the room of the Duke of Marchford. Of course.

"Bad cat! You come back here!" she hissed at the recalcitrant feline at the door to the duke's quarters.

The cat meowed defiantly in return.

Penelope dashed in the room. She had just left Marchford downstairs and with any luck she could retrieve the animal and be back in her room without him ever knowing. She searched around the room, trailing a finger along the edge of the bed. *His* bed. What might it be like to...

The cat! She must find the cat and stop these utterly inappropriate thoughts. The cat had found a hiding place under a dresser. She tried coaxing out the beast, but to no avail. She got down on her knees and bent over to pull the naughty cat out from his hiding spot.

"And a merry Christmas to you," said the seductive voice of Marchford. "How did you know exactly what I wanted for Christmas?"

Penelope, now with her head under the dresser, died of shame. He must be addressing her raised rump, since that would be about all of what he could see of her. She wiggled her way out and stood up with as much dignity as she could muster. It wasn't much.

"My cat is stuck under your dresser," said Penelope hopelessly.

Marchford attempted to suppress a smile. "How long have I waited to hear you say that?"

Penelope could not help herself and began to giggle. Marchford chuckled and then they both laughed.

"Thank you. I can't remember a time when I was so diverted." Marchford smiled at her. "You have indeed given me a happy Christmas."

"You are most welcome." If she had made him happy, she was happy too.

"Oh look, mistletoe."

"There's no mistletoe…"

He held a sprig of that mischievous plant over her head and before she could respond, planted a kiss on her lips. This time Penelope did not back away. She wrapped her arms around his neck and he gave her a warm embrace. He deepened the kiss and Penelope only held on tighter, shots of liquid lightning coursing through her at his touch. When they finally broke apart for a much-needed breath, Penelope could barely stand on her weak knees.

"I think I am going to like Christmas," said Marchford, his voice low and breathy. "Very friendly."

"And this is just the beginning. There are twelve days you know."

He glanced at his bed and back at her. "I am unfamiliar with these traditions. How friendly does this season get?"

Penelope snatched the cat, who had slowly vacated the dresser, her heart pounding. "I mean to say…a happy time and all but…"

"A happy Christmas to you, Penelope."

"Merry Christmas…James."

Nineteen

MILES THE PERUVIAN JUNGLE HOUSE CAT WAS A SOP-
ping mop when wet and a huge fluff ball when dry.
After an evening sitting by the fire and then sleeping
on her pillow, Penelope woke up sputtering on fur
and found Miles had fluffed up to a truly impressive
stature, even by Peruvian standards.

The animal was nothing if not appreciative for his
rescue and took to following her about the house,
pawing her gently with a large fluffy mitt if he felt
she was not paying him due homage. Penelope tried
putting him back in her room several times, but then
she would reach for a book and he would be sitting
on it, or she would grab her stitching and he would
be tangled up in it.

"Can we ship the dog back to Peru?" grumbled the
dowager.

"Doubtful," replied Penelope.

Of Marchford, she saw little during the day. He
had gone once more in search of the missing safe.
She spent most of the day absently poking a needle at
a sampler, though her mind was definitely on other

matters and she had to rip out more stitches than she put in. He had kissed her. She had kissed him. They had *kissed*.

It had been friendly—very, very friendly. But was it anything more? She waited impatiently for his return. When he finally did, his grim face told her that his efforts had been unsuccessful. Still, it was the day of the engagement ball for Sir Gareth and Lady Jane, to be held at Lord Felton's house, so there were still opportunities for discovering the culprits.

As Marchford predicted, a ball held at the home of Lord Felton, who had not entertained in twenty years, was something not to be missed. None who were lucky enough to be invited would ever consider declining the invitation, with the exception of Grant and his wife. She was feeling the ill effects of being heavy with child and decided to forgo the celebration, and naturally Grant would not stray out of doors without her.

Penelope was pleased, since the evening marked a success for Madame X, but even more excited, looking forward to the ability to look for clues as to Lord Felton's guilt or innocence. The fact that she could do so with Marchford only heightened her anticipation.

She was still trying to untangle her thoughts and emotions regarding the "friendly" kiss. She had gotten the merest crumb of what a man such as Marchford could offer; she wanted more. Yet she must take care to guard her heart, to avoid any discomfort when he chose another as a marriage partner.

The fact that she was theoretically employed in trying to find Marchford a marriage partner only made it that much more important that she not engage her heart in any matter that involved the handsome duke.

Call me James.

Penelope shook her head to banish the treacherous thoughts. It was a hopeless case. She needed to focus on the plan to search the house for anything suspicious.

Marchford made his way toward her, her heart beating with every step he drew nearer. "Find a way to check the kitchen and servants' areas," said Marchford in passing, adopting the cool reserve he showed in public. He caught her hand for a moment and whispered one more instruction in her ear. "Do not put yourself in danger. Anything suspicious, you come to me."

His breath was warm in her ear and sent a shiver down her spine. "I shall try not to be a witness to murder," she whispered back and moved on before he could reply. It would not do to be seen in conversation.

Penelope proceeded downstairs under the guise once more of preparing the dowager her particular blend of tea. Pen saw no need to change such an effective story, and if she was consistent, it only lent credence to the story. Even the dowager was beginning to appreciate tea in the evenings.

Downstairs, the passage on the right clearly led to the kitchens, but she purposely turned to the left. If caught, she could claim she got lost and in the meantime she would poke around to see what she might find.

The corridor was dark, probably leading to storage rooms or servants' quarters, and she was just about to turn around when she saw a light burning in the gloom. She proceeded slowly, catching a piece of intriguing conversation.

"How much longer must we wait 'ere?" asked a man with a heavy cockney accent.

"Not long now," said a smoother voice of a young man. "I am considering making myself known."

"Ought not to do that. Make a fuss. She'd not like it."

"Perhaps not. But it is my right after all."

Penelope strained to hear more of the conversation that was happening in a small room with the door slightly ajar. She stepped closer, but her slipper scuffed against something on the floor.

The men instantly stopped their conversation. "What's that?" asked the cockney accent.

Seeing there was no way to escape notice in the small passage way Penelope instantly stepped forward, calling out, "Hello? Is anyone there?"

The door opened and a young, attractive gentleman stepped out, candle in hand. He frowned at her, taking her measure in one sweeping glance. Her mind raced to come up with a plausible story that made her appear inconsequential and not a threat. "I was looking for the kitchens," she explained. "The Duchess of Marchford sent me down to make her tea."

"Companion, are you?" he asked.

"Yes, I'm afraid I've never been in this house before and I've gotten lost."

The man's face relaxed into a smile. "Wouldn't doubt you have never been here. The house has not been used to entertain for twenty years."

"Long time," she said, edging back, prepared to run if need be.

"I'm afraid we are both where we shouldn't be. I'm Justin Strader, Lord Felton's heir."

"Oh," said Penelope, now unsure how to proceed.

"You must be wondering why I am here in one of the servants' rooms."

"Well, I…it is none of my business, of course."

The man shrugged in a friendly manner. "I fear I am not on speaking terms with Lord Felton."

"I have heard there was bad blood between you," prompted Pen, hoping he would take her into his confidence.

"Not on my side, I assure you. I am Lord Felton's nephew, but he does not feel the man his sister, my mother, married is worthy of the title. He considers me rather low, I fear, and I don't doubt he somehow blames me for the sin of inheriting his estate."

"Not quite fair," agreed Penelope.

"I must confess, I have always been of that opinion," he said with a charming smile. "His animosity extends so far that I have never been inside this house. In truth, I have met the man only rarely. When I heard the house was finally opening up for a ball, I allowed curiosity to rule me and I convinced his groom to allow me to at least see the bottom parts of the house. There can be no chance of running into Lord Felton down here, and with all the bustle of the party, I am hardly noticed. You must think my presence an impertinence."

"Not at all," said Penelope frankly. "I find it rather shocking that Lord Felton would dismiss his own nephew."

"While he throws a party for distant cousins." His voice held an edge, but he smiled again the next moment. "Of course, they are wellborn. My mother ran off with the groundskeeper," he said ominously.

"Oh, well in that case, I understand," said Penelope with a laugh, and Strader joined in. "It is nice to meet you, Mr. Strader. I am Penelope Rose, companion to the Dowager Duchess of Marchford."

They bowed to each other and he offered to show her the kitchens, which she accepted. He was a nice man, surprisingly without malice, which she might have felt had she been so neglected by a relative. "I do hope you are able to take your proper place in society," said Penelope as they reached the door to the kitchens.

"I have no doubt that I will," said Mr. Strader. "Good night, Miss Rose." He bowed over her hand and disappeared back down the corridor.

Penelope considered him carefully as he walked away. He was simply dressed but neat and clean, well-spoken, and a pleasant sort of man. And he was young and would inherit an earldom. Mr. Strader was definitely going to have an entry in her matchmaking book tonight.

Now it was time to investigate the kitchens and see how easy it would be to bribe the staff into revealing something helpful.

❧

Marchford gave an obligatory look of feigned interest to a matron who was attempting to engage him in conversation with her young daughter. The daughter was pretty enough, but he could not imagine having to tolerate meaningless conversations on a daily basis. He kept an eye out for Penelope. She was always finding something of importance, and while he may not always agree with her, she never once made him consider faking a fit of apoplexy just to avoid a dull conversation.

Marchford broke away as soon as was socially possible and searched the ballroom for Penelope. Not only did he wish to hear her report, but also he needed to ensure her safety. Truth was he wanted to see her again. Of course the kitchens should be perfectly safe, but then again, he would have bet money the kitchens at the Grant house would have been safe too.

He found her delivering tea to his grandmother. Penelope threw him a glance, one that said there was something to say but nothing immediate. He wondered for a moment how it was that she could so readily communicate without words. And yet he knew her looks. Every twitch of an eyebrow meant something. It was a language he seemed to naturally understand. It was of course important in his line of work to have an accomplice with whom he could so easily communicate.

She was looking very lovely tonight in ice blue. Once again her décolletage was on display, and though it was not lower than any other fashionably attired lady in the room, she captured his full attention. Her brown hair was swept up into a bun, with a few ringlets of hair framing her face, a contrast to her pale skin. He did not have words to express how much he wished to thread his fingers through her hair and touch her ample bosom.

"I wonder what will become of her," said an elderly woman's voice.

Marchford turned to find the Comtesse de Marseille, dressed to kill in burgundy silk with enough gold and jewels to beggar a king. "I beg your pardon?" asked Marchford.

"I was speaking of Miss Rose, who has had a very surprising change in wardrobe lately."

"My grandmother insisted." Marchford was suspicious. The comtesse rarely initiated conversation with him, which could only mean she was pursuing some sort of society gossip.

"I wonder what will happen to her when Antonia marries. She must also be looking for a new situation." She gave him a condescending smile and glided away, taking her suspicious mind with her.

He went back to staring at Penelope. The comtesse was right about one thing: Penelope's situation was tenuous. She would need to move out when the dowager left.

And that was the one thing he could not allow.

Twenty

"THE HOUSEKEEPER AND THE COOK WERE BEYOND reproach, but the scullery maid was not above a monetary incentive to provide information," whispered Penelope.

"I am not sure I approve of your methods," said Marchford. It seemed the appropriate thing to say, although he was far from finding fault. They had met by design in a little-used corridor between the ballroom and the card room.

"Shall I go to a lonely corner to repent?" Penelope arched an eyebrow in a teasing gesture that made him want to reciprocate in a manner that would not be appropriate. Ever since those blasted "friendly" kisses, he had wanted more from her. And he only had himself and the mistletoe to blame.

"What else did you learn?" He needed to focus on the task at hand.

"First of all, I ran into an uninvited guest, Justin Strader, Lord Felton's heir."

"I thought they were estranged."

"They are. Mr. Strader apparently bribed one of the

grooms to allow him access to the house. Said he was curious to see it, since he will inherit."

"That is interesting." Marchford rubbed his jaw but could not think of any connection between Felton's poor family relations and the missing safe.

"Also, Lord Felton has been receiving some packages of late. He is a mite anxious about them, only wants the butler to receive them and then bring them into the study. Do you think it significant?"

"Perhaps. Perhaps not. Suppose I should inspect his study."

Penelope nodded. "What shall I do?"

"You will do nothing. You've done enough."

Penelope's face fell, and he was himself disappointed not to include her in the adventure, but his conscience would not allow him to put her at risk. It was better this way, though he was certain she would not share his conviction.

"As you wish." She spun on her heel and gave him her back, her posture rigid. She walked away without another word, giving him ample opportunity to admire her pleasing figure with her trim waist and the promise of a delightful swell at her derrière.

Marchford sighed. He was trying to protect her. She was having none of it, but still, it was for the best. Marchford casually wandered about the ballroom, making polite conversation and avoiding every member of the female species. He tossed back several drinks and shared some loud laughs with some of the highbred, ill-behaved members of the young male aristocracy. It was enough to convince his acquaintance that he was a bit bosky. If he should be caught where he shouldn't be, he needed an excuse for poor directional sense.

Despite his need to appear carefree, his eyes continued to find the figure of Penelope in her ice-blue gown. She made conversation with a few people and briefly attended his grandmother, who was radiant on the arm of the Earl of Langley. Penelope then sat down by the wall with the other matrons. He was sorry for her, alone in a ballroom.

He wished to go speak to her, to at least provide some company, but it would not serve. He should keep his distance. It was, of course, for the best.

"I see your grandmother's got herself a new companion," said one of the young bucks with Marchford.

"Miss Rose has been with my grandmother almost a year now," said Marchford.

"No, can't be. I'd have noticed her," said another with a look in his eye Marchford instantly disliked.

"Think I'll ask her to dance," said another, and without further comment or even asking Marchford's leave, he did just that.

"She's got a nice set on her. Just want to get my hands on her," said another man, too drunk to notice the flash of warning in Marchford's eyes.

"You will not insult her." Marchford's voice was low, but his hands burned to strangle the young inebriate. To further add to Marchford's fury, Penelope rose to greet the young man who approached and actually accepted his offer to dance. Wrong. It was just plain wrong. His Penelope did not dance. And yet, apparently, she did.

"Now don't get your back up. She's only a bit a muslin after all," said his drunk former friend.

Marchford grabbed the man's pinky finger and bent it back, pushing him outside the ballroom, into an empty corridor even as the man gasped in pain. "You will never insult Miss Rose. Are we clear?" Marchford hissed.

"Ow! Let go! What's got into you? Yeah, all right, sorry to insult. My mistake entirely."

Marchford released the man's finger, not sure whether or not he had broken it. He was certain he did not care. "Go back to your drink."

The man stumbled back to the ballroom. Marchford did not care to join him only to watch Penelope dance with another man. Could she not tell that man was beneath her? Why, the man had the intellect of wallpaper paste and the conversation of a fishmonger.

Marchford leaned on the wall, trying to regain his perspective and objectivity. He had other concerns that night beyond the dance partners of his grandmother's companion. He guessed one of the closed doors in the corridor led to Felton's study.

He stumbled, just in case there were unseen eyes, into the door he thought was most likely. He was in luck; it was the man's study. He closed the door as far as he could and still provide some light from the hallway lanterns to allow a search. He attacked the desk first, swiftly going through the papers on top and then the drawers. He wished he had someone to act as lookout. If caught, he might have difficulty explaining why he not only stumbled into the man's study but also into the man's desk drawers.

In the third drawer down, he found a false bottom and papers within. A wave of anticipation passed

over him. This would hold answers, he knew it. The
letters were not correspondence, but rather ledgers.
Marchford held more than a passing understanding of
ledger sheets and quickly ascertained that these were
not related to his household or even business accounts.
Instead, they seemed to be tracking deliveries from
different sources. But why?

He returned the papers to their original location
and continued his search through the room. In a
corner, he found brown paper stuffed into a trash bin.
On it was a post label, possibly one of the packages
the scullery maid had mentioned. But what had been
in it? He attempted to reconstruct the image from the
folds and so was kneeling on the floor when the door
opened and Lord Felton himself entered the room.

Concealed by the desk, Marchford crouched closer
to the floor. He stilled his breathing and hoped for the
best. If he was discovered, he would begin to snore and
pretend drunken stupor, but it was his preference not to
be known as a stumbling drunk who could not hold his
liquor at an engagement party of all the benign things.

Lord Felton walked in and stopped before the
desk. "Brown! Mr. Brown, I am in need of you!" he
called out the door and soon was joined by the butler.
"Where is the package that arrived today?"

"You had asked it be moved to your bedchamber
considering this evening's activities."

"Oh yes, must be foxed myself. Last thing I need
is some snooping fool. Can't trust them." Lord Felton
left and Marchford exhaled a long breath. Now he
needed to search the man's bedchamber, and for that
he needed Penelope.

He would drag her off the dance floor if need be, and he was quite determined the need would indeed be great. All for king and country, naturally.

❧

Penelope was having a curious evening. Things had started normally enough. She considered her match-making clients, but here she was at an impasse. She could not find a widowed and bereaved woman for Lord Darington, and there was not a gentleman she knew upon whom she would inflict his sister. As for finding a spouse for Marchford, she had given up. He would need to marry, true, but she could hardly bring herself to find him a wife.

Since she had no further business to attend, she sat in a chair by the wall to pass the time, watching the dancing couples until she was needed again. She did not mind it particularly, since it was how she had passed many a ball. Soon she would need to leave London and these soirees would be but a memory.

A well-dressed man interrupted her slightly maudlin train of thought. She stood, thinking he must have come in search of a chair. Instead, he boldly intro-duced himself and asked her to dance.

A man. A real live man had actually come up to her and asked her to dance. Penelope was stunned into accepting and glanced around to determine if she was to be the object of some joke. All she noted was the glare of Marchford and a knowing wink from the dowager. Something was definitely amiss.

But she still danced. She had not been asked in ages, and only then as a token in regard for her sisters.

Penelope actually enjoyed dancing, but was a bit rusty from neglect of the art. It all came back to her soon enough, and she enjoyed herself. It was quickly apparent that the man with whom she was dancing, although easy on the eyes and a fine dancer, would not be accounted among intellectual giants. Still, it was an opportunity to dance, and the fact that Marchford was so clearly displeased by it made her ridiculously happy.

Marchford disappeared for a while but returned at the end of the set. His approach was somewhat amusing. A few ladies attempted to divert his attention, but his eyes were fixed on Penelope, and none could turn his head. The unlikely coup won her a few looks of contempt, which Penelope could only cherish. She had never before been the object of jealousy, and she was determined to enjoy it.

The duke was taller than most men. In a dark blue frock coat and a golden waistcoat cut to perfection, he was the very image of a gentleman. Even more, his manner, his look, his address—he was a duke in every sense. And he was coming for her.

"I have need of you," whispered Marchford when she was parted from her partner for a moment in the dance.

"Perhaps I am dancing," said Penelope, which surprised herself even more than Marchford.

"Demands of king and country. I fear you must forgo the pleasures of your new beau's company." The words came almost as a growl. People turned their heads.

Penelope raised an eyebrow.

"My grandmother has need of your assistance," he said in a lazy manner, loud enough to be heard by the gossips.

Penelope made her apologies to her dance partner and followed Marchford to the side of the ballroom. She stifled a grin. The only thing better than being asked to dance, was having Marchford intercede to drag her away. "What would you have me do?" Her voice quivered in anticipation.

"I need a lookout," whispered Marchford, leaning toward her so none could hear, his breath hot on her cheek. "Meet me upstairs near the main bedrooms in ten minutes."

Penelope nodded, her heart pounding. He had said he needed her and directed her to the bedrooms. Nothing else mattered.

Getting up the main stairs unnoticed proved more difficult than she originally thought. The novelty of seeing a house open that had been shut for years made the evening's event a mad crush. People were everywhere and there was no chance of walking up the stairs without someone noticing. Out of habit, she had watched not only the guests but the servants as well, and noted the hidden doorway leading to the back stairs and servants' passages.

Penelope chose a moment when the future bride's brother announced a toast to slip up the side stairs. Upstairs, she found Marchford with a single candle in hand, most likely pilfered from a wall sconce.

"What are we looking for?" asked Penelope in a voice barely above a whisper.

"Not sure," Marchford answered in kind. "Felton talked about moving something up to his bedchamber. I need to search and I would like you to serve as my eyes while I do it." He paused and cleared his throat.

"If, that is, you are willing to become involved. I need not tell you this is highly irregular."

"I understand. We should be quick then."

Marchford nodded in approval. "You stand by the door. It will be dark, but that way you can see a candle coming and move out of the way before you are seen. The main stairs are here; the servants' back stairs are at the end of the hall. If someone comes, knock once if it is the main stairs, twice if the servants to warn me, then move down the opposite direction."

"What shall you do?"

"What I do best. Do not wait for me; just leave and return to the ball."

It was simple enough and Penelope was a little disappointed her role in the scheme was to remain outside without Marchford. "I understand. Good luck."

Marchford nodded and opened a few doors before finding the one he sought. He disappeared into the room, shutting the door behind himself. Penelope was instantly thrown into darkness. There was barely enough light from below to make out the gray outlines of the hall.

Waiting was an excruciating mix of nervous fear, lest she be caught, and boredom. She wished to know if Marchford had any success and steeled herself against the urge to poke her head in the room and ask him herself. The time stretched on, yet with her senses so alive, she could not tell if it was seconds, minutes, or hours. She was just about to give up her resistance and call to Marchford to see what he had found, when she heard someone coming up the main stairs.

They were not being particularly quiet, with slurred

speech and silly giggles. Penelope paused a moment. Was it one for the main stairs and two for the servants, or the other way around? Her mind spun as the light grew closer.

She knocked once and turned to flee to the side stairs. She was almost to the servants' stairs when she heard the unmistakable clanging of a maid carrying up a coal shuttle. Heart pounding, Penelope ran on tiptoes toward the inebriated couple still climbing the main stairs. No time to think. She must escape.

She slipped into the room, but Marchford was nowhere to be seen. She closed the door behind her and was immediately engulfed in darkness. "Marchford?" she whispered.

"Penelope?" hissed the voice of Marchford from across the room.

"Yes," she whispered back, walking in the direction of his voice.

"What are you doing here?" his voice was barely audible, but his disapproval was clear.

"Ow!" Penelope ran into some sort of table. "Drunk couple coming up the main stairs, maid coming up the back."

Marchford had her by the hand and moved her around something. How he saw in the dark she did not know, but she trusted him to guide her. "In here," he whispered and she felt the door of a large wardrobe. Nothing to do but climb inside with Marchford squishing in behind her. The wardrobe was much too small for this purpose and they were tangled up with each other, trying to squeeze inside.

Sitting most indecently on the lap of the Duke of

Marchford, Penelope hoped that the various parties in the hallway would pass and let them escape, but the hope was short-lived.

The door swung open and somebody entered the room.

Twenty-one

"A MAID, SHE'S COMING!" SQUEALED A YOUNG LADY. "Quick! In here."

The wardrobe door was still open a crack when the couple and their light fell inside the room. The illumination allowed Marchford and Penelope to move aside a fallen coat that was blocking the wardrobe door and close it swiftly, hoping they had not been seen. Penelope was sitting on top of the duke in a manner quite unladylike. After a few anxious moment, Pen doubted the couple, deep in drink by the sound of it, had noticed them. In truth, they were rather beyond noticing anything but themselves.

"Ah, my love, look. A bed," said the lady in a husky tone.

"Yes," said the young gentleman. "I do believe it is. Well, whatever shall we do?"

The young lady giggled and then the room grew quiet except for some wet smacking noises, leaving little doubt as to what the young lady of inebriation had on her mind. Unfortunately, in Penelope's present condition of forced intimacy, the idea of kissing was brought forcefully to mind with the man on whose lap she now sat and who was breathing hot breath on her neck. She desperately hoped that the couple would be leaving soon, for she was growing so warm with a mixture of embarrassment and desire she thought she might swoon.

Right on top of Marchford. Not an all-bad idea.

The bed gave a loud creak. "Oh!" said the man outside. "I fell."

"On the bed. How clever of you," purred the woman, who suddenly was not sounding quite as tipsy as she had before. "You look all hot. Allow me to loosen your cravat so you can breathe."

"Err, that is not my cravat."

"No, but I wager you can breathe better now."

"More like I can't catch my breath," said the young man in painful honesty.

"What can I do to put you more at ease. How about that?"

"Oh. Yesssss."

"Or this?"

Things grew quiet again except for a moan from the young man. It was intolerable. Penelope was sitting astride Marchford, his arms around her, his face tantalizingly close to her own. Her desire to kiss Marchford was pounding with intensity. She could not help herself and turned her head to rest her cheek on his. He responded immediately, running his hand up her back and down again, lower and lower, until his hand cupped her backside. Hot tingles shot through her, making her heart beat faster. She should stop him, but instead she wanted more.

The couple on the bed groaned again, and Penelope could only imagine what they were doing and how it would feel to be doing it with Marchford—James to her now. She nuzzled her cheek to his, brushing against the sting of the tiny stubble on his jaw. She turned, her lips trailing lightly across his cheek, in search of his mouth.

Her heart beat harder and she kissed the corner of his mouth. It was more chaste than she intended. It was dark, and she was aiming for his lips. He returned in kind and he did not miss. His lips were soft, and the kiss began as it had in the past—friendly, soft—but gradually it became more heated and urgent as he pressed into her. Or perhaps she was the one demanding more. The intensity increased, his lips moving over hers, a novel experience, but between the sounds of the couple on the bed and her own pounding desire pressed against him, she explored this new adventure with everything she had. Sitting on him as she was, she could not help but feel his interest rise.

"Wait, we shouldn't. In the master's room. Don't want to get you in trouble," said the lad on the bed with earnest concern.

"Don't you worry, my love. Drink," commanded the vixen, and from the sound, he did so. Shortly afterward, the bed began to creak and the soft moans of the couple drove Penelope's imagination wild. She knew the very basic facts about sex—having four married sisters was informative—but to be so close to the act was an educational experience. One that she suddenly wanted to be schooled in. And since she was conveniently sitting on a virile man, her education might soon be coming.

James's breath shuddered and he tried to pull back his arms, but there was nothing for it. The wardrobe was too cramped, and not being a small man, he took up much of the space. What little room was left, she consumed. He was trying not to ruin her, she understood, but she would have none of it. The truth was obvious in the dark wardrobe. She had been attracted to him since she met him. And now that she had him pinned beneath her in a situation from which he could not escape, she would give no quarter. Poor man.

She was going to be banished from London anyway, and she did not worry for a moment over the potential for him being less than discreet. Whatever they did in the wardrobe he would take to the grave. The revelation gave her a freedom she rarely felt, and probably should not have felt then, except that desire was such a powerful wave, it swept her along and refused to let go. She now understood why women would ruin themselves for this intoxicating passion. There may be a price to pay, but at the moment she could not bring herself to care.

She pressed her hands to his chest, feeling his muscles tense at her touch. She stroked down, exploring his firm abdominal muscles, his watch fob, the buttons of his vest, and the butt of the pistol inside his coat pocket. The last discovery was shocking only in that it did not surprise her. He stilled her hands with his, but that could not stop her. The noises outside increased in intensity and pitch, the bedpost banging rhythmically against the wall.

She pressed forward and this time her lips struck true, finding his and holding them hostage. If she triumphed in her victory, it was only for a moment before he began to show her why teasing such a man was not at all wise. The kiss that followed was so intimate, so unlike anything she had ever experienced or ever considered before, she was shocked into pulling back, but he caught her and pulled her back to him, one hand possessively on the back of her neck and the other sliding down over her backside.

She almost yelped in surprise, and he swallowed the sound before it could be uttered by deepening the kiss. He ran his hands up and down her back until her thoughts turned entirely treacherous and then stopped altogether.

The couple outside were now groaning and moaning together at a fevered pitch. James slid a hand between them and trailed a finger along the skin of her low-cut gown at the edge of her bodice. She had thought the gown too revealing before; now she cursed it for not being revealing enough. She pressed into him and his fingers slipped under her gown, running his thumb over her breast in a manner that made her wish she was with him on the bed instead of the unknown couple.

At that moment, the couple reached their climax and the young man shouted out and collapsed. For several minutes there was no sound. James and Penelope froze, his hand still trapped in her gown, not wanting to make any sound in the silent room. Although enough sense was returning to know they had traveled into dangerous territory, Penelope was mostly irritated at the couple for stopping and thus putting her own exploration at an end.

Soft snoring could be heard, and then the strange noises of drawers opening and closing. James slowly removed his hand from her bosom and peeked out of the keyhole. He shifted without a sound and ever so quietly drew a knife. He used the blade to lock the wardrobe with them inside. Taking a peek herself, Penelope saw a young woman carefully going through the room, searching for something. She did not appear at all drunk or exhausted by the throes of passion.

The woman had quickly dressed herself and was making short work of her search, coming close to the wardrobe. Pen hoped the makeshift lock would hold. James must have been thinking similar thoughts, for he held on to one of the inner hooks of the door so as to further prevent it from opening. The young woman came stealthily to the wardrobe and went to open it, pulling hard. When it refused to open, she quickly took a hairpin from her hair and attempted to pick the lock.

Penelope's pulse pounded as she grabbed one of the inner hooks and pulled toward her with all her might. The lady tried again to open the wardrobe, pulling on the door with surprising strength, but Marchford and Penelope pulled back, preventing her from opening the prize.

The young man on the bed stirred and the young woman paused, was still for a moment, then fled the room. After waiting a few more anxious minutes, Marchford opened the doors and they tumbled out. The man on the bed was snoring, giving no alarm that he would witness their presence.

"What was she looking for?" whispered Penelope.

"This," said Marchford, holding up a wine bottle.

"Why?" She almost mouthed the word.

Marchford shook his head and they examined the bottle in the pale light of the lantern. It was French and looked expensive. A close examination revealed nothing of particular interest until she examined the label closely.

"Some of these words in French have been spelled in a curious manner," whispered Penelope. "And does it seem to you that the bottle and cork are older than the label?"

Marchford examined the bottle more closely. "Yes, this label seems almost new."

The duke returned the bottle to where he'd found it. He motioned to the door and they were soon safely outside, leaving the lad to his fate.

Penelope breathed a sigh of relief at escaping the room and stepped forward in the dim hallway, forgetting the carpet runner down the hall. She tripped and landed hard, more embarrassed than hurt.

"Are you all right?" Marchford was there to offer a hand.

She was glad he could not see her cheeks burn in the dark hallway. Why was it not possible for her to appear as a sophisticated lady? She accepted his hand and put her foot down to a surprising pain.

"Ow!" She began to fall and clutched his shoulder for support. With surprising ease, he picked her up into his arms.

"Are you hurt?" he asked.

"I am sure it will be fine," breathed Penelope, even though she had no desire for Marchford to put her down. He carried her down the side stairwell without catching his breath.

"You will permit me to remove you from this location to a safer place." He adopted his usual reserved manner, yet she had witnessed the fire beneath the cool exterior.

Penelope wished to protest on principle, but she knew he could carry her faster than she could walk, and leaving their current situation was of utmost importance. More importantly, she liked being in his arms. She liked it a lot.

They returned to the main floor, the noise of musicians and people laughing loud in their ears after such quiet above.

"Let us go here, so I can evaluate your injury." Marchford carried her into a small side parlor, which was thankfully unoccupied. The room was decorated in rich tones of gold and scarlet and was dimly lit by two wall sconces.

Marchford gently set her down on the couch. "Would you allow me to inspect your injured foot?" he asked with all reserved politeness.

Penelope smiled in response. The formal nature did not correspond with the intimacies they had shared. Since he had already inspected her lips, her bottom, and her breasts, she figured he might as well have a go at the ankle as well. "If you must," complied Pen, wondering how to reconnect with this man, and yet at the same time wishing to push away the temptation.

She should not wish for something that would always be outside her grasp. Dukes may amuse themselves with insignificant companions if the opportunity arose, but they certainly didn't marry them. And Penelope Rose was not the type for whom options other than a respectable marriage would be entertained. She held her back straight, even as she swung her legs up to the couch to allow for better inspection. Her ankle was already beginning to feel better, and she guessed the roll was a momentary hurt rather than a long-term injury.

Marchford kneeled on the ground beside her and took her foot in hand. He carefully removed her slipper and felt around her foot in a manner that shot tingles up her leg and beyond. She did not wish him to stop.

"I cannot feel any swelling," said Marchford.

"That is not the foot I injured," confessed Penelope.

Marchford gave her the look of aristocratic displeasure. He cleared his throat and took the other foot in hand, giving it the same treatment. This time it was tender to the touch, yet still, she could not complain about the way he caressed her.

"I believe there is no serious harm," said Marchford, focusing on her foot. The harm was not to her foot; the harm would be to her heart if she tarried any longer.

"I am glad of it."

Silence filled in the gap between them, stretching out the moment. What could she say now? Was she simply to pretend the wardrobe never happened?

"Miss Rose, about what happened," began Marchford, staring down at her feet instead of at her. "I fear I owe you an apology."

"No!" Penelope swung her feet down. "You have nothing for which to apologize." She did not want the best kiss, albeit her only true kiss, to be so soon brushed into the waste bin of past mistakes.

"And yet I cannot rest easy with my behavior. I fear I have taken advantage." Marchford remained on his knees before her.

"You were not the one sitting in my lap. If anyone took the advantage, it was me."

"Do not be absurd. The fault was clearly mine."

"Fault? So I am a mistake you made?" Penelope rose to her feet, keeping the weight on her good leg.

"No, that is…you are no mistake, but I cannot look upon my own behavior without censure. Since I find myself at your feet, I shall beg for forgiveness. I warn you that if you deny me this boon, I shall be forced to either badger you until forgiveness is given or I shall attempt to even the score by doing something to place you in my debt. I wonder, what situation could I contrive?" The corners of his mouth twitched up.

"Fine, you win, but only because I concede you have more devious tendencies than I."

"I am pleased to see how well you know me."

"I shall content myself with providing you pleasure."

A collective gasp made them both jump. Someone had opened the door and had begun to enter the room. No, not just anyone, the Comtesse de Marseille, the most notorious gossip in all of London was standing in the doorway, her mouth open in horror. Behind her, several of her busybody cronies were with her. Other guests, seeing the crowd around the door stopped to look too, jostling from outside to see what was happening.

Penelope froze. She was standing before Marchford

who was on his knees before her. What could be the plausible explanation for this?

No one said anything for an eternity, though in reality it could have only been a few seconds. She started down at Marchford, hoping he had a plan.

He gave her a wink. He had a solution. She smiled. He smiled.

"Miss Rose," he began, his voice booming, "will you marry me?"

Twenty-two

SIMULTANEOUS EMOTIONS SLASHED THROUGH PENELOPE. Her heart soared at being proposed to by the one man, the only man, she could ever love. Yet her joy was instantly tempered by the realization that this proposal was forced by their audience. The growing crowd gasped again, and heat surged through her as embarrassment struck true.

The shock of such emotions proved too momentous for her single leg to hold, and she teetered off kilter. Marchford sprung up and caught her before she fell, sweeping her up in his arms.

"They need an answer," he whispered, and she knew beyond all hope that his interest in her was purely based on societal show.

"No," she whispered—or tried to. Marchford cut off the word with a kiss, winning them both another gasp from the crowd.

He broke the kiss and addressed the crowd, for whom the charade was intended. "I hope you all will wish us many happy returns."

The growing crowd tittered and congratulated,

even as the gossip spread like fire through the ballroom. The Comtesse de Marseille raised an aristocratic eyebrow and gave Penelope a piercing gaze.

Marchford gently set her back down. Penelope pasted on a smile and held on to his steady arm. She was soon mobbed by ladies wanting to speak to her, some noticing her for the first time, all asking some variation of the question of how she had landed one of the best matrimonial catches in all of London. Several were none too pleased and addressed her with open scorn.

"Step aside. Excuse me." The dowager pushed through and took Penelope's other arm. "Very tired, must retire, thank you, dear, for seeing me home."

Penelope proceeded in a dreamlike state to the ballroom, being escorted out with the duke on one side and the dowager on the other. The world seemed to be coming at her from a distance. Somehow, they made it through the gauntlet of the well-wishers, the curious, and the openly hostile and retreated back to the town coach.

"Why?" gasped Penelope as soon as they were alone in the coach. "Why did you ask me to marry you?"

"Needed to say something. Seemed the thing to do," said Marchford vaguely.

"James!" tsked Antonia. "What a thing to say."

Penelope's heart sank. She wasn't sure if the dowager was chastising his comment or his proposal to her.

"But why marriage?" pressed Penelope. "Why kiss me before the crowd?"

"I kissed you because you were giving the wrong answer." Marchford spoke as if the answer were obvious.

"But I do not wish for a proposal only because we were found in a room together. I do not want you to feel obligated to me."

"But of course he is obligated to you," chimed in the dowager. "At least he is now. Oh, we will have a time trying to win your acceptance in society. I warrant, James, you did not think this through."

"Indeed, I did not," said Marchford in a careless manner. He was staring out the window at the falling snow with a smile on his face as if quite pleased with himself. "Good thing you changed the venue to Lord Felton's. We could never have climbed the hill to the Wynbrook town home."

"Yes, I do believe it was a stunning victory," Antonia purred, easily distracted onto a topic in which she was central.

Penelope was shocked at how quickly the topic was turned. The dowager happily related the tale of all the people who had complimented her on the extraordinary feat of having Felton open his house to the affianced couple.

Despite the foot warmer, Penelope felt cold. Marchford's proposal had nothing to do with any interest in her, but rather a way to escape an awkward situation. It was all a charade. Apparently, she was good enough to kiss in the closet, but not good enough for an intentional proposal. Penelope had to admit she had powerful feelings for the duke, but to be married to a man who did not share her regard? That she would never do.

❧

He had done it. He had asked Penelope to marry him and he could not help but smile at the prospect. But why? James focused his attention on the snow falling outside the coach. Clean and white, it floated down from the heavens. Inside the coach was nothing but danger. He had steered the conversation away from his proposal, and his grandmother was happily prattling on about her societal success. She would not be put off for long, however. He was certain she would have much to say regarding his proposal to Penelope.

Penelope, on the other hand, said nothing but was glaring at him from the gloom of the coach. The small lantern swung with the movement of the conveyance, casting angry shadows across her face. She was silent for now, in the midst of his grandmother's conversation, but she would not remain so for long. He hoped for the possibility of safe passage through these waters, but he knew the course was treacherous.

His actions in the wardrobe floated back to him, and he ruthlessly pushed them aside. He had been tempted, yes, but it had been an extraordinary situation. Surely a man could not be blamed for reacting to a beautiful woman sitting atop him. His proposal had nothing to do with lust. It was simply a coincidence that the woman he wished to have in his bed was the one to whom he had proposed. A happy coincidence, but nothing more.

He would marry for logic and good sense. Penelope would serve admirably as a duchess. She was a sober, sensible girl, so unlike his own mother. In truth, he could not see any resemblance. It was true that Penelope was no aristocrat, but her father had been a gentleman, and her sisters all married well, so her connections, while not grand, were certainly respectable. It was not a brilliant alliance, but then he needed none. He was a duke; if that didn't give him license to wed where he wished, nothing did.

He ignored the nagging thought that this must have been some of his father's own logic. His father married for love. The present Duke of Marchford would never do such a thing. No. Never. He would marry Penelope and that would be the end of it.

At their return home, Marchford bid his grandmother and Penelope a very pleasant night and retreated, as quickly as he could manage and still appear ducal, into his study.

It was only a matter of minutes before the study door opened and Penelope boldly entered, closing the door behind her. She had removed her cloak and her form was remarkable in her pale blue gown. Some of her hair had escaped her hairpins in all the excitement and fell loose down her shoulder, enflaming the very passions he wished to keep at bay.

His eyes gravitated toward her cleavage, to the place his hands had explored only an hour ago. He longed to go back for more, but the stern look in Penelope's eye told him that event would be unlikely.

"Why would you like to marry me?" Penelope's voice wavered only slightly.

He ignored it. Emotions had no bearing to the matter at hand. "I have proposed in a public setting. You have accepted in much the same manner. I do not see the purpose of further discussion. We shall be married, and that is the end of it."

"Forgive me, but your reasons for proposing are very much of concern to me. Therefore, I must ask you to state them plainly." Penelope raised her chin.

Dangerous ground. Still, he could navigate this safely. "First, I proposed because we were caught in a delicate situation, and it seemed the best way to throw off suspicion from our activities."

"So you felt obligated."

Marchford continued. "Second, you are a sensible girl, whom I believe will perform the office of duchess admirably once you adjust to the position. You have a level head, you are intelligent, and I am certain you would meet the challenge of running this household."

"So you are looking for a housekeeper?"

He ignored that comment as well. "Third, you have proven to be valuable in the search for the spymaster and unraveling the plot that hangs above us. The safety and security of England herself is at stake. Unmarried, you must leave this house once grandmother quits it. As my fiancée, you could have leave to stay. Though I suppose we should dig up a female relation to stay for a while for propriety's sake."

Penelope shifted from one foot to the other, and he felt a pang for having kept her on her feet. Surely her ankle must hurt her. "Please, do sit, Miss Rose."

She shook her head in defiance and remained standing. "And are these the only reasons why you have proposed marriage?" Penelope pressed her full lips together to form a thin line.

"I believe three to be sufficient." More than sufficient. He had proposed. What more could she want? An inexplicable hurt was in Penelope's eyes, but he was certain she would overcome it. He did not consider himself at risk of losing her agreement to the union. He was a duke after all. Of course she would marry him, and the less spoken of any emotional attachments the better.

"I am sorry, Your Grace, but these reasons are not sufficient to me." She held her head high and blinked back tears. "I regret to inform you that I must decline your offer of marriage."

Marchford paused and leaned against his mahogany desk. Surely he had not heard her correctly. "I beg your pardon, Miss Rose."

"I said I will not marry you. However, since you have made it clear to me that my duty to king and country requires me to remain here to provide my services, such as they are, to the cause, I shall not publicly announce the dissolution of the engagement; however, I need you to understand I shall in no way actually marry you."

Marchford could not quite believe what he was hearing. Any woman of sound mind would have been well pleased to wed him in any circumstances. Which either meant she was not of sound mind or…well, he could not think of any other reason. "And why, I must ask, have you refused my offer? Do you harbor the hopes of making a better match?" The last was spoken in jest, so he was surprised to see her nod. What could she be holding out for? A prince?

"Yes, indeed, I do hope someday to be made a better offer than the one you have provided me."

"In what way? Forgive me, Miss Rose, but in what way do you find me lacking? I flatter myself that my understanding and temper are acceptable. My place in society and, I need not mention, my ability to allow you to live in whatever extravagance of luxury you should desire can only be seen as advantageous. I shall stoop to gross vanity and claim that I am not a hideous creature to behold.

"In addition, and I beg your forgiveness for mentioning it, but our time together this evening revealed a mutual attraction. In short, I would like to know in what manner you find my suit lacking?" Marchford prided himself in keeping a level head in all situations, but his voice rose slightly despite his best attempts to keep himself in check.

"You have declared that your proposal was based on three reasons. The first, because you felt obliged. The second, because you wish for a competent housekeeper. And the third, because of your duty to king and country. Should I ever marry, it will not be for the reasons of obligation, practicality, or duty. No, if I should ever wed, which at the present moment appears most unlikely, it will be for love."

Marchford gaped at her. "Love? What has that got to do with marriage?"

Penelope put her hands on her hips, unwittingly revealing her shapely form. "It has everything to do with it. If I wed, it will be because I am hopelessly in love with a man who is wildly in love with me!"

Silence. He had no retort. Falling in love was what she wanted? Practical, sensible Penelope wished to fall in love? How distressing.

"Do you not wish to fall in love?" she asked almost in a whisper, as if fearful of the answer she would hear.

"No!" He could only answer truthfully. "Indeed, I should like to avoid love at all costs."

"And why avoid the one thing that could bring joy to your life?" She turned away and was now addressing the bookcase instead of him.

"My father married my mother for love. It brought nothing but pain. No, I shall not marry for love. Save me from Cupid's poisoned dart."

She nodded in understanding, still not looking at him. "I believe there is nothing left to say."

"I disagree." He would not allow Penelope to simply walk away from him. He had asked; she had accepted. It was done. She was his. He just needed to appeal to her rational self. "I understand your romantic notions of true love. What girl is not brought up with such fantasies? But when you consider the proposal from a sensible light, I do not think you would be so quick to refuse the offer before you. I consider it very unlikely that another offer of marriage will ever come your way. If you could but think rationally, you would see that a life as a duchess must be infinitely better than a life as an old maid."

Her head snapped back at him, her brown eyes blazing. At once he realized he had made a foolish mistake. "So you consider my refusal to be that of a weak-minded female without sense or rationality?"

He took a step back and she took one toward him.

She continued, her voice rising. "You think that a woman in my low position should cling to any offer of marriage that comes her way? You think I should be grateful for whatever scraps fall from the master's table?"

"You consider me a scrap discarded from the table?" And now his pride was trod upon.

"I consider your proposal fit only for the dustbin." Her tone rose higher.

He swallowed down a lump in his throat. "I do believe you were correct earlier, Miss Rose. We do have nothing more to say. I wish you a very pleasant evening." He meant to say it politely, but he feared it must not have come across that way in a shout.

"Yes, indeed. Have a lovely evening, Your Grace." Penelope curtsied to him, which only made him want to wring her neck or kiss her senseless. She left before he got the chance.

He flung himself down at his desk and returned to sensible matters and rational concerns, but that night he dreamed of wardrobes, spies, and Penelope.

Twenty-three

MARCHFORD AWOKE THE NEXT MORNING TO THE orderly presence of his valet. A mental review of yesterday's momentous events was enough to bring a request for breakfast in bed. He was not afraid of Penelope, surely not. But he had heard that absence made the heart grow fonder, and he hoped that by removing himself from her view, she might begin to look more kindly on their present entanglement.

Happy that he had justified his cowardice as an act of kindness, he settled down to enjoy his coffee and toast in peace. He opened the freshly ironed paper and flipped past the commentary on the war (it was going poorly) and civil unrest (also poor goings-on) to the gossip columns.

"Damn!" Marchford slapped the paper shut.

"Is something the matter, Your Grace?" asked his valet.

Yes, indeed. The papers were not reporting his spontaneous proposal to Penelope with benevolence. They were gossip columns after all and made money on selling salacious bits of rumor and half-truth. Everyone knew not to trust the gossip column. And yet...

"Make sure my grandmother sees this." He handed the paper to his valet. Antonia would know how to best handle the situation. "And also ensure that Miss Rose does not." No need to upset her further.

He decided to leave for the club. Early. And stay late. Yes, that was a marvelous plan.

∽

Marchford did not come to breakfast, and the dowager never came to breakfast, so Penelope ate alone, glaring into her oatmeal and stabbing at her eggs with malicious intent. She had things to say to Marchford. Things she had been practicing all night to say.

After she finished her meal, she casually inquired of the butler the whereabouts of a certain errant duke. The bastard had gone to his club. Coward!

Instead of being able to confront him, she was left with giving the butler a fake smile and retreating to the morning room. Penelope sat with her needlepoint, though her mood made her more inclined to fling it to the wall. She considered what she would say to Antonia, which did not improve her disposition.

She had been the companion to the dowager for almost a year and now Penelope had received an offer most unexpected from the duke. She knew the dowager had vehemently opposed the last duke's choice in wives. Would the dowager also shun Penelope?

Miles the cat climbed up on her lap, or at least as much of him as could fit on her lap, and batted at her hand until she petted him. She sighed and rested back on the settee. Penelope stabbed her needlepoint again without care and took two stitches before realizing she had chosen an ill place and, with a grumble, pulled out the offending stitches. Miles decided to help with the thread, forcing her to hold up the work out of reach. In the light of the window, Penelope looked at her needlepoint with fresh eyes. The piece had detailed flowers along the border, which, like many samplers, had a verse of scripture to uplift, guide, and inspire.

Trust in the Lord with all thine heart; and lean not unto thine own understanding. Proverbs 3:5

It was a verse she had recalled a few days earlier. She had heard it many times as a child. Her father was particularly concerned about her propensity to organize, direct, and control. *'Tis not for you to be always in control, Penny. God will allow you to be put in circumstances beyond your control if only to help you learn to trust in the Lord, even when there is no hope.*

Penelope suddenly became aware of the message of her own work. Was she leaning on God or herself? It was not a difficult question to answer. Of course she was relying on herself. She took a deep breath. What would it mean to actually lean on God?

She did not have a ready answer. She prided herself on her ability to follow the commands of the Bible and live a sensible life. Though, with a sudden flash of insight, she realized the Bible never demanded living a quiet, sensible life, and in truth, the followers of the Bible often had the most remarkable adventures. In contrast, Penelope mostly followed the strictures of society, not the teachings of the Lord.

Trust in the Lord.

How was one do to that?

Miles batted at her again to get her to pet him more. She was lost and all she had for guidance were remembrances of her father, a sampler, and an extra-large cat.

Lord, please help. I need your guidance. She was not one to pray often, but she recognized she was utterly out of control. She could use some divine intervention, particularly as the dowager entered the room.

"I have no intention of actually marrying the duke!" cried Penelope before Antonia even had a chance to sit down.

"Oh dear." Antonia stopped. "Did you see the papers? I told the butler to remove them."

"No, I was told Marchford had taken them all." Penelope was suspicious. "What is in them?"

"Nothing!" the dowager answered quickly. Too quickly. And Penelope guessed she had been featured in an uncomplimentary manner.

"First time I make the gossip column and I am mocked," groaned Penelope.

"More like slandered," muttered the dowager, taking her seat. "Now what is this about you not marrying James?"

"He only asked because he felt trapped. We had been looking for something upstairs, in regards to tracking down foreign agents. I was not trying to do anything untoward." And yet in her denial, her actions the night before floated back. It might not have been what she intended, but it was certainly what happened.

Antonia waved a hand. "I know you are not the type to chase after my grandson. It is one of the reasons I have kept you. I admit I was…surprised by the proposal."

"You must think it a gross impertinence. I know you cannot stand grasping social climbers."

"Indeed I cannot. And I never cast you in that light." The dowager rapped her ivory handled cane on the floor for emphasis. "Now tell me, why do you refuse my grandson?"

"I do not wish anyone to feel trapped into making an offer of marriage."

"Admirable. But do you love him?"

The question stilled Penelope. Did she love him? She found she could not meet Antonia's bright blue eyes. "According to Marchford, love and matters of the heart are unnecessary."

"James is a nice sort of man, most of the time, but he is still a man. So I am asking you. Do you love him?"

Did she love him?

"My feelings are of no consequence," said Penelope, staring at the needlework in her hands.

The dowager stood, walked over to the settee, and sat beside her. Her thin, soft hand reached out and clasped Penelope's hand.

"I love him something awful," confessed Penelope in a small voice.

"And he does not return this love?" asked the dowager gently.

Penelope shook her head. "So you see why I cannot marry him."

"There would be few who would let a little thing like love prevent them from marrying a duke."

"I do not care to wed a duke."

Antonia squeezed her hand. "I would not be young again if it meant facing heartache. I am finally marrying my love, in spite of anything anyone might say. Do not consider the gossips, my dear. Follow your heart."

"My heart tells me I would be miserable as his wife."

"I do not think him immune to any feeling for you," said the dowager kindly.

"I do not know. But I do know I shall not be happy with a man who cannot express any affection for me." Penelope knew this with a certainty. She met Antonia's eyes, and the duchess nodded slowly.

"If that is the case, my dear, you must find another to wed. And quickly."

"How on earth would—" Penelope was cut off by the sudden appearance of the butler, announcing their first caller.

"Smile," hissed the dowager at Penelope. "Show no fear and do not speak of your doubts to anyone."

Penelope pasted on a smile and complied. They had a never-ending series of callers, all wanting to see for themselves the little nothing companion who had captured the most sought-after man in London. When this was over, and the ruse of the engagement dissolved, Penelope would need to leave London, of that she was sure.

❧

The home of Mortimer Sprot, in a nondescript part of Town, was small, as was everything in it. The parlor was small; the chairs were small; even the slight repast that was served was small. Apparently, those in service to the Crown were not afforded much in the way of comforts.

Marchford was not exactly certain where to put his

legs. They were too large to tuck under the chair, and if he stretched them out, they would extend into the next room.

"It is good of you to visit me, old friend," said Sprot.

"I have found something of interest," began Marchford, trying to fold his legs into some sort of dignified position. It was a lost cause.

"I am listening."

"I discovered that Lord Felton is importing wine from France, in spite of the blockade, and the labels are suspicious. I believe they may be in code."

The corner of Sprot's mouth twitched up. "I knew my faith in you was well placed. You have done well; however, Felton has been working for us. The labels are indeed in code, sent from our network of informants in France."

Marchford's shoulders slumped. "You might have told me this before I put myself in an awkward position."

"You must forgive me, my friend. I have learned to only say what is necessary at the time. I did not know Felton had aroused your suspicion. How did you come to suspect him?"

"The glassmaker who made the special decanters was commissioned to make several sets. He sent them to Felton."

Mortimer Sprot's brushy eyebrows fell over his sharp eyes. "Curious."

"I thought so. We found the other set in the home of Mr. Grant, but we supposed it was planted there to be used by the spies to pass messages during house parties. But I cannot think why Felton would be sent a set since he has not entertained in years."

Mortimer's frown increased. "Yes, indeed. More to it than meets the eye."

"That is not all. I discovered we were not the only ones looking for the wine bottle. A young woman, a courtesan of certain popularity, was also looking for the bottle."

"And did she find it?"

"No, she did not."

"You are a good man. Thank you. Your information is quite helpful."

"One other thing." Marchford shifted position as best he could. He was losing feeling in his right leg. "Lord Felton has a nephew and heir. They are estranged, but the young man was there yesterday, hiding in the servants' quarters, reportedly there out of curiosity to see his inheritance."

"Hmmmm. Curious indeed." The old man shook his head slowly. "And now I have news for you. We have feared that France may be planning some great offensive, and now we have confirmed that they have made invasion plans. Whatever they are planning, it will happen soon. More than that I do not know."

Marchford left the home of the spymaster more perplexed than when he arrived. He turned his horse in the direction of home, but instead found himself outside the home of William Grant.

"My friend! Congratulations!" Grant greeted him warmly and ushered him into his study, which he used as more of a card room since studying was not his primary interest.

Marchford noted a ledger open on the desk and credited Genie with having a positive influence on her new husband. "And to you as well. I hear your firstborn is coming soon."

"Ah, yes, the mysteries of life. There are signs that something has begun one day, only to be silenced the next. Apparently, this is part of the process, but I confess I will rest easier when the baby has safely made his arrival."

"His?"

"Naturally." Grant offered him a glass of wine, and they settled into chairs before the fire. "So you finally decided on a bride."

Marchford swirled the wine in his glass. "Perhaps."

"No, my dear friend, that will not do. What can you mean by 'perhaps'?"

"I mean that Miss Rose is not inclined to wed."

Grant stared at him a while and then burst into laughter. "You've got no luck. You propose to the only woman in London not prepared to marry you!"

Marchford did not see the humor in the situation whatsoever. "So glad my misfortune serves as amusement for you."

"Now do not feel sorry for yourself. Why, I have seen many ladies practically fall at your feet for the chance to be your bride. Simply choose one who so desperately wants to be a duchess."

"I do not want someone who wants to be a duchess. I want someone who wants me." The words were out of his mouth before he realized what he was saying.

Grant's blue eyes flashed in merriment. "Oh, I see now. You wish to fall in love!"

"No! Nothing of the sort!" Denial was pointless with Grant laughing so hard.

"Developed a *tendre* for Miss Rose, have you? What is keeping her from accepting your hand? The gossip columns are full of it."

"I do not know. Women are daft," grumbled Marchford and took another large mouthful of wine.

"How did you present your suit?"

Marchford frowned. "I was rather trapped into offering. Afterward, I told her it was a sensible, rational decision."

"Sounds like you both need the reassurance of mutual affection."

"Now you are daft."

"If you do not wish to succumb to the actual expression of dreaded emotions, why not show her your affection?" suggested Grant.

"How so?"

"The usual gifts might be sufficient. Jewelry. Flowers. Of course, we are talking about Miss Rose, so you may wish to choose something unconventional."

"Yes, indeed." The first ideas that sprang to Marchford's mind were unconventional indeed.

"You know the papers are saying that she trapped you into marriage by lifting her skirts."

"The papers are slanderous and wrong," Marchford said with frost in his tone that Grant would even bring up the subject.

"Naturally. But you are going to have to be even more charming to overcome such venom."

Marchford nodded in understanding. Let operation charm offensive begin.

Twenty-four

"MR. PETERS," MARCHFORD GREETED THE BUTLER THE next morning. "This is the twelve days of Christmas, is it not?"

"Yes, Your Grace."

"Is there not some child's rhyme about it? Something about giving ridiculous gifts each day?"

Even Peters could not help but have the edge of his mouth twitch up. "Yes, Your Grace. It is a game published in *Mirth without Mischief*."

"You are well informed."

"My nieces and nephews quite enjoy the game."

This was a new side of Mr. Peters. Marchford was vaguely aware he had family somewhere, but had never thought of the dour man's young relatives playing Christmas games. "Well then, can you tell me what day is today and what I am supposed to buy my true love?"

Peters's eyebrows did raise, but he recovered quickly. "I believe it to be the fourth day, so the gift would be four calling birds."

"What would Miss Rose want with four birds?"

"I am sure I could not say, Your Grace."

"And what of tomorrow?"

"The fifth day would be five gold rings."

"Five rings, I can do that. And what is the next day?"

"Six geese a laying."

"Six geese. Not sure where we would put them." Marchford rubbed his jaw. "And the next day?"

"Seven maids a milking."

"No. Now do be serious. Who wants seven maids and seven cows? Would it not be more sensible to have one or two maids milk all the cows? And where do you expect me to put seven milk cows?"

"I do not think the rhyme was intended to be applied literally, Your Grace."

"Well. I should hope not. At least the rings make some sense."

"Miss Rose awaits you in the breakfast room," said Peters with his remarkable lack of inflection.

Marchford wished to avoid the audience, but he dared ignore her no longer. He had already managed to avoid her entirely yesterday and had a vague awareness that it was not appreciated.

He entered the breakfast room to find Penelope draped in a warm shawl of burgundy brushed wool against the chill of the morning. She barely gave him a second glance as he entered and continued eating. Perhaps he had misjudged her and things were peaceful between them.

He settled his breakfast before himself—eggs, toast, and coffee. Everything just as he liked.

"Every last person in society thinks we are lovers!" accused Penelope just as he took a large sip of coffee.

She had the dubious delight of seeing him choke on his drink.

"I beg your pardon, Miss Rose," he said when he recovered.

"You might as well stop that Miss Rose nonsense and just call me Penelope, or my love, or perhaps my sweet pumpkin."

"I would never call you that." He was emphatic.

"The rumor has spread that I have forced your proposal by engaging in behavior most unbecoming a lady."

"What anyone thinks can hardly be of any relevance."

"Can it not? You have ruined me!"

"I have done no such thing." Though in truth, he also was concerned about the vicious rumors.

"Even if I married you, there would be nothing but whispers of how I trapped you. It is intolerable. Now I will be forced not only to leave London but possibly flee to the Continent."

"You shall stay here with me. Must dash!" Marchford fled the room, his eggs only half-finished. He had much to do.

❧

"I have laid out something special for you," said Penelope's maid with a twinkle in her eye.

"I am retiring for the night," said Pen to clarify. It had been another long day of members of society coming to look at the girl who secured an offer of marriage, using the most unconventional means if the rumors were true, from the Duke of Marchford. She felt like an oddity or a sideshow attraction.

She was left to face the never-ending barrage of morbid curiosity while Marchford made himself scarce. It was hardly fair! Fortunately, it was time for bed, which did not include needing any special garment besides a warm nightdress and a thick cap. It was getting quite chill at night.

"Here you go. Lovely is it not?" Abigail, the lady's-maid-in-training, held up a sheer night rail and a dressing gown made of similar gauzy material.

Pen stared for a moment, speechless. What fool would wear that to bed in December? And yet the maid seemed quite pleased with herself. "It is lovely," said Penelope slowly. "Wherever did you get it?"

"I talked to Madame Leclair, Her Grace's lady's maid, and she was kind enough to give this to me for you. Apparently the duchess bought it years ago and it did not suit her.

"I should say not," muttered Penelope.

"I have some ideas for your hair as well," said Abigail. "Please forgive me if this is forward, but I have been studying hard with madame, and I believe I should make a good lady's maid. I know I have not the experience others might have, and I won't pretend to be French, but I will say that I will work for you very hard and will seek to improve myself every day."

The light was beginning to dawn. "You would like to be the lady's maid for the next Duchess of Marchford."

"Forgive me, Miss Rose." Abigail lowered her eyes. "It was an impertinence to suggest it."

"No, quite right. I like a gal with pluck," said Penelope, not wanting to hurt the maid's feelings. Of course, if the maid wished to become the lady's maid for the next duchess, the last person she should address was Penelope.

Hope shone in the maid's eyes.

"But of course I am not at liberty to even entertain the thought of hiring a lady's maid at this time," tempered Penelope, not wishing to raise false hopes.

"No, of course. I did not wish to suggest, but I do enjoy working for you, Miss Rose."

Penelope doubted the maid would enjoy her work when she discovered the engagement was a sham, but Pen could do very little about that. She should be leaving for Bath soon anyway. "I simply wish to go to bed. The night rail you have does look pretty, I grant you, but perhaps too lightweight for winter. Something a tad warmer should do."

Abigail blushed furiously. "I did not think you would be quite concerned with warmth."

Pen began to wonder if the girl was daft. "A bit chill, do you not think?"

"Oh, you mean in the hallways. I should have thought of that. You could wear a warm wrap until you reach his room. Or..." Abigail blushed again. "I could send word that you would prefer the duke join you in your bedchamber this evening, so you did not catch a chill."

"You think that I...you believe that His Grace and I...me and the duke," sputtered Penelope.

Abigail bit her lip in a terrified gesture. "I meant no disrespect. I only thought that... Forgive me, but everyone was saying that..."

"Everyone was saying what?" Pen's voice was so low it dredged the bottom of her regard for one certain Duke of Marchford. He was going to pay for this. She wasn't sure how, but there was going to be a reckoning.

Abigail lowered her eyes, her hopes of moving up in the world plummeting. "Forgive me, miss. I spoke out of turn."

"No, you only informed me that I have apparently become fodder for the servants' gossip. I suppose I should thank you for letting me know. Thank you. That will be all for tonight."

The maid left without another word.

Penelope began to pace, wondering how she could make Marchford suffer for giving the world the impression that she had been less than honorable in her procurement of a very highly prized offer of marriage. Clearly to have caught such a man, Penelope must have sweetened the offer. After some time debating strategies, Penelope was no further in devising a suitably devious plan and had worn herself out with the silent raging.

Penelope sighed and decided nothing was being gained by her solitary irritation. It was time to go to bed, as she had planned to do an hour earlier. She attempted to change into a more sensible night rail, but found, much to her growing irritation, that the gown she wore was impossible to remove without some assistance. Her only choice to remove the gown was to call for the maid. The maid she had dismissed.

It was awkward to say the least. She could choose to sleep in her gown, but to be found in the morning in the same dress and have to explain that she was actually stuck in it, was even more distressing. Which led back to calling for the maid, who by this time was most certainly in bed herself and who believed, along with the entire staff, that Pen and Marchford were carrying on some illicit affair.

A fresh wave of righteous anger swept through her, warming her against the cold draft of winter. She grabbed the gauzy night rail and marched out of her room. Before she could think about what she was doing, she found herself at the door of the Duke of Marchford. Anger still churning through her veins, she knocked and, without waiting for a reply, opened the door and stepped inside, slamming the door behind her.

Marchford was sitting comfortably in bed, reading by the light of a lantern. "Miss Rose? Whatever is the matter?"

"This is the matter." She thrust the gauzy nightdress at him accusingly.

At Marchford's blank expression, she saw she needed to elaborate. She held it up so he could see the gown—and through the gown, in all its evocative glory. "The maid thought I should wear this to bed tonight."

Marchford frowned. "Not sensible. Catch a cold."

"Yes, indeed! But the maid explained she did not think that I would be in need of warmth since you would be performing the office yourself."

"Me?"

"Yes. Have you not heard? Everyone, even your own servants, thinks we are carrying about a secret liaison."

"That cannot be—"

"Yes, yes it is. You see what you have done?"

"I shall talk to the staff tomorrow."

"And tell them what? Can you imagine calling them all to attention before you to announce that you are not carrying about a scandalous sexual relationship with your grandmother's companion?" Penelope tried to ignore the rush of heat crawling up her neck and spreading to her cheeks. It was the first time she had said the word *sex* in mixed company.

"Yes, well, when you put it that way."

"And what other way is there to put it?"

Marchford sighed. "I deeply regret if my proposal led others to such wild and unfounded accusations. I had no intention of ever casting any shadow on your reputation, which to my mind remains exemplary."

Penelope fought against it, but she could feel herself soften at his charitable reply. She knew he had not intended for anyone to jump to such unfortunate conclusions. She was angrier at society, who valued her so cheaply that they decided she must have had to sell her own body to secure a seat at the matrimonial table beside a duke. "I know you did not intend for this to occur," she mumbled begrudgingly.

"Indeed. And forgive me for pointing this out, but coming to my bedroom late at night would only confirm such rumors. I suggest you return to your room, let us both get a good night's sleep, and we shall tease out what should be done in the morning." Marchford was himself, strong and in command, albeit sitting under the bedclothes with a red, wool cap on his head.

"Yes, of course, except for one thing. I am stuck."

"Stuck? Where?"

"In this gown. I cannot do the enclosures in the back."

Marchford looked at her as if she were daft. "So call for a maid."

"I cannot. I already dismissed her."

Marchford frowned, clearly ready to debate this conclusion.

"I cannot call back a maid who thinks I am carrying on an illicit affair with you. It would be humiliating. I simply cannot bring myself to do it." The words were tumbling out of Penelope's mouth before she could consider them. "Besides, I have decided a new course of action."

"You have?"

Everything was spinning out of control, and more than anything, she wanted to claim that control back. Sampler or no sampler, she wanted to be the one deciding her fate, even if it meant doing something utterly out of character.

Her words spilled out without thought. "Since everyone already thinks we are sleeping together and since I cannot escape from this gown without your assistance, I propose we actually do what everyone else thinks we have already done."

Marchford's eyebrows rose so far they disappeared beneath the red woolen cap. "Exactly what are you suggesting, Miss Rose?"

An excellent question. She did not consider her answer one jot before she blurted, "Everyone thinks we are lovers. So we might as well be lovers."

"Are you suggesting that we..."

"Yes! Sleep with me!"

Twenty-five

THERE WERE TIMES IN A MAN'S LIFE WHEN HE NEEDED to tread very carefully to avoid potential pitfalls, traps, and the failings that entangled weaker men. Considering the angry female before him who had just suggested sharing his bed for the night, Marchford knew this was one of those times. Standing over him, she had him at a disadvantage. He was in his bed-clothes and unsure whether it would be more proper to stand and reveal himself in his night shift or allow her to remain standing.

He motioned to a chair. "Sit!"

She sat but not on the chair; she defiantly chose the bed. He resisted both the urge to scoot away from her and the rather stronger urge to grab her and pull her under the covers to join him. No, he must be strong.

"Is this some sort of test of my honorable nature, Miss Rose?"

"Penelope," she corrected. "Now that we've been introduced, how about helping me out of this gown?"

Marchford weighed his options. He very much wanted to remove the gown, yet he suspected that tomorrow she would not look kindly to his taking the offer. "Penelope. I strongly suggest you return to your room. Call for the maid, and go to bed. It would be sensible."

"Yes, perhaps. But what has being sensible ever done for me? I was determined always to do the right thing. I never allowed myself to be out of control, at least not until I met you. And you see where it has gotten me? Everyone believes I am a seductress."

"The *ton* lives on gossip. Most people know not to believe half of it."

"Truly? In my experience, most people believe every word."

"Even if others believe the worst, it does not mean we should conduct ourselves with anything less than the highest level of propriety."

"Propriety? What of the kisses? What of everything else we did? Was that proper?"

No, it wasn't. In truth, even before she had entered his bedroom, his mind had wandered from his book to that day in the wardrobe. Yet another reason why he could not immediately rise from the bed—his interest would be immediately apparent. Her proposal had in no way lessened his firm interest.

"Penelope." He paused. He was not sure what to say. He wanted her in his bed. More than he cared to say.

"Yes?" She waited for him expectantly. "You were trying to come up with some excuse for kissing me."

"I have none other than the fact that I am only human and I failed in any attempt toward restraint."

"Did you attempt restraint?"

"Yes, though clearly my resolve was not up to the challenge."

She moved closer. "Which only leads me to wonder what a kiss with you might be like when you are not restrained."

Marchford's pulse jumped and beat a fast staccato rhythm. He was not unaccustomed to danger, nor even having females attempt a seduction to try to secure a proposal. Yet he never felt like his heart might burst around anyone but Penelope. Was this a test? Was she trying to trap him into declaring emotions he wished never to reveal? "Are you trying to confound me with lust to win a declaration of love?"

Penelope stood and her eyes flashed. "How dare you! How dare you accuse me of trying to entrap you into anything when you were the one to ensnare me!" She stomped to the door and Marchford was obliged to fling off the blankets and chase after her before she could reach the door.

"I apologize for my words. Forgive me. Careless thoughts."

Penelope turned, her eyes blazing. "I am tired of having my actions be consistently seen through the lens of a poor social climber who is intent on marrying a duke and is willing to do anything to achieve her goal. Do you think for one second I would accept you as a husband now? You who has allowed my good name to be trampled? Who do you think you are? Do you truly believe I would accept a man whom I could not trust? Whom I could not respect? Who does not believe me to be his social equal?"

Marchford stepped back from her wrath. "I

apologize again for any harm that has befallen your reputation as a result of my marriage proposal, though honestly I never thought I would need to beg forgiveness for making an offer. If you hold me in such obvious disgust, why offer to share my bed?"

Penelope flushed and began to pace. "I despise you," she grumbled.

"You despise me so much you wish to sleep with me?"

"Yes. No. Oh, I do not know what I am about."

"Which I am certain is my fault."

"Yes, yes, it is. I am glad you own it."

"Absolutely and without hesitation. I should take this moment also to apologize for the snow tomorrow and any other inconvenience, however slight, you may experience."

"Right now my main inconvenience is that I am stuck in this gown and I would rather cut it off than face that maid again."

"Here, I can be of assistance." Marchford grabbed his banyan robe and wrapped it around himself, offering an arm to Penelope. "Allow me to be your abigail tonight."

This won him a slight smile. She stopped pacing and accepted his arm.

"But first, allow me to give you something. It is after midnight, so this gift may be appropriate." Remembering Grant's suggestion that he enact a campaign of charm, he opened the drawer on his nightstand table and pulled out the red box from the jeweler. "Happy fifth day of Christmas."

Penelope accepted the box but stared at it without opening it. "What is it?"

"It is a gift. Open it," he commanded.

So she did. Even in the small light of the lantern, he could not miss how her eyes widened.

"Five gold rings, just like the rhyme." She blinked away tears. "It is beautiful, though I do not know what I would do with five rings."

"Choose one you like and wear it for me." He thought it a simple answer, yet she responded with a trembling bottom lip and an impulsive embrace.

He wrapped his arms around her, delighting in how her body melted into his. He wanted her. Now. Was it too late to reconsider her offer to share his bed?

"Thank you. I do appreciate the gift," she finally said, recovering from the unusual display of emotion.

Marchford made a mental note to buy her more jewelry. He would forgo the swans and the cows.

"I think it past time I went to bed." Penelope smiled up at him, then down at the rings.

He grabbed his candle, and they softly padded down the corridor to her smaller bedchamber. They entered, and he put the light on the stand by her bed. She had clearly moved beyond her rash offer, so he attempted to focus on the task at hand, not the woman before him.

"I am sorry to have disturbed you," apologized Penelope. "I was not thinking clearly. I cannot imagine why I said what I did."

"I have put you into a difficult situation. I thought my declaration would reduce the gossip, but it only increased it."

"They would gossip if you had not."

"But it was my fault you were in the wardrobe."

"And my fault I hurt my ankle."

And my fault I kissed you. But he did not say that. He understood her anger and frustration with the situation, but he was still genuinely confused about her interest in sleeping together. Was that simply what she said when she was angry? If so, how could he raise her ire at him again? He shook his head, banishing traitorous thoughts.

He cleared his throat. "I suppose there is much blame to go around, but I think we ought to place it squarely on the shoulders of the nameless, faceless society, and benefit from the clear conscious of self-righteous bias."

The comment earned him another weary smile from Penelope. "Yes, by all means, let us blame someone other than ourselves."

"Good, it is settled. Let me now perform the office for which I have come, and I shall allow you to get some sleep." He tried to keep his words light. He should not reveal how powerful an effect she was having on him. He wished now more than anything to take her to bed. He had been a fool to talk her out of it when he'd had the chance.

She slowly turned around so he could focus his attentions on her back. He stepped up gamely and attempted to undo the enclosures. Fortunately, from this position, she could not see if his hands shook. Her shoulders were rounded nicely, her back was straight as always, and although her gown was high waisted, according to the latest fashion, he could tell by the way the gown swished when she turned that she tapered into a nice little waist.

He cleared his throat and focused on the business at hand. Buttons. Millions of the tiny things.

"Good gracious, no wonder you could not do this without assistance," commented Marchford.

"I would need detachable arms."

"Indeed, I may be here awhile. How very tiny." He was in no great hurry. He was enjoying this considerably too much to rush the experience. With every button, a little more of her was exposed. At first his efforts revealed the milky white skin of her back. His fingers brushed accidentally against her, convincing him of her incredibly soft skin. He then brushed his fingertips across her skin in a manner that was not at all accidental.

Next, he began to reveal the edges of the petticoats. Lace was first to show and he was delighted it was a soft pink. He would not have guessed that staid, somber Penelope wore pink, lace petticoats.

At last he had undone the tiny buttons and was unsure how to proceed. At least, he knew exactly what he wanted, but despite being supposedly affianced to the woman before him, he was unsure how to convince her to stay with him, at least in a manner that allowed him to stay aloof. Truth be told, he was far from feeling emotionally distant from Penelope Rose.

"I will need some assistance in removing this gown if you are finally finished with the buttons," said Penelope in a matter-of-fact voice. She was trying to appear unmoved by the situation, but her shallow breathing said otherwise.

"Yes of course," he murmured, always ready to be of assistance to a lady. His lady. He helped her gently tug off the tightly fitted sleeves and pull the gown up over her head, revealing the marvel of Penelope in a state of undress. To be sure, she remained mostly covered, but her arms were now bare and the effect undressing Penelope was having on him was undeniable.

Penelope cleared her throat. "Enjoying yourself?"

"Quite abominably I fear."

She glared at him, but the intensity only enhanced his interest.

"This petticoat laces in the back." She presented him once more with her back side, and he once more was left to appreciate her figure freely and without censure. He ran his hands over the petticoat and smoothed the fabric down on either side to find her natural waist—just as he suspected, a narrow waist and nice rounded curves.

"That is not where the laces are," she chastised. "Besides, you could hurt yourself."

"How's that?"

"You'll see," she answered grimly.

He was taking too many liberties. He went back to his work and untied the laces, which had been tucked deftly into the petticoat. The lacy petticoat was the next to go carefully over her head. To his disappointment, more petticoats presented themselves, though with the removal of each layer her clothing became more sheer, revealing more and more of her shape underneath.

"One more thing," she said without looking at him. "Somewhere on the side there are pins. Could you help me find them?"

"Pins?" He looked carefully and found two straight pins, one on each side, which smoothed the bodice. "I never knew young ladies went around so armed. Do you not ever stick yourself by mistake?"

"Not if it's done correctly. The remaining petticoats lace in front. I can do the rest myself." She was dismissing him.

He remained planted to the floor. Somewhere in his mind, the rational English gentleman was wishing her a pleasant good night and leaving her to retire to his own bedchamber alone. He knew that was the right answer, but somehow the rogue within him refused to leave the room. He was alone with Penelope Rose, who was in a delightful state of undress. When would such an opportunity come again?

He realized the question was more than rhetorical. He wanted it to happen again. And again.

"Are you leaving?" she asked, her voice husky, her eyes glimmering in the candlelight.

"Do you wish me to leave?"

"No."

One word changed everything. "What do you wish?" Now his voice was raspy.

Penelope removed the pins from her hair, letting her brown locks fall free. James sucked in his breath. In the candlelight, with her brown hair falling in waves down to her waist, she was nothing like the well-disciplined Penelope of the day. This Penelope was a free, wild, beautiful creature. The desire to touch her was more powerful than he could deny, and he stepped to her, threading his fingers through her thick, silky hair.

"You are lovely," he murmured and pulled her close and kissed her before one or the other of them could talk themselves out of it. She was warm and the taste of her surged through him. He felt like a man waking up from a long sleep. The dreary sophistication of London society was stripped away, and he was truly, wonderfully alive. He deepened the kiss and she responded with a fervor that only sparked his desire with more passion than he had ever experienced before.

He walked her to the bed without breaking their kiss. Now he had a new plan to trap her into marriage. If he bedded her, she would be forced to marry him. It was a satisfactory conclusion and so he continued, pushing her gently down onto the bed. He flung off his robe and covered her, wearing nothing more than his nightshirt.

She squirmed beneath him in a manner that raised his interest significantly, almost painfully. He settled into kissing as she ran her hands up and down his back, and then grabbed his backside. All conscious thought stopped, and he kissed down her neck to the hollow of her throat and down farther to her chest. He lingered with his face in her full bosom. This is where he belonged, where he wanted to stay. He slowly slid a hand under her thin petticoat and worked up her leg to her thigh.

"No, no, we cannot." Penelope gasped, but her arms remained firmly around his neck, pulling him down on top of her.

"I assure you we certainly can," said Marchford with his mouth full.

"If we do this, you might feel some small obligation to marry me."

"When we do this, I shall feel an absolute obligation to marry you."

"No!" Penelope released him and pushed him away. "I shall not be accused of trapping you into marriage."

He was too much of a gentleman not to stand back up and allow her to scramble up beside him. "My dear girl, I am trapping *you* into marriage," he said through gritted teeth.

"Do not gammon me. You had no intention to marry me. You simply asked because we got caught." She was breathless and adorable.

"Yes, but—"

"And that reason is not good enough for marriage nor lends itself to any sort of affection on your part."

"Penelope, I fear my true feelings for you must be patently obvious." He gestured down to the tent he was making with his nightshirt.

"Mere lust." She waved a hand to dismiss it.

He was displeased his show of manly prowess was rejected in such an offhand manner. "I have desired women before you, but I have never offered marriage. This is no mere lust."

Penelope's chin wobbled. "What is it then?" Her voice was thick with emotion.

It was a legitimate question, but one he was not prepared to answer. He decided to evade. "We will be married."

Penelope shook her head. "You must tell me why."

"Because we work well together. Because we share an attraction neither of us can deny. You are a sensible girl and are able to tolerate my grandmother. These are all good reasons. I should think I do not pose an unworthy partner for you. My station and situation in life should make you very comfortable."

Penelope gave him a small smile with wet eyes. "Yes, but you see your situation in life would make me very uncomfortable. It would be different if there was…" She sniffed and cleared her throat. "Forgive me, but your offer is not good enough. Good night, Your Grace."

"Not good enough?" He grabbed his robe and wrapped it around himself to have some dignity. It was intolerable to be rejected by a woman while he was standing at attention for her.

"You have offered everything any girl would want, except what I want," she said in utter vagueness.

"And what is that?"

"I have already told you."

"I cannot recall," he lied.

"Love."

The word hung heavy and dropped to the pit of his stomach like a stone. He knew what she was going to say, but somehow hoped she would request something he was better able to provide.

"I want to be loved. I want to be adored. Anything less than that is a poor bargain." Her lips trembled, but her chin rose.

His tongue grew heavy in his mouth. He had never told anyone he loved them, just as the words had never been spoken to him. Was that true? He paused in thought. Not his grandmother certainly, not his mother either. No, he knew nothing of that particular malady, so how could he offer it with any authenticity?

"I hold you in high regard." It was the best he could offer.

One eyebrow rose.

"I have great esteem for you."

"But you do not love me."

"Dammit, Penelope, you are asking more of me than I have to give."

She walked to the door and opened it. She was a slight woman, especially in her disrobed state, but she was firm in her determination.

The walk back to his chamber was a long one, despite being a relatively short distance down the hall. What had happened? How dare she ask more of him than he was prepared to give? If she would not accept him as he was, so be it. It would be her loss.

The grief accompanying these musings was pushed beneath the rising confidence that whispered to him that he could change her mind. She was not immune to his charms, such as they were. He smiled to himself. He could persuade her. He could trap her. He was not proud of such tactics, but he quickly brushed that concern aside. He wanted to marry Penelope Rose without giving anything of himself away. Surely that was not too much to ask.

Tomorrow he would pay a visit to Doctors' Commons for a special license, and then, whenever he could contrive to entrap her, he would marry Penelope before she knew what was good for her. The game was on.

Twenty-six

PENELOPE HAD DIFFICULTY SLEEPING, KNOWING THAT just down the hall was the object of her powerful lust. How she had the strength to send him away she did not know. She needed to hold out for a declaration of affection, but she still wished to taste the delectable treats Marchford offered.

What irony that she had initially suggested they share a bed as a way to grab back some control for her life, and now she felt more out of control than ever. *If ye find yerself cut off from the vine, ye best drop the saw.* Grandma Moira's words floated back to her. It was true. She wanted to blame James, but she was as much a part of this as he. And tonight was her fault entirely.

She did want to marry the man, but she knew with certainty, however, that a marriage based on obligation and fleeting lust would end in misery for both of them. She would never be happy loving a man who could not love her in return. And what would happen when he pursued other interests? The prospect of being married to him while he carried on with a mistress was simply too horrible to contemplate.

After a restless night, she greeted the pale dawn with resignation. It would never work between her and the duke; she needed to let it go. She dressed modestly and glowered at the maid until Abigail performed her duty in silence. It was two days before the wedding of Antonia and Lord Langley, and there was much to be done. Pen would focus on her work and ignore handsome distractions.

On her way to the morning room, Pen became aware something was dreadfully wrong. A loud honking sound, a strange rustling, and a loud crash were coming from the usually peaceful morning room. Penelope opened the door slowly, with some trepidation.

"What on earth?"

"Geese!" cried Marchford. "I wish you a very happy sixth day of Christmas."

"Have you lost your mind?" asked Penelope, utterly aghast. Six large, white geese were running afoul in the sitting room. Some were standing on the furniture; others were walking about, pecking at things. One was pulling at the drapes; another was doing something untoward on the rug.

"Six geese a laying," explained James, with a mischievous grin. "I have got that right, haven't I? It is six geese today. I know how much you enjoy the Christmas holiday so…" He gestured at the rampaging geese.

"James Arthur Lockton!" cried the dowager as she followed the sounds of commotion. "What have you done, boy?"

"I am attempting romance," said James without apology, even when one bird flapped its wings and a china figurine went flying, crashing onto the floor.

"This is not romantic, you fool!" cried his grand-mother. "Langley! Peters! Help!"

"I tried to explain to Miss Rose that I am not romantic, but she insisted. This is my poor best, I fear." He surveyed the chaos before him with laughing eyes. "Oh look, mistletoe!" He grabbed Penelope and planted a breathtaking kiss on her lips.

Penelope's treacherous body sank into him. "You are horrible," accused Pen in a shaky voice when he finally let her free. "Utterly reprehensible," she added, trying not to laugh.

The commotion brought another member of the Marchford household, Miles the Peruvian Jungle Cat, who looked at the birds as vile interlopers into his domain. He joined the fray with a hiss and a meow, chasing the birds into a heated frenzy. Geese flew, drapes fell, tables toppled. Lord Langley and Peters rushed in to help, adding to the crazed, honking disaster.

"I did warn you," said Marchford with a hint of a smile, not offering to help in the least.

"Bad show, very bad show!" condemned Langley, holding one goose by a leg and the other by the neck.

"Get them!" shrieked the dowager. "Get them all out!"

"Yes, dear!" replied Langley, shooting Marchford another glare.

"You are a horrible man," said Penelope, feeling obligated to rush into the fray.

"Just wait," Marchford called after her with a wicked grin. "Tomorrow is swans and then come the cows!"

It took some time to get the geese out of the house and even longer to get the feathers out of her hair. And all the while she cursed Marchford, even as she was secretly touched that he would risk the ire of his grandmother to garner her affection.

That afternoon, Penelope was called to join Antonia and Langley to discuss wedding plans when she passed the door of Marchford's study.

"Miss Rose, a word if you please," the Duke of Marchford called out to her. He was sitting much as he usually did, at his desk, his head bent over his work.

She stopped and took a deep breath. Even the sound of his voice could set her heart to pounding. Wary, she walked to the door but did not enter. "Your grandmother has sworn to never speak to you again."

He looked up with a grin. "Truly? Should have filled the house with birds years ago."

"You are incorrigible."

"Naturally. Come in, please, and shut the door."

She did as was requested, wondering if there had been some new information in their investigations. "Do you have new information?"

"Indeed." He stood absently as she moved forward to take a chair. They both sat down. "First, I would like to update you on information regarding the case. I have learned that Lord Felton is actually working with the Foreign Office to import wine with secret messages on the bottle label. Unfortunately, this system has been compromised by the fact that we saw someone trying to intercept these messages."

"Interesting," said Penelope, greatly relieved to be speaking of catching spies and not anything else. "But why would the spymaster send one of the secret message decanters to Lord Felton's home?"

"Particularly when the man does not entertain," added Marchford. "Yes, there is some explaining to do."

"So what is our next move?"

"Sprot is talking with Felton. Also, at least one set of the special decanters remains at large in society. We need to find them, so I would appreciate your eyes and ears anytime you go out."

"Yes, of course. You have my full support."

"I am very glad to hear it. Especially since you will probably not like the next thing I must say to you." Marchford stood and strolled back and forth, his hands clasped behind his back. In a blue, tailored coat, tight breeches, and Hessian boots, he was a stunning image.

"I have been giving some thought to our situation," Marchford continued. "The facts as I see them are this. First, I have made a public proposal, which you publicly accepted. Second, you have privately declined such an offer for reasons of your own."

"I do believe I made my reasons clear," interrupted Penelope.

Marchford held up a hand to stop her. "Please hold all questions and comments to the end." He cleared his throat and continued to pace. "Third, society has made false accusations against you, which would only be confirmed if the engagement were broken, because it would be assumed I had been the one to walk away."

Penelope opened her mouth to express outrage at this assumption, but Marchford again held up a hand and she fell silent. Though it angered her, she had to admit he was most likely correct. The disillusionment of the engagement would only be seen as the duke coming to his senses. Who would believe she refused him?

"Fourth, between us there exists a mutual attraction neither can deny. Thus, in looking at the situation logically, soberly, I have decided there is only one course of action I can pursue." He stopped and gazed at her, his sage eyes gleaming.

"Which is?" prompted Penelope.

"I must trap you into marriage."

Penelope sat in stunned silence. "What?" It was all she could manage.

"I am going to trap you into marriage," he repeated.

"Wait, what?" She stood up, then sat back down. "I thought you already did that."

"Yes, a lesser woman would consider herself trapped by a public acceptance. You, however, are a hardened case and require more convincing. I believe that only the threat of bearing a child out of wedlock would induce you to accept my hand in marriage."

Penelope's jaw dropped. She couldn't help herself. "What are you suggesting?"

"As a friend, I thought it only fair to give you warning that I plan to seduce you to my bed...or wherever I can get you alone." He gave her a self-confident smile.

Her body turned traitor, her heart pounding, her hands sweating. Despite everything, there was a part of her that wished to offer herself to him that very moment. Infuriating man! "So you are telling me that you plan to force me—"

"Oh no. Not force. I am a gentleman, after all."

"You claim to be a gentleman, but then say you are going to seduce me into accepting your marriage proposal?"

Marchford looked up at the ceiling, considering her argument. "Yes, I suppose that is not exactly a gentlemanly action." His eyes pierced hers once again. "More the actions of a duke. I am giving you fair warning, that you must concede."

Penelope panicked and stood up, placing the chair between her and him. "I wish you would let me be."

"Do you?" He walked closer, and she backed up to the wall. He reached into his coat pocket and pulled out a folded piece of parchment. "I have acquired a special license so we will be wed as soon as you have been sufficiently convinced."

"You did not get a license." She was in disbelief.

"*Special* license," he corrected. "Returned from Doctors' Commons this morning."

She wished to tell him to back away, but she did not—could not. The desire to kiss him was overpowering. Instead, she put a hand on his shoulder. He trapped her, putting his hands on the wall on either side of her. She did not care to get away and instead tilted her head up to him.

His kiss was surprisingly soft, patient. She put another hand on his shoulder and pressed closer to him, her hand moving to the back of his neck. He increased the pressure as well, deepening the kiss. Colors swirled before her closed eyes, and she lost herself in the moment of the kiss, leaning on him for support as her legs gave way. He increased the intensity, pressing forward with his hips, showing her exactly what was on his mind.

"Ow! Stop!" she cried.

Instantly he pulled away, breathing hard. "You did not care for the kiss?"

"I did not care for the chair rail in my back."

James smiled. "Practical. Let us find a new place." He swung her around to his desk and lifted her easily to sit on it.

Her heart pounded audibly in her ears as he lifted her skirts enough so that he could stand between her legs.

"This can be settled very easily between us, here and now," he whispered in her ear.

She desired him so desperately she had to struggle to remember why she was saying no. "Here? On your maps?"

"My maps?" He looked beneath her with some dismay. "Well, I might move the maps." He shrugged. "I like my maps. Oh, and here is the diagram of that missing safe."

He handed Pen the diagram, and she couldn't help but laugh. James joined her, and it felt good to laugh together at the ridiculous situation they were in.

At the sound of a knock on the study door, Penelope jumped down and smoothed her skirts. James looked her over with satisfaction and then called for the person to enter.

It was the butler. "Her Grace requests the presence of the Duke of Marchford and Miss Rose in her sitting room to discuss wedding plans."

James groaned. "Save me."

"Come now. How bad could it be?" said Pen cheerfully, unsure if she was relieved or irritated by the interruption.

The Dowager Duchess of Marchford was holding court in her sitting room, surrounded by papers, fabric swatches, color palettes, and sample flowers. A harried Earl of Langley sat across from her and shot them a pleading look as they entered the door.

"Good. James, now stand here, I want to see which of these whites will go best."

James stood obediently, while Antonia held up fabric swatches, for what purpose, Pen decided it was best not to ask.

"I thought the primary decisions had all been made regarding the wedding plans," said Penelope.

"Oh, but the napkins, the napkins, dear. I cannot decide between the creamy white and the silver cream."

The two linens were indistinguishable to Penelope, but she held her tongue.

"I have decided that you and James shall act as my witnesses," said Antonia without looking up. She was not asking. She was telling.

"But surely there is someone closer in your family who would be more appropriate," protested Penelope.

"There is no one in my family I can tolerate better than you." Antonia gave her a quick nod of approval. "Besides, now that you are betrothed, it would demonstrate my approval of the union and start to undermine these vicious rumors. If I knew who was spreading them, I would end it quick, I can tell you."

"But you forget, I do not plan to marry Marchford."

"You don't?" asked Lord Langley, jumping into the conversation. "Whyever not? Anyone can see there is an attraction between you."

"It is complicated," said Penelope.

"Odd creature," muttered Langley.

"Forgive me, but are you not marrying for love?" defended Penelope. "Do I not deserve the same?"

Langley cocked his head. "The gel's right. Fell in love once, never could get over it. Finally had to go through with it." He smiled at his bride-to-be, who smiled in return.

"Thank you, Lord Langley. Perhaps you can help me." Penelope gathered her courage and decided to speak plainly. "Marchford has threatened seduction to force me into marriage."

Everyone in the room stopped, staring first at her, then at Marchford.

"Did he now?" asked the dowager.

"Indeed, I did," confirmed Marchford with surprising calm. Penelope had expected him to be ashamed and deny it, but she had underestimated him.

"Good for you," said Antonia.

"What?" cried Penelope. "You condone this behavior?"

"No, but you are being stubborn. You should marry James and be done with it."

"I thought you would defend me. Lord Langley, as a gentleman and a peer of the realm, you surely cannot condone this."

Langley gave her a weak smile. "I fear I have my own selfish reasons for agreeing with Antonia. First, if you don't marry him, someone else surely will. You get on with Antonia better than most, so if you wed, my life would be made easier. And second, I have learned never to disagree with my lovely bride. So my advice is to marry the lad. He's not so bad, even if he is a duke."

"Traitors! All of you!" cried Penelope.

Twenty-seven

THE NEXT DAY WAS NEW YEAR'S EVE, THE EVENING OF the traditional masked ball. Penelope had a difficult decision before her. She laid out two gowns. One was a modest gown of creams with a high neckline. It would be appropriate for tonight's New Year's Eve celebrations and would make the statement that she was not the wanton creature trying to trap Marchford into marriage that many in the *ton* believed she was. The other gown was red silk, with a plunging neckline. It would only confirm everyone's worst impressions of her.

Miles the cat rested his unnaturally large head in her lap, and she stroked the soft fur, in thought. The gown would also send a message to a certain duke. Should she admit that his ridiculous attempts at wooing her had actually captured her heart? No. Yes. She did not know.

She was looking forward to meeting her sisters at the ball. All of them, from eldest to youngest, were coming to Town to support her. They had heard the news and a flurry of letters was initiated between them. They were all married and busy with their own lives, but they were her sisters. She had helped to find each of them a groom, and now it was their turn to support her.

But which gown?

A shriek from an upstairs maid shocked her out of her revelry, and Pen bounded onto her feet. She ran toward the sound, down the hall, to the room where they kept the bathtub. A maid was standing at the door, screaming with all her might.

Her heart pounding, she ran to the door, afraid of what she might see. She rushed in to find…swans.

Seven swans to be exact—some swimming in the tub, some pulling down the drapes, some running about the room, and one pecking at the toe of the shrieking maid.

"I know they are supposed to be swimming, but they wouldn't all fit in the tub," said James, who was suddenly at her elbow, with a mischievous grin.

Before she could answer, Miles pounced inside, determined to defend his territory against another flock of marauding birds. Unfortunately, he found the swans to be substantial creatures with sharp beaks, and instead of chasing them, he was soon the one being chased.

"You are despicable!" cried Penelope, trying not to let James see how desperately she wanted to laugh.

Miles bolted out of the room, down the hall, and up and down several flights of stairs with seven swans in pursuit. This naturally brought the servants to chase the swans, the dowager to chase the servants, and Penelope to chase the dowager. All this with James laughing until the dowager began to chase him, cane upraised.

It was a long while before Penelope was able to rescue the cat and run back upstairs with her large bundle of yammering feline. She shut the door behind her with a sigh of relief. That man, he was horrible. Incorrigible. Utterly...sweet. Nobody had ever taken such notice of her as to ruin his own house to demonstrate their interest. Of course, he was displaying his determination to marry her, not any true affection.

She glanced at the two ball gowns. She knew which one she would wear. It was a masque after all.

⁓

Penelope relinquished her cape as she entered the ball in the gown of scarlet. Marchford did a double take in her direction. His jaw dropped open, and even in his mask, it was not difficult to judge his reaction. She touched her mask to ensure it was in place. She could be daring. Nobody knew who she was.

"Sister!"

Except her sisters. Penelope took a deep breath and turned to face her beautiful sisters in the glittering ballroom. Though they all wore masks, it was clear from the dazzling array of golden hair that these were the four Rose sisters. "My sisters! You are well met."

Amelia, Sophie, Mariah, and Julia rushed to her, their blue eyes sparkling behind their masks. Not for the first time, Penelope wondered how on earth she could claim these radiant ladies as full-blooded sisters. If this was fate's humor, the joke was certainly on her.

"Penelope!" they cried as one and all went to hug her, though she noted even her younger and more rash sisters had learned to have a care and did so with a dash of enviable elegance. They were all well dressed, in the height of fashion, and all in varying stages of expectant motherhood.

"How it is that you never told us?"

"You sly creature!"

"When did you first fall in love?"

"I always knew how it would be."

Her sisters all began commenting at once, not one of them feeling the need to stop to let the other speak. Penelope put up her hands to stop the happy cacophony. "Let's go sit somewhere we can talk."

Her sisters stopped short, exchanged glances with each other, and immediately agreed. They found an out-of-the-way parlor, dimly lit, that seemed perfect for a short confessional. They had hardly closed the door and removed their masks before the questions were put to her.

"What is this about?"

"Is something wrong?"

"Why would the gossip columns say such things?"

"You cannot take anything it says personally!"

Four concerned sisters stood before her, perfectly lovely in spirit and form, and ready to march into war for her. When it came down to it, they loved her and she them.

"Marchford proposed because we were caught in a slightly indelicate situation," began Penelope.

"If he has compromised you in any way," began her eldest sister Amelia, now the Countess of Stanton, her eyes blazing.

Had he compromised her? This was not the question she wished to discuss with her sisters. She paused, a fatal flaw.

"What did he do?" asked Sophie, her large, blue eyes growing even wider.

"Nothing, it was nothing."

"What exactly was nothing?" asked Amelia, her eyes narrowing. She was no fool and pounced on Pen's hesitation in an instant.

There was no use denying any impropriety; her sisters would see through the ruse. They were her sisters after all, and the single disturbing thing about them was they could turn from being fascinated with the most frivolous minutia of fashion one moment to being deadly serious and shockingly intelligent the next. They may look the part of the demure, empty-headed society female, but underneath worked the minds of scholars. And one sure thing they knew was when one of them was not telling the truth.

"There may have been a slight kiss," admitted Penelope.

Her sisters smiled and did not present her with the censure she expected.

"And then he proposed, quite right," said Amelia as if the case was settled.

"Not exactly. I hurt my ankle, and he was inspecting it when we were witnessed by some very malicious gossips." Penelope breezed over the compromising part.

"It hardly sounds like grounds for a proposal," said Mariah slowly, suspicious.

"I was surprised as well."

"He must truly be in love with you!" cried her more romantic sister, Sophia.

"No, I don't think his heart has been touched,"

admitted Penelope, trying to explain the situation without revealing too much. "I believe he is more interested in keeping me by his side, so I can assist him in his work."

"What work?" they asked in unison.

Fortunately, Penelope had anticipated this question and had a ready answer. "I have been helping him with some secretarial work to do with his business in Cádiz," said Penelope vaguely. "He says it is important and values my efforts. He was upset when the dowager announced her engagement because it meant that I too would be leaving."

"So he proposed to you so he could keep his secretary?" asked Mariah.

"Couldn't he just hire someone else?" asked Julia.

"Perhaps. We are working on a particular project, and he wants it to continue until completion. After that, I am sure he will look for someone to take my place."

Amelia frowned. "What are you saying?"

Penelope took a breath. "I fear the engagement is a ruse to allow me to stay in the house. He never intended to propose to me."

Silence. Four equally distressed blond sisters frowned at her.

"You cannot possibly be suggesting that he would refuse to marry you after making a public declaration," said Amelia, her voice grave.

"No, he has insisted that I wed him, but I have not agreed to such a union. You have heard the gossip, I am sure. I could not marry a man simply because he felt obligated, especially when society believes I sacrificed my honor to entrap him. Better to live a spinster than be shunned by society with a man who does not desire me. I would be a daily reminder for him of a terrible mistake. Bad enough to live with it for a moment, worse to suffer for the rest of our lives."

Her sisters gazed at her in silence, the thoughts clearly spinning in their heads but not making it to audible speech.

"But he's a duke," blurted Julia. "Trapping him into marriage is what half of London is trying to do."

"Fortunately, I do not count myself among that half," said Penelope with a sniff.

"The other half is male," muttered Mariah.

"I know you may think it foolishness," began Penelope.

"Indeed I do," said Amelia with brutal honesty. "If you had no intent of ever marrying him, you should never have accepted him publicly."

"You are rather stuck now," said Sophie gently.

It was precisely what Penelope had feared, but she was not ready to accept her fate. Being married to a man who did not return her affection simply would not do for her. If she were neutral toward him, it might be acceptable, but to live with a man she loved who did not love her in return would be unbearable. "I cannot marry him under these circumstances. You all must see that."

Silence greeted her again.

"It is difficult to end an engagement," said Sophie slowly.

"Particularly to a duke," said Julia.

"But not impossible," said Amelia firmly. "In order for you to retain your place in society, however, you must have another offer of marriage. It would be acceptable to dissolve this engagement if both of you announced that you were pursuing true love elsewhere and both left the agreement amicably. But you must be married."

"Why married?" asked Penelope. "I could retire to Bath or someplace where I was not known."

"You would have to retire someplace where they don't read the papers," said Julia with characteristic thoughtlessness. Her speech earned her looks of censure from her elder sisters.

"Were the papers so very bad?" asked Penelope.

"Sweetling," sighed Sophie. "There are some rather unkind inferences being made toward you. Did you not see?"

"They have kept the papers from me. I knew it was bad, but I didn't realize it was that bad." Penelope twisted the strings of her mask in her fingers.

"Given the talk, it would be best for you to marry and soon. If you were to walk away from this engagement without the protection of another, I fear people would assume Marchford had found you less than honorable and had abandoned you. You would find acceptance into any society difficult, even outside of London." Amelia laid the truth before her in the plain, straightforward fashion that had always been her way. Penelope had always preferred it, but now she would have welcomed a more comfortable lie.

"So I need to find a husband," said Penelope dully.

"Oh, I shall help," said Julia, clapping her hands. "You helped all of us. We shall help you!"

"Thank you," said Penelope weakly. The last thing

she needed was her adolescent sister trying to find her a husband.

"You are, of course, welcome in our homes always," said Sophia softly.

"Thank you," said Penelope again, this time mustering up the energy for a small smile. She had supporters, which was nice, but living her days shut up in somebody's back parlor was not the dream she had for her future.

"I believe we should circulate and try to gain the upper hand on the gossip, or at least contain the damage as much as possible," said Amelia briskly. "Gossip is fleeting. Tomorrow, something else will draw their attention. We can only hope someone else does something more shocking." Amelia had her own experience surviving nasty rumors.

"More shocking than a duke offering marriage to his grandmother's companion? Good luck!" blurted Julia, gaining furious frowns from her sisters. It was brutal but true.

"We shall defend you and remind everyone of your spotless reputation," said kindhearted Sophie, and her sisters all agreed. Penelope had good friends in her sisters, which in the end was all that mattered.

"Thank you all so much," said Penelope, this time with complete sincerity. "It is so good to know I have such supportive sisters to fall back on. Give me a moment alone to think, and I will join you all in a minute."

Her sisters gave her supportive squeezes and left her to sort through her scattered thoughts. What was she going to do? Marchford was certainly making an effort to charm her, and yet she knew he would break her heart if she married him. But how was she going to find a replacement so soon?

The clearing of a man's throat surprised Penelope out of her reverie, and to her surprise Lord Darington stood up from behind the high-backed chair. He had been sitting there the whole time! Her heart pounded and her mouth went dry. He must have heard everything.

"Forgive me." He bowed to her, solemn as an undertaker. "I felt it was right to make myself known. I would have done so earlier, except I judged it would only cause you further embarrassment if I did so before your friends."

"Yes, yes, thank you." It would have been worse if he had stood earlier, but now she regretted her candor acutely.

"These are matters that naturally do not concern me, however, as I have inadvertently overheard, I feel compelled to assist a lady if ever I can."

"I thank you, Lord Darington, but there can be nothing you can do to alleviate my current situation, which, as you have correctly stated, is not your concern." Penelope edged toward the door. She was quite desirous to leave the embarrassing situation. To her great surprise, Darington crossed the room in a few long strides and stood before her.

"I do beg your pardon but…" He paused as if unsure how to proceed.

Equal parts shocked and curious, Penelope knew she needed to hear whatever the man might say. "Do go on."

Darington began to pace, his hands clasped behind

his back, and Penelope could easily picture him walking the decks, the very picture of a sea captain. "I understand my sister has come to you to request a marriage partner for me, as I have for her. Since I am apparently, in the mind of my relations, in need of a spouse, and since you may find yourself in need of the same, I suggest an arrangement of mutual satisfaction." Here he glanced at her to gauge her reaction, which could only be confusion.

"I beg your pardon, could you clarify what sort of arrangement—"

"Marriage," he blurted, as if the very word itself might burn his tongue if it lingered in his mouth.

"You are proposing marriage?" Penelope was dumbfounded.

"Yes." He nodded. "A partnership between you and me."

"You cannot possibly be proposing marriage to me."

"Why not?" It was his turn to look confused. "You are a sensible lady. A practical choice. You know I am not good with conversing with members of the opposite sex. Marrying you would be…"

"Efficient?" Penelope supplied.

"Yes." He looked pleased. "Quite so."

"Forgive me, Lord Darington, but are you quite sure you are not proposing marriage to avoid awkward conversation?"

"People have been married for less worthy causes. You are a reasonable, intelligent person. There is no other lady I have yet met that I would consider taking as a wife."

It was a compliment, and Penelope felt it to its full

measure. The fact that she was so praised, and by an earl no less, was not lost on her. Of course, it was another marriage of convenience, but Darington was a good catch. Her answer was never in question, but she breathed deep, savoring the moment she had thought she would never live to experience.

"I thank you but—"

He held up his hand to stop her, taking a step closer. He was an attractive man, she must admit, in his own dark and brooding manner. "I do not ask for an answer now. I only propose this to you as a potential option for your current distress."

"Lord Darington, I am honored by your proposal more than I can say, but I cannot feel easy in marrying you for practicality's sake, and not because you have found true love." Besides, if she wanted a marriage of convenience, she could simply marry the duke.

"I never expected the fickle course of human emotion would play a part in choosing a marriage partner," said Darington coolly. He stepped closer still, looking down at her with his black eyes. "I never expected to fall in love. But perhaps your heart has already been touched."

Penelope turned away; he was too close to the truth. "Whatever do you mean?"

"Marchford is a good man." He bowed without another word and quit the room.

She stared after him. The man saw too much. But Marchford—what did he see?

Twenty-eight

PENELOPE'S BRAIN WAS AN UNHAPPY TUMBLE OF thoughts and emotions. Who would have guessed that she would receive offers from both a duke and an earl? It was preposterous. Only trouble was neither party had claimed any affection for her in particular, but rather saw her as an efficient means to achieving their own goals. It was always nice to be useful, but she would not marry simply to be obliging.

Returning to the ballroom without attending to her surroundings, she jumped at the sound of a woman's voice, realizing she forgot to put on her mask.

"I see you have finally made the papers, Miss Rose. You are to be congratulated, such a coup to have secured the proposal." The Comtesse de Marseille slid next to her. Though appropriately masked, Penelope knew that aristocratic tone with a slight hint of the French accent of her birth.

The comtesse linked arms with her—it was less an expression of friendship and more to prevent Penelope from running away. So trapped, Pen had little choice other than to listen politely to what the older matron would say. Pen prepared for the onslaught. The comtesse had a tongue as sharp as any sword.

"Thank you," said Penelope. She had never spoken words so insincerely in all her life. She glanced around but found she was very much alone in the corridor with the comtesse. No easy escape.

"I confess I had not thought you had it in you to secure such an alliance." The comtesse's perfume wafted around them in a pleasant cloud. Penelope knew the comtesse never complimented without barbs, and she steeled herself for them, but she did have to admit, the comtesse smelled nice.

"It was as much a surprise to me as to anyone," said Penelope in all honesty, not expecting such a denial to be believed.

"Was it?" asked the comtesse slyly. She stopped before entering the ballroom. The light, happy voices, and the bright sounds of a country reel were just steps away, but the comtesse held on to Penelope's elbow with a firm grip Pen did not expect from an elderly lady.

"The question is, do you truly wish to marry a duke? Someone so far above your own station?" The friendly tone of the comtesse never wavered, but the attack was launched.

Penelope's blood turned to ice at the sound of the comtesse's voice dripping with honey-dipped spite. "My sisters are expecting my return," said Penelope, desirous only of leaving the venomous comtesse behind.

"Your sisters, they are very pretty, no? They all made good matches, quite good. What an embarrassment it would be for them to have a sister so unequally yoked. You must know the talk surrounding your remarkable accomplishment has turned rather nasty. No one of any stature will admit you into their house. You would be considered as repugnant as any social climber."

"I had no intention—" Penelope was nettled into responding. It was naturally a losing battle.

"I believe you."

Penelope paused, waiting for the insult that never came. "You do?"

"Of course. Anyone with any sense can see that you are no social climber."

Penelope stared at the comtesse. Was she taking her side?

"I like you, Penelope Rose. You have more intelligence to you than the average chit. That is why I have come to offer you a solution for the current problem of your sisters."

"What about my sisters?" asked Penelope, wary of the comtesse.

"Your sisters, they are very kind. They will stand by you, no? But society, I fear, is so very cruel, and they will take their share in your disgrace. Their invitations will dwindle. Their husbands' careers will falter. Marital harmony will turn to discord. They will argue amongst themselves as to who must house you and how to minimize the damage to the reputations of themselves and their own children."

The trouble with the comtesse is that she knew how to fashion the truth into a spear and skewer you on the end of it. Penelope wished she could dismiss her speech as the pessimistic ramblings of a bitter old woman, but there was always veracity in her words. Penelope's sisters would be tarnished if they chose to stand by her.

"I wonder that you are even speaking to me, considering your low opinion of me," said Penelope coolly.

"Ah, but I have a very high opinion of you, my dear. Many a lovely thing has set her cap on getting a proposal from Marchford, but he has avoided all the traps with remarkable ease. I know you are no brash light-skirt, but still you have gotten him to propose. I know not what your secrets may be—oh, you can keep them. I care not—but I have come to offer you another solution."

Penelope was sure she would not care for this solution, but she was also certain there was no escape until the comtesse had said her piece, so she nodded for the comtesse to continue.

"There are people who marry and people who do not, or choose not. It does not, however, mean that such ladies must live solitary lives, serving as poor companions, always taking care to the comforts of others. No, some ladies choose to live their lives in utter comfort."

"I doubt very much I am such a woman." Was she actually suggesting Penelope become some man's mistress? Preposterous!

"I can help you," soothed the comtesse. "I have been known to help women such as yourself, who find themselves in impossible situations. I provide an alternative to isolation or scorn."

"I doubt very much becoming a…a…"

"Courtesan," supplied the comtesse with a slippery smile.

"Yes, *that*, would help raise my respectability in anyone's eyes."

She smiled sympathetically. "It is a strange world, my dear. Courtesans are accepted in the highest levels of society, where perceived social climbers are not."

Much to Penelope's dismay, a short reflection proved the comtesse to be correct. She knew of such women, though she held no acquaintance with any; that would be utterly inappropriate considering her situation. There was another level of society, a level that did not attend debutante balls as she did, and in that level such women were held in high regard.

"Such a change in occupation would in no way assist my sisters."

"They would have to disown you, of course, but then they would be clear of you. I would suggest you retreat to the Continent for a while, leave London to reduce the talk. It can all be done very neatly if you would employ my assistance."

Penelope became suspicious. "And how much would such assistance cost me?"

The comtesse graced her with a wide smile. "You are a shrewd little thing, aren't you? Now, my dear, don't bristle so. I meant it as a compliment. My services are a gift to you, and in return, you may repay me by doing small favors now and then if I should ask."

"What sort of favors?"

"Nothing of a vile nature, you can rest assured. Oh, now, do not blush." The comtesse laughed at her. "Ah, but you are a green one. You act as if you are a maiden still."

"Please allow me to disabuse you of several false

notions you have about me," began Penelope, rising to her own defense.

"Must away," said the comtesse, releasing her arm at last and floating gracefully out into the ballroom. "Think on what I have said."

Penelope glared after her. Odious woman! But with a small sigh, she realized much of what she had said was the plain, hard truth. Many considered her a fallen woman. She stepped into the ballroom and all eyes were upon her. The mask! It had been forgotten. She quickly turned aside and tied it on, but now everyone knew the woman in scarlet was her. Conversations died and heads turned as she passed. It was hardly fair for her to be punished for a sin she had not committed.

At least, not yet.

The whispers around her grew louder, and she was glad she was hidden behind a mask, so the gossips could not see how they made her face red. Sophie was suddenly by her side, coming to her rescue.

"Such a pretty ballroom," she said cheerfully. "Do you care for the decorations?"

Penelope glanced around, noting them for the first time. The ballroom had been transformed into a winter wonderland with thousands of glittering glass icicles hanging from the chandeliers, with silver ribbons abundant throughout the room. It was a marvelous effect and showed Penelope how distracted she must be with her own sad affairs not to notice such a lovely composition.

"It is quite well done," said Penelope.

"I shall pass your compliment on to our hostess. I am sure she will appreciate it."

"I am not certain a compliment from such a social pariah as myself would be welcome from anyone," muttered Penelope, flicking open her fan to avoid the accusing eyes of society.

"I would appreciate it." Marchford stood before her, strong and hale and impeccably dressed in a dark green frock coat and silver waistcoat. Even masked, she would know him anywhere.

"I believe my husband is needful of me," murmured Sophie, and she disappeared into the crowd, leaving Penelope to her fate.

Despite the masks, everyone was watching them, with only the paltriest attempts at hiding their interest. Masked faces peeked over painted fans, heads turned, conversations hushed. What were they to do now?

"Would you care to dance?" asked Marchford.

Penelope was amazed at his simplicity. After all, they were attending a ball.

"I have never seen you dance," Pen protested.

"I have not danced since before my brother died." Marchford's voice was soft and low. "And now I am asking you to dance, Miss Rose."

Denial was not possible. Marchford had chosen his timing well, for the reel had just ended, and they were beginning another set. They walked out onto the floor with the other couples, as if what they were doing was commonplace. Penelope was uncomfortably aware that people had now dropped any pretense of not noticing and were talking openly, with some even resorting to openmouthed stares and rude pointing.

"Look at me, Penelope," soothed Marchford. His

eyes behind the mask were warm and inviting. "Look only at me."

So she did. He was ever so handsome and ever so confident. The music began and she did not dare to look away.

"I may have forgotten my way," he commented as they passed in the dance. "You must instruct me if you will."

It was nonsense of course. Marchford danced well, and with his confidence, she began to relax and enjoy the moment for what it was. She was dancing with the most eligible prize in Britain. He might not be hers to keep, but he was hers for the dance.

The music swelled and she could not repress a smile. He returned it, and the rest of the disapproving eyes disappeared. All she saw was him. Despite the turmoil around her, she knew this would count as one of her happier moments, something to look back upon when things went horribly wrong, as she was certain they would.

"You are a fine dancer," said Marchford.

Penelope listened for a tone of surprise, but it was not there. He was Marchford, simply stating a fact. "It is easy with an accomplished partner," said Penelope with the same tone.

"A compliment." Now Marchford had a smug tone.

"Take it as you wish, Your Grace."

"James. You continue to forget to call me James."

Penelope wished he would be a little less perfect. It would make disliking him easier. "James," amended Pen.

They separated for a minute in the dance, and

Pen longed to be back at his side. It was insanity, the game her emotions were playing on her. "Have you been able to discover anything more about our investigations?"

"No, everything is quiet." He kept his voice low and whispered in her ear when they passed, so only she could hear. It was heady stuff to have a man such as the Duke of Marchford whisper in her ear.

Penelope took a breath and attempted to drag her wandering mind back to its proper place in the conversation. "I was accosted by the comtesse tonight." She murmured to him. Strange how they could have a private conversation in the middle of a ballroom.

"Determined to spread her poison?"

"What exactly was in the papers?"

Marchford took the opportunity of the dance to float away for a moment.

"Vicious woman. Believe nothing she says," said James when he returned. Which of course meant the gossip columns had indeed been unkind.

"She made me a curious offer. She warned me of the horrible repercussions of our alliance and encouraged me to consider a life of a…" Penelope could not bring herself to utter the word in the middle of the ballroom, even if she believed herself to be beyond the hearing of others.

A slight stutter in his footing indicated Marchford had understood. "Forgive me if I do not see how that would improve your situation."

"She offered to assist me in learning the trade."

"Vile woman!" Marchford said too loudly. "I do apologize, not you, madam." Marchford gave a bow to the shocked lady to his left, whom he had insulted by forgetting to keep his voice at a low register.

"I doubt she will ever dance near you again," commented Penelope.

"I shall have to soldier on without her company. But tell me, what gain is it for the comtesse for your change in occupations?"

"I have been puzzling over that as well. She mentioned something about owing her favors."

"Is that so?" James came slowly came to a stop, impeding the dance.

"James," hissed Penelope to get him moving again.

"That may be it," said James with a happy glint to his eye.

"The dance!" said Penelope. All eyes were on her now, fans went up, whispers, laughs—it was getting dreadful.

"Yes, of course," said James, snapping back to the present and taking Penelope's hand to join in the dance once more.

"What is it?" she asked once they had begun to dance once more.

"Talk later," he said. He danced away and back again. "I have not commented yet on your choice of gowns. Allow me to convey my deep appreciation for your modiste."

"I wish I had worn something less revealing," muttered Penelope.

"No. Never. You are perfection. Do not drink the poison of others."

At the end of the dance, he took her arm to lead her off the dance floor, but the musicians stopped and an announcement was made that soon they would mark the end of the year and the beginning of 1811. Footmen arrived carrying trays of champagne, and everyone was encouraged to charge their glasses. Marchford accepted two glasses, giving one to Penelope. People crowded into the ballroom in anticipation, but Penelope wished only to disappear away from so many staring eyes.

"I should go see how my sisters are doing," said Penelope, trying to step away.

"I am certain they are all well," said Marchford, holding fast to her arm.

"Your grandmother, I should check on her."

"She is with Langley, and I can assure you has no need of you at present."

"But… I need to…"

"Get away so you do not have to kiss me?" whispered James.

The countdown began.

"We truly should not do this in public," Penelope whispered in return.

"Ten, nine, eight, seven…"

"Allow me to disagree."

"Six, five, four…"

"But everyone will see," gasped Penelope desperately.

"Three, two, one…"

"Precisely."

"Happy New Year!"

Marchford whisked off his mask and did the same to hers. He enfolded her into his arms, dipping her down and kissing her in a confident manner that made her his. Some members of the *ton* gasped in shocked surprise. Others cheered. Undeterred, Marchford branded her with his kiss.

Twenty-nine

"WHERE IS YOUR GRANDMOTHER?" ASKED PENELOPE AS she was assisted into the carriage by Marchford.

"She is being escorted home by Lord Langley." Marchford climbed into the carriage and rapped on the roof to begin the journey home. He then closed the curtains, giving Penelope pause.

They had not stayed long after their kiss on the ballroom floor. If there had not been enough talk about them before, there was now. James appeared pleased with his public demonstration of affection. Indeed, Penelope was flattered that he was taking pains to show society that he was pleased with his choice.

"What were you thinking while we were dancing? You stopped in the middle of the set." Penelope was not sure why James had drawn the velvet curtains closed and decided to steer the conversation toward safe waters.

"I have always wondered where the Comtesse de Marseille got her money. She is a widow. She escaped from France during the Terror with presumably little in the way of financial comforts, and yet she lives like a queen. I suspect she is profiteering from the courtesan trade, most likely as a madam, or possibly even using the information she gains in such a profession for profit or blackmail."

Penelope shook her head. "Of her, I would not doubt anything."

"Indeed. If it would not put you into questionable company, I would suggest you accept her offer and find out more about her operation."

"I can certainly do so."

"No!" Marchford was firm. "I do not wish you mixed with that company, even on a ruse." He casually stretched and put his arm around her.

"What are you doing?"

James leaned closer, his gray eyes shining in the orange light of the lantern. "I did warn you I was going to compromise you."

Penelope's heart began to thud. "So you are keeping your word."

"Indeed. I will always keep my word." He trailed a finger down her cheek, across her jawline, down her throat, to her cleavage. He traced along the edge of her dress. "I love this gown."

"I wore it for you." Penelope decided it was time to be bold.

His hand stilled. "Did you?"

"Yes. You have been honest with me, and it has inspired me to be honest with you." She flushed hot. She knew what she wanted to say, but with his hand resting on her bosom, it was difficult to think properly.

"Do go on," he urged, his voice intense.

"You wish to compromise me so I will be forced to marry you."

"Yes." He leaned closer, blowing hot air down her cleavage.

Shivers raced up her spine and she was growing hot in certain unmentionable areas. "I also wish to compromise you."

"Then we are in happy agreement," he murmured, running his tongue along the edge of her bodice. He was making it impossible to think.

"I wish to convince you to love me."

He stopped and looked up at her. She hoped her words had not seemed as desperate as they sounded.

"Penelope," he began, but she put up a hand to stop him.

"It is all right if you cannot, truly it is. I have another plan. If I must enter into a marriage of convenience, I will, but not with you. Never with you. I received another offer of marriage tonight."

"What?!" Marchford sat upright and glared at her. "Who?"

Penelope was slightly gratified by his jealousy. It could only be a good sign. "He is an earl. The name is not relevant to this conversation. Suffice to say, I now have options."

"The hell you do," grumbled Marchford. "You will marry me. No one else. Me."

"I find your attitude positively primeval. Forgive my bluntness, but we cannot be wed without my consent, and you know the terms you must meet before I will grant such a request."

Marchford folded his arms across his chest. "Now you are being difficult."

"You might want to consider that fact before you

demand I marry you. I intend to be difficult my entire life."

Marchford raised an eyebrow.

"I thought I should warn you, as a friend."

Marchford surveyed her with displeasure for a few minutes, as they ambled along in the gently swaying coach. Finally he shrugged. "I can still continue my plan." He wrapped his arms around her.

"No, stop!"

He pulled back with a furious frown.

"We will return to the house any minute." The thought of being caught being indiscreet with Marchford in the carriage gave her chills.

"No chance of that," said James with a smile. "I told the coachman to give me a tour of Town until I signaled to go home."

"You didn't!"

"I did. Now where were we?" He put his arms around her once more and pulled her close for a kiss that curled her toes. Slowly, he laid her back on the plush velvet squabs of the coach.

She knew she should stop him, but she only pulled him closer. He tasted so good and smelled so good and felt so good, she did not wish him to stop. It wasn't until his hand began to creep up her leg to her thigh that alarm bells began to ring.

"Wait, no, I should not allow this," she gasped.

James stilled but did not sit up. Instead, he rested his head on her bosom, breathing hard. "What if I promised we could continue without compromising you?"

"This is all rather compromising," confessed Penelope.

"What if we continued without risking impregnating you?" He lifted his head, his eyes pleading. How could she say no?

"I...I am not sure it is wise."

"Probably not, but are you not even a little curious? Would you not like to find out what happens between a man and a woman in a way that will not cost you your maidenhood?"

"You can do that?"

"Yes," he whispered in her ear.

"As you wish," she said in a husky voice.

"Ask me to continue." He nuzzled her ear.

"Yes. Continue. Please."

And he did. Fingers worked to loosen her gown, allowing access to her breasts. After some heated attention there, his clever hands found their way under her gown. He worked his way up her thigh until he touched her in an intimate manner that made her jump.

"I fear I am not that sort of girl," she gasped.

"Of course you are not." He breathed heavy as well. "But you are my girl."

It seemed a good enough rationale at the moment, and so she opened herself to him, gasping at the sensations he was so quickly able to build. She could not help but press against him, wanting more but unsure what she wanted and where this all might end. Something was building inside her, threatening to explode. Heat surged through her, and she held on to him harder and tighter, not knowing where she was going but desperate to get there.

She threw back her head and cried aloud, only to have her mouth covered with his demanding kiss.

Suddenly the tension within her released and her body convulsed with waves of pure pleasure. She was left panting, wondering what on earth had just happened—and how soon she could do it again.

Penelope could not stop smiling. She tried but failed. She cuddled up against him, and he wrapped an arm around her. "Who won tonight?" she asked. "I fear I've lost track of the score."

"I definitely scored tonight," said James in a silky tone. "But so did you. And I need to take a long, cold walk outside to fully recover." He rapped on the roof for the coachman to take them home.

"I do like your games."

"Marry me and we can play them every night... and more."

More?

Thirty

THE NEXT MORNING PENELOPE MOVED THROUGH THE house with caution. First of all, mistletoe was still hung about the house like aerial mines. She moved about with one eye above her and one eye watching for James. Even worse, sometimes she wanted him to catch her, and other times she wanted to catch him!

Second, it was the first day of the new year, the day Antonia had chosen to begin her new, married life with Lord Langley. Despite Penelope's extensive experience with wedding day drama (she did have four sisters), all the wedding plans appeared to be moving smoothly. There was only one thing that gave her unease.

It was cow day.

The twelve days of Christmas was supposed to be a fun childhood game, but now she regretted ever mentioning it to the duke. She had no hope that James would forget or give some reprieve in honor of his grandmother's wedding. Antonia was resting before the momentous evening in her sitting room, writing letters, and Penelope crept in to join her. All was quiet.

Antonia had given specific orders that nothing of a bovine nature was to put so much as a hoof on her polished floors.

"If you would just agree to marry him, James would stop this wooing nonsense," grumbled the dowager in greeting.

"You don't think he would actually bring cows... do you?"

"James is a hardheaded boy. No telling what he will do."

"Good morning." The object of their discussion walked casually into the sitting room and sat down to read his newspaper. He looked well, as usual. In truth, Penelope feared he looked better and better every time she saw him.

She feared she was growing hot in unmentionable places at the mere entrance of the Duke of Marchford. She had not known what could happen between a man and a woman, and now that she did, a life of celibacy did not appeal. She must find a husband. And she knew whom she wanted to fill the job.

Except for the small matter of cows. Penelope shared a glance with Antonia, and they both turned to stare at the duke. After a minute, Marchford slowly lowered his paper, meeting their gaze.

"Ladies? Something I can help you with?" He was all innocence.

"What are you up to? You always were a devious child," criticized Antonia.

James merely smiled at his grandmother. "Was I?" He returned to his paper.

After a while longer, Penelope could stand it no

longer. "Well? Am I going to get eight maids a milking or not?"

James lowered the paper again revealing a smug grin. "As you wish. Peters! Bring them in!"

"No!" shouted Antonia. "You wouldn't dare!"

Instead of cows, eight milkmaids entered the sitting room all holding glasses of milk. The dowager let out a sigh of relief and put a hand to her chest.

Miles the Peruvian cat stalked into the room, wary of interlopers, particularly anything with a beak and feathers. To his delight, he instead found young women with milk.

"Oh, look at the precious puss-puss," purred one of the milkmaids.

"What a very large cat. Oh, he's so soft." Another milkmaid stroked his gray head.

"Would puss-puss like some milk?" A third milkmaid offered him a glass of milk.

It was a time of redemption for the twelve days of Christmas for Miles as eight charming young ladies sat around the large, king cat, petting him and offering him milk from a glass.

Marchford raised an eyebrow at the disturbing scene and walked over to share a private word with Penelope. "This was supposed to be a gift to you, not your ridiculously large cat-dog," said James in a low register.

"Peruvian cat," corrected Penelope, though it had been Marchford himself who had concocted the lie. "Besides, you owe him after the terrible swan incident."

"Who knew swans could be so vicious?"

Penelope giggled at the recollection.

James leaned down to whisper in her ear. "Happy

eighth day of Christmas. I am looking forward to our ride home tonight."

Heat surged into places she was only beginning to realize existed. She had always hated blushing, but this was far worse. She only hoped everyone was distracted by the eight milkmaids and the large cat, sitting in a most unbecoming manner, and would not notice her embarrassment. "You are abominable!"

"Yes, I am. I look forward to being ever so again tonight," James purred, enjoying himself as much as the feline before him. He took his leave, and Penelope could not help but watch him go.

Never listen to a thing a man says. Listen to what he does. Grandma Moira's wisdom once again came to mind. Perhaps she was being dim-witted, trying to get James to say particular words. Maybe she needed to stop trying to control everyone and everything around her. Perhaps his affection was being spoken in deeds.

Penelope could not stop the smile that spread across her face. She would accept his proposal tonight. Or maybe…she would let him convince her just a little bit more.

⤷

Penelope was dressed in a beautiful cream silk gown with extravagant lace overlays. It was terribly expensive; Antonia's sense of propriety demanded everyone connected with the wedding was perfect. Flowers adorned her hair, and Penelope almost felt like she was getting married herself.

The special license in Marchford's pocket returned to mind. They could be married at any point. A smile returned to her face and refused to leave. She gave herself a mental shake and attempted to compose herself. This was a wedding after all, not a time for giddy happiness.

Penelope joined Antonia in her room, in the midst of extensive preparations. The gown laid out for the Dowager Duchess of Marchford could beggar a small country. It was a marvel of pale blue silk with a gauzy white lace overdress studded with tiny diamonds. The effect, shimmering in the candlelight, was stunning.

"Penelope my dear, come here," said the dowager when she noted her arrival. "Do you not look lovely? Yes, I have the most exquisite taste."

"Indeed you do," agreed Penelope.

"I wish to speak to Miss Rose alone. All of you out," commanded the duchess, and five lady's maids fled the room, leaving behind a disarray of ribbons, silk, jewels, and fancy trinkets.

Penelope sat on a vacated stool before the Dowager Duchess of Marchford, wondering what the imposing lady would say.

"I was nothing but a mere slip of a girl when I first met Lord Langley. I loved him from the first moment I met him. Loved him and wished to marry him. When he rejected me on our wedding day, I rejected love and everything it did to me. My marriage to the Duke of Marchford was not founded in love, and it suited me well at the time."

Antonia paused and took a deep breath. "I need you to understand. I did not raise James to think well of love. I fear I poisoned him to it instead. If I was one to indulge in regrets..." She smiled briskly and blotted her eyes with a lace handkerchief. "But I am not, I fear. What was done is done."

"I understand."

"Do you?" Antonia's eyes were a piercing blue. "You must show James how to love you. He has not learnt it from me."

Penelope nodded and absently picked at the lace of her gown as she voiced her fear. "Do you think he could learn to love me?"

"Stupid gel," said Antonia in a kind voice. "I'm sure he already does."

Penelope met Antonia's eyes and then could not prevent herself from giving the elderly matron a warm embrace. "Thank you!"

"Yes, well. Very good. That's enough of that now. You are a silly gel, but we are all fools for love. Do not wait fifty years for love as I did."

"Indeed, I do not intend to wait long at all." Penelope grinned at her, warm and happy.

"That's a good girl. Now call the maids back in. We have much to do!"

❧

The wedding between Antonia and Lord Langley took place at St. George's with immediate family in attendance, followed by a celebration ball that evening at the town home of Lord Langley. There was little immediate family for the newlyweds, but a few cousins did arrive, along with several aunts, one uncle, and a lot (Penelope never could quite get a steady count) of children in tow.

The wedding was brief, beautiful, and heartfelt.

Penelope stood opposite James as the happy couple recited their vows. His eyes were only for her, and hers for him. He was even more handsome than usual, in a gleaming black coat of superfine and a snowy white waistcoat and cravat. She wished to speak with him immediately after but was foiled by the enthusiastic congratulations of the cousins.

The relatives were placed in the guest wing of Marchford House and would stay with Marchford a few days, which allowed Penelope to remain in the home, given the ample number of chaperones. After which, her plan had been to go live with one of her sisters until she could set up her own modest residence outside of Town. Except now, she was considering Marchford's alternative proposal of becoming his wife.

His *wife*!

Penelope had been concerned that she would face opposition in Marchford's relatives, but Antonia introduced her as James's fiancée, and none of the relatives dared to second-guess her. If the duchess accepted her, it was good enough for them.

The wedding ball was a crush, as everyone who was anyone attended the glittering event to begin the new year. They had been obliged to go in two coaches, with Penelope and the young cousins in one, and Marchford and the harried aunts in the other. Antonia was the only one who arrived comfortably, sharing Langley's town coach.

Penelope searched for Marchford's tall form and dark head in the crowd but was unsuccessful. She gave up after a while and hoped he could find her.

"Meet me in Langley's study," whispered his voice behind her. He had found her.

Happy tingles shot though her in anticipation as she worked her way through the crowd. She had not seen Marchford but knew he would proceed by a different route and meet her in the study, where they could be alone. She was waylaid briefly by well-wishers, but was able to push through, slipping into the study unnoticed.

He was there. She had barely closed the door before he was upon her, kissing his hello. Yes, it was time to listen to his actions. It was a most satisfactory greeting.

"I've missed you," he said in a seductive tone when they finally parted lips to breathe.

"I have missed you as well," answered Penelope, her arms around his neck, her head on his shoulder.

"I see my nefarious plot is working. I shall continue to press my suit in a manner most indecent." He picked her up and swung her around to drop her without ceremony on the desk. He hiked up her gown without regard to the lace, his focus elsewhere. He pushed her knees apart and stepped between them, kissing away any protest. Penelope was aware he intended to ruin her right there on the desk, and despite a slight concern for the gown (it was truly beautiful), she could not care less.

Marchford impatiently swept aside a tray of decanters so he could lean her back and Penelope glimpsed a familiar glass bottle.

"Wait, stop!" she cried.

"No, no, please, no stopping," said Marchford, his voice muffled from between her breasts.

"Look, this is important," said Penelope, though she honestly had rather let him continue.

"You best have a good reason to stop me." He stood up and glared at her.

She pointed at the glassware. "The decanters. Look. It's another set."

Marchford groaned. "Dammit. It is a good reason. You have a keen eye, and someday I'll thank you for it."

"Do you think Langley is involved?" asked Penelope.

"More likely he is another innocent on whom these were planted." He found the one with the hidden compartment and held it up to examine the bottom.

"You don't think they would still be using these to pass messages?"

"One way to find out." Marchford carefully twisted open the stopper and pulled out a tiny scroll of paper.

Tonight. Midnight. Third guest room on the right.

"It is probably an old message," said Penelope slowly.

"Most likely," agreed Marchford. He glanced at his pocket watch and gave her a smile. "Shall we inspect?"

Penelope jumped off the desk and nodded. "Yes, let's go!"

"Ah, if only you were as eager for me as you are for catching spies." James shook his head with a rueful grin.

"I cannot help it. You have drawn me into this intriguing life."

"I am very sorry to hear it. Since I have corrupted you, I should give you this." Marchford pulled something from an inner pocket of his coat and handed her a long, thin knife in an exquisitely wrought gold sheath.

"What is this?" Penelope turned the beautiful object over in her hand. It was smooth to the touch and heavy with gold. It was an old piece. Instinctively, she held it tighter.

"It was the knife belonging to my great-great-great—I actually am uncertain exactly how many greats—grandfather who gave it to his bride for protection. Or, depending on who is telling the story, it is the blade taken from my great-great-, you get the idea, grandfather by said bride who held him hostage for a brief while."

Penelope blinked. "Hostage?"

"The story differs depending on who tells it. One version has my grandfather saving his future bride, Gwyn Campbell, from hordes of marauding Scots. Another has this enterprising Campbell miss holding him hostage to secure a peace between the barons."

"Which story do you believe?"

Marchford shrugged. "She was a Scot and a Campbell, so anything is possible."

"And you remember her name even after so many years."

"Not too hard, considering." He pointed at the knife and she realized that engraved on the sheath in elaborate script was the name *Gwyn Campbell* on one side and *Lady Lockton* on the other.

"This is beautiful, but I could not possibly—"

"Tradition. Take it."

"But I—"

"For heaven's sake, you walk about with stickpins in your bodice. You can certainly add a small knife to your garter. Hope you never have call to use it, but it will do me good to know it is there for you if you do." Marchford crossed his arms before him in a manner that forbid discussion.

"Well…" Penelope hesitated. This belonged in the family. Marchford's family. Only his bride should carry this knife. "All right," she conceded. If they did not wed, she would return it.

She planned to keep it.

❧

Marchford smiled in anticipation as he and Penelope crept down the dimly lit hallway to the appropriate guest room. Either there was a spy waiting on the other side of the door and he would finally reveal the traitor, or, and more likely, the message was old and the guest room would be empty—perfect to continue what he started with Penelope in the study. Either way he was a winner!

"Stay back in the shadows," Marchford whispered to Penelope. He felt in his breast pocket for his small pistol. He had learned to be prepared, just in case. He glanced at Penelope and considered telling her to return to the ballroom, but that would defeat his object if the room were empty, which it most likely was. Besides, he recognized that look in her eye. Determination. Anticipation. She was as invested in this chase as he was, both for the spies and each other.

Marchford put his hand to the doorknob and opened the door slowly.

"Come in," said a woman's voice, one that was vaguely familiar.

Marchford put a hand on his pistol and hoped

Penelope would have the good sense to stay hidden. The room was lit only by the fire in the grate and a single candle, casting a warm glow to the rich furnishings. Dark woodwork and a velvet couch gave the room an opulent feel. A woman reclined on that couch, shrouded in darkness until she leaned forward into the candlelight.

His breath froze. His heart stopped. It was her. Of all the people in the world, it was her. He would have known her in an instant. After all the years, she had not changed. She was still the same—still exotic and beautiful and dangerous.

She stared at him, her eyes round and beautiful. "You are not who I expected."

He could not find his voice to answer her. After everything that had happened, that was all she could say? He bowed to her.

"Good evening, Mother."

Thirty-one

MOTHER?

Penelope entered the room without waiting for an invitation. A lady reclined on a burgundy velvet couch, her black hair loose and falling over her shoulders in wild curls. Her bosom was high and her gown low. Shockingly so. Her skin, much of which was on display, was a deep olive complexion. Her lips were red as roses, her eyes dark and seductive. She wore a gown of a delicate, almost sheer material, with some sort of gauzy wrap giving her the strong resemblance of the goddess Venus emerging from a frothy surf. She was a great beauty; there could be no denying.

Despite being caught in a rather compromising situation, her eyes betrayed no discomfort and her manner was one of confidence, a small smile showing she found the situation mildly amusing.

Marchford, on the other hand, looked as though he may be stricken by apoplexy. His jaw was clenched so tight, Penelope feared he might break a tooth. He turned rather white, his lips a thin line. Penelope's heart went out to him. He deserved better than to discover his mother was alive by finding her reclining in a spy's lair.

"Good evening," said Penelope, entering the room more fully.

"Good evening to you." Marchford's mother motioned to chairs before her. "Do sit. Be comfortable."

There was little chance of that, but Marchford sat as if in a trance and Penelope followed suit. Now, what conversation would be best? How long have you been a foreign spy? Which member of the aristocracy did you intend to seduce tonight? Why was it that you abandoned your son at a tender age and allowed him to think you were dead all these years?

"I believe it might snow," said Penelope, rejecting all manner of conversation topics before landing on the weather.

"*Sí.* Your English winters are quite cold, though the snow is quite beautiful. A pristine white blanket—it can cover a multitude of sins."

"And yet they are still there, seething under the pretty package." Marchford joined the conversation—and killed it.

"It is good to see you, James. You look well." His mother smiled at him, radiant and all the more beautiful with tears in her eyes.

Marchford spoke dully. "You look exactly as I remember you." It was spoken with dark solemnity.

"Oh! You are too kind." His mother fluttered a delicate hand to her chest.

Penelope could only agree with that statement. Trying to find fault with the woman who had hurt Marchford, Pen examined his mother, looking for a flaw, but was disappointed to find none. It only irritated her more. No woman of her age should look so well.

"Will you introduce me to your companion?" asked his mother, whom Penelope realized would also hold the title of Dowager Duchess of Marchford.

"May I present Miss Penelope Rose. My mother…" Marchford paused and surveyed her with what could only be sorrow in his eyes. "I do not suppose you are known anymore as the Duchess of Marchford."

"No, I have not been called that in a long time. I am the Marchioness d'Anjou."

"And is the marquis in Town?" asked Penelope.

"Oh no, he is quite dead."

Penelope was not at all surprised.

"What are you doing here? What game is this?" asked Marchford in a low voice. He had recovered from his shock and was back in control.

"I am certain you must have so many questions. You always were such a bright boy," said Lady d'Anjou.

"I am a lad no longer. And now I want answers." Marchford's voice was low and commanding.

"Yes, I am sure you must, but I must leave you now. Let us get together some other time, yes? Very soon. So good to see you." She rose majestically and glided to a side door.

Penelope eyed Marchford, wondering if he would allow her to leave.

"Mother." The word skittered across the room and lay dead at her feet.

She stopped and turned, waiting for her son's pronouncement. Silence fell heavy between them. Penelope held her breath.

"Tomorrow," he said.

His mother nodded and disappeared through a side door. Marchford turned and exited through the door he had entered. Penelope followed him down the corridor and into the main foyer. Coats and carriage were demanded, the cousins and aunts were left with a made-up excuse, and Penelope and Marchford were alone in the carriage in a matter of minutes.

Unlike the night before, Marchford barely looked at her, focusing his attention outside the carriage. The weather had changed to sleet, wet and cold, mixing in the dirty streets to form piles of muck and slick ruts in the road. The only sound was the rattle and crunch of the carriage wheels along the slushy cobblestone road.

Penelope wanted to comfort him, but she suspected that any offerings that smacked of pity would be instantly rebuffed. He sat silent as death and about as cheerful.

"Eventful evening," said Penelope.

No answer.

"How clever of you to have found your mother."

No response. Not even a grunt.

"I wonder if we should invite her to tea. I'm sure your grandmother would delight in seeing her." It was an impossible situation, and Penelope was attempting to draw him out with ridiculous conversation.

He looked up at her finally. "Yes, let's. I have always enjoyed watching blood sport in my drawing rooms."

"Perhaps we should lock them in and see which one survives."

His lips twitched. "What does it say about me that I am actually considering the idea?"

Penelope tried to give a small laugh, but it crept away on soft feet. "I am very sorry we found your mother in that room. It must have been a shock."

Marchford said nothing.

"Do you think she is involved?"

"I fear there is no other explanation for her to be in the room."

The carriage rocked slightly, and Penelope allowed her shoulder to rest against his as they sat beside each other. Strange how last night they were so close, and tonight even the smallest touch seemed awkward.

Pen found his hand with hers and gave it a soft squeeze. He held her hand for a moment and then threaded his fingers through hers. It was intimate, even though they both wore gloves.

Penelope could not think of a thing to say to make anything better, so she simply sat beside him in the dark carriage, holding his hand.

"I thought her dead," began Marchford. "I searched for her at her last-known residence. I searched for her in every place society might visit. She had disappeared. No trace."

"She must not have wanted to be found."

Marchford leaned his head back against the squabs of the carriage seat in an uncharacteristic slouch. "Not only did she never return to me, but she did her best to never be found by me."

Pen wished she could debate his logic, but it did appear that his mother had wished to never have anything to do with her son and must have taken pains to prevent herself from being discovered.

"Perhaps there is a reasonable explanation, once

we uncover all the information," suggested Penelope without much conviction.

Marchford shook his head. "My mother has made her choice, but I must always do my duty." The cold carriage grew even more chilled.

"And what is your duty now?"

"I will contact Mortimer Sprot and let him know we have found the spy."

Penelope took a deep breath, struggling against the heaviness in her chest. Better his mother to be dead than a spy. She kept that last reflection to herself.

Marchford squeezed her hand and released it. Penelope instantly felt him slip away and did not know how to reach him. He focused his gaze out the dark window.

"James." She did not know what else to say.

"I can take comfort in the fact that you have options. You can marry another and will not be trapped into an unwise alliance." His voice was like gravel.

"James, no," she breathed, her heart aching.

"You were right. You were always right. You do not wish to be connected to a man who can never love you."

"You don't mean that. You have had a shock."

Marchford turned to her, his face a cold mask. "You deserve better than to be mixed with us. Things are going to get ugly, far beyond any idle gossip. Get out while you can."

"No. I am not going anywhere."

"Your service to my grandmother is concluded and I release you from any bond of engagement you may feel toward me, as you have requested."

"My mind has changed." Penelope was desperate to get him to stop, and she wished she had married him while the chance was hers. She had been foolish to let him get away.

"You were right. I only asked you to marry me because we were caught in an awkward position, and I thought it would enable me to keep you as my assistant. I do thank you for your service to the Crown. In truth, your sharp eyes have led to the revelation of the traitor."

Penelope winced, regretting with painful intensity ever pointing out the spy's decanter. "I do not wish for your thanks. I only wish for you."

"Charitable of you. But you will see in time that this is best. I am only grateful that things between us never got so far as to require marriage."

"I can only disagree."

The carriage rolled to a stop. They were home, except she could no longer call it that.

Marchford met her eyes. "Forgive me, Miss Rose, for ever toying with your emotions. I do not love you. I can never love you. You are worth so much more than I can offer. I wish you health and happiness, and feel sure you will find these easier without me."

Tears sprang to her eyes as she bit her lip to keep from crying out. He had timed his declaration well, just as the groom opened the door to the carriage so she could not reply.

"Good-bye, Miss Rose."

Thirty-two

THESE WERE DESPERATE TIMES. IT WAS HER ONLY excuse. Penelope found the utterly inappropriate night rail her maid had brought a few days ago and laid it out on the bed. It was still a shocking confection of see-through gauze and expensive lace. She put it on carefully so as not to rip the thing to pieces.

She had considered it a useless garment, except tonight it would serve an important purpose. She was going to seduce the Duke of Marchford and trap him into marrying her. Not her best moment, but she would own her mistakes, and if this was one, so be it.

She donned slippers and covered herself with a warm robe; it was freezing in the hallways. She waited until everyone returned from the ball and retired to their rooms, and then a while longer to ensure everyone slept. Now was her moment.

She crept down the hall to Marchford's door and lifted her hand to knock. Was she truly going to do this? What strange circumstance had led her, sensible, pragmatic Penelope, to be knocking on the door of a duke, with the express purpose of bedding him and wedding him? Apparently in that order.

Her father, the country parson, would not be pleased.

She rapped lightly on the door. It was not exactly the right thing to do, but she could think of no better plan. Seduction and guilt would have to do. She rapped a little harder on the door. No answer. Perhaps he was asleep.

She turned the doorknob, her heart pounding. The door swung open. She tiptoed into the room, holding her candle aloft. Her small light flickered against the walls. The bed was empty. The room was empty.

He was gone.

How long she stood there in the empty room she could not say. Eventually, she crept back to her room and returned a minute later, placing the ancient knife he had given her on his dresser. She had no right to it now. She had no right to him. She shuffled back to her bed, tears running down her cheeks. This was a problem she could not fix. She was not in control. She doubted she ever had been.

❧

Snow can be treacherous but beautiful. Raise the temperature a few degrees and you have freezing rain, a weather condition none could enjoy. Yet Marchford spent the better part of the night standing outside the house of Mortimer Sprot in the cold, dark, and wet.

He knew he should report what he found—*whom* he found—but he could not. Sometime in the gray hour before dawn, he returned to his house. He needed sleep to clear his mind so he could think.

Instead, he found himself standing outside Penelope's door. What he wanted was her.

He put his hand on the doorknob. He should not, could not go in, yet there was no one else he needed to see. Everything had gone so terribly wrong; he wanted to talk to his friend, tell her what had happened. Of course, she already knew because it had happened to her too.

He cringed remembering the things he had said to her. The shock of pain in her eyes was more than he could bear. But there was no other choice. He loved her too much to allow her to be caught up in the nightmare that was his life.

The thought stilled him. Did he truly love Penelope? He shook his head. What did he know of love? He was trapped, but she could walk away. Her freedom was the only true gift he could give.

Marchford forced himself to pull away from the door and staggered back down to his study, to put distance between himself and temptation. He collapsed onto a dark leather couch. He could not think what to do. He had learned the importance of taking command of any situation, but this night was utterly outside anything he had anticipated or experienced.

There was nothing left to be done. And so he prayed, as he had not prayed in years, until he fell into a heavy, dreamless sleep.

&

No matter how dark the night, the sun always rises. After days of snow and rain, Penelope was shocked by bright sunlight on a crisp winter morning. She wrapped herself in a robe and sat in the window seat, her face to the rising sun.

Pen searched for a solution to the situation before her, but this was one problem she did not know how to fix. She recalled a similar empty feeling in her gut when her parents died of the fever. She tried to figure out how to bring them back to her, but of course, there was nothing she could do. Her father's teaching floated back. He would suggest prayers. But what should she say?

Her musings were suddenly interrupted by a loud rat-a-tat-tat banging. She jumped up and scurried out of her room. She began to fly down the stairs to the source of the noise but stopped short. Before her were nine drummers, drumming.

The aunts, cousins, and a gray-haired uncle emerged from the upstairs bedrooms drawn in wonder to the source of the syncopated beat. The drummers were military, all in their red coat regimentals with shining brass buttons. The younger boy cousins raced down the stairs and began marching about to the beat of the drum.

All Penelope could think was that James had changed his mind and this was his way of apologizing and wanting her back. She was more than willing to accept his apology and looked around to find him, hoping to see him smiling at her in his casual manner that befitted a duke.

Finally, Marchford stumbled out of the study in the same clothes he had worn to the wedding the night before. "Go! Not needed," he barked at the infantrymen.

Penelope's heart sank. The rhythm of the drums

ceased, and everyone watched in silence as the drummers filed out of the house. Marchford strode up the stairs, his unshaven face of such cold disregard that no one dared to ask him anything.

"Well, I never," said one of the aunts when Marchford had returned to his room. The entire extended family turned to Penelope as if she were going to explain the strange happenings, but Pen simply returned to her room. There was nothing she could say.

It was an unusually quiet breakfast. The younger members of the family had been banished elsewhere— Pen had not the energy to bother to inquire where— and the aunts, cousins, and great uncle all ate in silence, looking between her and Marchford. For his part, Marchford chose a suit of dark gray. He looked appropriate for a funeral.

Penelope wanted to speak to him but dared not with the eyes of his family on her—suspicious, resentful, curious, and haughty in different measures. There was nothing she could say under such scrutiny, so she focused on her eggs, determined to eat quickly and leave the awkward gathering. As the minutes dragged on, she could not stand to eat in silence any longer, and so she broached a subject she knew would be dear to the finer sensibilities of the aunts.

"The wedding ball was a great success, do you not think? Except some young thing wore emerald," said Penelope, throwing out the bait. "Thought she was too young for it. Caused a bit of a stir."

"As well it should. I despise seeing any young

thing in anything but white muslin," cried one of the aunts, unable to remain silent. "Who was it? Someone should speak to her mama."

"I am not certain, but I believe the mother had taken ill before the event, so the young miss dressed herself," said another aunt.

"But who served as chaperone?" asked the first.

"Her brother," said a cousin in a scandalized tone.

The aunts shook their heads. "Clearly not up to the challenge."

"Quite," said Penelope, feeling more relaxed for breaking the awkward silence. Marchford, however, remained beyond approach.

"You can never be too careful with the raising of girls. You must have a firm hand or they may turn out very wild," said one aunt.

"So true." Lady d'Anjou swirled into the room in a sweeping champagne morning dress of nothing less than silk, followed by a harried butler.

"Ah…err," stammered the usually unflappable butler. "The Dowager Duchess of Marchford?"

The aunts gasped; one shrieked, as if witnessing the dead rising, which in a sense she was. The uncle leaped to his feet, his mouth gaping open. The butler remained in the room for a moment, as if waiting to see if there would be blood, then turned on his heel and left. Marchford slowly rose, his eyes focused on his errant mother, his mouth grim.

"I am Lady d'Anjou now," said the black-haired beauty with a dazzling white smile. "Duchess of Marchford never quite seemed to fit."

One of the aunts snorted and another collapsed

forward onto the table, where several cousins began fanning her furiously to revive her delicate sensibilities.

"Well, bless me," stammered the uncle with delight. "So lovely to see you, Bella. So lovely indeed! How have you been—ow!" He looked down at his sharp-faced wife, and Penelope had no doubt he had just received a correctional kick in the shin. So chastised, the uncle sank back to his seat.

"Would you care to join us for breakfast?" said Penelope to break the icy silence that had fallen.

"Yes, that would be delightful," said James's mother, accepting a seat near him. "I know it is a tad early to call, but I thought since we were family..."

"I cannot, will not share a breakfast table or anything else with this...this...woman!" declared one of the aunts, rising to her feet as if to avoid sullying herself by breaking bread with the radiant creature before her.

The other aunts, cousins, and the reluctant uncle all stood as well. "If you will allow this woman into your house, I think it past time we bid you farewell," said another aunt, casting not only Marchford's mother but also Marchford himself a look of utter contempt.

Any words of reconciliation died in Penelope's throat. "I am so sorry you must be going. I do hope you have a pleasant journey home."

The aunts gasped again at not gaining preference and marched out of the room, the uncle giving a little apologetic wave. Bella gave Penelope a smile and a nod of approval. Marchford, however, had turned to marble, a frozen, impenetrable mask. With a wave, he dismissed the footmen so they were alone.

"I am sorry to cause a stir, darling," said Bella.

"You were always causing a stir," said Marchford with frost in his tone.

Bella smiled. "I suppose you are right. You have grown up so well. And have chosen a fine bride." Bella smiled at Penelope, and Pen could not help but feel gratified at her acceptance, followed by a grinding emptiness of knowing it was all for nothing.

"Miss Rose and I have come to an amicable dissolution of any claim I may have imposed upon her." Marchford's voice was without emotion.

"The engagement is off?" Bella's dainty eyebrows rose.

"Yes," said Marchford.

"No," said Penelope.

"Oh dear. There seems to be a difference of opinion," said Bella.

"Miss Rose, I believe we settled this last night," Marchford ground out.

"No, I fear it is far from settled," said Pen, choosing this moment to be bold. She could hardly lose anything more than she already had.

"Miss Rose, you need to return to your sisters." Marchford adopted a businesslike tone. "I asked you to marry me. You refused. The situation has been concluded for the best."

"I've changed my mind. I will accept you now."

"I understand your terms and cannot meet them. Besides, this is not the time or place to discuss the matter," said Marchford sharply.

"Oh, do not stop on my account. I cannot wait to see what happens next," said Bella with a darling smile.

"Mother." James turned on her. "I need to speak with you. Alone."

Penelope had to respect the request and rose from the table.

"But, my dear, if you will marry this girl, she should stay and hear this too," said Bella.

Penelope sat back down. She did not need much encouragement to remain.

James glowered at them both but apparently did not choose to continue the fight. "Fine. Mother, I have decided not to turn you over as a traitor. But I need you to tell me whom you are working for and then I need you to leave. And this time never return."

Instead of being insulted, Bella merely smiled. "And this is what you think of me? That I would abandon any loyalties to my late husband and aid the enemies of King George?"

"Abandoning is what you do best." Marchford's voice was like ice.

"I see." Bella blinked her large eyes innocently, but Marchford was unmoved. "I suppose you might be right, as always," said Bella in a light tone, dabbing her eyes with a lace handkerchief. "I do not know where to begin."

"I need names, any information you have. Then leave. If you need money, it will be provided for you." Marchford folded his arms across his chest.

"It is a fair offer. It warms my heart that you would consider my welfare after all these years. The bonds between mother and son—"

"Are gone." Marchford stood up. "You relinquished any right to call me that years ago. Now, I need names, dates, information. Anything more is irrelevant. Please do not insult me by wasting my time."

Bella's eyes shone. "Yes, you shall make a fine duke."

"He *is* a fine duke," said Penelope softly.

"Indeed. Very true." Bella's smile was dazzling. "You have grown up so well, I am convinced I made the right decision."

"And what decision was that?" asked Marchford.

"To leave you." Bella blotted her eyes again. "Forgive me for contradicting you, for I have my faults, but treason is not among them."

"I am not interested in listening to your denials." Marchford stated, "I am only interested in the truth."

"Then perhaps you will listen to me." To everyone's surprise, Mortimer Sprot appeared at the table.

Marchford sat down hard. "How do you do that?"

Mortimer merely gave a melancholy smile. "Forgive the interruption, but Lady d'Anjou invited me to share some information."

"You deserve to know the truth," said Bella. "I did leave you, but it was not of my desire." Bella looked up at the ceiling, as if reliving the events. "I was sixteen when I met your father—such a dashing duke. I fell madly in love. He is, to this day, the only man I ever truly loved, besides you, my dear one." Bella smiled at James, who only once more folded his arms across his chest.

"I had no idea what to expect when we returned to England and was shocked by the fierce opposition I encountered from the duchess." Bella's eyes gleamed. "I was not one to back down I fear, and I fought back. She always thought me very wild, and I expect it was true. I was faithful to the duke, though, while he lived. Afterward, I felt I had lost my only friend in the world. So I went in search of new friends."

Marchford's eyebrows fell even farther over his eyes. It was not much encouragement to continue, but she did.

"If I had but known what my indiscretion would cost me…" Bella sighed. "Antonia discovered it and demanded I take you and leave. I pleaded with her on your behalf. Frederick had inherited the title of duke, and she felt very little need of you. In the end, we agreed that I would leave, and she would raise you as she saw fit."

"And what is your role in this tragedy?" Marchford directed his question to Mortimer Sprot.

"I met Lady d'Anjou many years ago and requested that she provide the Crown with information only she was in a position to acquire," said Sprot.

It was nicely spoken, but Penelope caught the meaning. Bella used her liaisons with men of rank and power to gain information for the Crown. From Marchford's cold stare, it was evident he also understood.

"You were a spy for the Foreign Office?" Marchford asked his mother.

"Yes," said Bella simply.

"And you knew of it this whole time." Marchford turned on Mortimer. "You knew I was searching for her. Why did you not tell me?"

"It was my decision, darling," said Bella with sad eyes. "Some of my activities required that I become intimate with certain men, and I believed you would not like it."

"Like it? Of course I would not like it. Or allow

it!" Marchford stood his eyes blazing. "Now I know why I was never able to find her—because you were helping her hide." He pointed at Sprot.

"Yes, it is true. But the information we received was critical. The invasion plans themselves we would never have known without her work," explained Sprot, his sagging wrinkles making him appear like a perpetually sad hound dog.

"Why now?" Marchford began to pace at the head of the table. "Why reveal yourself now?"

"It was not intended," soothed Bella. "I was in Town only briefly on a mission, and we found a message about meeting in that room at midnight. I was attempting to discover the spy. Instead, it appears we were set up."

Marchford gave a mirthless chuckle. "I see. We played into their hands. I do hope someone is enjoying this little farce. But as for me, I am done." He glared at Mortimer. "I trusted you and this is how you repay me? You are no longer welcome in my home. I never wish to see your face again."

Mortimer Sprot bowed his head in solemn acknowledgment.

"I wish you all good day." Marchford stormed out of the room followed by Penelope and Bella.

Instead of being able to speak with James privately, they encountered the aunts, cousins, and sheepish uncle coming down the stairs in traveling clothes. The adults were all thin-lipped and silent, but the younger members of the party were not so circumspect, and despite many hushed warnings to be quiet, their little voices rang through the entryway.

"Why do we need to leave now, Mama?"

"But I want to play with Uncle James!"

"Why can't we stay until tomorrow?"

"What does 'hoyden' mean, Mama?"

Marchford stood before the family that was abandoning him with marked equanimity, his hands clasped behind his back. "I wish you a pleasant journey." He nodded to the aunts and cousins, shook the hand of the uncle, and saw all of them loaded into the carriage out front.

Marchford returned to the entryway, glaring first at Bella then Penelope. Somehow, without being seen, Mortimer Sprot had taken his leave.

"I suppose I should leave too," said Penelope with reluctance. Now that her chaperones were gone, she could not stay in the house with Marchford.

"Do not fear. I shall move in and provide the appropriate supervision," said Bella.

Marchford laughed, a cold and heartless sound. "I can only assume you speak in jest. Good day to you both."

He walked out the door, toward the stables, demanding his horse be saddled.

"James!" Penelope called after him.

He did not turn around.

Thirty-three

PENELOPE DID NOT APPRECIATE FEELING HELPLESS. SHE could not heal the rift between herself and Marchford nor the rift between him and his mother—nor the one between his mother and grandmother. She retreated to her room. What was she to do now?

Answer the first time when the Good Lord taps on the door of yer heart. He gets louder every time He knocks. Grandma Moira's words came back to her. Had she been ignoring God and trying to take care of things on her own?

Penelope went down on her knees in prayer. She did not know exactly what to say, so she simply poured out her heart, asked for help, and tried to cast her fears aside and trust in the Lord. It was an endeavor for which she was going to need some practice.

Miles batted her hand, insisting she pet him. He seemed to sense she needed comfort, so she sat on the floor and cuddled the fluffy cat. Her conversation with the comtesse floated back to her. Would it be worth exploring?

James had insisted she stay away from the comtesse,

but Penelope was in a unique position to try to gain information. Besides, if she could find something of interest, she knew James would have to listen to what she had to say. It was a way to stay connected even if she was going against his wishes. Besides, since James had repudiated any bond of engagement between them, he could have nothing to say about the matter.

Penelope got dressed and called for a carriage, with Miles following her about wherever she went. Once in the carriage, she petted Miles, who had curled up on her lap for the carriage ride. He was warm and furry and…there.

"Miles," she chastised. "Did you sneak into the carriage?" She cuddled closer to him, and he gave her a thunderous purr. Perhaps he knew she needed cheering.

The carriage pulled up to a sharp town house in the best neighborhood. Inside was exquisite, the best of everything without being ostentatious. Though Penelope could not appreciate Marseille's cruel wit, she had to admit the woman did have an eye for fine things.

A surprisingly young and handsome butler showed her into the gallery, a long hall with paintings along both sides and numerous marble statues. The Comtesse de Marseille was directing workmen who were taking down the paintings and covering the statuary with white sheets.

"Miss Rose." The comtesse gave her a sweeping glance with a critical eye. "What a pleasure. You find me at work this morning."

"You are doing some redecorating?"

"*Oui*. Poor timing, for it will not be finished before my Twelfth Night Eve ball, but I met the most talented painter—his ceilings are exquisite—and I simply must have it now." The comtesse came toward her in a gorgeous gown of burgundy silk. If these were her "work" clothes, her wardrobe must truly be substantial.

"It will be lovely, I'm sure."

"I have heard a shocking rumor. I hope you have come to confirm it for me," said the comtesse with glittering eyes. Nothing was more delicious to her than gossip.

"What rumor is that?" asked Penelope. It was dangerous to assume.

The comtesse linked arms with her and they walked majestically out of the hall. "Come now, do not be coy. I heard it from a reliable source that Marchford's relations left the house because his mother has returned from beyond the grave."

"Yes, I can confirm it is true." There was no point in denying it.

Her eyes flashed with malicious delight. "And how did poor Marchford react to the news?"

"Poorly," admitted Penelope.

"And what of Antonia?"

"They have yet to meet."

"Oh, if only I could be witness to their meeting!" The comtesse clasped her hands together at the rapturous thought. "Bella was a delightful girl, very beautiful, but oh, there was never such an inappropriate choice for a duchess as Bella."

Penelope found herself nodding her head. As much as she wished to be contrary, she agreed with the comtesse. Bella was not a good fit to be the Duchess of Marchford.

Entering an opulent sitting room, the comtesse motioned for them both to take seats and inclined her head to Penelope. "And how has this impacted you, my dear?" Her tone was understanding.

"The duke has decided it might be best for us not to wed." She clenched her hands together against the wave of unexpected emotion. It was the first time saying it out loud, and she almost choked on the words. Ironic that she had been so resistant to the one thing she now mourned as a great loss.

The comtesse surprised her by standing up and condescending to sit beside her on the settee. The comtesse put her hand on Penelope's clenched fingers. "I understand. When your engagement was announced, I knew it could never be, but I also felt it was an injustice to you."

"Why is that?" Pen was wary.

"Because I can see plainly two things. The first is that you are in love with Marchford. And the second is that you had not intended to marry him. I cannot abide social climbers, but you are not one. No, you come to love most unwillingly."

Penelope swallowed the lump in her throat. It was true. Everything the comtesse said was true. To find understanding in such an unlikely source brought tears to Penelope's eyes. She had come prepared for censure and criticism. Kindness struck home.

The comtesse offered Penelope an impractical lace handkerchief, but Penelope preferred a linen one of her own. "I had not intended to marry him." Penelope blotted her eyes. "But now that he is gone, I miss him so horribly." Penelope blew her nose.

"Yes, of course you do," said the comtesse. "But that does not mean you must be alone."

Penelope wiped her eyes and blinked at the comtesse.

"I can only assume you are here to talk of my proposal to you the other night. Even if you cannot be with your love, you still may find comfort in another."

Penelope instinctively shook her head.

"Your morals do you credit, but think of how you will live. You cannot marry Marchford even if he took you back. I may see your true nature, but everyone else will only believe you trapped him in a scandalous manner. You cannot remain in society as Marchford's discard. If you wish to retain any standing at all, your only recourse is through me."

"What would I need to do?" Penelope told herself she was just pretending to draw the comtesse out, but the comtesse was right about many things.

The comtesse smiled. "You needn't look so grim, my dear. This can be the beginning of a long career."

"I doubt it. Honestly, I cannot say why you would wish me to be a...a..."

"Courtesan."

"Yes, that. I do not have the beauty. I certainly do not have the requisite ability to flirt. I am a poor choice."

"My dear, you have cast yourself in a most unfavorable light. I have seen women much uglier than you make a nice living."

"Thank you." Penelope blew her nose at the backhanded insult.

"There now, don't take a pet. Women are as beautiful as they believe themselves to be. You already have enviable confidence in your abilities, if not your visage. You are not cowed by rank or prestige. You did manage to convince the duke to make a rash offer, which none have done before you. And I think with a little training, you could pleasure a man competently in the bedroom. Are you a virgin, dear?"

"Err…yes," whispered Penelope, her face aflame for discussing such topics so openly.

"That is good. We can charge a higher price for your first lover."

"Price?"

"Oh yes. I prefer to have everything negotiated in advance. You must be spoiled, pampered, cared for in luxury."

"Until he tires of me and I must move on to the next."

"But of course. You acquire more this way. The man, he gives only at the beginning of his infatuation. Once he feels your affection is assured, the gifts stop. It is an intelligent lady who knows when to move on to the next."

"How industrious."

"Indeed." The comtesse gave her a sly smile.

"And what is your role in this?"

"I am like that infamous Madame X, the matchmaker. I find men across Europe—rich men, lords, princes— who desire only quality and unite them with the highest paid, most sought-after courtesans in all of Europe."

"For a fee," added Penelope. Ironic that she, the true Madame X, would be sitting next to a much different sort of madam. And yet their work was not altogether different. "Business must be good."

The comtesse leaned forward with a Machiavellian glint in her eye. "Thriving."

"So you simply connect me with a man looking for a mistress?"

"No, of course not. We must first train you. I would never send out an untrained girl. It would be a disaster."

"Training?" Penelope could not help but ask. "And how much would this cost me?"

"My services are a gift to you, and in return you may repay me by doing small favors now and then if I should ask."

"You mentioned that before but failed to say what sort of favors."

"Sometimes I should request you entertain me with stories of conversations, such as you might hear from your lover."

"I see," Penelope said. Marchford was right; the comtesse was a madam for courtesans and brokered a little blackmail on the side. She did not say as much, but for what other purpose would the comtesse need information? It was good business for someone without a moral compass. Penelope was naturally horrified but a little impressed.

"I would like to think on it," hedged Pen. It was time to go.

"But what is there to think on? Come, let us begin your training."

"No, no, I really do not think I am ready."

"Do not be missish. Come with me." The comtesse stood and Penelope reluctantly followed. Truth was, she was curious. And wary. And more curious.

The comtesse led her down two flights of stairs. In the lower level, where most houses had servants' quarters, the comtesse had created additional and, Penelope guessed, secret living spaces. Pen followed her down a corridor of rich mahogany paneling and velvet. Penelope trailed her fingers along the wine-colored velvet wall.

The comtesse opened a door and escorted Penelope into a dimly lit room. "Another student for you, Mistress Lace." The comtesse left at once, leaving Penelope in a dark, intimate room of rich earth tones.

Mistress Lace, who was dressed in a provocative negligee, pointed to a leather chair with the riding crop in her hand. As her eyes adjusted to the light, Penelope noted that four other young women in provocative attire were sitting around a table. On the table was a naked man, face downward.

Penelope stifled a gasp and sat where she was directed.

"Our men come to us because they need to relax. They come to us because they have needs their wives cannot fulfill," said Mistress Lace. "Does everyone have their implements?"

The girls all held up an ostrich feather in one hand and a riding crop in the other. Penelope was supplied with the same, taking hold of each everyday item as if she were touching something illicit. What would she need these for?

"First we must soothe the man." Mistress Lace trailed her feather slowly up and down the man's body. "Then we must make sure we have his full attention." She gave the man a playful smack on the buttocks with her riding crop. The man flinched but relaxed again under the ministrations of the feather.

"Now it is your turn to try. You need to soothe

him, excite him, so that when he finally comes to you, he releases all his cares and worries."

The girls all took turns teasing with the feather and then slapping the man on his reddening derriere. Penelope was both intrigued and repulsed, and she did not care for the fact that she was definitely more one than the other. Who knew she harbored the heart of a wanton? When it came to her turn, she decided it was time to make her escape.

"Sorry. Just remembered a prior commitment. Do continue without me." She turned and fled the room. She was a little concerned her exit may be impeded, but she found her way back to the foyer and was given her cloak without comment, though the butler gave her a curious look.

Back at the carriage, she put out her hand to grab a handle and swing herself into the coach and realized she still held the crop and feather.

"Oh bother." She stopped and stood before the open carriage door, wondering if she should return the items. In her confusion, she was vaguely aware of a gray blur leaping from the carriage and running across the courtyard.

"Oh no, Miles!" Penelope dropped the items into the coach and ran after the cat, who had caught sight of an offending mouse in a doorway and taken chase, as any Peruvian jungle cat would do. The cat raced toward a side door and, despite his fluffiness, squeezed through a crack and was gone.

"Miles! Here, kitty, kitty!" Penelope stood outside the cellar door, hoping the cat would meander out, without success. She opened the door farther and stepped into the gloom. If she should be caught, she would have difficulty explaining her presence, but she could not very well leave an enormous cat behind.

She crept down some stairs and was presented with several passages. One led to the velvet hall, another to a door which most likely led to the kitchen, and yet another to a flight of stairs going down. She chose the stairs since it was the most likely to be devoid of people and thus most likely to be the path of the errant cat and mouse.

She wished she had a lantern as she descended into the gloom. She put a hand on the cold stone wall to descend. This was no lavishly decorated boudoir; this was a standard English cellar. At the bottom of the rickety wooden stairs, she paused to allow her eyes to adjust to the light. One small window near the ceiling provided the only light, seeping through the cracks in the shutters. The room was spare; a table, some crates, a large square object covered in a sheet in the corner, and debris cluttering the floor.

"Miles," whispered Penelope.

Somewhere near the large object, the cat meowed for her. She drew nearer until she found her jungle cat licking his paws. She did not wish to know the fate of the mouse. She picked up the cat and caught a glimpse of something curious just visible at the edge of the sheet.

She glanced around. She was alone in the room. She crouched by the object and slowly lifted the sheet. Metal legs with an intricate design. She dropped the cat and pulled off the sheet.

It was the safe!

She recognized it from the diagram. She stared at it, her heart beating. What was it doing here? With a growing sense of panic, she realized she must get out of the cellar. With haste she tossed the sheet back over the safe and retrieved the cat. She cringed at the squeaky steps, hastening up. Her heart was beating so loudly she feared it might give her away.

She reached the top of the cellar stairs but heard voices approaching her, coming from the direction of the kitchen. She dashed out of the cellar door and into the velvet hall to hide, her hands full of cat.

"What is this door doing open?" a cook chastised a scullery maid. "You know this is to remain locked!"

Penelope peeked out the crack of the velvet door.

"Sorry, ma'am. I just got the barley from the crate like you told me," squeaked the scullery maid.

"And didn't lock it again like I told you." The cook locked the door and both women returned to the kitchen.

Penelope breathed a sigh to relieve her tension. She had almost been caught—or worse, might have been locked inside the cellar.

"They using cats now?"

Penelope spun around to face a young man wearing nothing but a pair of breeches. He was a handsome lad and quite possibly was the naked model she had seen earlier.

"Some experimentation," improvised Penelope.

"Hope it don't have no claws." He shook his head and disappeared into a velvet room.

Penelope clutched Miles and fled out the door. Safe and breathless back in the coach, she returned back to

Marchford House with a good deal of information, a cat, a crop, and…now where was that feather?

❧

It is a curious thing about feathers, that sometimes they can cling to clothing, particularly a lady's gown, and deposit themselves in the most peculiar places. The man in the Carrick coat stood in the cellar of the comtesse, ostrich feather in hand.

He motioned to one of his associates. "Call the lads. We have a problem."

Thirty-four

PENELOPE RUSHED HOME TO TELL MARCHFORD WHAT she had found, but in this she was disappointed. Marchford had not returned and no one knew where he had gone or when he would return.

Unsure how to proceed, Penelope wandered into the sitting room, only to find it transformed by Lady Bella d'Anjou. The staid beige drapes had been replaced by ones of bright red. Luxurious throws and thick cushions in vibrant colors of deep red, gold, and evergreen littered the beige furniture.

"Lady d'Anjou!" exclaimed Penelope. She vaguely remembered Bella saying she was going to move in, but it was all rather a blur. Bella had not only moved in but had also redecorated, all within a few hours. Remarkable.

"Please, call me Bella." Marchford's mother greeted her with a bewitching smile. Penelope could easily see how a man, any man, could fall for this exotic beauty. "I understand you are responsible for the lovely Christmas decor, and I wished to continue where you left off. This room appeared untouched."

"I should certainly hope so." The former Dowager Duchess of Marchford, now the Countess of Langley, entered the room with a sharp rap of her cane on the floor. "No, Peters, do not bother to introduce me." She waved aside the butler. "But do bring tea."

Penelope unconsciously backed away from the two dowager duchesses. This was the scene the comtesse had dreamed of seeing.

"My dear Antonia." Bella rose majestically, her gown floating about her. "How lovely to see you."

"Good morning, Bella," said Antonia. "You are alive. How utterly disappointing." She took a seat, her eyes a sharp blue. "I see you have wasted no time in turning my sitting room into a bordello."

"Why thank you," replied Bella, regaining her seat with a wicked smile. "It does make me feel at home."

Penelope sat down on the edge of her chair, watching the combatants, wondering if she should leave or remain as a witness to the impending murder, though which lady would emerge victorious from this death match was at present uncertain.

"So you waited for me to vacate the house for an hour and then pounced back into our lives, ready to usurp the title of Duchess of Marchford," began Antonia. "Why, the ink on my marriage license was not even dry before you snuck back to Marchford House. I should not be surprised, since cunning and underhanded dealings were always your specialty."

"And making people feel welcome was always yours," said Bella with a smooth voice. "As for the title, you may keep it if you choose. It is not one I cherish, though it is certainly my due to use it as I see fit."

"You demand a place here? As if you have any right to set foot inside these halls." Antonia's voice was brittle.

"Oh, I agree I do not belong in this household, at least as long as you decided to rule over it with poison in your heart to anyone you deemed unworthy." Her words were spoken with such sugar, Penelope worried she might actually gag on the cloyingly sweet tone—and then be sliced to ribbons with Bella's stinging barbs.

Antonia rapped her cane on the floor. "Who are you to make judgments upon me, you licentious little tart!"

"Ladies, please!" cried Penelope, feeling much like an unwanted referee. The combatants were more than willing, but this behavior between them had hardened Marchford's heart such that now he doubted his own ability to love. He had just begun to emerge from his frozen existence, and Penelope would not allow him to be pushed back into the abyss without a fight.

"You both certainly live up to your reputation as being vicious to each other no matter whom you may hurt in the process," declared Penelope. "I can see now why James had a most miserable childhood."

"Nonsense." The dowager frowned. "James was raised by me."

Bella cast Antonia a murderous glance at this comment.

"I adore you, Antonia, but I should not like very much to be raised by you. Nor you either." Penelope gazed first at Antonia then Bella. "Forgive me for speaking freely before my betters, but both of you are so completely wrapped up in yourselves you cannot see what your fights did to James, and indeed are still doing to him."

"You have turned him against me," Bella accused Antonia, clearly choosing to hear only parts of what Pen said.

"If I have had any influence on his ability to discern good character and people of quality, then I consider my efforts to raise this child his mother abandoned a success," declared Antonia in an insufferably superior tone.

"I never abandoned him, as you well knew," cried Bella. "You threatened to have him sent away from the house and raised as a virtual pauper had I not left."

"I did what I knew was best. You must have agreed, since you made no effort, even after all these years, to return. Do not try to play the innocent with me, Bella."

"I had my reasons," said Bella stiffly.

"Enough!" Penelope attempted to once again intervene. "You both continue to fight and bicker and have chased Marchford away from you. Whatever this feud is between you, can you not find resolution? I understand, Antonia, that you did not approve of your son's choice of wife in his second marriage, but since he has long been in his grave, could you not forgive?"

"I have forgiven him. It is this jade before me I cannot abide," said Antonia.

"Bella, you were so very young when you came here. Mistakes were made on both sides, but you have returned now, and I can tell you that your son has never stopped searching for you or thinking of you with fondness. Can you not attempt civility with your son's grandmother for his sake?" asked Pen.

"There is nothing I would not do for my son," declared Bella.

Antonia opened her mouth for a retort, but Penelope stopped her. "You confided in me only yesterday that you had not raised James to be a friend to love. Now that you have found your happy ending, can you not allow James to find one as well?"

Antonia shifted in her seat, glowering at Penelope. After some internal struggle, her face relaxed and she sighed. "I have only ever wanted what was best for James."

"The one thing you both can agree upon is that James has grown to be a fine man," continued Penelope, thrilled with even a modicum of success in the reconciliation front.

Both dowager duchesses nodded.

"Good." Pen clutched her skirts beside her, trying to keep her voice calm as she said the boldest thing she had ever spoke. "I must declare that I intend to wed the Duke of Marchford, though thanks to you both, he now has no intention to marry me or anyone. I feel obliged to inform you both that I intend to marry him by any means necessary. If this should cause ongoing animosity between us, I should like to know now."

"If we were to object, what then?" asked Antonia with a frown.

Penelope took a deep breath. "I will still proceed as planned. But I would suggest to James that we live on the Continent until you pass away."

Bella's smile grew. "I give this plan my hardiest support."

"You would," muttered Antonia, but to Penelope

she said, "I would like to see my grandson conduct himself with a modicum of decorum, but somewhere between the geese, the swans, and the milkmaids, I am convinced this house will not be set to rights until the two of you are wed. So by all means, do whatever is necessary."

"Don't forget the nine drummers this morning," added Penelope, her heart pounding from her own boldness and Antonia's support.

"Swans? Drummers?" asked Bella, but Antonia waved off the question.

"Love matches are rare. You must not let him get away," said Antonia in a soft voice.

Relief washed over her. She had expected to join the ranks of the combatants, but now, somehow in the sitting room overrun with Christmastide, she had found acceptance. "Thank you, Antonia. Thank you, Bella. I shall do my best. But first, I must find him." Penelope stood and curtsied to the former duchesses. "Good day."

Silence fell upon the sitting room in Penelope's absence.

"She will make a fine duchess," said Bella finally.

"Yes," agreed Antonia. "All the Duchesses of Marchford are of a strong, determined nature."

"Indeed. They most certainly are."

Thirty-five

MARCHFORD DID NOT KNOW WHERE HE WAS GOING when he left the house, only that he needed to escape. He had never felt more betrayed. Without thought, he ended up at the door of William Grant, who greeted him with exuberance.

"Come in, come in," said Grant in a hushed tone, catching him before the butler announced him to the party in the sitting room. "No, you do not wish to go there. Come with me." Grant looked over his shoulder like a marked man and led him into the study.

"What is all this about?" asked Marchford as Grant cautiously shut the door behind them.

"Motherhood, babies, can't escape it. Everywhere."

"I'm sure fatherhood will agree with you. Congratulations," said Marchford.

"No, no, you don't understand. It is not so much that I am going to be a father as Genie is going to be a mother. It has brought here every female relation from both our families. I am overrun by women."

Marchford raised an eyebrow. "And this disturbs you?"

"They take no notice of me! Their conversations

are unguarded and have taken to speaking of... unmentionable things."

Marchford tried to think of what Grant's genteel female relations could discuss that would have him so disturbed and came up blank. "What things?" he asked in a hushed tone.

"Womanly things," whispered Grant ominously. "Birthing positions, breast feeding, what to do with umbilical cords—oh no, it is too much."

Marchford was taken aback. "That is too awful. Why don't you go to the club?"

"Can't. Baby may pop out any second. Must be here for it."

"But what have you to do with it?"

"That is exactly what I told them!" Grant poured himself a drink, which appeared suspiciously like lemonade. Ever since marrying Genie, Grant's drinking habits had taken a decided turn toward sobriety. "They laughed. Thought it was in fun. Said I was more sensitive than other husbands who abandon their wives. Now I am good and stuck!"

"And I thought I had problems." Marchford shook his head.

"What problems can you have? Grandma just got married. Going to marry Penelope yourself. All is right with you."

"My mother returned."

Grant dropped his lemonade. "What?"

"My mother is alive. She had been coerced by my grandmother to leave when I was young, then entered into service with the Foreign Office, whose agents kept her existence from me, and worked as a foreign spy. Now she is in my house with Penelope and most likely my grandmother."

Grant stared at him and then shrugged. "All right, you win. Your day is worse. Do you think it wise to leave the house? What if your relations kill each other in your absence?"

"Then one of my problems would be solved," muttered Marchford.

"And you could live happily ever after with Penelope."

"Cannot do that either. I broke off the engagement," sighed Marchford.

Grant stared at him again. "Now why do a fool thing like that?"

"Because my family is ready for Bedlam! She will be much happier in the future without me."

"Is that so? How did she take the news?"

"Poorly," Marchford admitted.

"For a smart man, you can be a true idiot." Grant waved off Marchford's defense. "You love her. She loves you. Anyone who has spent more than two minutes with the two of you together knows it."

"My character is that obvious?"

"Your affection for her is. Quick now, go back and tell her." Grant smiled at him with bright eyes.

Marchford shook his head. "On this I am resigned. I shall never marry. Penelope wants to be loved, but I am not capable of the emotion. She deserves better."

Grant shook his head. "And they say I am the slow one. You already are in love with her."

Marchford shook his head, but even he no longer believed the denial. He took up a deck of cards, and Grant was content to play and let the dangerous topic

of love drop. They spent much of the day hiding from
the womenfolk. Some might call it cowardice, but
they each accepted their discretion with equanimity.
The women were talking marriage and babies. The
only recourse for real men was hiding. So they did.

Around midnight came the word that Genie was
going into labor. Any callousness Grant may have
expressed disappeared, and he took up camp outside
her door. Marchford wished them both well, suspect-
ing that Genie was in much better condition than
Grant, and left for home.

His brush with marital bliss, along with Grant's firm
contention that he was already in love with Penelope,
had set his head to spinning. What he needed was a
good night's sleep.

He called for his valet when he returned home, and
the efficient man had him quickly dressed for bed and
retreated back to his own quarters. With a sigh, James
put the candle on the side table and pulled back the
curtains to the bed. It was a cold night, and the heavy
curtains would be appreciated. He sat down wearily
only to hear a sharp feminine squeak.

He bounded up and grabbed the light. "Penelope?"

Penelope gave him a sheepish wave as she peeked
up at him from under the blankets.

"What on earth are you doing in my bed?"

"Trying to stay warm."

"Why not be warm in your own bed?" He must
stay distant. He must not give in.

"Because I have news I must tell you. It cannot
wait for morning. Oh, and if you continue to be stubborn and say you will not marry me, I will be forced

to compromise you. Although, quite frankly, I have some mixed feelings about that, and so I am hoping to find you amenable."

James stared at her. In the dim light, she hardly resembled the Penelope he knew, with her thick, brown hair tousled around her. From what he could see at the edge of the blankets, she was wearing some sort of lace night rail that revealed more than it hid. He was suddenly very interested in what lay beneath the blankets. All thoughts of remaining distant died just as parts of him he had attempted to deny jumped back to life.

"Wait, what did you say?" James now was utterly muddled. He could not think straight with her lying in his bed in a state of dishabille. Had she said something about compromising him? Sounded like a worthy plan.

Penelope gave a short sigh, as if he were a schoolboy not quite keeping up with his lessons. "I have important information to share with you about our investigations. I came here tonight dressed in this most revealing night rail to get your attention, so I could tell you and possibly compromise you and force you to marry me. I sat waiting for as long as I could, but it was not seductive; it was freezing. So I crawled into bed and must have fallen asleep because the next thing I remember is you sitting on me."

There was much in her statement to respond to, so he needed to prioritize and comment on the most critical first. "Exactly what are you wearing, Miss Rose?"

Penelope's eyes danced in the candlelight and she sat up, letting the covers fall down. She was beautiful.

The lace and gauzy material did not seem appropriate for winter at first blush, but the provocative nature of the night rail ensured the one wearing it would not be going to bed alone, so perhaps it was good for warming after all.

"May I?" He pointed to the bed, and she allowed him enough room to lie next to her. He shouldn't be doing any of it, but he was so tired of fighting against his desire for Penelope he could not resist her. She curled up beside him, with her head on his shoulder and his arm around her waist. She fit him, just the way he always knew she would.

"This cannot change anything," he murmured, a poor attempt at pushing her away as he was holding her close. Her shapely body woke parts of him, even as it tempted his brain to go into permanent hibernation.

Penelope snuggled into him. "This changes everything."

"But you declared you wanted to be loved," he protested.

"By marrying you, I shall have years to work on that project. I am content to continue to find ways to entice you. I brought tools." She reached behind her and revealed a riding crop. "I couldn't find the ostrich feather." She sounded apologetic.

"Why on earth do you need a crop?" But now his imagination was running wild, and he was very much awake.

"I should begin by telling you that I went to visit the comtesse today."

"I told you not to."

"I know. When we are married you can hope for

better control of me, though I doubt you will have much luck in that regard."

"And the comtesse gave you a crop?"

"Yes!"

James was lost. "Why would she do that?"

"To smack you on the bottom, presumably."

Now she had his complete attention. "I think you should begin at the beginning and tell me all."

So Penelope told him the whole story of going to the comtesse's house and being asked to become a courtesan and provide information from her lovers. When she told him about her first "lesson," he had to bite his tongue to avoid crying out, though whether he was horrified or intrigued he did not wish to own.

"So I was correct at how she has become one of the richest ladies in London," commented Marchford, holding her closer. "You put yourself at risk and saw things you should not have seen. I am only glad you escaped without further incident."

"Yes. True. I really should be married now. I hope you can help remedy that." She ran her fingers up and down his chest.

Her hair spilled over him, seductive and silky. There was nothing left to do but give up and roll her over onto her back to kiss her thoroughly. She wanted it; he was going to give it to her. Far from resisting, she ran her hands up and down his back, pulling him closer and threading her fingers through his hair.

He paused for a moment, breaking the kiss, considering his actions with whatever brainpower he had left. He knew if he continued, he would be forced to marry her.

Her fingers did not stop. She ran her hand under his nightshirt and gave his naked bottom a squeeze. "Don't make me get the crop," she whispered.

James groaned. She was going to kill him. Oh well. "I am certain you should not have been at any lessons, but I cannot bring myself to entirely regret it." He moved down, kissing the soft, delicate skin of her throat, working down until he found the abundance of her bosom. He focused attentions on one and was gratified to hear her gasp.

"Oh, before I lose my mind, I need to tell you," Penelope panted.

He moved his attentions to the other breast, unable to speak due to his all-encompassing work.

"Miles ran into the cellar when I was leaving."

"Hmmmm." He could not care less about the cat.

"I found him in the cellar. Along with a safe."

James looked up. "A what?"

"A safe. It looked a lot like the picture from Lord Admiral Devine."

He bit his tongue to keep from cursing her. Why must she tell him now? "Penelope. I may appreciate you later, but now I wish that you would become a little less observant."

"Do you think it could be the one that was stolen?"

James groaned again. He did not want to think about this. Not now. "I don't know. Surely Devine is not the only person to buy such a safe. Or it could be planted there, just like everything else we seem to find is staged to confuse us."

"What should we do?" asked Penelope, her hands still clutching him tight.

James rolled off of her with a primal growl from that part of him that was in violent opposition to his decision to leave. "Don't leave. Don't get dressed. Stay here!" he commanded as he pulled on trousers. "It is most likely nothing. As awful as Marseille is, I find it hard to believe that a displaced comtesse would be in league with Napoleon."

"True," said Penelope thoughtfully, a lock of hair falling seductively over a breast.

James whimpered in pain and shoved on a jacket, forcing himself to look away. Leaving this bed must be the single greatest sacrifice he had ever made to the kingdom, and no one but him would ever know it.

He saw the ancient knife on his dresser and picked it up, showing it to Penelope. "I will take this tonight for luck, but it is yours. Stay here," he repeated. "You promised to entrap me into marriage, and I'm holding you to it!"

He couldn't believe he had left Penelope warm in his bed. He must be insane. But he knew what was kept in that safe: the codes would reveal much. Many lives of agents loyal to the Crown would be forfeit if the documents were discovered. While he wished nothing more than to stay and continue what they started, he would not, could not, do so at the risk of others' lives.

He rode through the dark streets, cold and damp, with a dense layer of fog thickened by coal smoke. When he got to the town house of the comtesse, he tied up his mount down the block and crept around to the side entrance Penelope described.

It was locked, but Marchford took two thin strips

of metal from his breast pocket and deftly picked the lock. Inside, he found a series of doors, and going from Penelope's description, he chose the door leading to the cellar.

He held only a small lantern, so as not to alert anyone to his presence. He needed to see if the safe was the same one that had been stolen or perhaps was a similar design that the comtesse had commissioned herself. Lord Devine could not be the only person to have a safe in his house.

Marchford listened a moment, but there was no noise. He crept down the stairs to the cellar. The small lantern had difficulty piercing the darkness, and Marchford had to steel himself against black corners. He pulled out his small pistol, ready for attack, but all was quiet. On the far side of the cellar was a large object covered by a sheet. He shuffled through the debris, goodness only knew what was on the dirt floor. He pulled off the sheet and the safe was revealed.

He inspected it quickly. It had marks on it revealing that it had been opened by force, but the secret compartments appeared to be intact. He heard a noise behind him and spun around. Two men rushed at him. Marchford raised his arm to shoot, but he was struck from behind.

The gun fell from his hand. A gray haze clouded his vision, the room tilted, he stumbled forward, and he fell to the ground.

Thirty-six

PENELOPE STAYED IN MARCHFORD'S BED AS LONG AS SHE dared, then was forced to sneak back to her own quarters before being discovered by his valet. Morning came, and she dressed in one of her nicest morning gowns and hurried down to breakfast, certain that Marchford had been delayed and would meet her there.

Marchford was not present, nor Bella either, whom Penelope guessed would be a late riser. Penelope was forced to wait in the sitting room alone, sure that Marchford would come for her when he awoke.

Most concerning was the absence of ten pipers piping, which Penelope felt sure would arrive if Marchford had anything to say about it. By midmorning, she was emboldened to ask the butler for Marchford's whereabouts and her worst fears were realized; he was not in the house. He had never returned.

Cold dread seeped through her at the news. She had prayed before for herself. Now she prayed for Marchford. She sensed he was in danger, and though she knew not what she could do about it, she knew she needed to act.

Penelope decided it was time to take her concerns to Bella. She would know how best to contact Mr. Sprot, who might be able to help or possibly even know where he was. She enjoyed tracking down spies when she was with Marchford, but without him, the cloak-and-dagger exploits had lost their luster.

"Good morning, my dear," said Bella when Penelope entered her room. She was surrounded by at least half a dozen maids, most of whom Penelope had never before seen. All were consumed with the process of making Bella suitable for presentation, which apparently was a lengthy process. The room also had been transformed, as if by magic, with lavender throws and pale pink satin pillows.

Penelope stopped short, taking it all in. "Good morning," she said, hesitating. She was beginning to feel some sympathy for Antonia, who must have been shocked to have her house turned upside down so rapidly.

"This"—Bella motioned down the length of her—"doesn't happen without expert help." She smiled slyly. "There was a time...ah, but those days are gone."

"Not at all," said Penelope honestly. "But I wished to speak with you privately, regarding a matter most urgent."

A small pucker formed between Bella's finely shaped eyebrows, and she dismissed her maids with an indulgent wave of the hand.

Penelope sat beside Bella, unsure exactly how much to say. "I found something in the home of the Comtesse de Marseille, and last night Marchford went to take a look. He has not returned and I grow concerned. I wonder if you could alert the Foreign Office to see if they can help."

Bella leaned forward, her eyes bright. "What did you find?"

"I...I'd rather not say."

Bella leaned back with a delicate sigh. "Very well. Bring my traveling writing desk and I shall write to Mortimer."

Penelope did so, and Bella scratched out a short note and addressed it. "The trouble is, the comtesse is above the touch of most of the law."

"Surely not!" exclaimed Pen. "Even a duke must follow the laws of the land."

Bella raised a sculpted eyebrow.

"Most of them anyway," amended Penelope. "At least some of them," she further muttered.

"The law is the law, but who to enforce it?" asked Bella sweetly. "You need someone of higher social class to give the authority. That is why James is so helpful."

"So he can enforce the law among the aristocracy, you mean." Penelope was starting to understand. "I do wish I knew where he was. Perhaps Mr. Grant will know his whereabouts. Thank you, Bella."

Penelope called for a carriage, and this time made sure Miles was shut securely in her room before she left. No more rampaging kitty cats.

She was surprised to see Bella standing in the entry-way, dressed in a long, fur-lined pelisse with a huge fur muff and a white fur hat. Bella gave her a wide smile. "I have decided to go with you."

"You have?" asked Penelope, not sure if the inclusion would be a help or a hindrance.

"Indeed I have. I have been a poor mother and some would say it is too late to start now, but I feel I must make some little push as amends."

Penelope accepted the company. It would take more than this to make amends, but she held her tongue. The ride to the Grant household was not far, and they arrived swiftly.

"I shall call on Mrs. Grant and ask her to inform her husband of the situation," said Penelope, hesitating. She was certain that wherever Bella went, a scene must follow, and she did not want to waste time on the astonishment of others at the resurrection of Bella d'Anjou.

Bella gave her a knowing smile. "I suppose that is my cue to wait in the carriage."

"Thank you. Ever so gracious of you." Penelope hopped out before Bella could change her mind.

Inside the Grant house, she found nothing but turmoil: maids rushing about, footmen racing up and down the stairs, and Jemima Price sitting on the lowest step.

"My goodness," said Penelope to the young maid, as there was no one else who would stand still long enough to ask. "What on earth is going on?"

"The good lady, Mrs. Grant, is having a baby," said Jemima.

"And she requires great assistance?"

"No, miss. Mrs. Grant is only having a baby. 'Tis the rest o' them is having the vapors. And Mr. Grant is the worst o' the lot, shouting and hollering, asking for this, demanding that. I hope the tot comes soon, or Mr. Grant might die of apoplexy."

Penelope gave Jem a smile. "I'm sure it will not come to that. But I suppose he will not be of much help to me today."

"Can I help you? Like I did before? This house done gone mad."

"No, there is nothing…" Penelope paused, an idea, rather mad itself, formed in her mind. "Actually, Jem, do you know how to pick a lock?"

Jem shrugged and chewed on her lip. "I ken the black art."

"Come with me." Penelope left the house with the young former thief turned chambermaid in tow. Back in the carriage, Penelope introduced the young miscreant and explained the plan.

"Oh yes," said Bella, her eyes gleaming with a devious glint, "I can cause a commotion for you. It was the comtesse who attempted to blackmail me years ago, after my indiscreet behavior. I refused, and she told the duchess, causing me to be banished. I do believe I owe her a visit."

Bella entered the town house of the comtesse, while Penelope and Jem waited in the carriage. At first, all was silent. They lowered the window, letting in the frigid breeze, waiting.

"How do we know when it's time?" asked Jem.

"I have a feeling we'll know."

Suddenly, an urn crashed through an upper-story window and shattered on the cobblestones below. Screaming could be heard from above.

"That's our cue," said Penelope and briskly hopped from the carriage. She and Jem crept toward the side door. They paused, listening to the commotion as the whole of the kitchen staff and downstairs' servants raced upstairs to attend to the crisis. Penelope and Jem slipped through the open side door and crept to the door to the cellar. It was locked.

Jem stepped forward and pulled a hairpin from the bonnet covering her red locks. Before Penelope had time to wonder how she was going to do it, the lock was open.

"Well done," whispered Pen.

"I practice on the liquor cabinet to keep up my skills," said Jem proudly.

Penelope chose to ignore that comment, and they both crept down the stairs. She had no lantern, so Pen once again relied on the light of a small cellar window to see. Her heart pounding, she held up her hand to make Jem stop on the stairs. She did not wish to put the child in danger.

She tiptoed down the remaining stairs into the cellar. Everything was much as she left it. Except that the safe was gone. She went to where it was, but it was most certainly gone. It was as if it had never been there.

"What are you looking fer?" whispered a voice behind her that made Penelope jump.

"I thought I told you to wait on the stairs," whispered Pen to the errant Jem.

Jem shrugged and skipped around the room. Pen did a cursory search, but there was nothing and, more importantly, nobody to see. Wherever Marchford was, he was not in the cellar.

"Let's go," said Penelope in a hushed tone.

"Lookee here," said Jem, picking something off the wooden stairs in a tone too loud for Penelope's liking.

"Hush, child!"

They quietly mounted the stairs, Jemima slipping around her and going first. The child was silent when she wanted to be. They reached the top and realized things upstairs had grown quiet. The staff would be returning any second. They needed to hurry.

"Let's just go," whispered Penelope, heading for the door.

Jem shook her red head and reached for the lock. "Leave 'em how you found 'em." Fortunately, she was faster locking the door than unlocking it, and the job was done in a trice.

They exited the side door and walked with haste back to the carriage. Bella arrived a moment later, her black hair tousled, her fur cap gone.

"Drive on!" she commanded, and the carriage rolled away as the butler and footman chased after her. She leaned back onto the velvet squabs of the town carriage and laughed. "Oh my word, I have not had so much fun in an age! Serves her right, the old—" She cut short whatever she was going to say with a glance at young Jemima. "Did you find James?" she asked Penelope.

"No. The cellar was empty. Even the thing I found in it before was gone."

"So you have no idea where he might be?" Bella's excitement waned.

"No," moaned Penelope. "Can you think of where he might be, or what could have happened to him?"

Penelope and Bella began to discuss options but were interrupted by Jemima, who was bouncing on the cushions in the coach. "Wanna see what I found?"

"Not now, Jem. We are busy with something important," chided Penelope. She talked more to Bella, but they were out of ideas. Remembering herself, she quieted herself to pray and realized she had not listened to Jemima.

"What did you wish to say, Jemmy?" she asked, trying to be kind no matter how distressed she felt.

"I know where the duke is," said Jemima, still bouncing.

"Where!" demanded Penelope.

"St. Giles," said Jemima, holding up a small piece of yellow paper.

"St. Giles?" Penelope asked.

Jem nodded. "Found this on the stairs. It's the wrapper from Lady Bunny's cheroots."

Penelope glanced at Bella, wondering if her more worldly experience would lead her to have a more ready understanding of the child, but she appeared just as confused as Penelope. "I'm sorry, Jemima, but I do not quite follow you."

"Yeah, people say that a lot," admitted Jem. "Trying to improve myself. Not talk cant and other rubbish."

"You are doing well. Now tell me about what you found in the cellar," said Penelope.

"This wrapper. I knowed it. It comes on the cheroots Lady Bunny sells in her store in St. Giles."

"Ah!" exclaimed Penelope, the light dawning. "So whoever was in the cellar also smoked cheroots from an establishment in the St. Giles neighborhood."

Jem giggled. "Not establishment really. Just a place they sells stuff we nicked. Rolls their own cheroots out back. Lady Bunny ain't no lady neither."

This was of no surprise to Penelope. "Let us see if Marchford has returned home in our absence and then I suppose we can go search St. Giles."

"Aw, no, miss. You can't go there. Really, you can't."

Penelope turned to Bella. "Do you think Mr. Sprot may be able to help us in this regard?"

Bella gave an adorable little frown. "I doubt whether any of his operatives could pass for residents of St. Giles. They are rather insular there and they know outsiders."

"Mr. Sprot does seem to be rather limited in his abilities," said Penelope dryly.

"I can go there. They know me." Jem was solemn.

"Thank you, Jemima." Penelope took a deep breath. "I will go with you."

Thirty-seven

PENELOPE GLANCED OUT THE CARRIAGE WINDOW. They were losing the light. Marchford was still missing, Mortimer Sprot had not responded, and Penelope felt she could wait no longer. She wore her oldest gown from the trunk in the attic, which even she had to admit was quite shabby, and her old but still serviceable wool coat. Instead of a bonnet, she wore a more practical knit cap, which Bella had eyed with horror.

Nobody believed Bella would ever be mistaken for a resident of St. Giles, so she was left to communicate the situation to Antonia, a conversation Penelope was glad to miss. In the end, Penelope and Jemima Price, now dressed in her old, boyish clothes, were the ones to pursue the lead into St. Giles.

At Jemima's suggestion, they stopped the carriage several blocks from St. Giles and walked into that most notorious of neighborhoods. Penelope clutched her workbag, full of the items she hoped would help her find Marchford, and nodded to Jemima to proceed.

It was approaching dusk, and the fog, dense with coal smoke, was so thick they could barely see a few feet before them. The cold seeped through Penelope's coat into the very marrow of her bones and clung to her no matter how brisk her step.

By the time they turned down a narrow street to the rookery of St. Giles, it was nearly dark, and with flame and candle beyond the touch of many in that poor neighborhood, there was nothing to light their way. Penelope glanced around, wary of attack, but she could see nothing but shadows.

Penelope could not see what she was stepping on or in, but from the damp squish every time she put down a boot and the heavy smell of rancid food and excrement, she was certain she would rather not know. The only comfort in the brutal cold was that few others were on the streets. Even the thieves and pickpockets were retiring early to find shelter from the freezing temperatures.

Finally, after a long slog, they reached their destination. Penelope had expected some sort of shop, but there was nothing of note about the darkened door, the same as a hundred other darkened doors they had passed.

"This is the shop?" asked Penelope doubtfully.

"Aye, miss. But not for any but St. Giles," said Jem from beneath her muffler. "I sure do hope you know what you're doing." She knocked a particular pattern and they waited in the cold.

The door opened a crack and a suspicious eye looked out. "Who you be and what's yer business?"

"I have come on urgent matters to speak with Lady Bunny," said Pen.

"Who you be is what matters. You ain't from here."

"I am," spoke up Jem. "Come on now. Bloody cold. Grim Reaper at our heels."

"Not my concern!"

"Shut the door!" called a voice from within. "Ye're letting in the draft."

"Indeed," said Penelope, putting her shoulder to the door. "How could you be so senseless?" She gave a firm push and forced her way inside, past the elderly man at the door. Jem squeezed in and the door shut behind them. "Lady Bunny if you please."

The man glared at them from under heavy eyelids. Finally he grunted and led them down a tight, dark hall to a room, revealing a poor tableau of domesticity. The room was cramped and small, particularly after Pen's standards had been elevated from living with the duchess. The only light came from a small coal fire in the grate, surrounded by grimy children. Adults sat around in chairs and were wrapped in blankets, for even inside the temperature was barely above freezing and Penelope could see her breath when she spoke. All eyes were on her.

"I am here to see Lady Bunny," she said in a calm, businesslike tone that was in discord with the worried chaos within her.

"Who are ye and what do ye want?" asked a woman from the corner. Instead of a blanket, she wore a wool coat and had a lace cap that marked her as the leader of this ragtag bunch. Her face was thin and her eyes sharp. She leaned forward into the paltry light, revealing two buckteeth that did remind one forcibly of a rabbit.

"I have come to call," said Penelope, recognizing

this to be an absurdity. "I have brought these for your hearth and table." She reached into her workbag and produced a small bundle of coal and a wrapper of bread. She handed her gifts to the old man, who was still standing at the door and took them readily.

"What do ye want in return?" The woman's voice was wary.

"I come to ask for your help."

The woman shook her head. "Do ye ken ye can prance in here and demand help from us for a loaf of bread? I do not know what brought ye here, but it is a fool's errand. Go home. Ye're not one of us. Ye're in danger here."

Penelope took a breath, her mind spinning. She needed this woman's help. The room was packed and smelled of wet wool and mold. Everyone was silent, staring at her as if waiting for her to do something remarkable. "Are you not curious what would bring a woman such as myself to your door?" asked Penelope, stepping farther into the room.

One side of Lady Bunny's mouth turned up. "We have lost our storyteller. Ye may stay and tell yer story. If we like it, we may escort ye out of St. Giles alive. If not…" She raised a thin shoulder.

"Well then," said Penelope, swallowing her fear. A man in a thick wrapper who was picking at his fingernails with a long knife vacated a wooden chair with a snarl, and she sat down. "My mother married for love and ended up with a country clergyman. Her sister married for money and ended up in Mayfair. I will leave it to you to decide who made the wiser choice." Penelope decided her best chance of securing the assistance of these suspicious folk was to tell a long version of her story. A very long version.

Jemima crept into the room, disappearing into the shadows with the other youngsters as Pen rambled through the story, telling first of her parents' death, then how five sisters came to London and how she had helped each one find love and marriage. All romances have their ups and downs, and Penelope made the most of them, giving the stories as dramatic a turn as she could.

When she came to her involvement with the Duke of Marchford, French spies, and English traitors, she was pleased to note her audience leaned forward. One woman even handed her a glass of something for her throat that was beginning to sound with a rasp. Penelope took a sip and tried not to gasp as liquid fire ran down her throat. Whatever it was, it did the trick, numbing her throat and warming her insides.

Now she was getting to the important part—the disappearance of the duke. She paused, wondering how much to reveal. She was not at all certain whether those around her could be trusted. It was time to take a chance.

Penelope told as much of the story as she could and withheld the names as appropriate. "So when I returned to the cellar, the duke was nowhere to be found and all I found was this." She held up the yellow wrapper from the cheroot.

"We ne'er did nothing to no duke," cried a man in the room.

"Of course not. But you may know of someone who did," said Penelope.

"Ye tell a diverting story, I grant ye," said Lady Bunny. "But we don't rat out anyone. Wouldn't be neighborly. Besides, what did this here duke ever do but look down on us and bar his carriage door as he rode by?"

"He gave you Christmas dinner, that's what." Jemima's voice rang out from the gloom.

Bunny's head cocked to one side. "That was him, was it?"

Penelope nodded. "I do not know exactly what has happened to him, but I hope someone here can help."

"Ne'er let it be said that we in St. Giles are less loyal subjects to the Crown than any who walk wi' privilege." Bunny narrowed her eyes in a shrewd manner. "There will be compensation for time and effort?" she asked Penelope in an undertone.

"Of course."

Lady Bunny nodded to a few men, and they left with a grumble and a grunt. "Ye best make yerself comfortable," she said to Penelope. "The lads will let us know if they find anything."

Penelope resigned herself to accept the hospitality of Lady Bunny and spent an uncomfortable night attempting to sleep in a wooden chair. It was a long, cold night and, throughout the ordeal, her mind continued to return to James. Where was he? Was he safe? Since she could not hold him in person, she held him in prayer.

When the light dawned the next day, Pen sent Jemima back to Grant's house and continued to wait. Surely they would find something. She could not imagine a world without the Duke of Marchford. Finally, Bunny called for her. "We found something.

Man hired some o' the lads to haul crates. Probably a smuggler. But one lad said he saw a dead man lying on the floor o' the warehouse."

Dead?

❧

James Lockton, Duke of Marchford, had never been so irritated. As if it wasn't bad enough he had been knocked unconscious and dragged into some heinous scum hole, he now had to continue to pretend to be incapacitated in order to work on his bonds. This required him to remain lying on his side on the floor, covered in a substance he did not wish to consider. He was not sure how long he had been unconscious or where he was—he could only guess somewhere south of the rotting pit of hell.

"Move it careful now, careful," growled a voice.

Through barely opened eyes, Marchford could just make out two men moving barrels out of where he was lying and could hear another giving orders.

"What about 'im?" asked one man.

"You just go on about yer business."

Marchford did not want to wait to find out what they were going to do with him. Nothing pleasant, considering they left him unconscious on a freezing, filthy floor. He redoubled his efforts to cut his bonds with his ancestor's knife he fortunately dropped in his coat pocket after Penelope returned it. Trying to cut free while bound was not an easy feat, and Marchford wondered if he was doing more damage to the rope or his wrist.

The men continued to load the barrels, though

what was in them Marchford had no way of knowing
There were only a few barrels left. When they were
done with the freight, they would be coming for him.
The men groaned as they lifted the last one.

"Why do I have to do it?" complained one.

"Because I gave you an order," said another in a
brisk tone.

"Don't want to. Ain't right."

"What's right is you doing what you're told or you
can go to blazes with him!"

"All right. All right. Just saying he looks mostly
dead already."

"Don't want him mostly dead. Want him completely dead."

Marchford's heart pounded, bringing back circula-
tion to his freezing extremities. Just another minute
more and he should be free. Footsteps came near. He
didn't have a minute. Marchford held his breath. The
stained, mud-caked boots of the man came slowly
nearer. His hands were still bound; the rope would not
give. The boots stopped beside him.

Marchford swung his legs around, suddenly knocking the man to the ground and the club from his hand.
Marchford tried to stand, but with his hands behind
him and his legs and feet numb from the cold and
lying motionless, he fell back down, on top of the
man's club. The man scrambled away from him and
yelled for help. Marchford tried once more to work
on the ropes with his ancient knife.

Two other men came running. "What are you afraid
of?" yelled one. "He's still bound. Just shoot him."

The other man obligingly took a pistol from his

waistband and aimed at Marchford. The rope broke at that moment and Marchford threw the knife, catching the man with the pistol in the throat. He gagged and fell to the floor. Marchford struggled to stand as the first man charged him. Marchford swung and connected, knocking the man to the ground.

The man in the Carrick coat drew a pistol. This was it.

"No!" shouted Penelope, rushing up from behind. The man turned, but she slammed into him before he could get off a shot, throwing the pistol to the side. Penelope, wonderful, glorious Penelope, knocked the man in the Carrick coat to the ground.

"Penelope!" roared Marchford in surprise and fear, charging to protect her. What was she doing here? The man in the Carrick coat rolled to his feet, grabbed Penelope, and put a knife to her throat.

Marchford's world closed around him. Penelope in danger made him physically ill. He had never known such blinding terror.

"Stop!" commanded the man in the Carrick coat, red-faced and breathing hard. He pulled Penelope close and held the edge of his knife to the tender skin of her neck. The artery pulsed under the blade.

Marchford stopped, desperate for anything that would save her.

"Justin Strader," said Penelope, whose voice was remarkably calm though her breathing was rapid. "You are the man with the Carrick coat?"

"Shut up!" hissed Strader, and he backed up, dragging her along with him.

"Mr. Strader, Lord Felton's heir?" asked Marchford,

trying to keep his tone conversational. He did not want to give Strader the satisfaction of seeing him panic, and he wanted to give Penelope the hope that only confidence can bring. "What is your business here?"

"None of your concern," said Strader, continuing to back up, holding Penelope tight.

Marchford took a step closer, keeping the same distance between them. He glanced at the pistol on the ground.

"Don't even think it," warned Strader. "I would slit her throat before you could grab it."

"And I would most assuredly kill you where you stand. But let us have enough of these unpleasantries. Let the young lady go. She can be of no consequence to you."

The man laughed without humor. "She knows my name."

"As do I, so the secret will hardly die with her."

Strader growled at him. "Need to think. Take her with me."

"No, you can leave, but she stays," commanded Marchford.

"That's far enough," warned Strader. He had backed out of the dank warehouse into a foggy London day, so thick with haze that Marchford could not see the other side of the street. Strader backed up to a horse and a wagon with crates in the bed, covered by a large piece of canvas.

"Let her go," Marchford commanded again, trying not to let the sheer panic seep into his voice.

Strader shook his head. "Take her for safe passage. Once I get where I need to be, I'll let her go."

Marchford doubted it. Once he got away, he would

have no need for Penelope and that would mean the
end of her. "Miss Rose is of great value to me," said
Marchford, trying to elevate her worth in Strader's
eyes. "I would give anything for her safe return."

"Would you now?" said Strader in an oily tone.
"How very interesting to know." He half threatened,
half carried Penelope into a seat of the wagon. "Don't
follow or she gets it!"

Watching for her chance, Penelope lunged off the
other side of the wagon, but the man Marchford had
flattened had apparently recovered and snuck around
behind, preventing her from escaping. Marchford ran
to the wagon, but Strader held the knife to Penelope's
ribs while the other man flicked the reins and the
wagon lurched forward, speeding off into the fog.

Marchford retrieved the pistol and his knife, and
set off on foot, running after the sound of the carriage
rattling down the cobblestones. He had one chance to
shoot Strader before he could stab Penelope.

Penelope.

The shock of seeing her still coursed through his
veins. He had no idea how she had come to be there,
but there was no doubt she had saved him. *Saved* him.
Time to repay the favor.

The fog was thick and the horses swift, even in
narrow lanes. Marchford's feet, legs, and lungs cried
out for him to stop, but he would not. Surely some
traffic would slow them down. He would catch them,
and he would save her. He ran out to a crossroads and
listened for the wagon wheels beyond the heaving of
his own chest. He heard nothing.

He had lost her.

Thirty-eight

THINGS WERE NOT GOING WELL FOR PENELOPE, BUT despite having a knifepoint stuck between two ribs by the duplicitous Mr. Strader, she never wavered in her knowledge that Marchford would come for her. It was just a matter of time. She only hoped she had enough of it left.

The streets were unfortunately light of commerce, it being a cold day and dense with fog. It was also later in the day than she realized, and the light was beginning to fail. Even if there were others out on the street, the fog was so dense she could barely see a few feet beyond her own nose. Her hope that someone would see her plight or that she could call for help of a passerby, or better yet a constable, waned as they progressed through the streets shrouded in the impenetrable murk.

"Don't cry out. Don't move," growled Strader as if he could read her mind. "I killed the last loudmouth I met. I will kill you too."

Penelope was effectively silenced. She was not surprised when the cart stopped before the town house of

the comtesse. She was shoved to the ground roughly
with Strader never letting go of her arm.

"You know where to go," Strader told the driver,
and the cart disappeared into the foggy gloom.

Penelope was hustled inside by Strader, who proved
to have a firm grip. She glanced around but still saw
nobody from whom to implore help. "Why are you
doing this?" asked Penelope. "What can you possibly
have to gain?"

"You must be daft," insulted Strader, his face she
had once found attractive twisted into something
repugnant. "Felton treated me as if I was nothing but
refuse. He will get his, he will." Strader led her to the
side door and up a flight of stairs.

She was pushed into a room of exorbitant beauty.
Everything was of the best quality, luxurious, and very
dear. The room was fashioned in rich tones, and even
the drapes and bed curtains appeared to have jewels
woven into the fabric, twinkling in the candlelight.
She was in the private boudoir of the Comtesse de
Marseille attended by a large bodyguard.

"You?" Penelope had never harbored a favorable
impression of the comtesse, but her working as a spy
for Napoleon was lower than she had thought possible. "You are working for Mr. Strader?"

"Of course not!" she retorted. "He works for me!"

Penelope's blood chilled at such an easy admission.
The comtesse could never allow such knowledge to
become known. It meant she had no intention of letting Penelope go. Ever.

"Why are you here?" Marseille demanded of
Strader. "I told you never to come here."

"Couldn't wait," said Strader, finally releasing Penelope's arm and shoving her forward. "This chit interfered and Marchford got away."

The comtesse rose majestically, her eyes blazing. "You let him get away? *Imbécile!*"

"Not my fault. He wants her though. He will come for her," said Strader. "I don't know where to hide her."

"Hide her? No, we must not do that." The comtesse gave Penelope a dark smile. "You may have a use yet. Prepare him a welcome."

Strader bowed and left the room. Penelope thought for a moment this might be an ideal time to escape, but the large guard walked forward and stood behind her in an ominous manner.

"Why are you aiding spies and traitors? Why turn your back on your adopted country?" Penelope asked, wanting to distract the comtesse from whatever plans she may be concocting for Marchford.

"England is nothing to me." The eyes of the comtesse flashed. "When the Terror came, we wrote to our English brethren for assistance, but no, none would come. My home was attacked by the mob and put to the torch. I was forced to sneak out in a cart of hay with naught but the clothes on my back. Those wretched peasants stole everything from me. Everything! And what did England do? Nothing!"

"But why work for Napoleon? Why support your enemy?" Penelope took a step toward the comtesse, but a large, firm hand grabbed her shoulder and pushed her down into a chair. The comtesse certainly had strong assistants.

"My enemy?" The comtesse's voice cracked with

laughter. "I care nothing for politics. My enemy is not a man. My enemy is poverty. I escaped the guillotine without a sou to my name. And I would be there still had I not changed my fate. No, I see very easily how this game is played. You may be born the better of those around you, but without the blunt, you are nothing. I am the comtesse. Shall I be counting every last farthing? No! It is an indignity."

"So you became a spy for Napoleon for the money?"

"I have done many a worse thing for the money, *mais oui*. And you shall not sit in judgment against me. You who trapped the Duke of Marchford into marriage."

"I did not!" The words escaped Pen before she could remember not to rise to the bait.

The comtesse gave her an unfriendly smile. "Ah yes, you have looked to your own interests. I would say you shall never live down the gossip, but I fear you shall not be bothered by any further unpleasantness. Truly, I am doing you a favor, no?"

Penelope's pulse began to pound in her ears. She needed to get away or she would have no future. "So you assist Napoleon and his spies, and use the information you learn from your ladies as blackmail… or maybe even to sell to France."

"*Oui*. Some information, it brings a worthy price. It is too bad you had to be so much trouble. You could have been very useful."

Light dawned for Penelope. "That is why you wanted me to become a courtesan, so I could spy for you against Marchford."

"Ah, you are too clever. I had plans for you with Marchford. Though I do not know what he sees in you. I have tempted him with ladies of much greater beauty." The comtesse focused on her reflection in the mirror, putting on a glittering diamond necklace.

Penelope didn't know whether to be insulted at being called plain or pleased to know, of all his feminine options, Marchford chose her. She chose the latter. "You also arranged for him to meet his mother."

The comtesse gave her another devious smile. "*Oui*. I learned she was working for Sprot and arranged for your little meeting. You and the duke were getting too close. I thought the rumors I started would be enough to prevent your union, but I realized I needed to do more to disrupt you. You are simply too dangerous to me, working as a team. I only regret not being there to see his shocked face when he saw his mother."

A bang at the door and a muffled scuffle got her attention. To her joy and relief, Marchford suddenly broke through the locked door. "Comtesse de Marseille," he greeted her as if walking into a drawing room. "Do forgive me, but Miss Rose is needed downstairs."

Penelope immediately rose along with her spirits. Marchford was here; he would fix everything. The sound of a shotgun being loaded and primed brought her attention back to the unfortunate situation. A man emerged from behind a curtain, pointing the loaded weapon directly at Penelope. Marchford slowly raised his hands. The large bodyguard searched his waistcoat for weapons and removed the pistol and knife. Satisfied he was unarmed, he nodded to the comtesse.

"How lovely of you to join us. We were waiting for you," said the comtesse as if Marchford was an errant schoolboy. "Now that everyone has finally arrived, we may continue the evening's festivities." Her eyes narrowed into hard slits, and she directed her attention to the man with the shotgun. "Take them to the cellar and kill them."

Penelope glanced at Marchford, but his face was a cool mask. Was this how it was going to end?

"You cannot possibly kill a peer of the realm, a duke no less, in a cellar, like you would dispose of a rat," cried Pen.

"I have seen all forms of aristocracy fall before the guillotine or ripped to bits at the hands of a mob," the comtesse snapped. "I assure you, no matter how blue his blood, and there is some debate about that, he can and will die same as all the rest."

"But we shall be missed. Many people know the last place Marchford went was to your house. How will you explain us being found dead in your cellar?"

"But you will not be found dead in the cellar. When you are no longer a bother to us, we can carry your bodies anywhere we like. I shall say the duke came to me desirous of escaping a lowering marriage. Perhaps seeing his mother again stiffened his resolve to avoid such low connections."

Marchford's jaw clenched, but he said nothing.

"He wanted to break it off, but you pursued him. You caught him, he repulsed you, and you shot him for it, then took your own life. Ah, what a romantic tale it shall be." The comtesse gave her a sickening smile and then turned to her lackeys. "Shoot her in the chest at point-blank, make it look like suicide."

"You cannot do this," said Penelope firmly. "Even

you cannot be so cruel, so utterly devoid of human feeling. Every fiber in your being must cry out against such inhuman cruelty."

"Ah, how sweet. Even at the end, you cherish antiquated notions of how a world should be. Well, I'll tell you the truth—all your honorable intentions don't mean a thing. I shall always win because I am not afraid to do whatever is necessary to win."

"And what is necessary to win?" asked Marchford with a detached air. "What is your plan?"

The comtesse raised an eyebrow. "Ah, you would like to know, but how desperate will you go to your death knowing that you came so close to stopping our plans but fell short. Members of Parliament have been meeting to declare your king utterly insane and put his idiot son on the throne. They shall die before the deed can be done, leaving behind only a feeble, mad king and chaos."

"Napoleon will invade." Marchford spoke without emotion.

The comtesse shrugged a delicate shoulder. "It was only a matter of time before England fell. You see, I know which side to choose. And to the victor, the spoils will fall."

Penelope stared at the vicious thing before her, so warped with hatred and pride. Of all the emotions sweeping through her, the one that came to the fore was pity. "I am sorry for you then. You may keep yourself alive for a little longer on this earth, but you have squandered your soul, and thus lost everything."

The comtesse stared at her and swallowed hard. "Take them." Her voice did not waver. She rose and swept her hands over her golden silk gown. "I must greet my guests."

Penelope realized with a start that tonight was the eve of Twelfth Night and the annual ball of the Comtesse de Marseille. She could not possibly be killed in a house with people dancing above. Her legs wobbled and her hands shook.

"Miss Rose." Marchford held out his arm and Pen took it. It was a comforting gesture. Whether Marchford had a plan of how to get them out of this situation or not, at the very least, they would leave this earth bravely, with dignity, and together. He patted her hand, and Penelope took courage. He was a calming presence, but the comtesse was right. He might be a peer of the realm, but he was not immortal.

They were led down the back stairs, the sounds of music a mockery in their ears. Penelope could feel the cold, hard edge of the shotgun in her back. She doubted whether the surly man behind her cared whether he shot her in the heart in the cellar or in the back on the stairs. If she called for help, no one would hear. If she bolted and ran, she would be shot. Nothing to do but proceed to the cellar and accept her fate with the resolve of an Englishwoman.

"How did you find me?" Pen whispered to Marchford.

"Went to the last place I knew spies had been," replied Marchford. "Thought to enlist the help of the comtesse. Didn't expect to find her the spymaster."

They walked down the servants' stairs and then on down rickety, wooden ones. It was going to be difficult for someone to hoist their bodies back out. Penelope shuddered at the macabre turn of her mind.

She stepped gingerly into the cellar, the freezing cold seeping through her wool coat, into her bones. The two men, one holding the shotgun, the other a lantern, followed into the space that had once housed the safe. Had it been two or three days ago? The time all ran together. The light of the lantern danced angrily on the stone walls of the cellar. The sounds of the ball above had been completely silenced. None would hear them scream; none would hear the shots. Once dead, the comtesse could arrange her little scene anywhere and anytime she wanted.

Marchford led her to the back of the cellar, near where the safe had been, and turned to face his killers, his face perfectly calm. He moved her slightly behind him, which she thought was kind, albeit utterly useless to protect her from bullets. Penelope wondered how he could remain so much at his ease. Her own heart was banging so hard against her rib cage she feared she might break one.

"Sorry, Your Grace, that it come to this," said the bodyguard with the lantern. "But I needs to do as I'm ordered, you understand."

Marchford gave him a short nod. "I would ask for your indulgence for a moment so I may address the lady."

"No talking. Time's up." The burly man with the shotgun took aim, but the other put his hand on the barrel, lowering it.

"Last request. What's right is right," said the bodyguard with the lantern. "All right, gov'ner, have your say."

To Penelope's surprise, Marchford went down to one knee on the ground before her.

"Penelope Rose." Marchford bowed his head before her. "Allow me to beg your forgiveness for bringing you into this adventure. I should never have let you get involved."

"I do forgive you if there was anything to forgive," said Penelope with fervor. "You always did what you thought was right in the service of your king and country. Besides, you would have had difficulty preventing me from becoming involved."

"True." Marchford met her eyes and took her hand with his left hand. Pen thought this a trifle unusual, but then again, she had a duke on his knees before her and two men wanting to kill her, so it was an unusual day all around.

"Penelope, I have one more confession to make. I told you that I proposed because you were useful, because we were caught, and because I wanted your continued assistance in this mission. Those considerations were all true, but not the reason I proposed." He paused and let his free hand fall to the ground, as if needing additional support. "I told you I could never love you, and that also was a lie. The real reason I proposed, the real reason I attempted to trap you into marriage, is because I love you."

Penelope had thought it was impossible to have her heart beat any faster or harder than it was, but she was wrong. He loved her. He *loved* her. Her heart beat so wildly she feared it might break free.

"I confess I hid this from you because I did not wish to be hurt. I feared marrying for love as my father did, so I convinced myself it was for other more rational motives. But now, as we face this night, I realize nothing else matters but to confess my love for you in the most ardent manner possible with the hope that someday you may grow to share my affection."

"I love you too!" blurted Penelope. There was no need to wait; indeed, they were out of time for all of Marchford's pretending. "I have loved you since the moment I saw you, or very nearly after, but I knew, or rather, I never dreamed that my affection could ever be returned. Our difference in position…"

"Enough talk of that nonsense." Marchford squeezed her hand. "I may have a title, but I also have relations who…well, you have met my mother. I declare you to be my equal in rank and my better in propriety and understanding."

"Not at all. You are the most intelligent man I know."

"And yet I am here in cellar with a gun to me," sighed Marchford.

Penelope shrugged. "Nobody's perfect."

"Enough talk," growled the man with the gun.

"Quiet, you!" chastised the man with the lantern. "Let them have their moment. Go on now."

Marchford gave the man with the lantern a slight nod and turned back to Penelope, giving her hand a slight squeeze. "Miss Rose, I fear I have not much to recommend myself to you, for you see what an abysmal office I have performed at either keeping you or my country safe. And yet I love you. I wish to have no one by my side but you. All that I have I give to you. You are my true companion, my friend, and the one woman my heart desires. Would you do me the honor of becoming my wife?"

Penelope blinked, but the tears fell anyway. "Yes," she answered simply. "Yes, I would love to be your wife."

"Truly?" Marchford looked up at her, his eyes wide and vulnerable.

"Truly," she said firmly.

He was on his feet and his mouth on hers before another happy tear could fall. She was loved by the man she adored. She could face her death beside him with a smile.

Suddenly he pushed her hard to the ground and a loud crack echoed off the walls of the cellar.

"James!" she screamed, but it was not he who fell. The man with the shotgun lay dead on the ground, a smoking pistol in Marchford's hand.

"But how?" cried Penelope, stunned on the ground.

Marchford and the man with the lantern dove for the shotgun in the dead man's hand. In an instant, she flung herself at the feet of the large bodyguard, tangling him for a moment and allowing Marchford to retrieve the shotgun.

James rolled on the ground and came up standing, shotgun in one hand, pistol in the other. The man stood slowly as Penelope backed away, and Marchford put himself between the man and Penelope with two long strides. He stood before her protectively and Penelope's heart soared.

"Now I'm going to give you the same courtesy you extended me," said Marchford to the man. "I give you the chance to surrender or be shot now."

The man put his hands up. "Sorry, Your Grace. I

knowed I done wrong. Just following orders," said the large man.

"When those orders are unjust, immoral, and illegal, you are honor bound not to follow them," said Penelope with feeling, picking up the lantern.

"Right you are, miss. I sees my mistake, I do," said the man, humble now that he was caught.

"Ordinarily I would not care as to your rehabilitation," said Marchford coolly. "But you may be of some use to us, which if done properly, could be used to mitigate your sentence and might just save your neck. Tell me everything you know."

"Nuthing. Not I. I was just hired for some muscle when it was required. I gots a family to feed, you see. I does what she says and asks no questions. That's the lay of it."

"So you can tell me nothing that could be used to help you? How disappointing for you. Since you allowed some charity, I was hoping to show you some in return," said Marchford.

"I knowed they had me move the safe that was here. Heavy too."

"Where to?" demanded Marchford.

"Just upstairs, to one of them velvet rooms."

Marchford shot Penelope a triumphant glance. "Now what of the attack of Parliament?"

"Nobody said nuthing about Parliament," insisted the bodyguard. "Why should I be in anyone's confidence, I ask? All I done is move wine crates, heavy ones, from the dock to a warehouse in St. Giles and from there to a house."

"Do you know whose house?" asked Penelope.

The man shrugged. "Took some wine to Lord Admiral Devine's house."

"Where there was the explosion." Penelope met Marchford's eye.

"Maybe there was more than wine in those bottles. Perhaps Devine was merely practice," said Marchford.

"But where will the next target be? Parliament itself?" asked Penelope.

"Difficult to do. After the Guy Fawkes incident, security of the building has been a priority."

"Then where?" asked Pen.

"I do not know, but I know who does." Marchford gave her a troubled glance. "I hate to ask you, but do you feel equal to some more excitement tonight?"

Penelope shook out her skirts and met his gaze with a smile. "Always."

Thirty-nine

THE TRAP WAS SET; IT HAD TO WORK. OTHERWISE, well, there could be no otherwise.

"I don't like it. I don't like it one bit," said Marchford, pacing in the cellar. It was the one place they knew they would not be disturbed.

"It is the only way," said Penelope, holding a dish of animal blood procured from the kitchen and splattering some on her gown. It was gruesome, but it was intended to be that way.

"If you are hurt, I will never forgive myself. Never."

"Then see to it that I am not hurt," said Pen, a bit distracted. She should be thinking of their next move, but instead James's proposal still rang in her ears. "I do have a question though."

"Yes?"

"Your proposal, was that a distraction tactic so you could find the pistol you dropped?"

"Yes. And I meant every word." He stopped pacing and came to her holding both her hands in his. "Did you only accept because we had witnesses?"

"No, I do wish to marry you." Penelope squeezed his hands.

"And...and you love me?" Marchford's voice was strangely tentative.

"And I love you," said Penelope with a smile. Strange how she had demanded to be loved and now it was him seeking reassurance in that regard.

"Good." James breathed a sigh. "Good. Because I cannot do this again, trying to convince you to marry me."

"All I needed to hear was that you loved me."

"I do." Marchford shook his head. "Probably be the end of me, but I do."

"Go now. We need to do this. I trust you." It was true; she did. And now they needed to take care of a certain comtesse.

"Keep this. For luck." He handed her back the ancient knife, which he had retrieved from the comtesse's boudoir while she was entertaining. Despite her unpleasant appearance, he pulled her close and hugged her, simply holding her for a moment. Penelope relaxed into him and breathed deep of his intoxicating scent and his calming strength. Even unshaven and with ruined clothes, he was attractive to her. Together they could do anything.

Marchford left and Penelope waited for the signal. Waiting was the worst part. She was primarily concerned something would happen to Marchford. In time, she was given the signal, and she crept up to the portrait hall, a long hall of statuary covered in white sheets. It was time to try her hand at an acting career.

"Your Grace," cried Penelope with what she

hoped was a convincing sob. "Please help me!" Pen stumbled forward toward Antonia, who stood among the covered statutes.

"Whatever has happened? Oh, my dear girl, are you hurt?" asked Antonia.

"They are trying to kill me, oh help." Pen staggered to Antonia, who directed her to a bench in alarm.

"My gracious, sit here. Don't move. I will get help. Whatever could have happened?" Antonia rushed from the room, encountering the comtesse on the way out. "Oh, my dear Miss Rose has been injured. I do not know how. Please stay with her while I get help."

"Of course, what a horrible thing. You can be sure I will know what to do." The comtesse smiled, waited for the dowager to leave the room, then locked the door behind her with a dreadful click.

"Who is it?" called Penelope. "Have you brought help?"

The comtesse swished in between the statuary. "Penelope Rose. You are causing much too much trouble."

"No!" cried Penelope. "Why do you wish to kill me? Isn't it enough that you have killed the duke?"

"But, my dear, you are so much in love with him. You should like to join him in the afterlife, no?" She shrugged her slight shoulders. "Whether you do or not, you shall be seeing him shortly." The comtesse reached down and pulled a long, thin knife from her stocking, approaching her steadily.

Penelope's heart was pounding, but the comtesse did not appear to be the least fazed by the events.

"You mean to kill me with your own hand?"

Penelope stood and backed away, remembering to feign injury. She needed to keep as much space as possible between her and the knife.

"I will do what needs to be done. I always have."

"This is not your first kill."

"No, indeed. I have made a bit of an art of it. In truth, the 'man' who bumped into you after killing the stupid footman, it was me."

"You killed the footman!" Pen was surprised.

"Now this will be easier if you sit still. Running about won't help you. I will do it quickly and then it will all be over." The soothing seduction of the comtesse's voice made Penelope shudder.

"Why must you kill me?" She needed no acting to make her voice waver. "I swear to you I will leave town. I will never say a word."

"You know I had my men kill Marchford. You know too much of our plans for tonight. No, my dear, you must die." The comtesse lunged at her, and Penelope ducked around a statue with a shriek. She was running out of room. The comtesse was slowly boxing her into a corner. From it, there would be no escape.

"But you can change your mind," pleaded Penelope. "You can call this all off. Tell whoever you are working for that—"

"Me, working for someone? Do you think there is anyone else? No! It is I who am the spymaster here. It is I who give the orders. The men, they work for me. What I do, I do as a favor for Napoleon himself. He has promised to restore my lands, my home, and more money than I could spend in a thousand lifetimes as a reward should I deliver him a weakened England, vulnerable to attack."

"You are doing this just to win back your house?" Pen carefully backed around the covered statues.

"It is mine! Mine, you understand! Ah, but you understand nothing, with your countrified mother and your clergyman father. You are but poor quality. Unworthy of notice. I don't know what Marchford ever saw in you, since you did not even share your bed with him. Who should care if you die? I am the Comtesse de Marseille. I may kill any who offend me."

"You are mad! You plan to kill members of Parliament for your own profit? I tell you the truth, I would rather choke on ashes than eat a fine meal with a snake like you! You are a traitor, a murderess, and a vile human being," cried Penelope.

"And you, my dear, have spoken quite enough. Time to die." The comtesse lunged again, with shocking speed for one her age. Penelope turned to run but tripped on her skirts and fell hard on her knee. This was not part of the plan. She was supposed to appear injured, not actually be injured.

"Help!" she cried as the snarling comtesse bore down on her, knife raised, the candlelight glinting off the blade. Remembering her own knife, she pulled it now, causing the comtesse to stop short. The comtesse narrowed her eyes and raised her knife as if to throw it.

Suddenly, one of the statues came rushing forward and grabbed the comtesse, pulling her off the ground.

The comtesse shrieked in surprise, the knife falling to the floor. Penelope quickly crawled forward and grabbed the knife, avoiding the comtesse's kicking feet.

"Enough!" demanded the statue. He put down the comtesse and whipped off the sheet. It was Marchford.

"But you are dead," stammered the comtesse. "I sent them to kill you."

"I am sorry to disappoint, but I am not quite dead yet."

"Then you will die soon," cried the comtesse.

"Perhaps you should consider just how many people you need to kill," said Marchford.

A nearby statue also pulled off the sheet, revealing Mr. Grant. "Best performance I ever heard, Miss Rose."

"I commend your courage," said the grim-faced Lady Katherine, tossing aside her sheet.

"Indeed. This has been quite illuminating," said Lady Devine, revealing herself. "Comtesse, you may consider yourself uninvited to my little soiree next week." It was perhaps the most unkind thing she had ever uttered.

"But…how…" gasped the comtesse. More sheets were removed, revealing more members of the *ton*, Mortimer Sprot, the local magistrate, and two large Bow Street Runners, who took command of the prisoner without ceremony. Last of all, in the corner of the room, closest to the door, stood the two Dowager Duchesses of Marchford.

"Very clever, locking the door, Cosette," said Antonia. "But of course, we had already gotten a key from the housekeeper."

"No," whispered the comtesse. "No! How could you? How did you possibly know?"

"For that, we have three people to thank," said Antonia, stepping forward so all could hear. "My grandson, the Duke of Marchford, is responsible for the capture of many a spy including this detestable spymaster, with the help, as you all have witnessed, of our lovely Penelope Rose. I look forward to the day when I may call her my own granddaughter. But they would not have succeeded without the help of my dear daughter-in-law, Bella, the Marchioness d'Anjou, who has been working for our king and country these past many years. To these three I shall drink a toast, for it is them we can thank for our safety from tyranny."

Penelope stared at her. James stared at her. The comtesse and everyone in the room stared at her. Much to the utter amazement of the crowd, Antonia and Bella gave each other the regal embrace of a duchess and linked arms together, facing their loyal subjects with beneficent smiles.

"Are they now on friendly terms?" Penelope whispered to James.

"Can't say. Still in shock. Perhaps the end of the world is nigh," said James, who appeared more shaken than at any time when his life was being threatened.

"Thank you, Your Grace," Penelope said to Antonia. "You also were essential to this plot. You played your part well."

"Naturally," retorted Antonia. "What else would you expect?"

Marchford chuckled and nodded to the Runners and the magistrate to take the prisoner out to wherever they put aristocratic traitors, most likely the Tower of London. To Mortimer Sprot, he simply said, "Thank you."

Mortimer nodded his head and disappeared among the statuary.

"Never a dull evening with you about," said Grant in his droll manner. "You are forever leaving dead bodies and treacherous spies in your wake. I merely popped over to announce the birth of my son and got caught up in all this."

"Oh, congratulations!" cried Penelope. "How is Genie?"

"Very well. She made it through the ordeal the best of all of us. For myself, it was touch and go there for a while."

"Congratulations, old friend!" said Marchford, giving his friend a hearty slap on the back. "You deserve to announce your good news. Where are Lord Admiral Devine, Wynbrook, and the others?" Marchford asked, looking around.

"Emergency meeting at the house of Lord Felton. They are negotiating the final agreement for the regency for the king. They expect a vote soon in Parliament," said Grant with an amused tone. "The lords have all abandoned you at the hour of your greatest triumph."

"Members of Parliament!" cried Penelope. "Strader had a wagon of crates."

"The comtesse spoke of her plans for tonight. They were targeting meetings in houses, not Parliament itself!" Marchford bolted for the door with Penelope running after.

"You'll never get there in time. It's too late!" cried the comtesse as she was being led away. She cackled in the very image of personified evil.

Marchford ignored her. She was no longer of any importance. "Grant, men, to me!"

Moments later, they were piled into carriages, racing to Lord Felton's house.

"When you met Strader at Lord Felton's house, where was he?" Marchford asked Penelope.

"In the servants' quarters, down the hallway leading opposite the kitchen," replied Penelope, gripping Marchford's arm to keep from sliding off the seat as the carriage took a turn a little too fast for her liking. When Marchford told the groom to "spring 'em," the man obviously took it to heart.

"Hiding bombs in wine crates, capital idea," said Grant. "If you are a traitor planning to bring down the government," he added to the shocked faces in the carriage.

"But why would Strader blow up his own inheritance?" asked Penelope. "Isn't he Felton's heir? It doesn't make any sense."

"Didn't you hear?" said Grant. "Felton won the lawsuit. Got Strader declared a bastard, effectively excluding him from any inheritance."

"I thought Strader's mother married the groundskeeper."

"She did," said Grant with a conspiratorial grin. "But not until after she bore the son."

"Which would explain the hostility," said Marchford dryly. "Probably thought he would get a better deal from Napoleon."

The carriage rolled up to the drive of Lord Felton's house and came to an unceremonious, jolting stop.

"Grant, you stay here in the carriage with Miss Rose," commanded Marchford, jumping out.

"Is the man daft?" asked Pen, hopping out of the carriage.

"Always has been," replied Grant, jumping out after them. "Let's get the people out of the house."

Penelope and Grant ran to the front door to warn the residents while Marchford and a few men ran around to the side. Two men were sitting on the now-empty wagon parked beside the house. The men ran at the sight of Marchford.

"Follow them!" Marchford yelled to the men with him. "Don't let them get away."

Penelope and Grant ran into the house without waiting at the door.

"Get everyone out of this house," Grant commanded the butler. "Everyone!"

Penelope ran ahead to the dining room and found Prime Minister Spencer Perceval and many other members of Parliament discussing the regency papers over dinner. "Get out!" she cried. "Everyone must leave. Now!"

"Miss Rose, whatever is wrong?" The Earl of Darington stood.

Penelope realized with blood and gore down her gown, she must look a horrible sight. "You are all in danger here. You must leave!"

The men stared at her, no one moving. Darington narrowed his eyes and stared at her as if he was reading her mind.

"You heard her. Everyone out!" Darington shouted, and suddenly everyone was in movement, heading for the door.

Within a matter of minutes, Penelope and Grant were standing on the grounds before the house with the entire household, down to the last housemaid, outside.

"Now tell us what this is all about," demanded an elderly lord.

A huge explosion ripped through the house, followed by another one, then another, blowing out all the windows, fire and smoke billowing from the gaping holes.

The shock of the blast caused the party to cover their heads as shattered glass and rubble were thrown everywhere. A few of the older men fell to the ground, and Penelope was steadied by Grant to keep her feet. She desperately looked around and grabbed Grant's arm. "Where is Marchford?"

Forty

MARCHFORD RAN INTO THE SIDE DOOR AND BARGED into the kitchen. "I am the Duke of Marchford. You are in danger. Everyone, outside!"

He ran on down the hall as the kitchen staff fled, though from their shrieks, they may have been more afraid of him than anything. So be it. He ran down the hall, opening doors. The first three were empty servants' quarters. The last was locked. He put his shoulder to it and broke open the door.

Strader stood up, a candle in hand. His look of surprise twisted into a sneer. "You're too late. The fuses have been lit."

Marchford put a fist to the man's nose, sending him flying backward. He grabbed the fuse from the bottle of gunpowder, throwing it down. "You're done."

Strader shook his head, wiping the blood from his nose. "You think this is all? I have slow fuses everywhere. There's nothing you can do about it now."

"Where are they?" demanded Marchford, grabbing the man by his lapels.

"I will see you in hell!" screamed Strader, the veins of his neck bulging.

Marchford dropped him. He needed to ensure Penelope was out of the house. He ran from the room with Strader lunging after him, but Strader's legs tangled in the fuses and he tripped, dropping his candle, lighting the fuse.

"Marchford! Marchford!" Strader screamed after him.

Marchford rushed to the door and only got a few steps before the concussive blast sent him flying. He rolled away and took cover behind a short stone wall as successive blasts tore through the house.

Penelope. It was his only thought. *Please, Lord, let her be safe*. Nothing else mattered. He got up and staggered to the front, where Lord Felton was staring at his burning house in shock, surrounded by various members of Parliament and house staff in various stages of disbelief and distress.

"Where is Marchford?" cried Penelope, her back to him.

She was alive! His heart soared! "Penelope!" He turned her around and pulled her into his arms. He would not let go. He would never let go.

She said something unintelligible into his collar and her body shook even as she grasped him with a surprisingly strong grip. She also was not letting go.

The most levelheaded of them all was Grant, who started a bucket brigade to put out the fire in the shell of the house and keep the fire from spreading to the neighbors. People poured into the street to gawk and help put out the fire. The house was most likely a complete loss. The only casualty, it appeared, was Strader himself, whom nobody particularly mourned.

Marchford suddenly reached for his coat pocket. Was it still there? "Thank goodness," he sighed.

"What is it?" asked Penelope, her eyes wide.

"The special license to marry you. I still have it." James grinned and held up the tattered paper.

"Best use it now," said Grant, joining the conversation.

"As soon as may be," said James with a smile.

"Not soon. Now," demanded Grant. "I know you both too well. Too much excitement. Too much trouble. Wed now before something else goes wrong."

"If it were possible, I would marry you right now." James gazed down upon Penelope. She was beautiful to him.

She grinned in return. "I would as well."

"Good," said Grant. "Come here."

James held out an arm for Penelope and they followed Grant down the street, away from the disaster. Grant paused before one of the new gas streetlights as fresh snow began to fall, dancing in the light of the lamp.

"Are you hurt?" asked a man in a black coat standing under the lamp. "Does someone need me?"

"Yes, Reverend," said Grant. "These two souls would like to be married."

"Married?" cried the clergyman. "When I came to help, I thought I would care for the injured and distraught."

"They are certainly distraught, hopeless cases," said Grant with a wide grin.

"I cannot possibly marry anyone. The banns must be read," said the reverend.

James turned to Penelope. "This is not at all how I pictured any wedding I might have."

"Nor I," agreed Penelope. She closed her eyes and looked up, smiling as the snow fell on her face. "But I have entirely given up trying to be the master of my own fate."

James's heart began to beat a little faster. Was she actually going to agree to this mad plan? Was he? He smiled at the picture of Penelope, snowflakes catching in her hair and eyelashes. After all he had gone through, he did not want to risk losing one moment together. And Grant was right; he should marry her before she came to her senses.

"Reverend, I believe this is what you need." He handed the special license to the reverend.

"Most unusual. Most unusual, indeed." He shook his head, but then he paused and gazed around. "But I cannot think of a more beautiful place to be wed."

Penelope threaded her fingers through his and he held her hand against the cold. "I love you." It was all she needed to say. She was ragged, her head uncovered, her hair a wild mess, her face was dirty, and her gown was splattered with blood. Yet in the halo of light of the streetlamp and the glistening snow, she was his angel.

"I love you too," he replied and meant every word.

"Dearly beloved…" began the reverend.

❧

Penelope was not certain if she was in a dream. Had she just married James under a streetlamp on a London street? No. Yes. She held James's hand. He was real; that was all she knew.

"Mr. Peters," James called the butler as they arrived home.

"My word, Your Grace," gasped the shocked butler. "Are you quite well?"

"Yes, never better," said the duke. "Best day of my life. Please arrange for a bath, so we may freshen up and prepare for guests tomorrow evening."

"Yes, Your Grace," said the butler, trying to recover from the shock of seeing Marchford and Penelope in such a grimy state. "Any particular occasion?"

"Twelfth Night tomorrow. Thought it a good day to have my wedding ball." He winked at Penelope, and she smiled in return. "And you can be the first in the household to greet my new bride, Penelope Lockton, the Duchess of Marchford."

Penelope smiled so broadly she thought her face might crack.

The butler stammered again and smiled himself, most uncharacteristically. "Yes, yes, quite. I wish you both every happiness!"

"Thank you, Peters," said James. "Let my mother and grandmother know, and tell them my mother may decorate as she wishes and my grandmother may invite whomever she pleases."

"That is certain to please and displease them both," laughed Penelope.

"As long as you are my bride, I care not."

"But what of the unpleasant gossip regarding our marriage?" asked Penelope, a cloud coming over her eyes.

"Gossip?" asked James. "The Comtesse de Marseille was revealed to be a traitor, Lord Felton's house was blown up, and most shocking of all, my grandmother and mother were seen making pleasant conversation. My dear lady, there is so much other more interesting gossip right now, I could have married the fishmonger's daughter, or even the fishmonger himself, and nobody would raise an eyebrow."

"I will fight off any and all tradesmen who might wish to take you from me," asserted Penelope with a grin.

"I thank you." James closed his eyes for a moment and opened them slowly. "I fear we must both be in need of sleep."

Penelope nodded. Now that the excitement was over, she was aware how her whole body ached. "I know this is not very wifely," she said as they walked up the stairs together, "but I desperately need sleep and a good wash."

"Yes, rest. I shall see you in the morning." James stopped under one of the mistletoe traps and kissed her on the forehead.

Back in her room, Penelope was attended by several excited maids, who had just heard the news they were now waiting on a duchess. They helped her remove the bloodstained gown, which she relinquished to them to be burned. The garment had served its purpose well. She did not need it anymore.

The maids provided hot water to wash, and Penelope did as best she could to remove the dirt and grime.

"May I express my best wishes for your future together," said Abigail. "And if I may suggest, there is a bath down the hall. Maybe you would like to relax in the hot water."

"Oh yes." Penelope wrapped in a dressing gown

and padded down the hall in her bare feet. She opened the door of the room with the large tub. It was mostly dark but for one candle. The smell of rose water and lavender soothed her senses.

She stepped inside and dropped the wrapper to the floor, walking to the tub. Suddenly, James emerged from under the water.

"Penelope!"

"James!"

"What are you doing here?" they both asked together.

"I fear my maid has taken things into her own hands," said Penelope, turning to find her wrapper. Husband or no, her cheeks burned at being caught naked by James.

"Come back!" James reached out and grabbed her hand. "My duchess, please join me." His eyes twinkled in the candlelight.

She glanced down. He was naked. She looked away, only to have her eyes drawn down again. He was very, very naked.

"You are the most beautiful woman in the world," he said, trailing one finger down her stomach, traveling below her belly button and beyond.

She caught her breath. Despite being exhausted, parts of her body were coming alive. She held on to his other hand and climbed into the tub, resting her back on his stomach. Warm water gushed around her, easing all the places of soreness and tension.

James grabbed a pitcher and poured warm water over her head, down her back. It felt so good she had to stifle a groan. He took some soap and began to work it through her hair, massaging as he went.

A satisfied sigh escaped her lips. Her body went limp as relaxation flowed through her. She had never known the simple act of washing hair could be so sensual, so utterly all-encompassing.

He poured water over her head again, washing away not only the soap, but also all the pain and anxiety of the past few days. She leaned back on him, her eyes closed. Never had she felt so relaxed, so happy, so safe.

"I love you," he whispered. "I hope you shall not grow tired of hearing it, for I feel I shall need to constantly remind you."

"I also may need to remind you of my love for you," murmured Penelope.

"Hopeless cases, the both of us," said James. His hands began an exploration of her body, and she floated in the water, allowing him to touch, massage, caress any part of her he so desired.

When he reached that secret place that made her catch her breath, she opened herself to him, knowing she was safe, protected, adored. Soon the tension built up so that she wanted, craved, *needed* more.

She turned around, straddling him in the tub, and he guided her to join him, completing her in a way she had not known possible. He was her other half, her mate, her love forever. She held on to his shoulders as he increased the pace, water slopping out over the side of the tub.

She chased after a building sensation within her, circling in her core, twisting up tension, until suddenly something within her exploded, filling her with an unspeakable joy.

James cried out and they both collapsed into each other, floating down into the warm water. Penelope doubted she could raise her head off his chest even to prevent from being drowned.

"I love you, my duchess."

※

The next day, Penelope stood next to James as they greeted the guests to their wedding celebration. Bella had expanded on the decorations, turning the entire house into a Christmas feast for the eyes. Never had Marchford House kept Twelfth Night with more merriment.

Antonia also did not disappoint. Despite the last-minute invitation, the ballroom was packed with friends and well-wishers, including Penelope's sisters and their husbands, all notable members of the *ton*, and many members of Parliament. It was glorious. Penelope was the last of her sisters to marry, and to a duke no less!

Penelope held James's hand, and the rest of the party seemed to slip away. She was married to the man she loved—to the only man she had ever loved. She had not thought it possible, but apparently nothing is impossible for God.

James's warm, misty-green eyes met hers. He was impeccably dressed, though she now had a preference to seeing him with less clothing. Still, he was a striking figure, and he was all hers. *I love you.* He did not need to say the words. It was there in his eyes. Suddenly bagpipes started up a deafening but joyous song.

"Ten pipers piping?" asked Penelope with a laugh.

"Yes. I am remiss, I missed a few," said James. "Still looking for a pear tree, but I expect a partridge will be on the menu tonight. As for dancing ladies and leaping lords, we will see what we can do at the dance."

"Oh no!" Penelope's joy diminished with a sudden realization. "You have given me all these presents and I have given you nothing. And it's Twelfth Night!"

James wrapped his arms around her. "You have given me the best present of all. You have given me yourself. And a very memorable Christmastide! There is nothing more I could ask for and nothing more I could want."

Everyone gathered around them, wishing them well. Antonia and Bella arrived, arm in arm of all things, with Lord Langley straggling behind them with a bemused smile.

"I am still stunned to see you both in each other's good graces," said James.

"We found something we agree on," said Bella.

"We approve of your choice of bride," said Antonia, giving Pen a warm embrace.

Penelope was flooded with a warm swell of joy. It was no small thing to win over two such imposing ladies. And Antonia was not the hugging type.

"However, I find the decor something appalling," continued Antonia.

"And the number of persons in attendance is hardly what I consider the small, intimate affair as we agreed upon," countered Bella.

"That's better. Everything is making more sense to me now," said James.

His mother gave him a kiss on the cheek. "I shall be leaving soon, but I want you to know how proud I am of you. I love you with my whole heart."

"Thank you." James blinked away emotion and cleared his throat.

"Ah, you are all misty for me!" Grant was next in line and slapped him on the shoulder.

"Thank you, Grant," said Marchford. "For everything."

"It was nothing. Love to force my friends into marriage under streetlamps." Grant smiled. "Can't stay long. Must get back soon."

"Is anything wrong?" asked Penelope.

"Oh no. Nothing has ever been so right. But I like to watch when the little one sleeps and eats, and opens his eyes. Never been so amused by an infant."

"You are well on your way to becoming a good father," said Penelope.

"Goodness. There's something I never thought I'd be accused of. Best of everything to you both!"

Penelope's sisters came next, surrounding her with love and kisses. Then they descended on Marchford, giving him the full dose of the Rose family love.

"We are so happy for you," said Amelia.

"We wish you all the best," sighed Sophie.

"Much joy to you!" declared Mariah.

"Sugar and spice, Pen, you married a duke!" exclaimed Julia.

The Earl of Darington was next, with his sister, giving Penelope a pang of regret. "Oh dear, I have not found spouses for either of you."

"I told you she was Madame X." Kate glared at her brother. "And I don't want a husband."

Penelope covered her mouth with her hand, realizing she had revealed herself. This marriage thing was making her soft in the head.

"You have employed your time far better," said Darington. "You saved my life, and for that, I thank you. We wish you every happiness."

The line continued until they had greeted every well-wisher. The chairs were cleared away, the music started to play, and they began to dance.

"You dance divinely, Your Grace," said Penelope.

"Only with you, my duchess." James's eyes smiled at her in a way that was for her alone. "Only for you."

❧

Three months later, Penelope sat on the settee surrounded by her sisters and Genie Grant. Miles the cat and Genie's adorable tot were the only males allowed in the room. Miles rested his large, furry head on Penelope's lap as she stroked him while listening to the complaints of ladies.

"I do love him, but I confess I miss sleep. Grant says to use a wet nurse, but I wouldn't miss a moment with my boy," said Genie, cradling her baby boy.

"My little one has a foot or something stuck in my ribs," said Amelia.

"I am craving the most odd things," sighed Sophie.

"My back is killing me," declared Mariah.

"La, I'm so fat!" exclaimed Julia.

"I've been feeling a little queasy myself," added Penelope with a small smile.

Her sisters were quiet a moment, then turned to her, their eyes as wide as their smiles. "Are you?" they all asked together.

"Yes!" Penelope could not help but smile as all the expecting Rose sisters and Genie exclaimed their joy and happiness to hear a little ducal heir was on the way.

"What is all this squealing?" James strode through the door, strong and tall as ever. "I can only assume you are being attacked or—"

"I told them." Penelope rose with a grin.

James strode forward and clasped her hands in his. "Very good. All according to plan."

"*Your* plan?" Penelope raised an eyebrow.

"Well, someone's plan who is vastly smarter than me." He raised his eyes for a moment and came back down for a kiss on Penelope's lips to the cheers of her sisters.

The Lord's plans were very good indeed.

Acknowledgments

Huge thanks to my editor, Deb Werksman, who nicely pointed out the original beginning of this book needed some love (and an additional chapter); this book is so much better because of you. Thanks to my agent, Barbara Poelle, who believes in me more than I do. I am very appreciative of my beta reader, Laurie Maus, whose initial feedback on my chapters is so helpful (should have listened to you more). Thanks to my kids, who are very supportive of my writing and even suggested a lemonade stand in front of the house to sell books—someday I'll write something you can actually read. And to Ed, who is my rock.

About the Author

Amanda Forester holds a PhD in psychology and worked for many years in academia before discovering that writing historical romance was decidedly more fun. Whether in the rugged Highlands of medieval Scotland or the decadent ballrooms of Regency England, her novels offer fast-paced adventures filled with wit, intrigue, and romance. Amanda lives with her family in the Pacific Northwest. You can visit her at www.amandaforester.com.